"Clandestine somehow manages to exceed Torsion in its plot twists and revelations, with characters more compelling than ever. This masterpiece of a sequel prompts deep thought while simultaneously tugging on all your emotions, and the deliciously detailed world-building makes this a must-read for any sci-fi lover."

—AMELIA E. CLAWFORD, AUTHOR OF
ALL THAT THERE IS(N'T) TO KNOW ABOUT FROGS

"Aliens, assassins, and overworked college students. Clandestine is suspenseful, funny, and heartwarming; a great fall read."

—SAVANNAH-ROSE ROUSSOS, AUTHOR OF THE FOUND

"Clandestine offers the perfect mix of banter, found families, science fiction, corruption arcs, and so much more. I definitely recommend this to anyone who's looking for a unique read or a large cast to get attached to."

—NOIR ELLE, ADVANCED READER

"Clandestine is the exact book you NEED to read if you want heart-wrenching, thought-provoking sci-fi. I'm trying to find the right words to describe it, but I'll I've got is RAHHHHHH ASTRA."

—DALLAS, ADVANCED READER

"Clandestine is a thrilling read for anyone who loves academia, morally grey characters, sci-fi, and multi-povs. It's full of characters you will care about and get attached to, and the plot is enough to keep you reading more!"

—DANNI GRACE, ADVANCED READER

CLANDESTINE

SERA AMOROSO

Clandestine

This is a work of fiction. Names, characters, places, and incidents either are the
product of the author's imagination or are used fictitiously. Any resemblance to
actual persons, living or dead, events, or locales is entirely coincidental.

ISBN: 978-1-7372310-2-8
First Edition: April 2024
Cover design by Jessica Sanders
Interior formatting by Riley Perrie

For Amelia,
I hope you laugh at all mentions of frogs.
P.S. Thank you for not hating me for the ending.

Content Warning

I intended this book to be PG-13. However, please be advised that the cast is 18+ and there is on-page death, mentions of violence, blood and gore, depression, manipulation, anxiety, and other potentially triggering topics. If you are a parent and your child is under the age of 13, I would recommend reading it first.

Table of Contents

Prologue

There's not much that a person can do when they're stuck indoors. Astra didn't realize how hard it would be to fight off the urge to fall asleep. She was currently quarantined in her dorm room, under several thick blankets, due to yet another experiment gone wrong. All hell breaks loose when you leave Alyssa Clark by herself, apparently. Of course, Astra was a stubborn girl who didn't let the supposed sickness keep her from working. Sniffling once in determination, she tapped away at the keys until she was satisfied with her word count, then set the computer aside. It was getting late, and she knew no one would bother her anyway.

She fished her notebook out of her bag and opened it. It had been almost nine months since she and her friends had taken over the school. Recently, Astra had been going through the leftover files in the room underneath it. There were hundreds of thousands of them, and Zola had told her it would take years for someone to even begin to put a dent into the to-be-read pile. Luckily, Astra wasn't a normal person, and after a month of scouring, she was almost halfway through.

Then, Alyssa accidentally let a disease loose in the school, causing the infected students, Astra included, to be confined to their rooms. Every so often, Astra would employ Henry to bring her some files, and she continued her hunt at a snail-like pace. At least it kept the boredom away. Meanwhile, Astra knew that Zola was off firing all of the old staff and putting out ads for new employees. Nasra was in charge of finding and interviewing every single student who ever knew about Parkes' old experiment, and the rest of the group were left to their own devices.

She was upset to be stuck in her room, angry that her immune system wasn't kicking in. She knew it was a side effect, but she hated it all the same. She'd get over it as soon as Alyssa was able to come up with a cure. Still, it had been days since she was ordered to stay in her dorm, and she hated the idea that she had to be there and not work. Of the files that Henry had brought her, there wasn't much to be found. Still, she took notes, steadily weeding through Parkes' journals, lab notes, employee records, and experiments.

Every single time she found something related to Destiny, she'd have to stop and collect herself to keep from punching the wall in her anger. Parkes never should have been trusted, but they were all too naive to have seen it. If it weren't for Isaac...

Astra paused. Getting lost in her memories wasn't good for her work ethic. She pulled the most recent stack of files out from underneath her bed and got to work. Most of it was useless. There was nothing out of the ordinary for Parkes, just records, thousands of them. He was very organized, she had to give him that. She skimmed through most of the records. They weren't interesting to her anyway.

It wasn't until she pulled out a file labeled *Project Checkmate* that she realized. It was an old tradition, playing chess. She had learned it from her parents; she had even played the game with Parkes once, back when she was younger. Mostly, he played with her father, who claimed all of his kids' work as his own in front of guests and allies. It was for their own safety, after all. No one had to know what they did.

She read through the file carefully, and couldn't keep the hatred from welling up inside her. She picked up a cup and threw it across the room. Astra never allowed herself to get angry. It was a risk she couldn't take. Still, she granted it to herself just this once. She had to. Her technology wasn't just in Parkes' hands, it was spread across the globe. It was recycled, used, and then retired to a facility to be studied, kept safe, once Parkes had to go into hiding.

Syn's Technology Research Facility, he called it. After synergy, because he and so many people had worked together to make it happen. Astra scoffed. Parkes must have thought himself so brilliant. She didn't often make mistakes like this, underestimating her opponent. If anything, she overestimated. So how could she have overlooked the thought that Parkes hadn't destroyed the designs that came before his last project? The android's predecessors, shut off and dismantled though they were, were trophies. And this facility was the biggest trophy case that ever existed.

Authorities had spent years trying to convict Leroy Parkes of the crimes he had committed, but they had no evidence. When he died, that was perfect for the police. Not for her, unfortunately, without anything to show for it, authorities couldn't take his work, and that made things harder for Astra. She could easily break into a police station and remove her tech. But to infiltrate a research facility that prized its work and rarely hired anyone, was strict on its internships, and would have her file on hand? That was risky. There was not a lot she could do on that front. She had to tell someone. She couldn't do this on her own. Astra's eyes narrowed, and she made a split-second decision as she grabbed her phone.

Xavier Zhang didn't like surprises. He was no stranger to secrets. He kept them loyally his entire life. Then again, it wasn't like he had a choice. Now, in the wake of his father's death, he was without a mentor, surrounded by people he barely knew, trying to recall his siblings back from their various locations across the world. He was tired, of course. Days cooped up in a darkened conference room trying to put your father's affairs in order would do that to a person. He had finally gotten around to it, after the disasters of last year.

It was tedious work, but he did it without complaint. Well, without complaining out loud. When his phone rang, he was grateful for the distraction. He picked up without bothering to check the caller ID. "Hello?" All that he could hear on the other end was static. He frowned. His eyes widened in recognition when he heard the breathing, a rhythm he could recognize anywhere. "Astra?"

"Hello, Xavier. I have a favor to ask of you."

Blame it on the Business

Xavier crossed his arms and rolled his eyes. He should have been used to these kinds of meetings by now. He had attended them ever since he was twelve years old. This time, though, he would like to throw himself out of the window. Especially with his mind occupied by his earlier call with Astra. Plus, it was exhausting, going through his parent's work. Lists of people and places, jobs, technology, it was endless. Even with all the files he had already gone through, he hadn't even made a dent in his to-do list. It didn't stop him. If there was one thing he was, it was persistent. This was his legacy, his responsibility.

Still, he hated listening to these people talk. They droned on and on about bills, missions, what his father did better than he did, contracts, and death threats. Not from outsiders, but from those within the room. It had taken everything he had to keep the previous meeting attendees from killing each other. Xavier was more convinced that he was babysitting, rather than facilitating discussions between diplomats and hosting spies. This was his job now, and this was just a step up the ladder of life. He only wished that his father had spent more time teaching him.

Xavier had always followed his father around, carefully retracing his footsteps and sticking to the examples Ares Duke had provided. Unfortunately, Xavier was only human, and he made mistakes, too. His impatience led to three different shattered ties – former allies of the Duke family. It might not seem like a lot, but that meant that there were three more people out there with information on the Duke family, people that would report that information back to their organizations or sell it to the highest bidder.

There might as well have been a target on his back because of this. If he cared more, he might have been more protective of his own life, but he wasn't. Xavier didn't mind when he was threatened. It was something he was used to. No one could hurt him the way he hurt himself. No one. The only things that bothered him were these stupid meetings and the workload that accompanied them.

Yet, he persisted. He didn't always agree with the people he worked with, but he respected them. He enjoyed the thrill of the hunt and the jobs he was assigned but hated the worry in his siblings' eyes when they were the ones left behind. It would kill him if they were the targets. Xavier wasn't the oldest—that title belonged to Arya and then Jaxson—but he was protective. It was drilled into him by the oldest two, to watch out for the younger ones. Astra, Cassidy, Tessa, Griffin, Zale, and Yvette—they were his responsibility now, even out of his sight. He missed them.

Astra had been right when she told him he wasn't ready to take on this role. Maybe it was the grief, but it stung more than the eulogy she gave for their father. Astra had the innate ability to know things she shouldn't have. She was ever present in his life, never faltering, rarely changing. They were a team, though Astra was more than that. She was his closest friend. Xavier remembered meeting her the first time that Ares brought him to the mansion all those years ago. She was small and quiet. That was useful on the missions they went on. Xavier had come to rely on her quick thinking and direction.

He needed that direction now. All he had been doing recently was regurgitating the rules his father had put into his head, repeating the same things he remembered Ares saying at these meetings. Didn't he want to be different? With Astra gone for good, Xavier could feel that his family was falling apart. It wouldn't be long until the others found out and followed her lead. Despite Astra's status as a traitor in the family, she was still well-loved, and Xavier knew that at least Tessa and Griffin would leave to support her if they had to. He knew that it was their choice but that didn't stop him from worrying.

No, Xavier didn't care about himself, but he cared about them. He would never forgive himself if anything happened, something that he could have prevented. He couldn't protect them if they left. Deep down he knew that his fear was really because he knew he couldn't protect himself.

Xavier zoned back into the conversation, catching his sister's eye. "What?"

Cassidy sighed and closed the file in front of her. "Thank you for your time, everyone. We'll reconvene in a few hours."

Xavier watched as his father's friends exited the room.

Jaxson and Tessa lingered but ultimately left when Cassidy glared at them, shooting Xavier worried glances as they walked out.

"Seriously, Cass?"

"It's obvious you weren't paying attention, and I've lived with you long enough to know that something is on your mind. What's wrong?" She stared at him.

Xavier glanced away. Sometimes looking straight at Cassidy made his skin prickle, her eyes were ocean blue and held the wrath of the sea inside them.

"It's Astra," he said flatly.

"Oh." Cassidy's voice betrayed her.

"You're still mad," Xavier said. It wasn't a question.

"Of course I'm mad. She betrayed us! She's never coming back." Cassidy rarely yelled.

"Maybe we betrayed her," Xavier whispered. He knew they were both still angry, but he also knew that it was also partly his fault.

"What?"

"You heard me. The truth is, we've all betrayed each other. We've lied, stolen, left each other behind for the greater good of our mission—but was that really worth everything that we lost?"

His words were sharp, but his voice was soft, trying to keep the situation from escalating.

Cassidy raised an eyebrow. "Well, that certainly came out of nowhere."

"It was a long time coming." Xavier looked down. He didn't know confessing that would be so easy and yet so difficult.

"Hmm. Anyway, what does this have to do with Astra?" Cassidy looked down, tracing the scratches in the hardwood of the table with her fingers.

"She asked a favor of me," Xavier said.

"And what was that?"

"Help. Recovering the last of her inventions, everything that Parkes stole from us and recreated. She's located it and she wants my help retrieving it."

Cassidy looked up, eyes wide. "Really? And? Are you going to?"

Xavier sighed and looked away. "I don't know."

"Why not? She is still our sister." Cassidy sounded frustrated.

"Do you want me to do this or not? Aren't you the one still angry with her?"

"Anger does not easily replace loyalty, Xavier. She still is our sister, despite the fighting and everything else that we've been through. Astra is a Duke—same as me, same as you. It was her choice to leave but that doesn't mean we have to cut her off."

"So, a begrudging help is what you want me to do?"

Cassidy crossed her arms. "I never said you had to do it, I just said you should consider it. I think you're misplacing your anger."

"Okay."

"Okay." Cassidy surveyed Xavier quietly. She stood up.

Xavier's eyes snapped back towards Cassidy. "Where are you going?"

"To get food. We're reconvening in a couple of hours, and if I'm going to have to listen to more of this nonsense, I need to eat."

Xavier laughed. Cassidy just smiled and left the room.

Xavier stared at the wall. He had memorized every dip, scratch, and bullet hole in the fading grey wallpaper. "I do owe her some favors," he mused. "We'll see, Little Star. We'll see."

Xavier sat in silence, just staring into nothingness. He didn't realize how long he had been thinking until Cassidy returned to the room.

"Still deciding, huh?" she asked.

"Wouldn't you? It's a hard thing to do, Cass."

"Take your time X, it's not the end of the world if you don't figure it out in a day. But it is the end of the world if you mess up with Dad's clients. They're not the kind of people you want to cross and we need to let them down gently."

"Shouldn't they be afraid of us?"

"Don't get cocky. You're not invincible." Cassidy plopped down into her seat. "You don't get a second life, Xavier. Be careful."

Xavier sighed. Cassidy was right, and despite how much he hated the idea, he had more important things to focus on. So he did. When the meeting restarted, he listened, advocated, debated, and tried his absolute best to keep his father's clients happy. Unfortunately, the Duke family business wasn't an easy one to run, and he was tired of needing to defend all the changes he wanted to make. As time went on, Xavier found himself not really paying attention. Instead, he just got impatient, tapping his nails on the table, biting his tongue to fight the urge to lash out. In the end, Xavier lost his patience, ignoring Cassidy's warnings. He kicked everyone out of the conference room and sat there in silence.

He'd worry about their feelings later. Though, later he knew that Cassidy would yell at him for his uncharacteristic outburst. Diplomacy may not have been his strong suit, but he usually did it just fine. He'd have one of the staff smooth things over while he sorted everything else out. At the moment, all he knew was the thumping in his chest and the feeling of his nails cutting into his palms. It was like a comfort blanket. He used to think that he was the best at concealing his feelings, but now he understood. The only reason he could conceal them in the first place was because he had chosen not to feel at all.

A bad decision, as it only built up until he couldn't stand it any longer. He was used to being able to tell his mother if something went wrong. Now, if he had the urge, he'd have to talk to her gravestone.

His mother had always taught him that all good things must come to an end. It shouldn't have surprised him when Astra stayed at Torsion. Their mother didn't sugarcoat their lessons. She taught them to fight and to blend in, but she also taught them how to mourn: quickly and discreetly.

Later that night, Xavier sat alone in his room, staring at the files that covered his floor. He knew them all by heart. Mission after mission, near-death experiences, and diplomacy. Xavier didn't call himself brave, but he was resourceful. Loyalty was prized above all in this household. The ability to keep his mouth shut and the willingness to sacrifice everything just to keep the family safe were hardwired in him. He should help Astra. Shouldn't he?

He still owed her for the things she did at Torsion, taking on the job when everyone else deemed it a lost cause. In the past, he had risked everything for her, saving her even when protocol required that he leave her behind. Xavier picked up one of the files: Astra's latest mission. He didn't mean to be sentimental, but he was. They didn't try to persuade her not to go. They didn't do anything—they trusted her and they let her leave. *'The weakest link,'* he had called her.

"We were only ever as strong as you were." Xavier skimmed the file thoughtfully. He frowned. He thought back to that day, Astra's face when he said it. The change in her eyes as she pushed him away. She was angry, he was angry. Xavier knew it was his fault. He just didn't want to admit it.

"You made your choice," he said aloud. "You have to do this on your own." Xavier shook his head and started organizing the files so he could read them better. "I'm sorry," he whispered. "I can't help you this time."

No Rest for the Wicked

Astra winced as the needle went into her skin.

"You're all set," Alyssa said. She set the syringe down. "You know, you fought that off hard. You're doing better than everyone else; that's why I saved you for last. You should be able to leave your room in a few hours."

"Thanks. Though, I am going to remind you that this is your fault."

Alyssa tsked and shook her head. "I'm sorry, okay? I didn't mean for this to happen."

Astra smiled. "I know you didn't. That's why I'm giving you such a hard time. You did well."

Alyssa frowned, confused. "Is that drug getting to your head? I've never heard you really compliment someone before."

Astra shrugged. "It could be the lack of sleep." Alyssa had always been self-conscious of her own work. Praise seemed like the best way to throw Alyssa off her tracks. Though maybe it was too out of character, maybe Alyssa would be too weirded out.

"You didn't sleep?"

"Of course I did, but I also worked. Time stops for no one, Alyssa. Henry, however, stops for food."

Alyssa rolled her eyes. "I should have known. Next time you get sick, I'll make sure he stays away from you. You need rest."

"I need answers."

"Astra!"

"What?"

Alyssa just shook her head. "You're a menace to society and a problem to yourself. You know that, right?"

"Of course I do." Astra crossed her arms. "But, habits take longer than a week of sickness to die out."

"Will I ever understand you?"

"Probably not."

Alyssa laughed. "You're so weird. Now sleep! Doctor's orders."

"You're not a doctor yet."

Alyssa glared at her. "Astra Aracelli. If you do not go to sleep, I will confine you to your room until you do."

Astra raised an eyebrow. "If I didn't want to stay here, I wouldn't be here. I can and will get out."

"Please?"

Astra looked away. "Fine," she said, exasperated. "I'll sleep for a few hours, then I'll leave my room and continue my work out in public, where I can get more files without needing Henry's help."

"I really need to talk to him about not doing that."

"You'd cut off my only source of entertainment?"

"Astra, you can read a book, watch a movie, play a video game—do anything that involves not going through those files until I say that you're healthy."

"Killjoy."

Alyssa just smiled, raising her hands in mock surrender, and left the room. "Rest!" She yelled, closing the door.

Astra huffed and leaned back on her bed. She didn't know what to do if she wasn't working. There was no life for her outside of her work. When she was younger, she had learned how to play chess, video games, sports—just about anything to help her assimilate with the people around her, but it brought her little joy. If she wasn't actively working, then she was plotting. But this time, she had nothing left to do until the machine brought her a response to her call.

Astra hated to admit it, but she was bored. She got up and stared out the window. She considered opening it to let the breeze in, but that would tempt her to hop out of it and climb to the roof.

If Alyssa caught her out of her room, she'd get lectured, and listening to Alyssa rant for half an hour was not on her to-do list for the day. Astra sighed. She could work on her codes if she wanted.

Astra grabbed her computer and sat down on her bed. Even though she had technically graduated and all she had to worry about was helping to run the school, there was still some work to be done. A gap year is what they called it. Many of the graduate students would either leave to take an internship somewhere else, get a job, continue on to get their Master's degree, or maybe even a Ph.D. She had considered doing that, but she couldn't bring herself to take more classes, not when she wanted to go home. That was the end goal, the only reason she still worked, still lived.

She loved her education, she had even grown to love Earth. She loved the challenge and the knowledge she gained, but she didn't want to be distracted. She needed her home and her people like humans needed oxygen. She would never be complete without a colony. So, she focused on going through files and assigning incoming student applications to the others to vote on.

Torsion's application system was a little annoying to get used to. Even though she had done the exact same steps herself, she couldn't help but make fun of the way they did things. The university only accepted a small group of students every few years, after the previous group completed their bachelor's degrees. The applicants had to take several tests, write long essays, and do personality assessments as part of the process.

Each packet that came in was at least thirty pages long, and thousands came in per day. While the system automatically rejected people that didn't meet the requirements, there were still a lot of applications that passed through. Astra did the brunt of that part of the sorting, tossing applications she didn't like and forwarding the ones she did like to the group. Astra had suggested taking in a bigger class this year, and after a bit of back and forth, they agreed to take on twenty new students for the upcoming year. All they had to do now was choose them.

She was a bit annoyed with how long it took the others to finish reading the applications, but she couldn't make them go faster without forcibly controlling them, and overusing the nanobots for something so unimportant seemed tacky. So, her friends did what they wanted to. They researched, worked, then slept for 15 hours straight. Astra didn't understand the appeal of it all.

When Astra was done with the applications, she opened her coding program and began adding to her latest project. She honestly had no idea what she wanted to do with it. Her mind began to drift to other things, like Xavier, and her stolen technology. When she finally came back to reality, she realized she had created something like Zola's code from last year.

Something that would be useful for hacking.

Astra began to think. She had done hacking jobs before, and if she was going to retrieve her tech, she certainly needed to be good at it. She had thought about using Zola's codes before, but without a way to get the codes close enough to the facility to take control of it, she'd have to do it her own way. She saved her code and set the laptop on her bedside table. She grabbed her notebook and began to write. All she needed were a couple of passwords and a specific set of files from the lab.

Astra groaned. The files. She wouldn't be able to get to them until Alyssa let her out of her room. Astra glanced at her phone. When she had taken Zola's codes to control the group, she had only ever planned to use them to finish the mission that the Dukes had assigned her to. But this was an emergency, right?

She bit her lip. *'Whatever,'* she thought. No matter how much she would try to persuade herself that it wasn't the most morally correct thing to do, she knew that nothing would stop her. "I was never raised to be particularly ethical anyway."

Astra grabbed her phone, typed out the few lines she needed, and hopped into bed. She brought her heart rate down through leveled breathing and willed herself not to move. Breathe in, breathe out. For this to work, Alyssa had to see her asleep. Zola's code couldn't do everything, but it was good enough. It wasn't long before Astra heard footsteps in the hallway. Alyssa poked her head into the room.

"Astra?" Alyssa said, softly. She walked over to Astra's bed and lightly tapped her on the shoulder.

Astra did her best to move and act as if she had just been woken up. "Hmm?"

"So you did go to sleep as I told you," Alyssa said. She raised an eyebrow.

"What?"

"I suppose you're free to go now."

"Really?"

"Yeah. That cure is almost instant, and I can't force you to take a nap for too long. Just, don't overwork yourself, 'kay? Or you'll be right back in here."

"Yes, Mom." Astra rolled her eyes. "Any luck keeping Henry from bringing me files?"

Alyssa laughed. "Nope. Should've known—he never listens to me."

"Of course he doesn't. What did you expect?"

Alyssa nodded. "True, true. Anyway." She stared at Astra pointedly. "Before you go back to work, eat."

Astra stared at her. "Eat?"

"Yes, eat. If you don't, I will put you back in here."

"I thought we agreed on me sleeping."

"We agreed on healthy. This isn't healthy. Go."

Astra rolled her eyes. She grabbed her bag, threw her laptop into it, slipped her phone into her back pocket, and hopped out the door. "Fine!" she called back, still frantically tugging her shoes on. "I'll eat! Just close the door!"

Astra sprinted down the stairs and towards the cafeteria. Now that she was out of her room, she was free to finally hunt down what she needed, and she didn't want to waste any time. She grabbed a sandwich and tossed it into her backpack. She was halfway out the door before she realized Alyssa would probably get on her case if she didn't drink water, so she doubled back to grab a bottle, and continued on her way.

It had been a while since she had been in the lab, so she wasn't sure what to expect when she got down there. There were papers, books, granola bar wrappers, old water bottles, and more strewn all over the floor. All of the whiteboards was covered with random notes, prompts, and doodles, as well as sticky notes. Files were stacked on every available surface. Astra sighed. She placed her bag on a nearby chair and cracked her knuckles. "I guess I'm the clean-up crew."

Astra sorted the papers into piles on one specific table and collected all the trash. She took several files that she knew were useless to the hunt and put them back in the file room. No doubt Zola had used them when she was going through staff's files and forgotten where they'd gone. Astra rolled her eyes. She wasn't a librarian. Eventually, Astra cleared all the trash out and was left with a clean workplace. *'Finally.'* Astra checked her watch. It was getting late.

She pulled her notebook out and began going through the files. She may have already been halfway through them, but once she found the ones she wanted, they would need to be more closely read. If Xavier decided to help her, she wouldn't be able to spend as much time on it. As the night went on, Astra started to get hungry. "Okay, maybe Alyssa was kinda right," she said aloud to herself as she ate.

Astra turned to the pile of files she still had yet to read and sighed. "I really am not going to be able to do all of this, am I?" she asked herself. She had a million things to do and while she technically could do it all, she didn't really want to. She wanted to focus her energy on the more important things. "I guess I'll finish sorting and ask someone to look at it more in-depth and take notes so I can save time." Astra furrowed her brow. One problem: asking someone to read and take notes on all of Leroy's work would be suspicious, especially since she wanted to do this under the radar.

Astra's childhood tech was special, and allowing her friends to trace her back to the Duke family would be dangerous. There was really only one person who wouldn't suspect her and would have the time to do it. Not to mention, they were the only person she trusted to do it. Astra picked up her phone and checked the time. It was 6 a.m. Not bad, but certainly not ideal for them. But that would work in her favor. Astra called anyway.

"What?" The sleepy voice at the end of the line made Astra smile. A person was much easier to persuade when they were tired.

"Aiken, will you do me a favor?"

Family Values

There was one room in the house that Xavier still hadn't touched. His father's study had always been off-limits, and it felt weird—almost illegal—to enter. When he was a child, Xavier would often sit outside his father's door, patiently waiting for him to come out. Ares would open the door, pick him up, and take him out to the gardens to tell him about his day, the biggest smile on his face. Xavier smiled softly at the memory. He had such a good family, didn't he? Even if it was broken.

Xavier placed his hand on the doorknob. Once he opened the door, there was no going back, but he had to put his father's affairs in order. He had to go through and find anything that might pertain to the next group of people that would come to meet the new leader of the Dukes. He had to. It was his duty to protect the family. Xavier turned the knob hesitantly.

The door swung open. Xavier stepped inside, flicking on the lights as he went. He took a deep breath. It smelled like his dad, smoke and green tea.

Xavier stood frozen in the doorway for a second, shook his head, and then moved further into the room. His father's study was covered in dust; after all, it had sat untouched for almost two years. There were days when Xavier had caught a glimpse of what was inside the room from the doorway, but he didn't want to know what was in there anymore. It was just darkness and the outline of books in the faint light of the lamp on his father's desk.

Ares rarely ever turned the lights on in his study, something that Xavier had always found a little odd. It seemed his father worked better in the dark, and Xavier knew better than to ask. Entering the room was forbidden, so his younger self had always believed that it was just as much a sin to peek through the crack in the door. Xavier dragged his fingers along his father's desk, leaving a trail in the dust. He wanted to clean the room before he touched anything else. He turned around. There was a supply closet down the hall, and it didn't take him long to find the duster.

Once he had rid every corner of the office of dirt, Xavier sat down at his father's desk. There was an overwhelming feeling of power that immediately fell upon him when he pressed his palms into the wood. This was his now. Xavier started looking through the drawers. There wasn't anything out of the ordinary—pens, papers, to-do lists. A small notepad sat in front of a picture of Ares and Caliste, and next to the photo was a small frog statue that Zale had made in one of his pottery classes. There were files detailing his father's clients and friends, and Xavier set them to the side to look through later. In one drawer, there were photos. Xavier smiled softly as he looked through them.

There he was, learning how to shoot a gun for the first time. Cassidy cooking. Astra building her first computer. There was Griffin, walking a tightrope, light as always, the thrill of the fall in his eyes. There was Jaxson and Zale building a table. Zale still had the scar on his hand from when Jaxson accidentally drove a nail through the side of his wrist. He had taken out a chunk of skin, and Zale hadn't been able to write for weeks. Jaxson stayed with him in the hospital, and did his chores the whole time as an apology.

Xavier quickly wiped away a tear that slid down his cheek and continued to flip through the photos. Yvette and Tessa racing each other. His parents. Arya. Griffin and Jaxson laughing while they baked, the treehouse his dad built in the backyard, Astra and Cassidy's matching dresses, Yvette playing the piano, his mother teaching Tessa to sew. Christmas photos, baby photos, the chess set, Griffin's guilty expression after he broke a vase. They all looked so normal. Xavier wished he could go back to being innocent.

He set the photos in a stack. He had to remember to get a photo album to keep them safe in his room. Xavier continued to look through the desk drawers. There wasn't much else in there that wasn't work-related. He was surprised to find contracts that dated back to before he was born. "Don't you have filing cabinets for this? Why aren't they being used?" he wondered aloud. After Xavier had completely emptied the desk, he stared at the piles he had made and groaned. It was going to take forever to go through them all.

Xavier located his father's semi-empty filing cabinets and began organizing the contracts by dates. He noticed a couple of names that seemed familiar, as well as those that he had already met with. While snagging a pen and carefully writing them down, he decided that it would be good to read up on the files and the terms his father had set, just in case they tried to double-cross him. Xavier already knew that the penalty of betrayal or anything of the like, no matter how severe, was death. His family didn't do mercy. It was the reason why they had done so well.

While he was going through a storage room to find a bin to keep the contracts for later reading in, he found a photo album that was mostly empty. There were more photos of old pets and a few more pictures of him and his siblings learning the family trade. He dropped it into the box and took it back to the office.

Once he was situated, he set the files in the bin and delicately placed the photos into the album. Of all his siblings, Cassidy was the only one who stayed in the house with him. After his father's death, they had been scattered and assigned to different countries and cities to keep clients under control. In just three months, their kill count had doubled. Yes, there was no such thing as mercy, but even they weren't exempt from feeling guilty.

Yvette was the one who suggested the meetings with the family clients, instead of just emailing them the changes. It was a pain, dealing with people who wanted jobs done, only to find out they were no longer offering certain services. Though Yvette was right, it was way more personal, and it showed the fact that they were changing. Yvette was with him through it all, the meetings, the filing, the grief-fueled target practice. She was the youngest, but one of the strongest. Yvette had taken countless jobs, doing more in a month than Xavier could have ever done in a year. When she spoke to Xavier, he listened. Yvette had even set up the first few meetings. His sister's diplomacy and calm demeanor are what got him and these people through the first weeks' worth of meetings.

Not everyone was happy with the changes. Some clients took it well, the fact that assassination was off the table, so long as the family could still be hired on as body guards. Then, the subject of no longer stealing and selling information came up. That was an even harder conversation. When Xavier announced that they would be taking their weapons off the market, he got coffee thrown at his face and what he hoped was a bunch of empty threats.

Yvette was with him through all of it. She was set on making sure the family paid for their crimes. She knew the pain of murdering former friends, same as him. Xavier knew she took it harder. However, Yvette was adamant that atoning didn't mean that they were done with the job. What it meant was that they were changing the rules. Xavier was not above killing. He was not above destroying anyone and everyone that ever caused them any problems. But they were done making and distributing weapons to the wrong people. They were done taking blood money just to stay afloat. Yvette made sure of that, and he knew it was a good decision.

When he was younger, Xavier hadn't known what they were doing. His first missions included dropping off news and packages to his father's friends. He followed his older siblings on shorter missions, keeping watch and learning the ropes. Then he upgraded to assassination. Before he knew it, he and his siblings ruled the world from underground. Anyone and everyone who ever cycled through the halls of the Duke family mansion knew it. They were ruthless. They could bring empires down with a flick of their hand.

It all went south when Leroy stole tech from them.

Their father had trusted him enough to welcome him into their home. Leroy had walked the halls, he ate at their table, he worked with Ares, he was more than a client, they were friends. Leroy barely knew the family, and only Ares by name. Xavier and his siblings weren't allowed to talk to clients, it was for their own safety. Still, Xavier thought Leroy was safe, that he was kind. One second, he was working with Ares, the next had taken everything he could carry and fled, killing his own brother in the process.

They spent years cleaning his mess up, only to find that he was still working. They planned to take back what was theirs, but they had no easy way of getting near him. They had been so close. Then Arya died. Then their mother. Then their father. It took a lot of time to recover from the death of one family member, let alone three. Only once Astra infiltrated Torsion did they have a chance, and even after that, there was still work to do.

Xavier dropped his head down on the desk and heard a hollow echo. He frowned. He began to tap on the desk until he reached the side of the desk where the echo was strongest. Xavier felt around until he found a thin dip in the wood and he pried the side off of the desk. There were more binders inside. He pulled them out one by one. When he picked one up, a photo fell onto the floor. It was a photo of him. Xavier flipped the binder over. His name was printed onto the front of it in bold gold lettering: Xiwang *'Xavier'* Zhang. Third of the Duke children. *Dum Spiro Spero*. Xavier smiled. "While I breathe, I hope," he read aloud. "Makes sense."

Xavier looked at the other binders. Arya, *abore et honore:* by labor and honor. Jaxson, *dat deus incrementum*: God gives growth. Cassidy, *malo mori quam foedari:* death before dishonor.

Tessa, *non semper erit aestas:* it will not always be summer. Griffin, *regnat populus:* the people rule. Zale, *carpe maria:* seize the seas. Yvette, *fiat iustitia et pereat mundus:* let justice be done, though the world would perish.

Then finally: Astra, *ad astra per aspera*. Through adversity, we go to the stars.

He sighed. The logical thing would be to open his own binder first, but he didn't. Instead, Xavier opened Astra's and began to read. He found pictures, notes on her work, pictures she drew, old homework assignments, newspaper clippings, and mission reports. Then, he got to his father's notes. He had listed her accomplishments and how proud he was of her. He had repeated her mother's words and congratulated her on her success. The last page of the notes was a letter of farewell to her as she went to Torsion, obviously one never sent. When Xavier flipped to the end, he found a folded piece of paper, taped to the inner back cover. He pulled it off and opened it.

'Dear Astra. If you're reading this, it seems that I have suffered the fate that all of us do. I'm sorry that you couldn't be with me, but as you know, it was unsafe to do so. Astra, remember your roots. Do not allow yourself to become angry. Stay close to your family; it is not yet time for you to die. As for me—my absence has been too long, and my time is nearing. Be careful, stay mindful, and try to return home. Thank you for allowing me to look out for you. You'll do well when you grow up. Sincerely, Ares.'

Xavier folded the note up and returned it to its place. He knew he had seen something very personal, something he never should have read. He turned a couple of pages back, trying to find any context for why his father would tell Astra that. He had not known his father was going to die, and it didn't seem like his father had known it either. So why would his father prepare something in advance for this, especially dated only a few years ago? Xavier flipped through the binder, abruptly stopping at a diagram and a drawing about five pages after his father's notes had ended. This was obviously Astra's doing, though his father's handwriting was sprinkled through it. What he saw shocked him.

Xavier dropped the binder onto the floor and threw his head

back, staring at the ceiling. Thoughts whirled around in his head as little pieces fell into place. Xavier didn't realize he had been missing so much. He sighed. "Well, Little Star… looks like I'm helping you, after all."

4

Notes on the Dead

Astra set a stack of files down on the lab table. "Well, Aiken—you ready?"

Aiken stared up at her. "This seems like it could take a while."

"Of course it does. That's because it will."

Aiken frowned. "Why?"

"It's meant to. There are more files in the box there." She gestured toward the container. "As long as you keep going through them and taking notes, it'll be fine."

"So, instead of being stuck on tank duty, I'm stuck on studying-Parkes'-insane-brain duty." Aiken crossed his arms. "I'm not an intern Astra."

"Think of it as a learning opportunity!"

Aiken huffed. "Yeah, right."

Astra sighed. "Look, I can't do all of this right now. I have a lot on my plate and you're the only person who's not actually busy."

"I am busy! I'm working on my plants."

"Aiken, half the time you spend working on your plants is just waiting around for them to grow."

Aiken pursed his lips. "Okay, you got me there."

"Aiken, I'm counting on you, okay?" Astra turned away and grabbed her phone. "You're the only person who can help me. You have to!" She typed a couple of commands in the program on her phone and turned around, raising an eyebrow pointedly. "You said that you would."

Aiken hesitated. Something was telling him that he should help Astra. After all, she had done a lot for them. She had helped them in so many ways, he couldn't even recall them all… "Fine, I'll do it. But my research takes priority."

Astra smiled, but it didn't look completely right. "Of course.

Well, I'm off to go help Zola hire new staff. Good luck!" She sprinted out the door so he couldn't see the look on her face.

It was a good excuse, and one that made sense. With Leroy gone, they had petitioned the school to make Zola acting Dean. They loved her in the interview process, and with a few called in favors from Astra's family, it was settled. Astra, despite not taking classes, was allowed to stay there, and took on a temporary staff position as well.

As Astra walked away from Aiken, she thought back to everything they'd been through. The files, the manipulations, the clones, the loss of his hand. The longer she thought about it, the more an unfamiliar feeling formed in her stomach. It wasn't until she was almost to Parkes' former office that she realized it was guilt.

Aiken stared at the stack of files in front of him. He really didn't want to do this, but Astra was right… he did have the time, and he did agree to do it. Sighing, he grabbed a file, opened his notebook, and began to read. These files were of the androids and his experiments. This particular file was filled with diagrams and notes on Destiny. Aiken was impressed by Destiny's inner workings—the fact that anyone could do this and confuse a man who spent his life working with robots was incredible.

The more he read, the more intrigued he got. One note stood out to him, and he frowned. It read, *'I believe that Destiny was made flawed on purpose. She is a frail imitation of the real thing. Ares has always had a thing for art.'* Ares? Aiken shrugged. It could be a code name. Maybe Leroy didn't want to credit himself. It was a plausible explanation; many people had been killed over inventions. Then again, Leroy liked being recognized, so maybe it was his partner. Aiken wrote it down in his notes. *'Leroy believes Destiny was created faulty. I'm unsure what that means.'*

He continued on. The next file contained plans and notes for the android copies he was going to make. *'I want to do what Ares could not. I want to make humans out of metal, fully controllable.*

They can burn the world all they want. They are not restricted to petty ideals.' Aiken snickered. *'Leroy was absolutely insane,'* he wrote. *'He seemed to want world domination.'* Leroy had planned everything. His ideas were listed very clearly, and Aiken knew Astra would want to look at them herself. He stuck a sticky note on it, telling himself he'd give it to her later.

The next three files detailed Parkes' beginning stages. There were codes, blueprints, notes on his employees, letters, and graphs of the androids. Aiken pulled the letters out and began to read them. Most taunted whoever or whatever Ares was. Each letter referred to the project as Project Checkmate and always ended with, *'Your move, Leroy.'* Aiken raised an eyebrow. At least he was creative.

Aiken noted the letters. *'Parkes likes taunting his adversary. I don't know if you who or what Ares is, but each letter is addressed to him and tells him that it's his turn. It's like they're playing a game of chess.'* Aiken spotted a file labeled 01, and instantly knew what it was. The file could only refer to Cassian, the oldest of the androids and the first replacement model. Sure enough, he was right. The file contained a diagram of Cassian, his base code, what he was meant to do, and the trials that he was a part of—except for the last one. Aiken's guess was that Parkes didn't have time to put the latest trial in, given that he was dead. He yawned.

Aiken frowned, looking at his watch. He could have sworn that it had been only an hour ago that Astra gave him the files, but his watch read midnight. He had been planning to hand Astra his notes along with the file he set aside for her that night. Oh, well. Astra would probably still be awake; she never seemed to sleep. He grabbed the files and his notes. He'd drop them off with her and then go to sleep.

The walk up the stairs seemed longer and harder than usual. Aiken found it hard to focus. *'It must be the sleep deprivation,'* he thought. By the time Aiken made it to Astra's floor, he was out of breath. *'Or maybe I'm out of shape. It could be a side effect of trauma.'* Aiken yawned. The group had almost unanimously decided he needed therapy, so he started doing sessions online. It was difficult, there were days when he couldn't even identify the feelings he had. It was all numb, and doing things filled the hole that numbness left.

He raised his hand to knock on the door. Astra opened it before he could. She raised an eyebrow. "What are you doing here?"

Aiken held up the files and notes. "I thought you might find my findings today interesting."

Astra nodded. "I didn't expect you to bring it, but I probably will."

"There's also a file in there that you'll want to look at."

"Okay—I'll check it out. Sleep well, Aiken. You need it."

Aiken rubbed his eyes. "Yeah, I'll go sleep right away."

Astra held his gaze. "You better." She closed the door.

Astra watched as Aiken's heart rate settled as he fell asleep. She was surprised at how easy it was to control him now. She turned to the documents Aiken had given her. She picked up the file first. *'Leroy Parkes' Plans, '* read the sticky note on the front.

This time, Astra didn't skim the file. Instead, she took it slow, thoroughly absorbing all the information inside.

When she finally put the file down, she was upset. "I'm glad you're dead," she muttered. "I will destroy everything you've built. I will find your body and burn it. I will kill your friends, cripple your allies, and raise your enemies. You don't deserve anything you've accomplished. You deserve the fate that has befallen you. No one outruns death."

She sat there in silence, breathing heavily. The monologuing was almost cliche, but it felt better to say it aloud than write it down. It meant that once she said it, it was gone. No one could hold those words against her. Astra's heart thumped in her ears. Her father had always told her it was good to disburse any feelings of bitterness. Astra counted in her head until her breathing leveled.

She closed her eyes.

'I am calm,' she thought.

Astra opened her eyes and grabbed Aiken's notes. They were simple, mostly references to the experiments and things he thought were important. She paused by the note about Destiny, about her *'intentionally'* flawed design. Astra scoffed. "She was, but Father didn't make her." Astra had always found Parkes' confusion regarding who actually made the tech amusing. Granted, her father was protecting her and her siblings. But she did wish that she was recognized. It was all the better for her still—she was meant to live in the shadows.

Astra's thoughts were interrupted by her phone ringing. She frowned. It was Xavier. "Hello?"

"Hi, Astra. Sorry I took so long to get back to you—a lot was going on around here. I had to dispatch some more of our siblings to keep the peace between the people that I insulted."

Astra laughed. "That seems like you."

"I'm not as diplomatic as the rest of you."

"You were supposed to be."

"You know that I'm more of an *'act first, ask questions later'* type."

"True. So, do you have an answer for me?" There was silence on the other end of the line. "Xavier?"

"I found something I shouldn't have."

"What?"

"I went into Father's office to clean and look for files. I found binders meant for us instead."

"Binders?" Astra frowned. "What does that mean?"

"You know how we've all been apart for so long that we didn't open the letter he gave us in the will?"

"Yeah."

"Well, after I found the binders, I looked for it. I read Dad's will and it gave us instructions to find the binders. There's a secret compartment in his desk. Anyway, they're filled with gifts for us, notes on us, and things he wanted to tell us but didn't."

"So it was meant for you. Why do you think you read something you shouldn't have?"

Xavier was silent for a second. "Because I didn't read mine." He sighed. "I read yours."

Astra's heart sank. "What?"

"I read yours, Astra, and I know what you are now. I know who Father is, and I'm going to help you. I have to keep you safe, even though I know that our roles have flipped."

Astra leaned against the wall. "So, you're going to help me because you're scared I might die?"

"Yes. Because you're my sister and I care about you. We all do—even Cassidy, though she's still mad."

Astra nodded. "Okay. Thank you."

"So, what do I have to do?"

Astra smiled. "I've thought about it, and this is the best course of action. You're going to apply for an internship at Leroy Parkes's secondary research facility," Astra said. "And I'm going to make sure you get in."

5

A House Divided

Xavier stared at his computer. It was long past midnight, but he wanted to finish the application. He had just started about five minutes ago and he was already bored. Astra was right—it was a long and inefficient process. They no doubt wanted to weed out anyone who didn't fit their standards, much like the process for selecting students for Torsion University. Astra had already informed him about the process that went with choosing the students: how picky they were, and how she wouldn't have even gotten in if it weren't for the glitch in the system.

If Astra had gotten in by the skin of her teeth, Xavier could only hope to get into this research facility without interference. Xavier stared down at the blank space where his essay was supposed to go. He considered leaving it blank, but they would most likely bring it up in whatever interview he had to do, so he took a deep breath and began to write.

Xavier didn't really know when he fell asleep. He was awoken the next morning to his phone vibrating—someone was calling him. He picked up the phone. "Hello?" he murmured, hyper-aware of how tired he felt and sounded.

"Did you just wake up?"

"Yeah, why?"

Astra laughed. "First of all, check the time. Second of all, check your email."

Xavier looked at his watch. A shock ran through him. "It's noon?" he yelled.

"Yep."

Xavier shook his head. "I swear it was nine a.m. three minutes ago. Wow, I must have passed out. "

"You probably did. You started on that application way too

late. It didn't even come in until four a.m., and then I had to make sure it was accepted."

"I had a lot to do," Xavier complained. "I'm a very busy person."

Astra ignored his comments. "You have an interview at three p.m., so it's a good thing I woke you up. Dress nicely, okay?"

"Three p.m.? Dress nicely? Ugh!" Xavier slammed his head down on the table. "Ow," he mumbled. "I don't wanna go."

"You have to." Astra paused. "I'll call you back in an hour to make sure you're ready."

"I hate you."

"Too late, you've already agreed. Good luck!" She hung up before Xavier could retort. He slowly stood up, the only thought in his head was to get caffeine. He trudged down the stairs. He didn't want anyone to see him. He was always up early, and if Cassidy found out, she would be making fun of him for days.

Just when Xavier thought he had successfully made it to the coffee machine without being noticed, he heard a voice behind him. "Long night?"

Xavier facepalmed. "Hi, Cass."

She pressed a cup of coffee into his hands. "Astra told me what's going on. I'm glad you decided to help her."

"You're not mad at her anymore?"

"No, I still am. But family comes first, always. Drink up. I'm going to go find you proper clothes. You can't show up in sweatpants as you do at our meetings. You need dress pants. And a button-down. Do you think you can fit in Dad's clothes?" She waved her hand. "Nevermind, I think your measurements are in one of the files upstairs, I'll figure it out. Gosh, do you even own anything dressy?" Cassidy ran up the stairs, leaving Xavier to hold his coffee in bewilderment.

One of the staff members passed by and nodded to him. Xavier blinked wearily. It was going to be a long day.

Cassidy forced him to shower and comb his hair. Xavier faced himself in the mirror and gave himself a half-smile. When had he become so lazy? He washed his hands in silence, contemplating what he had just agreed to. Putting his life on the line was the norm in his family. Feeling unsure was not. He heard a knock on the door.

"Are you ready?" Xavier could hear Cassidy's irritation even in her muffled voice. "You're going to be late!"

Xavier swallowed. "As ready as I'll ever be," he muttered to himself. He opened the door. "Let's go."

The drive to the airport was short. According to Astra, Leroy wanted to keep an eye on his projects, so they were always nearby. Astra had set up the first interview to be over the phone just before the flight. She had even sent him a script. The second interview would be conducted in person as soon as Xavier arrived sometime in the evening. Xavier read Astra's instructions over and over until he had memorized them.

Cassidy tapped him on the shoulder and handed him a computer. "It's time."

Xavier sat still, trying to push his father's calm and collected presence forward. He shoved his qualms about the mission behind him. As the connection stabilized, revealing his interviewers, he straightened up and finished his facade.

His name was Xavier Duke, and he ruled the world.

* * * * * * * *

The interview went well, unsurprisingly. Astra sure knew how to put together a plan. Xavier settled back into his chair. He could see the clouds out the window, bathed in the golden light of the setting sun. He was fully calm now, not just faking it. He glanced toward the front of the plane, where Cassidy was sitting, absorbed in her phone. "How's it going?" he asked.

"I have to do your work for you," she sighed. "That means I'm taking care of business when you're away. Since you're incapable of doing it yourself, apparently."

Xavier rolled his eyes. "I'm not diplomatic," he said. "I told you that."

"Maybe not. But you're still a member of this household, and you need to do your part."

"I am."

"Now you are." Cassidy glared at him. "After months of doing nothing at all. You were a mess. You moped around the house like you had nothing left."

Xavier sighed. "I feel different, Cass. Something's changing."

"Dad's not holding us together anymore. Mom died a long time ago. You shouldn't be worried about her not being here to help."

"You were closest to her."

"Tessa was closest to her," she corrected. "But what daughter isn't close to her mother? We were all young. We saw what happened to Mom when Arya died. She was… different. When Dad sent us all on these missions to teach us, she told him not to. She warned him. We would've turned out differently if we had waited until we were older. If Mom succeeded in keeping us from the business until we were 18, like Jaxson."

"No one suspects a child. Not even Parkes," Xavier said.

"That is good reasoning."

"Of course." Xavier looked back out the window. "We shouldn't be talking about this. We should be preparing for what's awaiting us when we land."

"What's awaiting you."

Xavier looked at her. "You're not coming to see me off?"

"Of course not. Astra only prepared you. I'm staying on the plane. Since you're the only one with the interview, you're the only one who gets to disembark the plane and live. If I stepped off, they'd shoot me. They're very intense, according to Astra," Cassidy said.

Xavier frowned. "That's not concerning at all."

Cassidy put her phone down and smiled. "You'll do fine. You passed the first interview. All this one does is determine what level you'll be placed at when you enter."

Xavier blinked. "So I get a level of classification to get in?"

Cassidy threw a pen at him. "Did you not read what Astra sent you?"

"I read the instructions."

"You're hopeless."

"I also haven't left the house since Father died."

Cassidy sighed. "Look, I'm sorry. I know you and I are different; we have different ways of dealing with things. But you need to be ready. What's waiting when you get there is certain death if you aren't careful. You have everything you need to survive, so long as you keep yourself together and you remember your training. You were built for this."

"Cass—"

"No. You listen to me. You've done this countless times before. You know how to do it, you know what to do, you know how to protect yourself. You can't let that go to waste just because you're sad!"

Xavier sat there in silence. He looked down at his lap, not wanting to look her in the eye. "I know, I know, I know."

"Then why don't you act like it?"

"It's hard, Cass. I never want to feel like this, but I've never felt like this before."

"Then pull yourself together."

Xavier raised an eyebrow.

"You heard me. Do it internally. Deal with it silently. Because right now, you are the weakest, and you cannot afford to be."

Xavier nodded. "Fine." He narrowed his eyes. "But if I die here, you're not taking over."

Cassidy stared at him. "Why not?"

"You're not ready. You're not as old as Jaxson is. You're not as level-headed as Tessa, and you cannot lead if you yell. A leader is there to be encouraging, to play on the strengths of those below them. A leader guides and teaches those in their care how to succeed. They don't berate them."

Cassidy looked shocked. She opened her mouth to speak but Xavier raised a finger to shush her.

"If you're going to critique me, I can do the same to you," he said levelly. You're like how I was: cocky. You think you can take on the world. You think you're invincible, that nothing can kill you until you're ready to die. That has never been the right way to treat life. I called Astra the weakest of us, but she never was. None of us were weak. We all had equal strengths and different skills, but still, we worked together. A house divided crumbles. Don't divide your people as I did."

Cassidy stared at him. "That was a switch up. It seems every time you speak you have something to say that I never expected."

Xavier nodded. "I told you. I'm not the person I was."

6

Sick

Astra headed towards one of the lower floors, passing students on her way down. She had rarely left her room recently and it felt strange to be around so many people again. Some of them greeted her as she walked, others turned away, unable to look her in the face. Astra sighed, stopping in the middle of the hallway. It was normal for people to be afraid of her. She knew that her appearance wasn't entirely human. She wasn't going to ignore the way people cringed when they looked at her for too long. Humans had a natural tendency to realize when something wasn't quite real. Perhaps that's why Leroy's project failed.

Astra didn't know what to think now. Since Leroy's death, everything had been falling into place. Her friends were busy with school and work, the students avoided her, so no one really had time to ask questions. She was left alone. Now, Astra had to take care of multiple other problems that took that peace and time away from her. She had every right to be angry. Xavier had agreed to do what she asked of him, but she didn't know if he would be safe. He had the tendency to be reckless. She had to make sure she had an insurance policy for him. He wouldn't like being babysat, so she'd find someone to cover his tracks.

Luckily, she knew where to find just the right person.

After a few more minutes of staring straight ahead and disrupting foot traffic, Astra opted to take one of the passageways instead of the stairs. She didn't like being looked at. They knew she was part of the reason the staff was being replaced. Every so often, she got a notification from Zola about the applicants. Almost every single one was a familiar name. Her family kept their promises. Torsion would be cared for, and her friends would be safe. That gave her a sense of relief.

Astra arrived at the final dorm level and knocked on the first door. To her surprise, Alyssa opened it. Astra frowned. "What are you doing here? Shouldn't you be doing doctor-related stuff?"

Alyssa grimaced. "That's the problem. Come on in."

Astra stepped in hesitantly. "I thought that the transfer went smoothly. What's this?"

Cassian looked up at her and waved. "Hey."

She smiled back at him weakly and turned to Alyssa. "What's going on?" she whispered.

"They're getting sick."

"Sick?"

"They're not losing memories—there's no sign of aggressive behavior—but they are immunocompromised. I've been trying to get ahold of Aiken to see if he has anything that might be able to help... but he's been ghosting me."

Astra nodded. "Aiken's flighty. You'll probably be able to get ahold of him soon. Where's Isaac? Doesn't he share a room with Cassian?"

"Isaac didn't show any signs of sickness. Neither did Willow, Morgan, or Eric. They've been moved to the lab, but the other five have been quarantined."

"I was just in the lab. I didn't see them there."

Alyssa laughed. "Right, I forgot—you were quarantined too. Mary and Elena have been repurposing the room that they found Aiken in when Parkes kidnapped him. They've turned it into a second lab, so we can monitor the health of clones without anyone getting concerned or curious."

Astra pursed her lips. "A good idea." She turned towards Cassian. "How are you feeling?"

"Horrid," Cassian admitted. "I liked it better when the only disease I had was the fact that I was made of metal." He groaned. "I hope you figure something out soon."

Astra nodded. "We'll try!" she said encouragingly. "Alyssa's the best in her practice, if anyone can help you, it's her." She turned and whispered to Alyssa. "You can help them, right?"

Alyssa nodded. "I think so. So far, I think it's not contagious to us. But Castor did infect William, so it can be spread to them."

Astra frowned. "This has to be unique to them."

Alyssa nodded. "Probably. I'm going to keep getting blood samples until I figure out what's wrong."

Astra nodded. "Okay. I'm going to go to the lab and check on the others." She paused. "Wait. Can we be carriers of the bacteria?"

"I don't think so, but it'll probably be killed by extreme cold or heat. Just go stand in the freezer before you go."

"Okay." Astra left the room. She didn't have time, so she took another passageway and just let her anger heat her skin until she lit the passageways up with blue light. There's no way bacteria would still be on her after that. It took her a few minutes to calm down before she went inside the lab. When she opened the door, she nearly hit Mary in the face.

"Whoa! Watch it!" Mary yelled. Her frustrated expression melted to a face of concern once she saw Astra. "What's up? You look stressed."

"Alyssa told me what was going on. How are you guys?"

"Oh, we're fine. Elena went to find Nasra to help her set up the monitors. I need to go get some wiring. It's good that you're here. Do you think you could watch them?"

Astra nodded. "Of course."

Mary smiled. "Thanks so much!" She dropped her pliers and wrench on the closest table and sprinted out of the room.

Astra watched her go before delving further into the room. "Eric? Willow? Morgan? Isaac?"

"They're asleep." It was Isaac's voice.

"Oh. Hi, Isaac."

"Hi, Astra. How are you?"

"I'm fine. What are you up to?"

"Trying not to die. You aren't carrying the disease, are you?"

"I shouldn't be. How do you think you guys are okay?"

Isaac looked her in the eye. "I think it was you."

"Me?" Astra frowned. "How could I keep you from getting sick?"

Isaac tapped the back of her hand. "Your blood. You seem to have immunity. Every other student in that quarantine was fighting for their lives, but you treated it like it was a mild version of the common cold." Isaac looked down. "I went back to the machine because Morgan told me that you were alone with it. It's not what they think it is, is it?"

"No." Astra wasn't sure where Isaac was going with this, but she was sure she wouldn't like it.

Isaac nodded. "I saw the machine, I touched it—cut my finger on it—and something came out of it. I couldn't get rid of it. I didn't go back to my room because I was literally glowing. I burned everything I touched for about an hour. When it was gone, I knew I couldn't tell anyone, but I also wasn't sure how to tell you. But I'm sure how to now. Whatever that thing was made to be, it's strange. Because," Isaac held up his hand, "every single time I cut my pointer finger, now, I bleed blue."

Astra stared at him. "Let me see." She peered at it, and sure enough, there was a faint glow in his finger. "Huh. I have an idea."

"Really?"

Astra smiled. "You'll hate it though." Before Issac could object, she grabbed a syringe off the cart and inserted it into his finger.

"Ow!"

"Be quiet."

"Wha—you didn't even ask!"

"You had a problem. I gave you a solution. You don't have the right to be angry." She drew blood until it came out red. She grabbed a bandage and wrapped his finger. "There. You're all set."

Isaac stared at her and then looked down at his finger. "You seem like you know what you're doing. Have you done this before?"

Astra stared at the vial in her hand. "Nope. This is a first. I've never seen anything like it."

"Did I ruin the machine?"

"No. It was designed to start on blood, not run on it. It'll be fine." She turned back to Isaac. "What I want to know is how you got this into the others."

"I didn't. Once Castor infected William, they realized we had to be quarantined. Nothing else. They don't have your blood."

Astra slipped the vial into her pocket. "Good. Then you need to come with me. Before Mary gets back."

"Why?"

"Because I have a job for you, and you probably won't like it either."

* * * * * * * *

Astra and Isaac sat together in the airport, silently.

"How are you going to explain me being gone?" Isaac asked finally.

"I won't."

"You're not going to elaborate on that?"

"Why should I?"

Isaac shrugged. "Fair enough."

Astra sighed. "You really don't understand the stakes here. The quicker you leave, the better it will be for me. When you return, no one will even notice you left."

"That's comforting," he said, sarcastically. "But really."

"Isaac, if you die, they won't even remember you."

"What?"

Astra tapped her fingers on her phone. "By now, the other clones don't know your name; they don't know who you are. And when I return, I'll make sure the rest of the students and our friends don't either."

Isaac sighed. "There's really no going back, is there?"

"Not until you've finished the job."

"I will."

"Of course, you will. You have a lot of potential. I know I can trust you for this mission. You were made after Destiny, modeled to be better than her. If Leroy Parkes succeeded in making a perfect version of my work—despite the fact that it was never meant to be perfect—then you cannot fail. It doesn't worry me. He tried so hard to make multiple of you, and they still had flaws. But he was wrong about one thing. Those flaws make you stronger. You're human. You'll succeed."

"And if I don't?"

"Then I'll remake you." Astra passed him a bottle of water. "Drink all of it. When you do, I'll have your memories."

Isaac nodded. He downed it all in one go, making a face once he had. "So, I'm safe now."

"It'll take a couple of hours to kick in, but I'll be able to save everything you see and revive you. That's only a worst-case scenario. I pray it doesn't come to that."

"I don't understand why I need to do this. Why can't you go with him?"

"I just can't." Astra looked up at him. "You can fly under the radar. You'll keep suspicion away from him. If I go, I'll just make it worse. They have a file on me from school. They'll know something's wrong."

"Still, if I die–"

Astra cut him off. "That won't happen." She stared at him. "I promise. I always take precautions. You won't die. Even if you get caught, I believe you'll find a way. You'll do well," she said. "Do you promise to keep my brother safe?"

Isaac nodded firmly. "With my life."

7

Arrivals

Xavier stood in the airport checking his watch as if it had the ability to tell him what the hold-up was. It had been half an hour since he was supposed to be picked up and nobody had shown up yet. He sighed. Some people used tardiness as a way of intimidation. Xavier just found it tacky and unprofessional. Maybe it was a habit, but he was never late, nor ever early. Xavier prided himself in getting to places exactly on time. That was one thing his siblings didn't agree with him on, to the point that they began to just take separate transportation.

A few minutes later, he heard someone calling his name. "Xavier? Xavier Zhang?"

He turned around. A man in a plain suit waved at him. "Are you Xavier?"

He nodded.

The man smiled. "Great! I'm Mr. Lavoie. I'll be taking you to the research facility. Come with me."

Xavier followed, wary. As soon as he had gotten back onto the field, his instincts had kicked in. He had almost forgotten what it was like. The familiarity was almost comforting, being on edge, knowing half the world wanted you dead. Xavier slid into the backseat of the car. '*Let the show begin,*' he thought.

At least the scenery was beautiful. Concrete turned to dirt, to fields, to trees. Xavier considered rolling down the window to feel the breeze, but ultimately decided not to. It was always better to be silent and speak when you're spoken to.

Several hours passed without a word from the driver. Xavier began to think that they wanted to kill him. He tightened his hand around the knife in his pocket. It was easy to smuggle in his luggage, and a quick trip to the bathroom allowed him to conceal three other portable weapons on his person.

He tried to calm down. He glanced toward the driver. Lavoie kept both hands on the wheel, back straight, eyes alert on the road. He barely gave Xavier any attention. Xavier relaxed. This man wasn't going to kill him, at least not now.

About twenty minutes later, they slowed down and the dirt roads turned back into concrete. When they arrived at the gates, Mr. Lavoie spent several minutes arguing with someone on the phone. Xavier rolled his eyes. Either they were still trying to impress him, or they were extremely unorganized.

Xavier wished he could go with the former. He disliked jobs that were easy, but in the aftermath of their boss's death, it was no wonder they were having problems. Xavier resisted the urge to roll his eyes. He doubted that the driver was like the people on the inside, so he wasn't going to be able to guess what was waiting for him. Still, he had assumed that he'd be able to get in and out quickly. *'Then I can go home, and finally get my life in order. Astra, why do you have to be so convincing? I could have 100 problems, and you would be the source of all of them.'*

Eventually, the gate opened and they were allowed in. Xavier followed Mr. Lavoie into the building, up several flights of stairs, and finally into an office, where he was left alone. The place was pristine; he could almost see his reflection in the marble floors. It didn't take him long to spot the cameras. No wonder why they felt safe leaving him alone—he never left their sight. Sighing, Xavier settled into his chair. He had a feeling he was going to be waiting for a very long time.

* * * * * * * *

Back at Torsion, Astra tracked Xavier's progress through a device she had coded into his watch. He had gotten inside alright, but he had been stuck in the same room for several hours. Astra knew not to be worried. Her brother could take care of himself and it wasn't like this enemy was any worse than others they had faced. It was

45

Isaac that was the issue now. It was easier to get him in—they had a file on him and they still thought he was made of metal instead of flesh and bones. That was just one of the things she had kept from him.

They wouldn't question what he did, so long as he followed her instructions exactly. Astra sighed. Isaac could be controlled. She wasn't so stupid as to let him leave without an insurance policy, one that was far more complicated than just downloading his memories onto a hard drive. Unfortunately, Xavier couldn't be. And that could prove to be disastrous.

"Astra!"

She instinctively closed the page she was looking at and turned around, hiding the computer with her body. She recognized the silhouette that had appeared. "Oh. Hi, Zola. What's up?"

Zola frowned. "Don't you remember? You were supposed to be helping me with hiring today!"

"Of course!" Astra stood up and closed her laptop. "I got a little sidetracked. Sorry."

Zola looked at her. "You're acting weird."

"No, where would you get that idea?"

"Something seems off." She peered at Astra. "Are you still sick?"

Astra flipped her hair behind her. "Of course not. You're being paranoid, Zola. The idea that I would be acting any differently is preposterous. I'm not an idiot; I was just startled."

Zola laughed. "You're using unnecessary words again. Are you sure you're fine? It's okay if you're feeling a little off. I won't tell Alyssa." She raised an eyebrow. "Gosh, you act like you're trying to impress someone, or hiding something, which is normal for you, so maybe I shouldn't be so concerned."

Astra glared. "I'm not hiding anything. I'm just… slightly stressed."

"Hmph." Zola sighed. "You're so confusing. One day you

seem as if you like us, the next you're cold as ice. Is there anything about you that's real?"

"Don't you trust me?"

"Of course I trust you. But it's hard to trust someone with so many secrets."

"So you don't trust me," Astra said flatly.

"Don't put words into my mouth, I do trust you. It's just the things you hide, I feel like you don't trust me," Zola retorted.

"As if you don't have secrets."

"At least I don't go around parading them."

"What's that supposed to mean?!" Astra frowned, half-yelling the question.

"Geez, don't scream in my ear. I'm just saying, you walk with purpose, which is fine. But you speak like you're going to die at any moment." Zola paused. She continued quietly, "There's nothing wrong with living, Astra."

"There's nothing wrong with *me,* Zola. Just because I don't live the way you do doesn't mean there's a problem."

"I wasn't saying that! I'm just saying, have you ever thought about, oh I don't know, being a little bit more normal?"

A mirthless laugh escaped Astra. "That's rich coming from you. None of us are normal, and who wants to be anyway?"

Zola rolled her eyes. "Fair. I give up. No point in arguing with a brick wall. Come help me with the files. I conducted the interviews, I just need a second opinion on who to hire."

Astra grabbed one of the files and opened it, scanning through it before looking at another one. "Are you favoring anyone?"

"Not really. I mean, I have some ideas, but I want your input first."

Astra knew every single one of their names. While not everyone who applied was directly connected to her, it seemed that only people she knew she could trust had made it through the process. That was one perk of having her siblings controlling which applications actually made their way into Zola's hands.

Astra disregarded Zola's recommendations entirely. Some of these people were not fit for the tasks she was going to give them. Slowly but surely, Astra pushed Zola to pick the people she wanted. They were almost finished when the name on one of the files caught Astra's eye. She picked it up and opened it. "Huh."

"What? Is it bad? Should I throw it out?"

"No, her file is impressive. She should be our final hire."

Zola nodded. "I trust your judgment." She gathered the files of the people they chose. "I'll make sure to give them all calls tomorrow. Good luck with whatever it is you're doing."

Astra nodded and mumbled a thanks as Zola left.

Of all people, why did Tessa want to work at Torsion? It would work well in her favor, but why? It had been years since the two had even seen each other. Astra smiled. She could feel a backup plan forming. "Thanks, Tess," she said to herself. "I didn't ask for your help, but it'll still be good to have it."

Astra opened her laptop. Things were going to be happening a lot quicker with her sister by her side. She had to make sure she adjusted accordingly.

* * * * * * * *

Xavier was correct that they were going to keep him waiting. He sat there for what seemed like hours. Not once did Xavier move to check behind him or look at his watch. To another person, that might seem odd. But Xavier wanted to stand out. He wanted his interviewer to not know what to expect. In order to pass this interview, he had to be himself. Well, as much of himself as he could be, given that most of him was a lie.

Luckily, he had plenty of time to prepare himself. Did he regret being a puzzle built of pieces of every character he had been forced to play? Of course not. But it would be nice to know exactly who he was, instead of just wondering if his own personality was an act.

He groaned, staring at his watch. He was beginning to get

48

bored now that he had played out almost every single scenario in his head. He wondered if they were going to keep him there until he went in search of them. Still, he stayed put and tried to ignore his brain shouting at him to get moving.

He was startled by the sound of the door opening and he turned around. A tall old man smiled at him. "Hi. You must be Xavier, correct?"

He nodded.

"I'm so sorry to keep you waiting. You can call me Mr. Parkes."

"Parkes?"

"Yes, Clay Parkes. You've probably heard all the mess with my cousin. His death was a surprise to us all."

Xavier stared. "You don't seem concerned about him dying at all."

Clay shrugged. "People die. To be fairly honest, not many people in the family got along with him, not since he left and dragged Isaac into his problems." He took a breath in and smiled. "But you're not here to learn about my family history. You're here to work."

"Yes, sir."

Clay chuckled. "Well, you're polite. That's a plus." He pulled up a chair and sat down in it. "So, tell me, Xavier. Who are you?"

"What do you mean?"

"Well, what kind of person are you? Tell me about yourself."

Xavier raised an eyebrow. "Did you not get my resume?"

"Of course I did."

"What about my application? Cover letter? The essay I wrote?"

"I received those as well."

"So, you should already know about me. Tell me about me. Better yet, tell me about you."

Clay Parkes looked taken aback. "You certainly are interesting, Xavier. Where'd you get your attitude?"

"Probably my sisters. They annoyed me so I annoyed them."

Clay smiled. "Yes, siblings do that to you. I noticed in your resume that you're good with all sorts of technology, and you seem to understand coding very well. Your education is remarkable. "

"I like to think that I'm good at everything you just mentioned, sir."

He nodded. "You know, I like you. I don't say that about many people. You're a smart kid, and I'd be stupid not to bring you on."

"Sir?"

"You're hired. You were hired when we saw your application, but this meeting sets my decision in stone. Lavoie will show you to your room, and later you'll be taken around the facility, tested on your knowledge, and assigned to a section to work."

"Thank you, sir."

Clay shook his head. "No need to thank me." He looked up at Xavier, suddenly serious. "I assume you know what goes on here and how we run the place."

Xavier nodded.

"Then you know the stakes. And you know what happens if you mess up. You be careful, boy, especially with that attitude. You don't want to lose your head."

8

Neuroscience

Nasra stared down at her notes until she was seeing double. No matter how hard she fought to focus, her thoughts kept straying.

Alyssa had called her that morning to check on the sick clones. Their condition was getting worse. When they had first begun to show symptoms, it had been like a common cold. Now, they could barely get out of bed. David could barely breathe. So far, there was no explanation for what was happening.

Cassian hadn't woken up yet, but she had checked the vitals of the other four and found the same problem. They were acting as though they were immunocompromised, but they showed no signs of it from a medical standpoint. Outside of the external signs, their bodies acted as if they were healthy—stronger than the average human, even. There was no sign of a virus, no parasites, no bacteria that wasn't supposed to be there, no cancerous tissue. Nothing.

What was especially strange was the fact that every single non-clone exposed to the clones were completely fine. Healthy, every single one of them. It reminded Nasra of earlier, when the clones didn't catch Alyssa's experiential disease that put half the school in lockdown. At this point, Nasra was beginning to think that something was attacking the clones specifically. And for that, she had no answers.

Alyssa opened the door, and Nasra jumped.

"Oh, it's just you," she said, placing a hand over her heart. She laughed. "You scared me."

Alyssa half smiled. "Sorry, didn't mean to. Find anything yet?"

Nasra shook her head. "It's the same as always. Nothing internal, no strange brain waves, nothing in the heart or lungs," she said, counting the points on her fingers. "I pulled some red and white blood cells out to study later, but I haven't looked at them yet. What about you?"

Alyssa sat down on Nasra's bed and sighed. "Well, Cassian just woke up. He's developed a rash on one of his arms; it's nothing like I've ever seen before." She rubbed her eyes, looking visibly fatigued. "I assume that they're all suffering from the same condition, so the others will probably start showing signs of it as well."

Nasra groaned. "That can't be good."

"I honestly couldn't tell you. If this disease is deadly, I wouldn't be able to think of a cure until I figured out the source. And if it's something that is caused by the cloning process, then even if they did die, we have a responsibility to not do it again. We can't risk it—not if they'll suffer and die the same way."

Nasra nodded. "What about the brain tissue?"

"Didn't you already check their brain waves and vitals?"

"Well, yeah, but not the brain itself. Just because there's nothing wrong with the function of the brain itself, doesn't mean that the consciousness transfer didn't cause brain trauma or stress. Their body could be failing because their brain is sending the wrong signals, and causing it to attack itself."

Alyssa stared at her. "Why didn't you think of this sooner?"

Nasra shrugged. "I don't know. I just thought of it because it hasn't been affecting us. It could be a them problem."

"Then why is it contagious? How come the other clones are having the same problem?"

Nasra shut her computer and rested her head in her hands. "I don't know…" She rubbed her eyes. "I just want to find a solution, okay? I want to be able to look at them and know that they're healthy, and that…" Her voice cracked. "…That when I agreed to clone them I made the right decision." Nasra looked up at Alyssa. When she continued, her voice was small. "Cassian warned me that there was a moral obligation that came along with the idea. Do you think I made the wrong choice?"

Alyssa awkwardly patted Nasra on the shoulder. "Nasra, you didn't do anything wrong, okay? This isn't your fault. We are going to figure this out, and they're going to be fine. Now, where are those cell samples? You go ahead and test your theory—I'll take a look at the samples while you do."

Nasra nodded and stood up from her chair. Her hands shook slightly and she clenched them into fists to stop the movement. "Okay. Brain surgery. Got it."

Alyssa smiled. "Your first brain surgery! Finally, a chance to put your major to use."

"Alyssa, I don't have a doctorate degree yet. Just because I'm studying neuroscience doesn't mean I'm qualified to do this."

Alyssa glared at her. "You can. I believe in you."

"Okay. I'll do my best." Nasra took a deep breath. "So, where's the closest sterile room?"

* * * * * * * *

Three coffees and a power nap later, Nasra was ready.

She ended up working with Nicole. She was desperate to get out of her room, and even though Nicole ached and coughed with every step she took, she was stubborn.

Nasra's hands trembled as she started. However, as time passed, the nerves wore away. Despite the blood and the pressure, Nasra didn't mess up, and by the time she stitched Nicole's head back up, she was determined to find something. Her research was not going to be in vain.

Alyssa made sure that Nicole was stable while Nasra did her part. Nasra analyzed the brain matter until she was sure she was about to fall asleep on her feet. Even though the tiredness had settled into her bones, Nasra didn't stop working. Alyssa took Nicole to another room, and Nasra started writing. She was barely able to finish writing up her report before passing out in her chair. That was how Alyssa found her, hours later, when she came in with the test results.

Alyssa didn't want to wake Nasra. She looked so peaceful, but she shook the girl awake all the same. "Wake up."

"Huh?" Nasra said, groggily.

Alyssa held up a folder. "I got the results."

Nasra sat up, suddenly awake. "Well?"

Alyssa pursed her lips. "Do you want the good news or the bad news first?"

Nasra waved her hand. "Good news, please. I've heard too much bad news today."

"Well, I did find something. It doesn't act like a typical disease, and the white blood cells aren't attacking it, so I don't know what it is. I'll check with the others later; see if they know anything about it."

"And the bad news?"

Alyssa sighed. "Whatever it is, you're right. it's only attacking the clones. It seems that it can travel by air, since the clones didn't really touch each other, but they did get infected from being in the same vicinity. Since there's a possibility that we could be carriers, it's best to stay away from the healthy clones for now. The real bad news is, though I think we can develop a cure, and if we don't do it fast, this thing will kill them."

Nasra slumped back into her chair. "That's what I was afraid of."

Alyssa nodded. "What about you?"

Nasra gestured to the equipment and notes in front of her. "Nothing. No trauma, no stress, nothing. The brain's completely fine. There's also no strange mental activity, like psychological trauma or things of that sort. It's so strange, and I don't know what to do."

"Do we know what caused it?"

Nasra shook her head. "I've been over my results dozens of times and they seem healthy but they don't look it. There's no internal symptoms for a cold or any other sickness."

"Right. So this disease only shows itself in blood, from what I can tell, it feeds off of white blood cells, and can only be seen through a microscope. The disease presents itself externally, and cannot infect other humans, only other clones."

"What about animals?"

Alyssa frowned. "I can check, I've got some spare lab rats."

They were interrupted by the sound of the door opening. "Did you guys try looking at their nervous systems yet?"

Nasra's eyes lit up. "Elena, you're a genius!"

Elena frowned. "I just got here, I wanted to see if you needed any help, and now I'm a genius?"

Nasra got up and hugged Elena. "Alyssa, when I said that something internal is causing their bodies to attack itself, I only checked brain signals, not the nerves. If something fried their nerve endings, that could cause a mutation to solve the problem, but not all mutations are helpful to the body."

Alyssa tilted her head in curiosity. "And that means?"

"Okay, so, if the nerves told the body to make something, and their instruction was faulty, they would make a mutated version of how it's supposed to be."

"Huh?"

Nasra rolled her eyes. "There are many reasons for why a person gets sick. One is stress. It affects your body's ability to defend itself against infection. And you know how tumors are just mutated lumps of cells caused by a problem with the way that cells die?"

Alyssa nodded. "Yeah."

"So, say a clone became a carrier of a sickness, but because they can't get sick like we do, the virus had no choice but to mutate in order to infect the clones. With the nervous system giving off the wrong signals, there's a chance that their bodies naturally weakened and the virus found an easy way to not only infect them, but continue to mutate and make it worse. So, we would have to not only find a cure to inhibit it, but destroy it completely. Otherwise it could mutate further."

"Yeah, but that doesn't explain why they can't infect us," Alyssa argued.

"Their cells are naturally different from ours," Nasra said, matter-of-factly. "Since we used lab-grown ones, there's a possibility that their cells are incompatible with ours, meaning that they can only infect one another. That's why they weren't able to get your disease when they were exposed to it and most of the school got infected. It would also explain why it's only attacking them, not us. That also means we can't do organ or cell transplants without using lab-grown pieces."

Alyssa stared at her. "That's an insane theory."

"You've heard me say weirder, now I'm gonna go test it." Nasra ran out the door, leaving Alyssa in shock.

Alyssa turned. "Elena, what have you done? You just put this thought into her head, and if she's not right she's gonna be devastated."

Elena frowned. "Hey! I was just trying to help."

Attachment Issues

Aiken stared at the pile of files on his desk. Even if he wanted a break, he had made a promise. And when it came to promises, Aiken did his best to keep them. Astra had agreed to let him choose which files he wanted to look at and in his own time. That was how he ended up with Leroy Parkes' experiment records. He knew that Astra would love to take a look inside of Parkes' head–and honestly, he couldn't wait to peek inside either.

He chose to start with the journal entries, notes on the original model, and Parkes' anger with Ares, who Aiken decided was definitely a coworker or partner of some kind. It seemed that Ares was always avoiding Parkes' questions, as if he didn't want him to know what was going on with the android that he built. He carefully took notes of everything that stood out to him. Leroy sure was bitter, and he certainly had his disagreements with his brother.

Aiken understood Leroy's pain and frustration. Though he had only known Henry for a short time, they had their fair share of squabbles. It came with the closeness. Henry's ever present quips and their shared hatred of being wrong. Their arguments never lasted; the human urge to be safe and close to the people around them overpowered the idea that they had to always be right. Though Aiken's sense of what was right and wrong was certainly changing, he was almost sure Henry would take it in stride. They were friends. Henry had to.

Parkes had some of the same ideas, the same problems that Aiken had. Was it strange, relating to a murderer? Maybe. His family had taught him that even if you don't like someone, that doesn't necessarily mean that their ideals were wrong.

Then there was Astra.

She liked to lecture them, tell them that you can learn from the people who oppose you. It was strange hearing her admit that she didn't know everything. *'It's not good to always be the smartest person in the room. You should always be learning from other people.'*

Aiken had almost been convinced that Astra was just being humble, lying to avoid hurting their feelings, but there was something genuine in her eyes when she said it to him. He couldn't help but feel like she was telling the truth. He wanted to believe her; he wanted to believe everyone. It wasn't until he arrived at Torsion that he realized just how cruel the world could be.

Aiken glanced at his watch. Astra would probably still be up, and he wanted to share his notes with her immediately.

Aiken grabbed the file and his notes. He headed towards Astra's room. She nearly ran into him as he went to knock on the door.

"Aiken." She didn't sound surprised. Astra never sounded surprised. He ignored that mental note and held up the file.

"I was reading through Parkes' journal and I found some things you might be interested in, I made a page of notes." He paused. "Also… Parkes' brother is named Isaac. Like our Isaac? Do you think they're connected?"

"Of course not. It's just a name. Don't be silly."

He nodded, mildly embarrassed. "Yeah, of course… Speaking of which, where is Isaac anyway?"

Astra stared at him. "Isaac?"

"Yeah, we were just talking about him—"

"I don't know an Isaac. There's never been an Isaac here. There are only eight clones. I don't know what's gotten into you. Are you tired? Have you been getting enough sleep?"

Aiken faltered. What was he talking about? Leroy's brother? "Oh yeah, Parkes had a brother named Isaac, that was it." He laughed awkwardly. "Yeah, we don't know an Isaac. Sorry, I guess I am just really tired. Are you gonna come with me back to the lab?

It's quieter, better to study than anywhere else."

Astra nodded. "Sure. Then you can tell me what you find as you find it."

"Great idea!"

Astra let Aiken run ahead of her as they made their way back to the lab. She honestly thought he would fight harder than this, but Aiken's mind was extremely open to suggestions. She had coded Isaac out of everyone's memories the day he left, so it was interesting that some thought of him still lingered before being erased. Either way, it wouldn't affect her that much.

Astra sometimes wondered if she had gone too far. Was this a sign that her morals had finally been pushed to their limit and snapped back at her?

Of course not. If she could kill without remorse, she could deal with a little manipulation. When they got to the lab, Astra busied herself with confirming that she had successfully wiped Isaac from everyone's minds. Her friends were easy enough, having already been exposed to the commands she gave them. They responded quickly, and Isaac was erased just as quickly from their heads. The harder part was the students.

They had already been taught not to speak about secret things, and Astra had learned that if it seemed like a person didn't know something, the other students wouldn't go out of their way to fill them in. Still, Astra had to go a step further. She never trusted anyone to keep quiet. Several trips later, Astra's mechanical spider had dumped millions of nanobots into the water pipes of the school.

She finally controlled the place, so she could do whatever she wanted. No one knew it was her doing, so no one would be able to stop her. That was her father's teaching, and his words. '*It's not my responsibility to make you feel important. It's nobody's responsibility, and it's better if you aren't important anyway. Important people are killed. If you don't matter to yourself then you don't matter to anyone. So watch your own back.*'

Astra winced, trying to push the memory out of her head. Her father was kind for the most part, but when he wanted them to hear him, they would. Everything that he said and taught was like a knife in her brain at the times she least wanted to hear them. She felt that her own fears were repetitive. It bubbled up inside her, the ache of guilt in her stomach, the idea that she would be so angry, she'd explode if she was betrayed like this. *'You don't care about morals; you don't care about anything,'* she repeated to herself. *'You don't care.'*

Astra had never liked surprises. Not even on her birthday. Yet, her father still liked to keep her on her toes and throw situations, questions, and ideas at her, expecting her to counter. He never was surprised when she excelled, so she taught herself to be the same. Astra had never heard him say, *'you've outsmarted me; I didn't think you could do that.'* The truth was, he always expected the best of them. That's why they never failed.

Astra stared at Aiken as he worked, taking notes of Parkes's ideals, every so often passing her a page full of scribbled thoughts and arguments. He was brilliant, just like every other person at the school, but Astra found his mind more emotional. She knew very well what it was like to lose emotion to intelligence, she had seen it in herself and other people—but not Aiken. Never Aiken. He was too soft, too curious, too *human.* That's why she asked him to do the job; he would understand Parkes in a way she couldn't.

Eventually, Astra turned back to her own work. She kept tabs on her brother and Isaac, making sure that both of them were safe. Every so often, she'd type another line or two of her essay, but it wasn't long before she grew bored of that.

It was easy to pretend that she was invincible once she was in the shadows. But, she was known here. And to stay unknown, she'd have to destroy everything. Despite the fact that she was almost sure she was heartless, she didn't want to do that to her friends.

Aiken yawned.

Astra snapped back to reality, suddenly aware of her own fatigue, and how nice it would be to just fall asleep. It was a bore to be human in her opinion. Their bodies were faulty and so were their minds. She couldn't remember when her thoughts changed, when she no longer minded feeling like and being human. It was a shame she couldn't stay on earth and study them further.

"Aren't you tired, Aiken?" she asked, though there was no need to. She knew he was, but it was a courtesy she wanted to extend.

"I'll be fine."

"If you're tired you can go. You don't have to get everything done in one day. I asked for your help, not that you'd overwork yourself."

"I'm fine, Astra."

She glared at him. "The dark circles under your eyes say otherwise. If you stay up you'll have to double your caffeine intake which isn't good at all. This isn't worth sacrificing your health over."

Aiken didn't take his eyes off the files. "But I want to help."

"You are helping. And you won't be able to help if you exhaust yourself every day, especially since you've still got to do school and research. Just because you're the least busy of us doesn't mean you're not busy in general." Astra motioned for Aiken to stand up. "Go to sleep. I'll finish up here by myself."

Aiken stared at her. "Are you sure? I don't mind staying up with you. Besides, you should get some sleep as well."

Astra shook her head. "Go. I'll be fine. I took a nap and I have stuff to do."

Aiken nodded, though Astra could see in his eyes that he didn't really want to leave. "Okay." He yawned again. "See you tomorrow."

Aiken trudged up the stairs towards his dorm room. His eyes hurt and he was almost half asleep by the time he had reached his destination.

Henry greeted him as soon as he came in the door. "Hey, long day? You look tired."

"I am tired."

"Not too tired to get me food, I hope."

Aiken stared at him. "Are you serious? It's one a.m.!"

"Yes, and I want tacos."

Aiken rolled his eyes. "Fine."

Henry raised his eyebrow. "No fighting back today?"

Aiken shook his head. "Are you paying?"

"No."

Aiken threw his hands in the air, exasperated. "The way I get treated here! I need so much coffee!" He left the room and headed toward the cafeteria.

Henry stared at the closed door and frowned. Aiken usually kept the banter going for longer. "That was strange." He shrugged and went back to scrolling on his phone. If something was wrong, Aiken would tell him later. Maybe he was just tired.

10

Watchful

Katya was beginning to get frustrated. She had worked on the telescope day and night for weeks, continuously getting perfect results… until now. It wasn't easy. Her results were always impressive, drawing the eyes of professionals worldwide—even from outside of her field. Perhaps that was why Elena had been so on edge recently. It was either the nightmares, or the rapidly growing pile of issues in the school that needed fixing. Despite multiple reassurances, Parkes' death loomed over her shoulder and terrorized her in the night. Katya had to pretend that she couldn't hear Elena waking up screaming on the other side of the wall.

They had turned in most of the staff. Authorities were overwhelmingly grateful for their cooperation. Katya assumed that this was the only way to keep Elena away from being suspected of murder—not that she would actually be prosecuted if she was caught. There were a lot of governments that had wanted Leroy Parkes dead. That would be enough to earn judicial silence, a thank you gift for her service. When Katya had asked what would happen to the staff, Astra had only replied that she *would take care of it*. Katya shivered. She was sure that her definition of *take care of it* was completely different from Astra's.

Katya didn't know what had happened to the staff who had fled when the authorities swarmed the area. She could guess, but she had a feeling she didn't want to know. Zola had told her that they would be caught and arrested, but Katya knew that wasn't true. She also knew better than to snoop… but Katya was curious. Astra kept logs of every single staff member—who was caught and who was not—and she knew some of those people marked off on the list hadn't gone to court. They probably never even made it out of the school.

There were a lot of rooms and tunnels that weren't publicly accessible. If Katya searched long enough, she was sure she would find their bodies. Whether they were dead or alive… well, that was up to Astra. When she first met Astra, Katya had the impression that she wouldn't even hurt a fly. The more she got to know her, the more she realized that that was the furthest thing from the truth. She barely knew what Astra was actually capable of. But then again, did she really know any of her friends?

Katya sighed. There were days she loved being by herself with her thoughts and her hands, busy recording the readings on the telescope. She'd hole herself up inside the telescope for hours. Other days, she dove down the rabbit hole and found herself questioning her friend group and what they really wanted.

Katya gently adjusted the telescope, trying to find a good angle. She hadn't been getting clear pictures lately, which was strange, given that the telescope had seen further than this before. Now, it seemed like there was nothing but blurry space and black spots where stars should've been. She made a mental note to look at the lens later. It could just be scratches causing the issue, or maybe it was the programming. She was no good with coding; so she would probably call Zola or Henry down to fix it. Katya scrolled through past images in the computer and sent a few of them to the printer.

If she could pinpoint when the telescope started acting up, that might help. She was sure it was probably the lens, but it didn't hurt to check. Katya moved the telescope one more time. To her surprise, it was clear, and she could see just fine. She frowned. She moved it back to where it was and then back into place. Sure enough, it was the same, blurry space, clear night sky.

There had to be something blocking the lens. To her knowledge, there were no satellites in that area, and the International Space Station was nowhere near there right now. She had hacked several sites to get that information. Well, Henry had, but that was close enough. Unless the programming had a blind spot, something or someone was blocking her, and she was going to figure it out.

Katya returned to her dorm room, curious and a little discouraged.

"What's wrong?" Zola asked.

They had once again switched dorms, this time, with Alyssa rooming with Mary, Katya with Zola, and Nasra with Elena. Astra still kept to herself in her single room.

"Hmm?"

"You don't seem happy. I thought everything was going good with the telescope?"

"It was, but something doesn't seem right."

Zola raised an eyebrow. "What'd you find?"

Katya plopped down on her bed. "So. I was testing the range as I usually do, and it was… weird. There were lights that weren't supposed to be there, a random blind spot, and missing stars."

"Doesn't it take light years for a dying star to fully disappear from our sky, or something like that?" Zola asked. "That could be what you're seeing."

"That's not… well, technically, that can happen, but they fade over time. Stars just don't disappear overnight. We'd know if a star was dying way before it went dark," Katya said.

"Okay, so are you sure it's not the programming that needs fixing? I could take a look at it later; a little troubleshooting won't hurt." Zola rummaged through her bedside table to find a notebook and a pen. "Look at the telescope computer," she murmured as she wrote it down.

Katya fell backward onto her bed and stared up at the ceiling. She turned to face Zola. "What about the fact that there's not a problem if I move it to a different part of the sky?" Katya questioned. Zola shrugged. "It could still be the programming. Or some government satellites blocking your view."

"Trust me." Katya laughed, almost mockingly. "I would know

if it were a satellite." She was getting a little frustrated that Zola didn't believe her.

Zola nodded. "Of course you would. Fine. I trust you, you know your stuff, I don't. This isn't something you'd lie about." She paused. "Now, it could just be a mistake. We can go together and look at it. I'll check the programming, Elena can check the telescope, and if there's truly nothing wrong with the machine, I'll help you figure out what's really wrong with it."

Katya sat up. "Promise?"

"I promise."

* * * * * * * *

Elena kicked the panel back into place. It was almost therapeutic for her, being that violent with the machinery. She had to take her anger out on something, and pretending she was fine and everything normal was the best way to do it. Unfortunately, she wasn't in a good mood, and everyone could see it. After being dragged into this mess, she needed something to calm her down, but no matter how many relaxing things she did, she still saw blood when she closed her eyes. So Elena worked.

When Katya and Zola came to her to ask for her help with the telescope, she was grateful, for the distraction. She searched through all the wiring, checked every port, corner, and crevice of the thing, and couldn't find a single blemish. Not a single scratch, frayed cord, or melted motherboard. It was a good thing that she knew how to keep things from overheating, otherwise it would have been a pain to replace. "Well, I couldn't find anything in the telescope. Zola, anything?"

"No, but I'm not done yet."

Elena walked over to Zola, who was currently searching through the machine's base code. She elbowed Katya aside so she could have room to peer over Zola's shoulder. "How long is this going to take?"

Zola stopped and glared at her. "It'll take even longer if you

66

keep breathing down my neck."

Elena backed up. "Sorry."

Zola turned back to the computer and started scrolling through the data. "There is literally so much information here, it could take hours, maybe even days to search through all of this."

"Didn't you write this?" Katya quipped.

"Yeah, but I didn't leave any bookmarks where a problem could be. Only where I left off. And I double-checked it. There was no problem with the code when I put it in."

"Then why don't you believe me?" Katya asked loudly.

Zola winced and moved her head away. "It's not that I don't believe you, I just want to check. Things can be misleading, we all know that. Code can be corrupted, whether it be a mistake in a backup, or a virus that was downloaded by accident. It happens. We look at a lot of government websites."

"Wouldn't it be faster if you just made a command that searched through the code for you? Doesn't this code do exactly what you want?" Elena asked.

Zola stopped and facepalmed. "I am so tired," she sighed. Zola grabbed her phone. "I haven't really used it since we made the clones. We did do a lot of work, and I had to go through all the staff files myself. Speaking of which… we're almost done hiring new staff."

Elena made a face. "Great…" she said, sarcastically. "Just what we need. More people."

"You're not going to get arrested," Katya said.

"Who said anything about me being arrested? Why does everyone automatically think that's what I'm referencing–stop bringing it up!"

Katya took a step back and avoided looking in Elena's eyes. "Sorry, I didn't mean to upset you."

Elena sighed. "It's fine. Just weird to think about."

Katya looked back at her and grabbed Elena's hand comfortingly. "You don't have to talk about it if you don't want to."

Elena nodded uncertainly. "I know. I… think I'm ready to. I just don't know how."

"It takes time."

"I know, and I am looking into getting help. It's just easier to not think about it."

Katya nodded sympathetically. "Well, if you ever want to talk about it, I'm here–"

The two were interrupted by an elated cry. "I found something!" Zola held up her phone triumphantly. "I got it–let me just reboot this, and put this in here…" She moved the telescope and beckoned Katya over. "See! Everything is in the right place now."

Katya looked through the telescope. Zola was right. The blind spot disappeared and stars were back in their proper places. She frowned.

"How did that happen?"

Zola shrugged. "We map a lot of constellations and the program has the ability to project them over an area. It's to check for those dying stars we talked about earlier. It could have been a glitch or an accidental mistype that caused a map to cover your lens instead of transmitting in real time."

"Oh."

Zola smiled. "I know you want another mystery Katya, but we're done. No more adventures for us. Now, I'm going to go get food." And on that note, she turned around and left the room.

"I can't believe it. I could have sworn that was real."

"It's okay," Elena said reassuringly. "It's not the end of the world." She paused, hesitant to switch the subject back to herself. She waited a bit, staring at Katya who was looking over the computer screen and comparing the differences between the star maps. When she spoke again, her voice was small. "Katya… am I a horrible person?"

Katya looked at her in surprise. "What?"

Elena shrugged, her form showing confidence, but her eyes betraying her. "I know, I know, I'm focusing on it too much, but do you know how it feels? I killed someone, Kat. Sure it was in self-defense, but I still did it. It was partly for revenge too. Was it the wrong thing to do?"

Katya patted Elena on the back. "You worry too much. It wasn't your fault. Any court would agree. You aren't horrible for that. Mistakes happen– just look at this!" She gestured to the telescope. "I know that's not the same, but I don't have any related experience."

Elena sniffed and closed her eyes tightly to avoid crying. "You're right. It's just hard to forgive myself."

Katya smiled and pulled her in for a hug. "You just think you deserve the same fate. That doesn't mean you do, but it does mean that you're compassionate. You're not a terrible person for thinking you deserve something you don't. That's not justice, it's just anxiety." Katya let go and looked back at the computer. She paused before she spoke again. "I think Zola was right. I do want another adventure."

Elena laughed. "We both do. And we both want something we can't have."

Katya looked surprised. "I know what I want, but what do you want?"

Elena sighed. "I want to change the past. I wish Parkes was still alive and in jail. I wish I never killed him." She paused. "I want to redeem myself."

11

Pursuing Atonement

Despite her earlier conversation with Katya, Elena didn't feel comforted. Not anymore, at least. It's easy to say that you feel okay in the moment, but not when you're alone with your thoughts. She had sat alone in her dorm for a few hours before Nasra came in and pulled her away.

Elena glanced over to where Mary and Astra were looking over blueprints of the catacombs. Nasra had brought the idea up a while ago, and after voting, they finally decided it was time to block off the major entrances. It was a labyrinth down there, mostly unexplored. Elena only knew one room: the place she killed Leroy Parkes. It was still the file room to everyone else, but to her, it was like an open closer with a monster waiting inside.

She had to confess: before she knew who he was and what he did, she admired him. After all, he was the Dean, he had been a good role model. Elena knew that Aiken was grateful that Leroy was no longer terrorizing them. She knew that no one blamed her for it, but nothing made her feel better. She wouldn't until she felt that she had finally atoned. She did everything she could to make up for it.

Anything they asked her to build or fix, she did without question. She spent hours writing down everything that happened during the cloning process and countless more storing it properly. On the days that she helped Astra, Elena learned where all the files in the back room were. She was nowhere near as knowledgeable about where everything went as Astra, but she could find what she wanted pretty easily.

When they asked her to help, Elena had jumped at the chance. Maybe changing things would help dull the ache every time she walked near the file room door. Elena placed a sticky note above one of the entrances. Astra had agreed to block the area off on the condition that they explored each passage and took everything out of the underground rooms, just to make sure they weren't missing anything.

There was a number for every entrance. Elena had no idea she enjoyed cartography until she started. When she agreed to help, Katya had whispered a theory to her. Elena had scoffed at the idea. If Astra was truly capable of killing someone, she had no doubt she'd be capable of cleaning up the evidence.

So far, Elena had mapped out five different rooms. She hadn't found much: gears, papers, a couple of empty bins. They had so much storage space and nothing to do with it. Granted, Leroy probably didn't want people to find out what he did underneath the school. Plus, she had only explored five passageways and their connecting rooms, marking them as she went. There was a chance that someone had been there before her, but if Elena was being honest, she didn't care. She didn't want to know what happened underneath the school while she was there; she barely wanted anything to do with it now. The people she had become attached to were the only thing holding her in place.

If murder was to be her legacy, it would be for a good cause.

Elena returned to where Astra and Mary stood to retrieve more sticky notes. "So," she asked, "how many more rooms do you think we can do today?"

"Ten," Astra answered. "Fifteen total. No more, no less. Fifteen is a good number, so no matter how much time you have left, stop at the fifteenth room, then go help Nasra or Zola."

Elena frowned. "Fifteen is a good number," she restated, the confusion evident in her tone.

Astra looked up. "Yes. Fifteen is divisible by three, which is also a good number. And so is five, so is twenty."

"So, why not twenty rooms?"

Astra shrugged. She turned away from Elena. "Mary, these are the files you need, I can take care of the rest, 'kay?" She handed a few folders to Mary, waved goodbye, and quickly scurried away. She turned back towards Elena. "I don't know. It just seemed like a good idea. Feels right."

Elena laughed. "You are so strange. How do numbers mean so much to you?"

Astra didn't feel like telling her that fifteen was the number of days that she was kept in her room. For fifteen days, she was quarantined. For fifteen days she felt trapped. On the fifteenth day, it was as if she was released from a prison that she could have died in. Metaphorically of course. "I don't know, it just seems right."

Elena nodded. "Okay. Ten more rooms it is."

Astra smiled. "Great."

Numbers had meaning in her culture. They were a symbol of power, peace, and equality. She couldn't remember a time when she wasn't surrounded by numbers, data, and lists. Once she was adopted by Ares, the tradition continued until Astra could rattle off statistical problems in her sleep. She would have made a great engineer if she wasn't so obsessed with coding.

Well, she was a great engineer; she had made so many beautiful things. It was a pity that so few people knew. Then again, most of the things she created were either only useful for manipulation, or for weaponry.

Astra looked up just as Elena turned around to go back to her work. She remembered something. "Actually, Elena, before you go back to finish, can you help me with something?"

Elena frowned. "Sure, what's up?"

Astra clapped her hands together. "How would you feel about doing me a favor?"

"Depends on the favor."

Astra sighed. "Well, I want to do something nice for the school—everyone's constantly on edge because of the constant watch from the authorities, and we can at least be kind to our guests while they're here."

Elena raised an eyebrow. "That seems sinister. What do you want to do?" She mimicked shivering. "Ooh, Astra's doing something nice for once, scary." She laughed.

Astra glared at her. "Just because I haven't done anything nice yet, doesn't mean it's sinister. I just want to make food for them."

Elena blinked. "Like a school-wide picnic or something?"

"Yeah. Plus, we'll make the cops more comfortable and less suspicious of us."

"You think food is going to solve that?"

Astra shrugged. "Food solves a lot of problems. Besides, you know what it feels like to be an outsider, even in your own friend group. There's a point where we need to be kind so people are reminded we're human."

Elena huffed. "Fine. So where do I come in?"

"I need you to help me cook and distribute water and other drinks." Astra looked back down at the blueprints. "Maybe set up and clean up, but I should be able to do that myself."

"That's it?" Elena scoffed. "It feels like there's more to your idea."

"Would you rather I ask someone else?"

Elena shook her head. "No… It just seems out of character for you." She paused. "I'm glad you thought of me, and I'd love to help. I wasn't expecting it, that's all."

"What were you expecting?" Astra questioned.

She shrugged. "I don't know. Something crazy, I guess. Like when I asked for your help to get parts for my project."

Astra laughed. "I guess you don't know me as well as you thought you did, huh?"

Elena elbowed her, smiling. "Hey, I think you're cool. You're kinda creepy though. Like a witch."

"A witch?!"

"Yeah! Are you gonna put a spell on us? Curse our first-born children? Perform a little mind-control?" Elena poked Astra in the side between each word, making her laugh louder.

Astra shook her head. "Ah, El, you're too funny. Get back to work, I'll see you later."

Elena smiled and returned to placing sticky notes over the passageways, content to see happiness sparkling in Astra's eyes.

Astra watched as Elena returned to her work. She sighed. "Witch, huh? I guess I've got mind control covered, at least." She pursed her lips. "It makes it easier to get the job done, so don't hate me too much."

Astra turned back to the maps that Elena had already given her, marking the places she wanted to block off. If she was going to pull this off, she needed easy access to the kitchen area and the loading dock. Lucky for her, she had the plans to herself, and no one to question her choices.

Astra wanted the authorities gone. Since the school was under her control, the authorities would inevitably end up questioning what she knew, why the other students listened to her, and how she was involved in Parkes' death. She didn't have time for those questions. In order to get authorities off her tail—while simultaneously keeping Elena safe—she had to be able to control them.

Astra scribbled notes down on a scrap of paper she had torn off the corner of one of the blueprints. She couldn't help but remember the days when she ruled the criminal underworld. Those resources were so easy to reach for, back then. Sometimes, she wondered if she relied on them too much. Astra shook her head, forcing the thoughts out of her mind. She couldn't become distracted. Not now. She still had to be on the lookout for her ride home. She expected to get a signal within the next few months.

It was yet another reason why she didn't want to take classes. Leaving in the middle of a semester raised eyebrows and drew eyes. She had made a promise to keep these people safe. Besides that, Astra also needed her tech in the right hands. Her family would watch over it, but she needed to still be able to pull the strings behind the scenes. She couldn't do that if she was constantly being watched.

It would only take a moment for her to whisper her idea into the ears of passing students for word to spread like wildfire. There was a time in her life when Astra would have said that she was fully prepared to die for a mission. It was unfortunate that this one depended on her staying alive because somehow, it made things much harder.

12

The is the Enemy

Xavier didn't consider himself to be a morning nor a night person. He woke when he wanted and slept when he had to. However, he found himself getting angry when he was woken up at 5 a.m. by the knock on his door. He'd been up earlier than this before, forced to pull all-nighters, even passing out from exhaustion some days. Still, there was something especially irritating about bending to the will of people he could just kill if he wanted to.

He stumbled around the room getting dressed before following Mr. Lavoie down to the dining hall for breakfast. He hadn't seen this many drowsy people regretting their life choices since the time that he and Cassidy broke into a random college in the U.S.

As he ate, Xavier couldn't help but feel acutely aware of how vulnerable he was without a weapon. Unfortunately, the butter-knife he slipped up his sleeve didn't provide much comfort either. He buried his complaints underneath a mask of curiosity and followed Mr. Lavoie to the offices.

These were the department heads, the people who ran the show. They were businessmen and cowards, and even though Xavier put his best foot forward, he could barely hide his disgust for them. He murdered people like these for a living—not just because he had to, but because he wanted to. They were the lowest of the low, rubbing elbows for an hourly salary that could feed a family for a week. Even though no one called him out for it, with every frown and slow handshake Xavier received, he knew they knew he hated them.

When he had finally finished meeting all of the supervisors, Xavier disappeared into the bathroom to wash his hands. The phantom feeling of blood underneath his nails was growing stronger, and every single moment he spent with those people he felt nauseous. He didn't want those emotions affecting the part he was looking forward to: the lab.

When he first entered, all Xavier could think about was retrieving his sister's tech. Then, the wonder hit him. The lab was beautiful, completely pristine, fresh with the scent of bleach—like someone had just sanitized it. The people within these walls were innocent compared to the board members he had just met. He wasn't inclined to blame them; it was their job to work with what they were given.

Still, Astra's tech was passing through unworthy hands, and all he wanted was to retrieve it and leave. He was a little annoyed by that thought, but Xavier allowed himself to be amazed by what was around him. The thrum of the machines flowing through the ground, the scent of metal chasing the coattails of the bleach that still lingered. He knew he could feel at home in a place like this. He couldn't wait to get started.

He was introduced first to the head of a station whose workers were studying what seemed like nanotech. Once he got closer, his suspicions were confirmed. Astra had often used him as her guinea pig, and after days of drinking tasteless liquids full of the stuff until she was satisfied, he knew the design by heart. He noticed a kid, around his age, messing with a clump of them.

"What's wrong?" Xavier asked. He couldn't help it. He liked to be right.

The man turned around to look at him. "You're new, aren't you?"

Xavier nodded.

"Normally, I wouldn't talk to anyone who came into my station, but since it's your first day, I'll make an exception."

Xavier found the guy to be funny. Xavier already knew what was wrong, and how to fix it, but he was here to learn, not to teach. Still, he allowed himself this one moment of pride.

The man pointed to the petri dish underneath a microscope

that he was working with. "I'm having trouble with the clumping; they're supposed to be in smaller groups than this. It could cause problems once they're absorbed into the bloodstream."

Xavier snickered internally. *'That's what happens when you try to reverse engineer something that isn't yours and is way more advanced than your technology.'* He pointed to a section of the bots. "Try changing the polarization of some of them, then neutralizing the others. They won't clump together as much so they won't cause a clog, and they'll keep the ones that don't have the magnet moving. They'll move in smaller packs, and bump the neutral ones along."

He frowned. "Huh. How'd you think of that?"

Xavier shrugged. "I guess I just know my magnets."

The guy smiled and held out his hand. "I'm Alejo by the way."

"Xavier." He shook Alejo's hand and returned the smile. He had a feeling he was going to like working with this guy. "It's nice to meet you."

"Of course it is. When someone your age is in the same field as you, isn't it nice to know you're crushing the competition together?" Alejo laughed good-naturedly. "Well, unless you're the kind of person who hates sharing."

Xavier chuckled. "I don't hate sharing, but I am competitive. My focus isn't nanotech, though."

Alejo frowned. "Then how come you're so good at it?"

Xavier shrugged again. "I have a wide variety of interests, but I'm more of a coding person, so I'll see you around. If you ever need any more help with your magnets, you can always come and find me."

Alejo smiled wider. "I will. Have fun!" He returned to his work, and as Mr. Lavoie pulled Xavier away, he caught a glimpse of Alejo chuckling to himself as he wrote down Xavier's suggestion.

Xavier met a lot more people that day. It was a whirlwind of names, careers, and focuses. When he got to the coding section, his skin prickled. He was ecstatic to find computers being assembled and being set up, websites being created and hacked, and programs being tested. These were his people.

Xavier had always admired security hackers. Those were the people who tested systems that could potentially be hacked by competitors and made them stronger. In his childhood training, he used to hang over the shoulders of his father's employees, watching them do it. Eventually, they let him learn and he grew to be better at it. It used to be one of his big interests, but he was never able to beat Astra at it, so he settled into web design and smaller hacking jobs. Since information drops were his side job, Xavier was familiar with coding secrets into websites.

Mr. Lavoie had left him with the station manager to take a call, and it didn't take long for Xavier to make some friends. There was an older man named Stephan that showed him some of the minor upgrades he had made to the basic PC to make it run faster. "I wanted to eliminate the middle man," he said. "I even wrote the manual myself."

The more time he spent, the more he found himself genuinely interested in what the people around him were saying. Xavier had always found it hard to be impressed, but these people were geniuses. He loved being around them.

When Mr. Lavoie came back to escort him to the dining hall for lunch, Xavier mapped out some of the lab rooms and stations on a napkin. He wanted to memorize everything that he saw, so that when he got the chance, he could get in and out before anyone even realized he was gone. It wouldn't take him that long to figure out where everything on the main floor was, but he still had to locate Astra's tech. Luckily, thinking ahead was his specialty.

Xavier went back to his room for the rest of the day, opting to sit and read over going back to the lab and working. He had all the time in the world to work.

What he didn't have was enough time to build trust.

He wanted to be out within a few weeks. A challenge, even for him. Not many people were allowed to roam freely, so Xavier needed to find a shortcut. All he needed was to make friends with his manager, swipe a key, and take out some cameras. Seemed easy enough, but it wasn't. He wasn't really good at making friends, especially with an enemy. Xavier made a mental note to check out the ventilation system later that evening.

There were always people watching him. When Xavier left his room for dinner, he noted the cameras outside his door, memorized every face that he passed on his floor. Now that he was officially hired, he may have lost Lavoie, but there were eyes everywhere. He needed to turn the cameras off in his room. Xavier slipped a stick of butter into his pocket. It wouldn't shut off the cameras, but it would blur them.

Later, Xavier carefully found blind spots from which to launch the butter at the cameras, then clambered into the vents as silently as he could. They were expectedly cramped, his shirt catching on edges as he rounded corners, but Xavier was free up there so long as he kept quiet.

He carefully lowered himself from the vents onto the lab floor. Having memorized the camera layout, it was easy to avoid the cameras as they spun around and swipe some of the nanobots. He clambered back into the vents and retreated back to his room, dropped into his bed, and buried himself underneath the covers.

He texted Astra as soon as he got back. The now blurry cameras couldn't see him, but he didn't doubt that someone would notice. He had a plan if they asked, but he had a feeling they wouldn't. No one likes cameras on them. They would be cleaned if a watchful eye caught them soon enough, but for now, Xavier asked his questions in plain sight, asking for advice on how to use the nanobots. He spent a couple of hours trying to set them up before Astra managed to get control of them. He then dutifully dumped them down the sink.

He went to sleep triumphantly that night, knowing that he was now no longer alone in the facility.

Miles away at Torsion, Astra watched the bots progress through the water pipes from her phone. While her help was limited, it was there when Xavier needed it.

She just had to wait until Isaac arrived, and then he would be fully protected.

13

Tessa

Astra wasn't partial to the area where she worked. There were days when she'd sit in her room and days when she'd sit in the lab. Sometimes it was the cafeteria, the front steps, underneath the stairs, or the roof. Today she occupied the garden, nestled in a small open patch surrounded by rose bushes.

Did it hurt when she shifted and the thorns dug into her skin? Of course, it did, but only a little. That small amount of pain was the price she was willing to pay for secrecy and a little peace and quiet. Today, she was monitoring the trackers. For the most part, Astra left them to their own devices, only nudging people here and there to stay away from things she didn't want them to see.

Other days, Astra would plant herself in a corner and orchestrate every move of every single person on campus. Astra didn't really care what the other students did in their free time, she was more concerned about her friends. Still, she wanted the other students out of the way, and she would only use them where she needed them. Astra focused the most on the progress that Aiken was making, and how Isaac was doing. Isaac was under quarantine at the moment, and thanks to the nanobots in his blood, he would be safely controlled until he was allowed to roam Syn freely.

Astra's plan was contingent on Aiken and Isaac. Without them, everything would fall apart. She never lost sight of where they were, and though she was paranoid that something would happen, deep down she knew they would do as they were told so long as no one interfered.

Right now, her problem was Katya. Stubborn, curious, intelligent Katya. Astra had noticed too late that Katya had discovered the blind spots, and it was only a desperate coding session and some late-night changes that kept her from being discovered.

Katya, like Astra, instantly noticed the changes in the sky, but she wouldn't know what they meant. Astra, on the other hand, kept note of every time the night was brighter, or stars disappeared from their usual places light years away.

Astra wished her rescue would come sooner. Whenever she peered through the telescope at the sky, she was grateful for the modifications she put in. It allowed her to see further, to the very outer limits of her galaxy, and that comforted her, even if it was only for a short time. Testing the telescope's limits and breaking it was something she didn't have time for, so she kept her mourning moments brief. Still, the thrill of the hunt for something out of place in her sky made her long for home even more.

When Astra first got to earth and met Ares, he told her the story of how he had begun his empire. He was charged with tracking ships, weaponry, technology, and researching human behavior. He also kept those humans from finding out what they really were. When the wars started, Astra's people scattered, some even left Earth to join the fight. When Ares died, it only got worse. It was her fault for not going with them, a choice that left her stranded, with only her wits to keep her alive. She prayed they heard her call. For the first time in a long time, Astra didn't want to be alone.

Astra sighed. Oh, the way she was falling apart. If only she was older and wiser. She remembered the curiosity and love she had in her youth. Though her memories of her younger years were hazy, she had not forgotten the love, the tradition of her people. She missed having Ares there to guide her. His death was a warning that she would not live as long as she hoped. Still, she needed to try. She didn't want to drag innocent people into her mess.

Astra could argue that the people already tangled in the web she had spun were not innocent. Still, that didn't mean they deserved the fate that followed her. Astra touched the file in her lap, lightly tracing the ridges and edges of the paper. It was Tessa's application, Tessa who would be coming to the school today. She sighed. Astra hadn't seen Tessa since her father's funeral, and even then she hadn't talked to her. Though Tessa's eyes had followed her, burning holes into her back, Astra stuck to Xavier. By the time Astra had been ready to face her, Tessa was gone.

Astra closed her eyes, wincing at the thought. It had been so easy to think that Tessa was coming to help her. But what if Tessa was coming to hurt her? To spy on her or take her home? She was a fool to think that Xavier would let her go so quickly. Though, to be fair, maybe he was, maybe she was overthinking the situation. She leaned back and then hissed in pain as the thorns stabbed her back. She had forgotten where she was.

Deeming the spot too painful for reminiscing, Astra got up and headed back towards her dorm room. Zola had informed her that Tessa would be getting there around noon, which meant that she had about two hours to do nothing. Astra hated sitting around, but there wasn't really anything to do now that she had sent Isaac on his way. She decided to change directions and headed towards the lab instead.

When she reached it, she found Aiken dutifully going through files. "How's it going?" she questioned.

Aiken hummed. "I haven't found anything you would find important, but I have to say, this is fascinating. Leroy Parkes has the wildest ideas, they almost make sense."

Astra laughed. "Are you that impressionable?"

"No!" Aiken glared at her. "I'm just saying…" he trailed off.

Astra shook her head. "Hmm. Have fun!" She disappeared into the file room. She began to lose track of time. She could have sworn it had only been 30 minutes when Zola came to get her. Astra steeled herself for anger, but when she saw Tessa standing in the foyer, all the air left her lungs. It took everything inside her not to just hug Tessa, pretend everything was fine and throw all secrecy out the window. Tessa wasn't like Xavier, she was quicker and calmer and more forgiving.

When Astra beckoned Tessa to follow, she did, silently. Astra took Tessa to the roof, and when she was sure that they were alone, she finally turned to face her sister. Tessa looked the same, a mischievous glint in her intelligent eyes, long red hair, freckles speckled across her nose and cheeks. Astra smiled, and Tessa matched her grin.

It was Tessa who broke the silence. "How are you doing?" she asked.

"I'm doing well."

"Then why do you look so tense?" Tessa took one of Astra's hands in her own. "It's like if someone even breathes wrong you're going to shatter."

"What's that supposed to mean?"

Tessa laughed. "Out of all of us, you're always the one put together, it's different now."

Astra raised an eyebrow. "That didn't clarify anything."

Tessa shook her head. "If you didn't get it, then I'm not going to elaborate."

Astra rolled her eyes. "Okay. Will you at least tell me what you came for?"

"What I came for? To see you and help you of course."

"And to work at the former estate of our family's worst enemy?"

Tessa took a deep breath. "I heard from Xavier about everything that happened. I'm here to help you, to do whatever you need me to do, and to spend time with you. I fear that if I don't I'll never have the chance to do so again."

Astra nodded. "Okay. I believe you. You're hired."

Tessa laughed. "That's it?"

"Well, I helped choose you earlier, I just wanted to make sure."

"Did you think I would lie to you?"

"I don't know what I think," Astra said. She stared at Tessa for a long time before turning around again. "Come with me, I'll show you where you'll be staying. For your position, you'll be working with the nursing students as a lab assistant."

"Sounds fun," Tessa said.

"You love to help people, it's only right."

"Fair enough."

Astra stopped in front of a door. "Here you go." She handed Tessa a set of keys. "Those go for the nursing labs, and the big one is a master key for the doors on this floor. You'll also be serving as an RA."

"Seriously?" Tessa huffed.

"What? You're great with people."

Tessa made a face. "I'll try, but if I don't like it, you're moving me."

Astra sighed. "Fine. You should start tomorrow, and help me figure things out."

Tessa nodded. "Wait. There's one more thing. I'm not going to be responsible for any blood that's spilt, okay Astra?"

Astra smiled. "Don't worry, I'll do the dirty work. Now, go rest. I have some things to do." She hesitated, then hugged Tessa tightly. She let go quickly and disappeared down the hall, once again headed towards the lab.

* * * * * * * * *

Henry typed his last thoughts quickly. He had gotten used to rapidly finishing his work due to college deadlines and it felt wrong to stop now. Though Aiken was there when he arrived, the boy was long gone, probably foraging for food. He had been there for hours already, struggling to put the words on paper. He wasn't very good at it, and he never had to be. Now research papers and proof of work was all that filled his days. That and being pulled into random side projects by Alyssa or Elena.

Footsteps coming down into the lab drew his attention. He assumed it was Aiken returning, but was pleasantly surprised to see Astra enter the room.

"Hello Henry," Astra said.

Henry just nodded in greeting, returning back to his computer. He saved his essay and submitted it, then leaned back in his chair. He stretched, closing his eyes. This break wouldn't last forever, but he still welcomed it.

"Still working?" Astra questioned.

"Always. I just finished one assignment, but I have three more to do. What about you, how'd that meeting with the new staff member go?"

"Pretty good. Tessa, that's her name, Tessa Lynn, is starting tomorrow," Astra replied.

"So soon?" Henry finally looked up at Astra. "Doesn't she need training?"

Astra shook her head. "Nope. Well, maybe, but Zola will train her if she needs it. It's not really my job." She smiled at him, the corners of her eyes crinkling. "Anyway, I have a few things to do. Let me know if you need anything. Have fun!" She disappeared into the file room.

Henry frowned. He could have sworn Astra's eyes were brown, not black. He shrugged. He wasn't really the observant type.

14

A Bullet-Ridden Legacy

Xavier woke with a start. Now that he was getting into the routine of being at the compound, he was excited to wake early. He did feel tired, but there was a pep in his step when he walked. In the past two days, while he still expressed the want to stay in the coding section of the lab, he had also gotten to shadow higher-level employees and learn what they did. Syn placed emphasis on making sure their employees could do multiple things. Xavier had spent days running around doing odd jobs to practice.

Xavier thought it was a good idea that every person could run almost every station and be moved around. If he was thinking critically, that meant their turn-over rate was high. Of course, at Syn, that meant those employees didn't even make it out of the building before they were killed. Xavier wondered if Clay Parkes actually beheaded people. *'You don't want to lose your head,'* Clay had warned him. It would be the ironic thing to do, but it would probably draw too much attention. Hiding bodies, especially dismembered ones, on the grounds of the facility was probably a bad idea. Especially if they had to deal with the bones. Maybe they had an incinerator, or a wild animal kept somewhere in the lower rooms.

Xavier's mind drifted. He had killed many people in his lifetime, and one of the most bloody ways he had hid a body was throwing them into a meat grinder at a butcher shop. It had taken him days to stop throwing up every time he thought of it. He hadn't thought about what would happen to the people who consumed what that shop sold. After all, he still refused eat meat of any kind. Xavier tried not to think about the staff cooking humans into food, but his mind wandered all the same. He assumed, that just like every other meat, they would taste like chicken. It would be unexpected, easily masked by other flavors, and with the food choices here…

Xavier shook his head aggressively. He was not here to die, and if he went out, it would not be a brutal death by unintentional cannibalism. Xavier forced himself to think of the day's work. There was a lot still to do, and while he preferred some jobs over others, he was looking forward to them all. He wasn't sure what he was doing today. Xavier had impressed the girl who ran engineering, and if he was being honest, he found what they were doing interesting. He had so much to do before he could even get to the point where he could work with the androids and he wanted to get there as quickly as possible. The least he could do was make sure he enjoyed the process.

He wasn't really the inventing type, but working with your hands and creating something was a great way to pass time.

Xavier thought that he finally understood the appeal. His younger self had often questioned why his siblings spent so much time cooped up building things. He just wanted to see Astra in person and apologize for the one time that he taunted her by stealing her tech and hiding it in his room. She broke his nose for it, but he had found it so entertaining. Then he found out that these people were putting their heart and soul into what they built, and he believed he was finally aware enough to admire it.

Xavier had never been stupid, not intellectually, but there were days that he could be dumb enough to believe that he was always right. On one particular day, his father had pulled him into the lab and gave him a bullet. *'Xavier,'* he had said. *'You will respect your family, you will respect their work and their ways, even if you don't understand them. And if there is a time where you break this rule, you will shoot yourself with this bullet and you will die for your arrogance.'*

Xavier remembered fearfully asking his father if he meant it, only for Ares to chuckle and slap him on the back. When he realized that he was joking, Xavier had been so angry he had chucked the thing across the room and locked himself in the bathroom to cry. Later, he found the bullet in his room, and for every single time he hurt his siblings, Ares added another bullet to the collection. He learned later from Jaxson that their father had given this talk to everyone.

When Xavier finally had the courage to ask why he had done that, Ares had turned to him and said: *'Xavier, in this world, we are nothing. We are made of the people who surround us, and the ones that we trust. For every person that you hurt, there is a consequence. It's important to remember the lives that we've taken, to honor the people they were. No matter how corrupt they were, we owe them that. So keep these bullets as a reminder. One day, you will die. You should pray that the people around you will have enough mercy to remember you.'*

Xavier stared at his reflection in the mirror. He had kept those words close to him every single day. When Ares died, Xavier took the first bullet he gave him and put it on a necklace and took it with him everywhere. He added a bullet to his collection for every person he killed and every time he got in an argument with his siblings. The latest was for his anger at Astra, cutting words he'd regretted since they left his mouth. Xavier glanced at the bathroom door, knowing that when he left this room he'd be in danger. If he died here, they wouldn't remember him. Xavier had his heart set on leaving a legacy. So there, in the bathroom, he made a vow to himself. If he lost the game that he was playing, he'd take the joking advice his father gave him, and shoot himself in the head.

It was a deathbed attitude that he brought with him as he went down to breakfast. He greeted the people around him and waved to his friends. If they had known him well enough they would have recognized the somberness in his voice. They didn't. There were some days that Xavier wished his father had been consistent, that he hadn't told them to stay in the shadows and yet reminded them to plead for recognition.

It could have been a cruel joke. Or maybe it was a reminder that no matter what they did, they weren't special, and they certainly weren't good. For people to remember them, they had to do something to be remembered and Xavier no longer wanted to be remembered for his removal of the so-called *'corruption'*. That meant people would remember him for being a killer who claimed to do good. When he got home, he would beg Tessa to help him. Xavier wanted to be remembered for acknowledging his mistakes. Even if it took him forever to fix things, he'd do it.

Mr. Lavoie took an unusual amount of time to come get Xavier. He was almost alone in the dining hall by the time Mr. Lavoie arrived. Lavoie's behavior told Xavier that his job today was going to be different than normal. He only hoped that it would be a welcome change. Xavier was taken to the nanotech station, where Lavoie left him with the instruction to wait until someone else came. So he was shadowing an employee from here. Xavier had several ideas of who would be replacing him. He was not at all expecting to see Alejo.

The boy smiled and waved at him as he approached. "Hi Xavier!" Alejo said, excited. "Did Lavoie tell you that you're shadowing me today?"

"He did not."

Alejo smiled wider. "It's a surprise then, huh?"

"I had no idea you were such a high level employee," Xavier answered.

"People don't expect me to be. But don't worry, today is not going to be like what you've experienced with other people."

Xavier frowned. "What do you mean?"

"Well, in other circumstances, you watched the managers while they worked, correct?"

"Yes."

"We're going to be switching jobs. You'll get a task, and I'm going to be watching and evaluating you."

Xavier raised an eyebrow. "That is new. Are you sure you trust me?"

Alejo shrugged. "It's not about trust, it's about knowledge. If you can't hold your own in a test like this, how do we know you can actually apply what you claim you know?"

"What happens if I fail this test?" Xavier asked. "Do you kill me?"

"No," Alejo responded. "If I don't like what you do, I'll show you how to do it right. It's not me you should be worried about."

Xavier liked Alejo's answer. He wasn't sure if the kid was lying or not, but he did feel a little better. "Okay, and what if I pass the test?"

"Then you've impressed me and I get to tell my boss that you did well."

"Is there any reward that I get?"

Alejo pursed his lips. "Job security?"

"Huh."

"That and you get better privileges."

"What kind of privileges?" Xavier asked, curious.

"You get access to projects, higher-level tech, they take the cameras out of your room, stuff like that."

"Is there a major project going on right now?"

Alejo nodded.

Xavier pressed further. "Is there any way I could earn hearing about this project?"

Alejo smiled. "If you are smart enough Xavier, you will figure out what it is on your own."

"And what if I want to work on it?"

"Don't worry, if you impress me and everyone else, you will."

15

Logic

Xavier enjoyed the time that he worked with Alejo. The constant moving and problem-solving kept him on his toes. It reminded him of old times, fighting with his sisters and countering everything that Ares threw at him. Alejo really put him to work. Xavier never struggled through the equations, but his hands shook when he had to work with wires.

When the day was over, Alejo simply put his clipboard down and shook Xavier's hand. That's how he knew he did well. Xavier only hoped it was good enough to give him access to some of Astra's stuff.

The Syn compound was nothing like he had ever seen, and being unprepared was an unfamiliar feeling. There was a time when Xavier wouldn't leave his mother's side. Even on his first mission, he thought of her. When she died, he had tried to escape her, but her kindness and her teaching followed him. Tonight, he wanted to honor her memory. He would follow in her footsteps and leave his father's anger behind. His own need to succeed would be the end of him, that air of pride and insincerity. He would let his mother's diplomacy, his sister's calming presence fill him. He would do his best to fulfill this cause, like old times, or he would die trying.

Xavier returned to his room in somber silence. He wanted to be arrogant, but the unknown made him sick to his stomach. He didn't eat dinner that night, he just sat there in the dark, waiting. He couldn't sleep, not until he had an answer. Did he truly impress Alejo? Xavier began to rethink Alejo's expression, the grip of his hand, the weight of what that meant. He hadn't felt this anxious to prove himself since his father had tested him. Xavier shuddered. Unlike his younger self, he was not allowed to fail this test. There were no second chances. Xavier did not move from his seat until the sun rose and a familiar knock resounded, calling him to breakfast.

There was no expression on Lavoie's face. Per usual, the man just walked Xavier to the dining hall and left. Xavier could barely eat, but he forced himself to down some water and a few bites of oatmeal, just so he wouldn't feel sick later. It was both strange, and comforting. He remembered when Astra or Cassidy would do the same, practically forcing food down his throat so he wouldn't pass out. It was strange how life had come to this. He used to be a king, and here he was, a stranger, nothing, no one. And this time, being no one was more dangerous than it usually was. Xavier smiled to himself. All good things come to an end. It was kind of ironic, his 'reign' was not really good.

Lavoie returned and rather than taking him to the lab, Xavier realized that they were going towards Clay's office. Xavier fought to keep his face blank, his expression neutral, and his heart rate under control. There were two reasons that he was going there. Either he did make a good impression, or he was walking to his death. When they arrived, Lavoie didn't even knock, he just opened the door, gestured for Xavier to go inside, and left. Xavier braced himself for the worst and went inside.

"Close the door behind you, will you, Mr. Zhang?"

Xavier frowned, but did as he was told. In front of Clay Parkes's desk were two chairs, one of which was now occupied by Alejo, whose face was completely blank. His posture was rigid, and his hands were folded on his lap.

"May I ask what's going on, sir?"

Clay closed the file that he was reading and smiled at Xavier. "Yesterday, I assigned you to Alejo, having an idea of the kind of performance that you would give. However, his report was completely different than what I expected."

"In a good way, or a bad way, sir?"

Clay laughed. "Sit down, Xavier. It's quite more complicated than that."

Xavier did as he was told, even though every instinct in him was screaming at him to run. Xavier often leaned towards fight over flight, but Clay was a killer, and he had no doubt that Alejo was too. If he had to fight his way out, he would. But getting Astra's tech back to her meant more to him than his life, like many things, so he just sat there, prepared to take whatever judgment or punishment that he was given.

Clay smiled at him, which surprised Xavier. "What's wrong, kid?" Clay asked.

Xavier groaned internally. His concern for the situation must have shown through, and he had to choose his words carefully. "In my experience, you only get called to the office when you're in trouble." Xavier had always been taught that being honest was the best way to avoid getting in trouble. His mother was especially strict with this rule.

Clay laughed again. "Don't worry, you're not in trouble Xavier. I'm just going to try to pick your brain."

"Okay?" Xavier frowned.

"Alejo, would you like to explain?"

Xavier turned to Alejo, who still had no expression on his face. Despite the fact that whatever this meeting was would be good for him, that scared him. In the short time that Xavier had gotten to know Alejo, he had always been extremely expressive.

After staring him down for a few seconds, Alejo's shoulders relaxed, and he gave Xavier a curt smile. "Xavier, what kind of person are you?"

"Excuse me?" Xavier was taken aback. This was not the kind of question he had been expecting.

Alejo's smile fell. He leaned forward. "You are the most extraordinary person that I've ever met. You took every problem that I gave you in stride, you worked with this tech as if you were familiar with it, though you never should have seen it in your life, and you coded laps around previous trainees." Alejo stared at him for a second before continuing. "What goes on inside that brain of yours?"

Xavier faltered. For the first time in his life, he had no answer, no quip, there was only confusion as he struggled to find something to say that wouldn't betray him. "I think, I was raised to be quick-witted, to understand what people told me, to follow orders, and to analyze technology well. Someone very dear to me told me that if I pay enough attention to the pieces, I can solve any puzzle. The same goes for technology. It's just numbers and wires put together. If you have a logical brain, you think fast, and you don't get distracted, it's possible to do anything. I got nervous, definitely, but I did all that I could."

"Huh." Alejo sat back in his seat. "Are you thinking what I'm thinking, Mr. Parkes?"

"Of course I am. Or at least I assume I am, if you're referencing your report."

Xavier turned back to Clay, aware that Alejo was intently watching his every move. The thought was unnerving. "What do you mean sir?"

Clay Parkes tapped the file on his desk. "This is the report that Alejo gave me on you. In it is a detailed section of the way that you work with code. We have a project going on at the facility, a security program, built to protect itself. If someone tries to hack it, it will counter. Eventually, it will learn the user and fix problems and weaknesses before a hacker even tries those areas."

Xavier frowned again. "Sir, it's extremely difficult to eliminate the middle man. You're talking about coding an AI so intelligent that it can anticipate anything that the human brain throws at it, it's impossible. Without that human element, the analysis and knowledge of true creativity and desperation, an AI will ultimately fail."

Clay sighed. "If my cousin could do it, I can."

"I'm sorry?" Xavier connected that sentence very quickly, to a facility that he knew, and a person that he hated. Clay Parkes must have known what his cousin had done using his sister's technology.

"Have you ever heard of androids, kid?"

Xavier nodded. "I have."

"Then you should know that it's not unattainable."

Xavier sighed. "Okay, it's not impossible. But it is difficult to do so without a brilliant mind that can think quick enough to analyze patterns and…" he trailed off. "Oh." Xavier threw pieces together, trying to figure out what Clay was proposing.

Clay smiled. "Yes, you can see why we called you in here."

"You want me to work on this project?" Xavier questioned. "I mean, I consider myself quick-witted, but I haven't worked with anything remotely close to AI." This was the truth, Astra made sure to keep him far away from her pet projects, something about not wanting him to break them. If he even breathed close to what she was working on, she would kick him out of the room.

"Work on it?" Clay scoffed. "You're not going to work on it. I mean, you will work on it, but not really, not in the way you're thinking."

"What do you mean sir?"

Alejo sighed loudly and rolled his eyes. "Xavier, we're going to be modeling the program after your brain."

Xavier was stunned. "What?"

Clay nodded. "Humanoid androids would be almost impossible to do from scratch, even with your mind. Luckily, we have a blueprint, well, pieces of it, and with your help, this program will be online in no time."

Xavier couldn't help but laugh.

"What's so funny?" Clay asked.

Xavier shook his head. "Nothing sir, just, Alejo told me that getting onto your main project would be difficult. I had no idea I was extraordinary. I don't mean to brag, but it's strange to me."

Clay smiled. "No, Xavier, this isn't the main project. This is an extra layer of defense for it. You are extraordinary, I'll give you that, but you're not ready to be put on the project. I'm sure you will, but it will take time. For now, you'll work with what we give you. Go with Alejo and practice for the rest of the day. You start work with the program tomorrow."

Xavier nodded. "Yes sir." As he left the office, he smiled. He was one step closer. If he continued at this pace, he'd be out with Astra's tech by the end of next month.

"You excited?" Alejo asked him, smiling. He fell in line with Xavier, both briskly walking towards the lab.

Xavier nodded. "Very."

16

You're On Your Own

Astra sat at her computer, staring straight ahead, not even comprehending the words on the screen. She still couldn't believe that Tessa was there at the school; there for her. This was what family was, not Xavier's harsh words or her parent's expectations. And maybe the unquestioned loyalty wasn't something they had earned. But she would still fight for her own survival as she did before. Except this time, perhaps it was okay not to be alone.

She had always been taught that she didn't need help. Astra remembered the words drilled into her head as a child, long before she came to earth.

'You will be on your own Astra. Help is not freely given because you will have to be strong. Even though you are connected to us, as we all are strong together, we must also be strong separately so that all of us will live. You will learn to survive off of your own wit and self-discipline. If you need help, don't be afraid to call for it, but also do not rely on it. You cannot bring us down because you can't do something yourself.'

Astra remembered the lecture a younger girl in her class had gotten. After a few weeks, she hadn't seen that girl again. Astra knew she had just been sent home, but she couldn't help but feel bad. The city raised her people, so someone would've taken care of the girl after she left the facility. Still, children weren't meant to be on the streets. Those kids were rejects, the motivation behind every student's work.

Astra couldn't remember when her motivation switched from working just to keep herself from becoming one of them, to working to make sure those kids would be helped. It was definitely her parents who changed her mind. Her people didn't live off of the idea of family, just loyalty. Loyalty to the point of death. It was ingrained in her. So when did she stop feeling that way? When did her mind change?

Astra sighed. Her childhood was many things, but the word *'consistent'* was not something she could use to describe it. She was a child soldier. That was the easiest way to explain. She had no true home to return to, her only *'parents'* were dead, and the thought of even using that word would have made her younger self sick.

'I am on my own,' Astra thought. *'It is time I accept that.'*

Astra closed her computer and left her room. It was a common habit. Her family was used to her roaming the halls, looking for something to give her inspiration. It was usually those times that Astra would seek Arya out. Her older sister was comforting and wise in a way that Astra wanted to be. Arya was the first person Astra had ever told about her home and her culture. The only person she had mourned as if Arya was a part of her people.

Unlike Ares, whose sharp words and stories had told Astra what Earth was like, Arya had taught Astra what Earth was like. She could have written down from memory what both had said to her, and they would have been drastically different. Ares could see the good in other people but he never focused on it. True to their culture and world, Ares was angry. He had one goal, to correct and consume. The same goal she shared. Conquer. Conform or be destroyed. She had never questioned it before.

Meanwhile, Arya had shown Astra the world. She had talked for hours about places she wanted to visit, museums, gardens, and oceans. There were buildings full of history that Arya wanted to enjoy. Astra hard listened intently, for the most part. Sometimes, she got lost in Arya's eyes. The way they sparkled when she talked about things she loved. When Astra had told Arya about the stars, she had finally felt understood. If Arya was still here, Astra knew she would have no problem renouncing her old life and staying.

She wanted to go back to her childhood. Those midnight trips down the hall, up the stairs, to the left, and into Arya's room. Astra often buried herself under Arya's covers with a book or some machine she was tinkering with. Then she'd talk for hours. She'd tell Arya what she was working on or what Ares was worried about with his clients. Then there were the days that Arya asked about her home. Astra was sure that her own eyes sparkled the way Arya's did when describing the city.

"You know, if you find the tallest building, and you stand at a certain spot at a certain time, the buildings glisten. It's perfect for watching meteor showers or just watching the way the light hits. And in the evenings during the colder months, all the windows turn to prisms and the whole city is in rainbows, it's beautiful. I wish you could see it."

Astra scoffed. She had promised a lot to Arya. It was not easy burying her. Sometimes Astra thought she had buried her wonder with her sister. She hadn't enjoyed much since then. Astra wandered the halls of the school for hours, lost in thought. When she had finally moved on from reminiscing, her brain filled with formulas and bits and pieces of code.

Even though she wasn't taking classes, Astra couldn't stop working. After hours in the lab, she'd tinker until she fell asleep. Sometimes, Henry would join her. The two worked in silence, though every so often Henry would talk aloud about his project. Astra knew it was in an effort to make her laugh. Sometimes she did. Most times she didn't.

Astra wandered into the cafeteria and grabbed a sandwich before heading back towards her room. As she excited the stairwell on her floor, Tessa blocked her way. Astra frowned. "What—"

Tessa cut her off. "We need to talk."

Tessa pulled Astra back into the stairwell and up to the roof. They stood there in complete silence for a while, just surveying the grounds before Tessa spoke.

"I must confess, my goal for coming here is not what I told

you."

"Oh?"

Tessa nodded. The light breeze blew the hair away from her face. In the light of the setting sun, Tessa looked just as solemn as always. There was a beauty in the way that Tessa held herself. She was often the bearer of bad news, since her soft demeanor and diplomatic style of speaking had always made the people around her more comfortable. Astra noticed for the first time that Tessa had cut her hair. Tessa never cut her hair, no matter how inconvenient it was to have to tie it back.

Tessa didn't look at Astra. The light of the setting sun illuminated her, and Astra could read her like a book.

"You came to try to convince me to come home, didn't you?"

Tessa nodded again. "I wasn't sent by anyone, I hope you know that." She finally turned to Astra. "We're redoing everything that Father stood for. We want to be our own people, do something good for once. And it's hard to imagine a life that you're not in."

Astra stared back at her sister. Tessa, the kindest, the glue of the family, the loved. "Tessa, I can't do what you want me to do. I'm not that girl anymore. I'll always be your sister, but my loyalty belongs to something else. I cannot change that."

Tessa didn't turn, she continued staring into the sun. "Astra, do you know what it's like to be selfish?"

"Excuse me?"

Tessa finally turned to look at her and gave Astra a soft smile. "You are always doing things for other people. What about yourself?"

"Tessa..."

"I'm just saying. Don't you want to come home?"

"I want to do what I said that I would do. I want to follow through with getting my tech back and going home. I'm not a quitter, Tessa. I love you all, but I have to do this. And if this is selfishness, then let me have it."

Tessa sighed. "Astra, have you ever forgotten what your goal in life was?"

Astra hesitated before shaking her head. "Never."

"Come on now, I know you're lying. You're really going to look me in the eyes and say that you truly believe you're doing the right thing? You're really not angry?"

"Do you think I am made of glass? I'm not fragile Tessa, nor stupid. It is wrong what Xavier said to me, but that is not why I'm leaving."

Tessa moved closer to Astra. She took her right hand, entwining their fingers together. "I'm not saying that. However, you have a tendency to forfeit your own happiness. I know you're having questions. Do you really want to leave?"

Astra looked down. "I'm not sure what I'd have left if I didn't."

"You'd have me."

"I want to say that would be enough." Astra laughed.

"I wish for you to have a kinder tomorrow Astra. I hope that you find yourself."

Astra looked back up. Tessa's expression hadn't changed, it was still soft, her slight smile and sad eyes held no ounce of pity. It was sorrow that Astra saw in the lines of Tessa's face. "If I stay, I will not go home immediately."

"You don't have to."

Astra nodded. "I want to find answers, Tess."

Tessa removed her hand and pulled Astra into a hug. "Then go search for them. You were always good at that."

Astra smiled half-heartedly as she leaned her head on Tessa's shoulder. "I was, wasn't I? I only wish that I was as good at making a home for myself as I was at solving problems."

Tessa laughed. It was soft, and almost sad. "It's okay. I don't expect you to have all the answers."

"You may be the only person who doesn't."

"Or maybe, you might be the only person who does."

17

Greet the Stars

Katya sat in the observatory, staring at the telescope. *'It was just a glitch,'* she kept telling herself. She had no proof it was anything more, but in her mind, she wanted it to be. She wanted to find something that would mean she was right. So she stole Zola's code. She hadn't meant to cause any harm, but she couldn't help it. She had snagged Zola's computer and copied the code onto her computer. She had asked Henry for help understanding how to run it, and she was set. He hadn't even asked any questions.

Now, her computer was hooked up to the mainframe of the telescope and she was ready. She held the list of search parameters in one hand and balanced a notebook full of instructions on her knee. She didn't want to be wrong. Katya typed the parameters into the computer and let it run. She began to drum her fingers on her leg. *'Let me be right, let me be right, let me be right.'*

By the time the program had ended, Katya was rigid, clenching her teeth and her fists together tightly. She checked the results and then slowly relaxed, releasing the tension from her shoulders and the breath from her lungs in a long sigh of relief. There, on the screen, was all the proof she needed. Someone had messed with the telescope, it wasn't a glitch at all. She just had to figure out who.

Katya sat there for a long time, just processing the implications. She didn't know who would even want to hide that sort of thing. It wasn't like it was important information that stars were missing. It wasn't life-threatening, it was just another discovery that would fuel astronomer curiosity for a while. Stars technically could disappear instantly, but they should fade. Maybe they'd discover a black hole over there. That didn't account for the blurry space or the random lights, but that could just be the telescope.

Whoever had messed with it and went through the trouble of hiding the fact that they did that, was more than capable of accidentally messing with the telescopes' range.

Katya made a mental note to ask Astra and Elena to come to take a look at the lens, then packed up and returned to her dorm. Like usual, Zola was there, tapping away at her computer. For a second, Katya considered showing Zola what she'd found, but then she would have to explain that she had stolen Zola's tech in the first place. Instead, she sat on her bed, pulled the two maps out of her bag, and compared them. The first was how the sky should look. The second was the allegedly projected map that Zola had found and rebooted the server for. The same map she found trashed and covered up in the system.

How Zola hadn't discovered it was beyond her. The map disappeared from the code when Zola rebooted the computer, but Katya's search revealed it wasn't a projection at all. It was real. The more Katya stared at the screen, the more uneasy she got. So much was unaccounted for, and if this was the map that was real, and what she thought was real was fake, then this was way bigger than just a black hole a couple galaxies over and missing stars. Katya contemplated it for a long time. If she didn't figure it out soon, she feared the questioning would consume her.

* * * * * * * * *

The next day, Katya and Elena took the lenses off the telescope and inspected them thoroughly. Elena spent a few hours cleaning and polishing each one before putting it back on the telescope. Katya sat at the server, searching for something else. She didn't find anything. No more strange images, no explanation, no warning signs that could account for the missing stars and blurry spaces. The random lights on the map were also something that eluded Katya. They weren't stars, or satellites as far as she could tell. But they were too small to be anything that she knew.

She could ask someone to hack into a satellite, maybe get closer if the telescope wasn't able to see them. She had wanted to launch a satellite of her own to connect to the computer, but she just didn't have the materials. All Katya knew was that she had to be the first to figure it out. Katya knew scientists, they were ruthless when it came to new discoveries. If anyone else had seen what she did, she was certain she would never be able to take credit for it.

Eventually, Katya abandoned the server and shadowed Elena as she inspected the base of the telescope for any tampering.

"Did you find anything?"

Elena shook her head. "Nothing. Whoever did this was quick, and knew what they were hiding."

Katya fiddled with the hair tie on her wrist. "Do you think one of the old staff members could have done it?"

"No, I'm pretty sure we got all of them. My guess is it was a student. That, or someone broke it for the sole purpose of using the telescope, found these anomalies, and was smart enough to know how to cover their tracks. Which should be extremely improbable since besides our teachers, no one knew we were making this, and most of the school board was arrested."

Katya sighed. "Do you think we'll figure out who did this?"

Elena shrugged. "Not sure. Besides, I think you'll be able to report this way quicker than anyone else. You're smart, and you have the resources you need. Don't worry about other people, you're better than other people. You can do this, regardless of who was trying to get there first."

Katya smiled half-heartedly. "Thanks El."

"Of course. Now, I have things to do, so I've got to go, but I will see you later. Maybe let's eat dinner together?"

Katya nodded. "Sure. Have fun!"

Elena disappeared, leaving Katya alone with her thoughts again. She would have a few minutes before Astra showed up to help her take a look at the map. Astra would not be an astronomer, but her attention to detail could prove useful. Katya printed the map out and dropped it on the table. Like clockwork, Katya heard the door open behind her as she finished marking the inconsistencies.

"Hi Astra," she said.

"Hello Katya." Astra came up behind her and leaned over her shoulder. "What do you need help with?"

Katya passed Astra the map. Astra's face was unreadable as she scanned it. "What's so important about this?"

"Do you see those small lights and the blurry space, and those black areas? The ones I circled?" Katya tapped on the paper. "They aren't supposed to be there."

"Okay…" Astra sat down, still staring at the paper. "So, you're a researcher. Why do you need my help?"

Katya plopped into the chair opposite of Astra. "The problem is that someone went through great lengths to hide this. Someone who knew this was happening, and had the coding skills to cover their tracks. Eventually, I want to figure out who did it, but right now the more pressing matter is why. What was the point?"

Astra frowned. "What do you mean?"

"Well, the night sky is pretty consistent. Things don't just move or disappear without warning, at least, all natural laws state that. Whatever this phenomenon is, I want to know. It could be dangerous. Or, it could be something else…" Katya trailed off.

Astra watched her expression change. "You're still thinking about aliens, aren't you?"

"Is it that obvious?"

Astra nodded. She tossed the map onto the table. "Listen Kat, I don't think you're wrong, or crazy."

Katya cocked her head and stared. "You don't?"

"No. Many people have come to the same conclusion as you. And whether the unknown can be attributed to aliens or to humans, that's something you get to discover. There's a lot of things we don't know, secrets we haven't uncovered. The universe holds just as many, if not more secrets than this world does. We haven't even begun to scratch the surface."

Katya smiled. "You really think that?"

"I don't just think that, I know it. The government hides way more than what we've been able to uncover just by hacking websites and satellites. They may know something we don't. Or, say that your aliens theory is correct. Why shouldn't there be things out there beyond our understanding? I mean, you are human after all. There are bound to be things that you don't know. Hopefully, you'll be able to figure it out in your lifetime. Or at the very least, witness it."

Katya laughed.

"What?"

"Nothing, you're just surprisingly encouraging."

Astra rolled her eyes, trying to hide a smile. "I guess I'm just in a good mood."

"How are things going for you, by the way?"

Astra shrugged. "Better. The new staff have definitely taken pressure off of me, and with everything calming down, I've had some time to myself. I've gotten to reflect on things, journal, tinker without the stress of a grade, it's nice."

"I'm glad you're doing better."

Astra paused before she began to speak again. "Kat?"

"Yes?"

"I think you're going to achieve your goals."

"What do you mean?"

Astra looked down at her hands. "Well, you're going to graduate, write about this discovery, probably get government funding, and your name will be known. You'll get to reach the stars like you've always wanted to. And I really hope you find the answers you're looking for."

"Well, I definitely didn't think you were the sentimental type, but thank you for that, it means a lot."

Astra smiled, and nodded. "Well, I have to go finish some administrative work, but I'll take the map with me and let you know if I see anything interesting."

"Thanks Astra."

Astra was halfway out the door before she stopped and turned around. She sighed. "Katya?"

Katya looked up from the computer. "Yes?"

"When you get to the stars, go ahead and greet them for me, okay?" Astra shut the door, leaving Katya with her work and the strange request reverberating in her mind.

18

The Grandmaster

Xavier sat on his bed fiddling with some spare parts. Somehow, he always found himself back here—shut in his room working. It was good for him, the silence. He thrived there. After the adrenaline and excitement wore off, Xavier realized exactly what the offer meant. Despite the comfort of the familiar environment, Xavier could not wrap his head around Clay Parkes's reasoning. His brain being the model for their security AI? Was this a joke?

Deep inside, he doubted it, but he wanted to think that they knew. He wanted to stay on edge. Maybe he was wrong, maybe they were all wrong. Maybe if they realized he was a spy, they wouldn't kill him. Still, even if they didn't know, he did not think that he was worthy of the honor of being a blueprint. Him. A model for the biggest advancement in security tech since—he paused. He couldn't even remember when something this complicated was introduced to AI.

This was what Astra was afraid of when Destiny was stolen. If technology became too human, they would be more susceptible to corruption, dangerous if they got out of control due to their physical and mental strength. Could he allow himself to be caught up in such a morally incorrect project, right after he agreed to fix himself and the way he thought? Xavier thought about texting Yvette, asking her what she'd think of him doing it. Breaking the law was one thing. Disappointing his youngest sister, now that was almost like sentencing himself to death.

Xavier sighed. On one hand, he wanted to do it. On the other hand, he knew that it was for all the wrong reasons. He used to like compromise. Now, he didn't know if he could forgive himself if he did. He couldn't pretend like his actions didn't have consequences, not anymore. He wanted to be a better person. He owed it to himself to try.

A few hours later, Xavier begrudgingly went down the stairs to dinner. He was worried he would run into Alejo and have to explain why he was feeling down. He started on the project tomorrow, and after his happy outburst in the office, he couldn't be caught regretting agreeing. Xavier picked at his food. He wasn't hungry. The knot in his stomach reminded him that he was not one of them, and he never would be. It was in that moment that he made the decision. If he was to appease his conscience, then he would have to sabotage everything he could to offset the fact that he was working for the enemy.

When Xavier returned to his room, he began to formulate a plan. He knew the camera in the corner was pointed at him, like Clay Parkes himself was boring a hole in his forehead. Xavier couldn't help but smile. This devious, malicious, hateful, part of himself was something that he should have gotten rid of. Unfortunately, it was useful, and at this point, he didn't know if he would ever lay it to rest.

The next morning, Xavier woke up bright and early. Although he was still mulling over the consequences that could come, for now he was just excited for the destruction and chaos he would cause. Alejo greeted him as soon as he entered the dining hall.

"Hello Xavier, are you ready?"

Xavier grinned. "I'm really excited, I was thinking a lot about what this security AI would have to do, will you tell me more about it?"

Alejo matched his smile. "Of course. Get some food and we can discuss."

The two made their way to a corner of the room. Alejo stabbed his eggs and chewed thoughtfully.

"So, what do you want to know?"

* * * * * * * *

Alejo talked a lot, and the amount of information that filled his brain was enough to keep him from paying attention to the directions Clay was trying to give him.

Clay sighed. "Mr. Zhang, are you listening?"

Xavier pulled himself into the present and nodded. "Yes sir. Well, not really. I was thinking about something."

Clay Parkes just shook his head. He pointed to the chess set on the table. "You will be playing Alejo. We'll be recording your brain signals to better model the speed and way in which you react. That will help us recreate the patterns in the AI's code. Understand?"

Xavier nodded. "I believe so. What happens if I lose?"

"Then you play until you win."

"That's it?"

Alejo spoke before Clay had the chance. "Well, the AI is supposed to learn how to counter new attacks, right? So, even if you're losing, you're also learning, and we can modify things here and there to compensate."

Xavier nodded again. "That makes sense."

He was in that room for hours. He used to think he was bad at chess, mainly because Astra would beat him every time. Now he was countering Alejo's every move, he won every single game. By the end of the day, Xavier was mentally exhausted, and yet he still hadn't lost.

"Interesting…" Clay said. "I think I may have to bring in new people to play you."

Xavier leaned back in his chair. "I hope that won't be too much trouble."

Clay shook his head. "I doubt it. You're dismissed."

Alejo helped Xavier remove the wires and monitors attached to his body before disappearing out the door and down the hall. Xavier hesitated at the door, staring at Clay's unreadable features, before heading towards his room.

Upstairs, Xavier made a decision. There was no time like the present and he would be lying to himself if he said he didn't miss the adrenaline. He sat there in his room until sunset, fiddling with the machinery in his hands. He had picked it up from one of the downstairs labs a few days ago. If he was going to do this, he had to run some kind of interference. After making sure that the cameras were subtly moved so he could sneak away, Xavier left his room.

One thing that he remembered about the Parkes family is that they preferred the dark. Maybe it was some sort of metaphorical thing, maybe they genuinely felt safe underground, but he was sure that if he was going to find anything, it would be downstairs in their most secure room. Not many people were roaming the halls thanks to the curfew, so Xavier found it easy to slip around the staff. *'Just like the old days.'* He thought to himself.

The lower he went, the colder it got, the more difficult the checkpoints and locks. Xavier picked and hacked his way through each one. Even though some were more time consuming, he didn't find many particularly troubling. Part of him thought that perhaps he would reach a point and someone would jump out at him, because someone this smart shouldn't be leaving their prize possessions unguarded. Then again, he'd always been this good. His younger self wouldn't be panicking.

Xavier steeled himself as he entered yet another hallway, except this one was different than all the ones before. It resembled those at Torsion where the lab started, and he grinned. It may have been too easy, but he wasn't worried anymore. There was a hum of electricity beneath his feet as he walked, colder air wafting through the air vents above him. The hairs on the back of his neck stood up. He was excited, Astra would be so happy to hear the news. He hesitated when he reached the doorway at the end of the hall. There was no door, and when he tentatively reached a hand through it, nothing happened.

He stepped into the room and gasped. This was a tech genius's heaven. He immediately recognized the style: the wiring and the air ducts, the panels, computers, the androids themselves displayed in the center of the room. This was his sister's work. His expression turned from wonder to displeasure, heat welling up in the pit of his stomach and on his cheeks. If his father was still alive, there was a particular punishment for thieves that he was fond of. Xavier wouldn't have minded if they still enforced it…

Xavier shook his head aggressively, clearing the thought from his mind. He would love to torture someone for hurting his siblings, but Yvette? She wouldn't approve. Xavier stepped closer to the displays, looking for anything that would indicate how close they were to completion. Xavier looked up into the face of the one closest to him. He shuddered. They looked too human.

It was something that Astra had always been afraid of. The flaws in her art were not there because she couldn't perfect it, but for the safety of anyone who encountered them. He still remembered what she had told him when he found her first messing with Destiny's body. "I don't want to be a creator, Xavier. I'm simply replicating things that I've seen before. They shouldn't be too real because that threatens humanity and if you threaten humanity, what are you left with? Absolute power and the absence of morality. That, brother, is something that you should fear. If we ever reach that point, humanity is doomed."

Astra had always been careful, and she was usually right. As he searched around the room for records, he wished that he hadn't been so caught up in being right. He had lost his sister for good, and he knew nothing would change her mind. Xavier stopped at the base of one of the other androids and just stared. It was easy to believe that this was Astra's handiwork, even without the intentional mistakes, it was hers. A black folder caught his eye as he turned to keep moving. It almost blended in with the bottom of the display case. He picked it up and flipped through it.

Then, he ran. He didn't care about whether or not the folder was in the same place as he found it, all he cared about was getting out of there and back to the safety of his room. If he was caught down there, he feared that they would realize he wasn't who he said he was. Or worse, maybe they already knew. He sprinted through the halls, no longer caring about secrecy. She had to know, he had to tell her. Maybe Astra would kill him, but at least she would know what to do. Xavier rounded a corner and ran into something hard.

"Umph." He looked up. A boy about his height was standing in front of him. "Sorry."

"For what? It did not hurt."

Xavier's eyes widened. He immediately made the connection. This was an android, most likely the test run he had read about in the folder. Xavier cleared his throat. He had to pretend he had no idea this thing wasn't human. "Still, I should have been watching where I was going. I just realized I broke curfew by a couple of minutes, I wasn't paying attention to the time. You won't tell, right?" He held out his hand. "I'm Xavier, nice to meet you."

The android took his hand, squeezing it just a little too tightly for Xavier's liking. "No, I won't, not if you won't tell them you saw me. It's nice to meet you too. My name is Isaac."

19

Motivation

Astra sat on her bed, computer in front of her, phone in hand. She checked the clock every few minutes, waiting for the right time. At 10 p.m. exactly, Astra wrote the code and looped the video feed to Xavier's room. She had long since hacked into that camera, and after making sure that the microphone feedback was listening to periodic shuffling of sheets and faint breathing, Astra called Xavier.

He answered the phone automatically, confirming that what she had done worked. "Hello?"

"Good evening, Xavier."

"Do you have a new job for me?"

"No. I have news." Astra couldn't see Xavier's face, but she imagined that he was frowning, waiting to hear what she said next. "There's someone else in there with you."

"What? Why?"

"Because I wanted to keep an eye on you."

Xavier's frustration was evident in his voice. "Do you think I can't do this by myself? Astra, we've worked together for years, don't you trust me?"

She hesitated. "I do." It wasn't a lie. "But he is there as an insurance policy. To get you out if something goes wrong."

"He?"

"His name is Isaac."

There was silence on Xavier's end for a while and Astra almost thought he hung up. "The android? The one I literally just met?!" Xavier half-yelled.

"Be quiet! Just because I covered the mic in your room and looped the video feed doesn't mean that something in the hall couldn't pick up the sound of your voice."

"I'm pretty sure all the rooms are sound-proof."

"Still."

Xavier sighed loudly. "But Astra, you sent me an android."

"No I didn't."

"What?"

Astra closed her eyes. "It's hard to explain, but Isaac isn't an android, not anymore."

"Well, you better start talking."

"I can't."

"Why not?"

"Xavier…"

"No! Why all these secrets? You can't keep your motives clandestine forever."

She hesitated, the thought of spilling all her worries crept to the forefront of her mind. Still, she held her ground.

"It's not up to you anymore. Please, just do your job."

"Astra, you expect me to trust you, and do what you ask, which I will, because we're family and I love you. But you have to tell me something, do you really want this to be the hill you die on?"

"I said I can't tell you. Respect that, Xavier. Please."

He sighed. "I hope you know what you're doing."

"I do. Stay safe. Isaac is on your side, I promise. I'll explain later, but for now, please just take me at my word. Don't ask unnecessary questions."

"Fine."

"Keep me updated."

"About that…"

The hesitation in his voice made Astra's skin prickle. "What?"

"I found some of your tech."

"Great. You can work on stealing it so I can retrieve it and Isaac will help you smuggle it out."

"That's not the issue Astra."

"Then what is?"

"They're not there to be tested. They're there to be prepped.

Astra, they're going to use those bots as weapons."

Astra was silent for a minute. "Thank you for telling me. I'll deal with it." Astra hung up and waited a few minutes before letting the video loop end. By then, Xavier was in bed, and no one would have any knowledge that their conversation had taken place. She turned her computer off and placed it on her desk. She decided to go to the only place that she knew would make her feel better: the roof. She needed to contemplate. Processing this new information, she needed to find some sort of peace before making a decision.

It was chilly outside, a light breeze rustled through the trees in the courtyard below, illuminated by the full moon. Astra stared up at the sky. Her heart longed for the beyond up there, her home, her people. She wanted to walk the silver streets again. To the people of earth, her home was a mystery, a secret, a myth.

For her, the city she grew up in was a haven built of stardust. She missed it, and yet, she was content to stay here on earth. Astra wanted an in-between she could never have. The choice was killing her. Astra walked along the roof, staring down at the flowers below her. There was a garden on her home planet where a special flower grew. It was blue and white and shone like the moon. It was beautiful. When the planet mourned, it bled from the center, like they did. They were all connected. She had been taught this since she was old enough to understand.

So maybe, she could have both worlds. She'd just have to let herself spread. Astra could do that. She could lead her people here, and continue conquering just like she had been taught. Astra looked down at her hands. In the light of the moon, she looked almost blue. She could pretend she was finally home, she could pretend this was her home. If there was anything that Astra was used to, it was knowing that wherever she went, whether she made a place for herself there or not, she didn't belong. She would always belong among her people.

Astra looked back up at the moon, scanning the sky for anything that would be out of place. There was nothing. She was suddenly reminded of what Tessa had told her just a few nights ago. It finally clicked in her head. *'Astra, do you know what it's like to be selfish?'* Tessa didn't mean she would be selfish for leaving. Tessa had meant it would be okay for her to stay. Astra sighed. If she could convince herself that it would be okay, then she would.

Astra returned to her room at midnight. It was probably the earliest that she had ever gone to bed, but she was especially tired for some reason. Right as she was about to turn off her light and settle into bed, her phone rang. She didn't recognize the caller ID, but she answered all the same.

"Hello?"

"Hi, Astra. Thank goodness I got ahold of you, I was a little worried that I had the wrong number."

Astra sat straight up. "Isaac. Is something wrong?"

"No, why would you think that?"

Astra sighed in relief and fell backwards. "I'm not sure, I guess I'm just always prepared for the worst."

Isaac laughed. "I'm fine. I just wanted to give you a little bit of an update. You know, since I finally ran into Xavier."

"How is it going?"

Isaac sighed. "Your brother is absolutely insane, Astra. I'm not sure how he survives."

Astra smiled and shook her head. "Isn't that everyone's impression of him? He hasn't accidentally exposed himself yet, right?"

"Nope. For someone so reckless, he at least knows how to cover his tracks."

"That does sound like my brother."

"Does he know that I'm here yet?"

"Yes. I told him. I'm not entirely sure that he's happy about it, but he knows."

"Good."

"Oh, how are the others? Still sick?"

"Yes. Nasra and Alyssa are working on it, so if I get any updates from them, I'll let you know."

There was silence on the other end of the phone before Isaac spoke up again. "Astra, may I ask you a personal question?"

She frowned. "It depends on the question."

Isaac hesitated. "If you couldn't come into any of Parkes's facilities without being noticed, then how come you were able to apply to Torsion and get in without any problems?"

Astra nodded unconsciously, without even realizing he couldn't see her. "That is a good question. In all honesty, if Parkes had recognized my name among those applicants, I would have been dealing with someone trying to kill me. He didn't. Originally, I was going to disguise myself, sneak into the school, and gather evidence. I wasn't supposed to get involved. Then I saw Destiny, and I had to get her. Despite what they told me, I didn't just want Parkes in jail, I wanted him suffering, I wanted him dead."

Astra stared up at the ceiling, fidgeting with the corner of her blanket. "I got what I wanted, I got everything. Yet, I lost everything. You know, my sister Tessa was the one who told me to apply. She said that if I didn't make it, we would find another way. When everything happened, I thought I would never see her again. I hate to admit that it hurt, what they said. My family stopped caring when my mother died. When I found out I got in because of your glitch, it was something that made me realize I wasn't there by design. He truly didn't know who I was, though I think he did get a little suspicious. I'm surprised Destiny never told him."

"So, if it wasn't for what happened, you would be here?"

"Two years ago, I could have snuck into that facility and no one would bat an eye. But they have records, and I'm in those records. I'm a student, part of the group that was still around when Parkes' died, they know me. They may not associate me with my family, but they know me. It's for the best. I have to leave, I can't stay with them forever."

"Leave?"

"Don't question it. If you really want to know, I'll tell you later."

"Okay." Isaac sighed. "There's something about Xavier. I saw him again today, in the cafeteria. He doesn't trust me, I can tell. I'm not sure that will ever change."

"He doesn't have to, he just has to work with you."

"I suppose."

Astra sighed. "Your job is not to make him trust you. Your job is to protect him. The same way that his job is to find and deliver my tech to me, not to know everything. Sometimes I think you guys are obsessed with being in control. You are just a piece in a plan. That doesn't mean you're not important, but you overthink your place. Also, Xavier has found out that the androids in the facility are being prepped for use. Keep an eye on them. If something goes wrong, you do not want to be responsible for it."

"Okay. I'll do what I can."

"Thank you Isaac."

Astra hung up and groaned, before rolling over and staring at the wall. So much for an early bedtime.

20

Cellular Degeneration

The steady noise of the printer releasing paper into her hand was a glorious sound to Nasra's tired brain. She had spent hours just looking at a screen and analyzing the data she had gathered until her eyes watered and burned. When she finally figured it out, she couldn't wait. Nasra separated the pages into two stacks and stapled them together.

She didn't even bother to lock the door as she left the room. The fact that it was very early morning and the sun hadn't even risen didn't click in Nasra's head as she ran. Nasra burst into Alyssa's room, waving the stack of papers in her hand. "Alyssa! Alyssa!"

"What?" she said groggily, raising her head up from the table where she had fallen asleep the previous night.

"I finally got the results!"

"Oh?" Alyssa rubbed her eyes. "What'd you find?"

Nasra skidded to a stop in front of her. "Okay, so my cell theory was way off, which is kind of good, and fun fact, all the clones are universal blood donors! But that's not the point. I figured out what's wrong! I did find mutated cells, but those aren't the problem surprisingly."

"Huh." Alyssa looked at her blankly.

"Yeah." Nasra handed the papers to Alyssa. "Look at this."

Alyssa skimmed through it. "These results are inconclusive Nasra."

"Exactly!"

Alyssa stared up at her, confused. "What?"

Nasra grabbed the results from her and flipped to one of the pages. "Here, stable blood pressure, lower white blood cell count, like we saw earlier, but look. Their organs are fine, their brain is fine, heart working normally, and no sign of stress related damage or anything."

"So, your results are that they're fine? Didn't you just find stress related damage in Nicole? And you're saying they're perfectly healthy?" Alyssa questioned.

Nasra laughed. "No, not in the slightest."

Alyssa frowned. "What?"

Nasra sighed. "I'm getting ahead of myself. This is one set of results. So, you know how a couple of days ago, you put together a test medicine to see if it would work? And we tried it and it didn't."

"Yeah, that's old news."

"That's the thing, it did work, for some of them." Nasra held up the second set of results. "But for the rest of them, it made them worse." She held them out.

Alyssa stared at Nasra for a second before accepting them. "This is a degenerative disease?"

"Yep." Nasra nodded solemnly. "No sign of mutated cells, but definite signs of brain damage and stress."

"So, do you think the mutations have something to do with those getting well?"

Nasra shrugged. "I haven't gotten there yet, those are still in the lab downstairs."

"That should be our next course of action," Alyssa said. "Hand me the other results please?"

Nasra obliged. "What do you think?"

Alyssa responded with a question of her own. "Hmm, Nasra, whose results are whose?"

"Well, excluding the ones who didn't get sick at all, Cassian, Nicole, and David are doing better. They had it the worst previously, and they are the ones with the mutated cells. Castor and William are the ones doing the worst. They are exhibiting the exact same symptoms, to the same degree. When I ran the tests they were identical. They don't have mutated cells and are consistently getting worse."

"That's so weird."

Nasra nodded. "Anyway, I moved the three to a different room. I want to make sure that they are fully healthy before letting them interact with Morgan, Willow, and Eric again."

"Good call," Alyssa said. "So, what we know so far is that some of the clones didn't get sick, those who had it the worst have mutated cells—"

"White blood cells. I forgot to mention, they have a lower count, but they're noticeably different."

"—Okay, mutated white blood cells for the healthy ones, and a deteriorating brain for the still sick ones. Anything else you noticed?"

Nasra shook her head. "Nothing, they're all perfectly normal."

"Except for the brain disease," Alyssa retorted

Nasra facepalmed. "Well yeah, but I thought that was implied."

"It was, I'm just give you a hard time."

"I'm already having a hard time," Nasra groaned.

Alyssa got up. "Well, I'm going to get some coffee, then I will go see what I can find with those samples you got. Take a break, and join me when you're ready."

Nasra smiled. "Thank you, and good luck."

Alyssa left the room, and after making herself a cup of instant coffee, went to the lab. The grogginess and dull ache in her bones alleviated as she walked and sipped on the coffee. She tasted hazelnut and a hint of vanilla peaking through. She stopped in the hallway and took a long swig from her cup. The warmth spread throughout her body, and she sighed happily. "Whoever bought this needs a raise," she muttered to herself.

Once she reached the lab, she plopped into the closest chair and pulled up her computer. She spent a while just staring at the model of her current medicine components, occasionally changing things around to run tests. A second tab showed a model of the mutated cells. She made a mental note to pull some more of them to run actual tests.

Hours passed by, and Alyssa barely made any progress. The screen started to look like a mass of words and variables, fuzzy and unreadable. It was like her brain shut off and she just forgot everything. Alyssa shook her head. Her data tables slowly came back into view. She just couldn't focus on them. Alyssa sighed and dropped her head on the table.

She repeatedly hit her head on the hard surface, just enough to make a sound. "Why. Can't. I. Figure. This. Out?!"

She heard the door open behind her. "Hey Alyssa, sorry to bother you, is this a bad time? I can come back."

Alyssa looked up and turned around. "Oh, hi Mary. No, it's not. What's up?"

Mary tried to smile, but it turned out more of a grimace, her mouth pressed into a thin line. "Bad news, some of the students are getting sick again. Clear signs of a relapse of your disease."

Alyssa groaned and rubbed her face. "Why me?" she mumbled, voice muffled by her hands.

Mary placed a sympathetic hand on Alyssa's shoulder. "I'm sorry." She slowly moved to hug Alyssa, head resting on her back. "You won't be going through this alone."

Alyssa nodded, reaching up to grasp Mary's hands. "I know," she said, voice barely above a whisper. "I'm just so tired. I can't keep up, how am I supposed to just do this all?"

Mary moved to rest her chin on Alyssa's shoulder. "You won't do it all. I'll be there to help, so will Nasra. Astra's in the downstairs lab with some of the students right now, checking in on them and taking notes of their symptoms. You have an army of friends who will help you, don't lose heart.

Alyssa nodded, clenching her eyes shut so that she wouldn't cry. "Thanks," she said. "You're the bestest friend I could ever ask for."

Mary smiled and squeezed her before letting go. "Now come

on. Let's go take care of the students downstairs, then you have to take a break. Nasra can take over while you sleep."

"But..." She paused. "Nasra was already up all night, is that fair?"

"Don't worry, she offered. Besides, look at you, I don't think you're really in any state to look at these results. Just handle the sick people downstairs, that's your job. Then go to sleep."

Alyssa nodded again, almost mechanically as she slipped out of Mary's grasp. "Alright, okay, I'm gonna go downstairs now."

Mary patted her lightly on the back. "I'm gonna go make you some tea, you don't need that much caffeine."

Alyssa gave a hoarse laugh. "Always taking care of me, huh? And I'm the older one."

Mary raised an eyebrow. Her attempt at a serious look melted into a playful smile. "You deserve it. Now go. I'll see if I can stop by later."

Alyssa grabbed her jacket and left the room, almost running down the stairs. There was something about good conversation that left her exhilarated. When she reached the lab, she paused to catch her breath. She was facing a lot, and the thought of it fell on her immediately, washing away her positive mood. Every ounce of energy left her body like the tide withdrawing. She took a deep breath and raised her hand to open the door only for Astra to open it for her.

Astra grinned. "Hi Alyssa. Glad you're here! I did the most that I could because I don't want you to be too overwhelmed but I don't know much about this." She held out a folder which Alyssa took, frowning. "I've gotta go, but that's all the notes I took! Good luck!"

Astra pushed past her and disappeared down the hall. Alyssa stared after her, wide-eyed. "What... You know, I don't have time to wonder about that." She looked down at the folder that Astra gave her and flipped through the papers inside. There wasn't much, just a list of names and their associated symptoms. Alyssa sighed. She pushed the door open. Time to face yet another one of her messes.

The people inside greeted her with weak smiles. Alyssa sat with each and every one of them, making sure to ask questions about school, faking a cheerful attitude. Her exhaustion must have showed because the more she talked, the more the students seemed to shorten their answers and push her to finish.

Alyssa smiled. "Okay, so, like usual, quarantine, I should have an updated vaccine for you guys by the end of the week. You'll get food delivered to you, and I'll make sure any assignments you have this week get waived. Sound good?"

A chorus of agreements and thank yous followed Alyssa out into the hall, up the stairs and into her dorm room. Alyssa removed her shoes and collapsed on her bed, not even bothering to get underneath the covers. As soon as she closed her eyes, she was asleep.

21

No Matter What

Aiken sighed, taking a sip of tea. The steam pooled around his face, the burning of his tongue followed by the taste of honey-tainted oolong. His mother had mailed him the tea last week, and when he had spoken to her yesterday, she insisted he try it. He didn't like oolong, he much preferred jasmine, but he drank it anyway. It tasted like home, and in some ways, he felt like he had to.

He had spent almost every waking moment going through the files Astra gave him. He wanted to make her happy, so he read as many as he could. It had been a few months, and in that time, he had gone through hundreds of files, notes, journals, and videos. There were even audio recordings that Aiken would listen to when he was eating or before he went to bed. Each word he read brought him closer to the man. So much so that he didn't even think of his hand unless it hurt or he caught a glimpse of it out of the corner of his eye.

Some days, Astra would stop by and bring him files she was particularly interested in. Today was not one of those days. Aiken wondered if he would ever finish. A part of him wished he never had to. Granted, there was a whole storage room that held file after file on different staff members, projects, and just thoughts that Leroy had. There were hundreds of thousands of files that Aiken hadn't even seen, much less touched so he didn't have to worry about that at the moment. The more time he spent working, the more he had started to see patterns in the words. Impatience, anger, pride. Aiken couldn't help but be proud for Leroy. He had done what most people could not: take control.

Leroy was better than the friend that he stole from. Sure, he stole, but what he made was no longer machine, it was art. It was human. Aiken had seen it first-hand. The androids turned clones were so human, too human? Aiken frowned. He had no idea where that thought had come from. No, he admired Leroy, didn't he? Then why was he angry with him? Aiken shrugged and took another sip of tea.

Aiken had learned a while back that he shouldn't ask questions. It was so easy to fall into, doing what you're told and not looking back. These particular files weren't useful, Astra wouldn't even care about them. That meant he should probably toss them aside, but he didn't want to. Aiken was drawn to a lot of things nowadays, Leroy especially.

His words, his work, his ideals. Aiken couldn't get enough of it. He flipped through the files skimming for something important. He ignored Leroy's thoughts on his employees, and devoured Leroy's journals. He talked a lot about his achievements, especially how young he was when he got what he wanted. Leroy was a genius who monopolized on what already existed, made it perfect.

Maybe that was theft, but one could argue that it was all about who got there first. Aiken would argue for Leroy. He was a great man, a great mind… Aiken shook his head and looked down at the journal he was currently holding. This one depicted the process of recruitment for students and staff. When he came across the requirements for students, he paused. They were extremely detailed.

The students had to be smart, but not too smart, exceptional, but pushovers, willing to do anything, yet complacent. Aiken wasn't sure how he felt about that description. He made it into Torsion, all on his own, didn't he? Yet, they were the ones who defeated Parkes.

Defeated. A bitter taste filled Aiken's mouth. He was partially responsible for the downfall of a man he now idolized. Of course, then he had viewed Parkes as evil. After all, Parkes was going to use him for spare parts, turn him into a monster. Aiken couldn't blame him though, a man like him needed to fuel his genius. In fact, Aiken would do anything to even be compared to him. He wanted to be the monster that Leroy was going to create from his body. Before he was rescued, before Elena killed him. The thought pained him, but Aiken was going to make sure that Parkes's death was not in vain.

He would take his work and make it better. He would be better. And maybe… Aiken smirked. Immortality wasn't a fairytale anymore, was it? Leroy must have his own ideals, videos, memoirs, hidden around here somewhere. With that, well, Aiken could bring him back, couldn't he? Now that would be the work of a genius. Maybe he would be forgiven. Aiken closed the file and threw it aside. He would set out today to do what no one had done before: bring back the dead.

Aiken had just started to get up when the door slammed open and Henry came in. He turned to meet Henry's eyes, and smiled. "What's up?"

"Aiken, I know you're working but will you please—"

"Sure." Aiken didn't think before answering, any previous thought gone from his mind.

Henry frowned. "What?"

"You want me to hang out with you? Right? Or help you with something?" Aiken's expression didn't change.

"Yeah, I wanted to know if you wanted to work on building computers with me." Henry emphasized the building, but Aiken didn't look fazed.

"Okay, let me just finish this up and I'll meet you in our dorm, sound good?"

"...Okay." Henry just stared at Aiken before walking away. "Huh. He must be really stressed if he wants to do stuff like that," he muttered to himself. Henry walked up the stairs, confused. Then he got a sandwich from the cafeteria and the confusion was lost. He was so happy that Aiken was finally making time for him in his busy schedule.

When he got back to the dorm, Henry kicked his shoes off at

the door and hummed happily while sipping on a smoothie. The cafeteria rarely sold smoothies so he appreciated the rare times he could grab one. Henry flopped down on the floor and pulled a box of parts out from underneath his bed. He had always been a fan of tinkering, working with his hands. From his family's mass sewing hang-outs, to his older brother teaching him how to make pottery, Henry had learned that in order to succeed, you have to get your hands dirty.

Plus, sitting on the floor was very enjoyable. Henry's old apartment had heated floors. He remembered waking up early on test days to a cup of tea and a bowl of sticky rice that his mother gave him. He would curl up on the floor with a blanket and eat while his brother or sister quizzed him. They never had to be up that early, but they always were. His mother always sent him off with a hug and a handful of yeot candy. He was always happy on test days, and he always passed.

Henry missed the tradition.

Nowadays, he'd wake up on his own, trudge down to the cafeteria, let himself into the kitchen. He'd make his own breakfast and tea, eat yeot on his own on the tile floors, clutching a small knitted pig that his sister made him for his 10th birthday. After the test, he'd call his mother and let her know how he thought he did. It wasn't much, but it was something, and he was so grateful for that.

Henry was pulled out of his thoughts by the sound of the door opening. He looked up to see Aiken trudge in, dutifully remove his shoes and sit down across from him.

"So," Aiken said. "What did you want to do?"

Henry grinned. "So, there's a bunch of old parts in here, I just want to see what we can make from it."

Aiken made a small humming noise. "Sounds easy enough." He reached into the box and pulled out a couple of gears, boards, and wires. "I don't know anything about computers though."

"That's the fun of tinkering! It doesn't have to be working, and besides, I can show you the basics."

Aiken fiddled with the parts in his hands until Henry pulled them away from him. "Here." Henry replaced a couple of the parts and started connecting the boards together with the wires Aiken chose. "It won't work until it has a power source, so just pretend whatever you put together will work out. Sometimes, if you do that, it does."

Aiken raised an eyebrow. "Really?"

Henry shrugged. "That's how everyone else learned. Invention is just imagination come to life, isn't it? You're supposed to fail over and over and over."

"You don't." Aiken stared at him, the familiar softness accompanied by something different that Henry couldn't quite pinpoint. "I've never seen you fail."

Henry sighed. "Failure is just as subjective as success, Aiken. I used to fail, at least in my own eyes, but it was never academically. My parents never got on me for doing badly in school or anything like that. I was never compared to my siblings, even though their achievements far outweighed mine. I'm honestly confused as to how I got it, the guilt that is. I mean, there are days that I think I failed myself if I do just a little worse than I'm used to. Sometimes, when you grow up seeing the people around you be the best, you expect the best of yourself."

Aiken frowned. "That's interesting to think about."

Henry nodded. "I have a great family, they're always there for me, even thousands of miles away, I know I can still talk to them whenever I feel like it. They never made me feel like I was less, for anything. I put that on myself. We do it to ourselves because when people always believe in us, we want to keep that pride. We don't realize that it's always given, you don't have to earn it."

Aiken's mouth fell open. "Wow," he breathed. He looked down at his lap. "I want that."

"You have that." Henry smiled softly. "You've got me, and I'm proud of you, always. All of us are.”

"No matter what?”

"No matter what.”

22

Strength in Numbers

Mary hummed quietly to herself as she sketched, blissfully unaware of the state of the girl sitting across from her.

Elena groaned. "Can you not?"

Mary frowned. "What?"

"The humming, it's distracting, and we need to get this done."

"We are getting this done."

Elena scoffed. "You realize that they're asking us to modify an MRI machine with virtually no experience and no idea what we're doing?"

"We've built things before," Mary said, frustrated. "We do have experience, what are you on about?"

Elena sighed, dropping her head into her hands. She looked back up at Mary. "I mean with this." She gestured to the papers scattered on the table. "We basically have no idea what we're looking for, we're making this all from scratch."

"Not from scratch, we're modifying an MR...I machine." Mary trailed off, mumbling the ends of her words when she saw the look on Elena's face.

"Again, not what I meant." Elena groaned again. "You do know how an MRI works, right?"

Mary nodded. "Of course I do, I'm not an idiot."

"Good. Well, keeping a person in that machine for too long is not recommended, any type of long-term exposure to x-rays can severely damage a body."

"I know that, what's your point?"

Elena sighed. "Don't you get it? We're trying to monitor their brains without x-rays, in a way that can't be done by other types of monitoring systems, we're trying to do the impossible!"

"We've done things like this before," Mary said.

"Yeah but that's different. I wasn't doing it. Alyssa and Nasra were, and they had the skills and prior research to prove that what they were doing was even possible. We don't have that with this. There is nothing that proves that what we're doing is going to be even remotely successful."

Mary sighed. "Look. Just do what I do. Consider everything as always attainable, even if it isn't. You may not be the one to reach it, but you've done what you can, and that's enough."

Elena frowned. "How are you so confident?"

"I'm really not. I'm just thinking, compared to what we've done, this is easy. Think of what we've done that was impossible for all the people who came before us. It's not that different."

"I guess you're right."

Mary nodded. "Anyway, I was thinking along the lines of going off of echolocation. Pinging noises to look inside the skull cavity for anything out of place. Since Alyssa said that spots are starting to show up on the brain tissue."

Elena stared at her for a minute, silent, a stunned look on her face. "Mary. What the—you don't know anything about being a doctor, you have no experience with brains in any capacity and you came up with that?"

"Is it bad?"

"No! No no no, that's genius! I mean, we don't know if it'll work but it's a start."

Mary grinned. She looked back down at her sketch. "I'll keep working on it then."

Elena sighed and shook her head.

"What?"

"Nothing. Well, I think something is really keeping me from focusing. At least, that's what it feels like."

Mary nodded. "It's normal when something bad happens. You focus on it until you can't think. It affects everything, your mood, sleep schedule, confidence. I'm not going to tell you that you need to get over it. What I do think you should do, is try to find something that brings you joy and comfort. Maybe it won't be so difficult."

* * * * * * * *

Nasra leaned against the wall, staring into space. Alyssa had forced her to stop working, recruiting Katya to help her in the meantime. The girl was currently doing CT scans of the sick clones while Alyssa ran blood tests in the next room. Nasra was pleasantly surprised to find that Katya was very good at using the machinery. She was a quick learner, and that gave Nasra an emotional boost.

The door opened next to her and Nasra turned. "Oh, hi Henry!"

He smiled, holding up two cups. "I got you both some matcha. Thought it would help with the stress."

Nasra smiled back and took them from him. "Thanks Henry. Kat!"

Katya looked up. "Hm?"

"Henry brought us matcha!"

Katya grinned. "Yay! Let me finish this." She turned back to the screen.

Nasra nodded. "Okay." She turned back to Henry. "So, what brings you down here?"

"Like I said, matcha for you two."

"Really, nothing else?"

He shook his head. "I was bored. Aiken just went back to filing. Astra's not responding to my texts. Elena and Mary have been put to work, and the rest of you are in here."

Nasra laughed. "Now, that's something I've never had a problem with. Usually, whenever I get free time, I sleep."

Henry shrugged. "I'm not tired, besides I know myself enough to know how to schedule breaks."

Nasra shook her head and took a sip of the matcha. It was still hot enough to spread warmth throughout her body without burning her tongue. She smiled. "Well, at least one of us has healthy

136

habits.”

Katya came up behind her and took the other cup. “Thank you Henry,” she said. “That’s the last of them, I sent the scans to the printer next store, so Alyssa will probably bring them over. I’m gonna go eat dinner, okay? I’ll be back.”

“Okay. Bye!” Nasra smiled at her retreating form before turning back to Henry. “So, how bored are you?”

Henry grimaced and gave her a thumbs up. “Depends on what you’re gonna make me do. You are going to put me to work, right?”

Nasra laughed. “You know me too well, come on.” She waved her hand, beckoning him to follow her. “We’ve got a lot to work on.” She opened a small door to a side room where Castor was sitting next to a CT scanner. The room was bare, pure white, and Castor’s tan skin and dark clothing stood out in comparison. “Hey Castor! How are you feeling?”

“How do you think I’m feeling?” he quipped. His smile still reached his eyes, despite the sickness.

“Pain level on a scale of 1 to 10?”

Castor shifted in his chair. “I don’t know, like a 6?”

“Hmm.” Nasra stared at him. “Alright.” She cupped his face in her hands and turned it a few different ways to get a better look. “Any pain when I do this?” She pressed the spot on the back of his neck where his spine ended.

Castor yelped and pulled away. “Yes, ow.”

Nasra pressed her lips together in a thin line. “Well, let’s see what Alyssa—”

The door slammed open. “Nasra!”

Nasra turned to Alyssa. “Did you get the papers Katya printed?”

“Yep! Hi Henry, what are you doing here? Shouldn’t you be building computers or standing confused in the middle of the hall or something?”

“That was one time—”

"I don't care. Castor, looks like you're stable, neither getting better or worse. You do have a bit of a fluid build-up in your brain though, which we'll drain if it gets worse."

Henry rolled his eyes. "Really Alyssa?"

"Shut up, I am talking to my patient."

"That would explain the pain," Nasra mused. "Henry, could you bring Castor back to the quarantine room? Castor, sleep."

"I will." Castor gave her a faint smile.

Henry nodded. "I can do that, that's easy. Anything to get me away from her bossiness and bad attitude. Come on, Castor." He helped the boy to his feet.

"I don't have a bad attitude," Alyssa protested.

"You're always making fun of me!"

"That's because it's funny. You're too smart, and I need to find something to poke fun at. I do it to everyone, especially Mary. It's called friendship."

"Yeah, sure." Henry chuckled, and lightly hit her with the back of his hand. "It's all in good fun, don't worry. But don't be mad when I hit back. After all, I wasn't the one who tripped over her feet and spilled cereal everywhere last week."

"I—" she paused, huffing in defeat. "I don't have a response for that."

"Yeah, that's what I thought." He shook his head, smiling, and walked Castor out of the room.

Nasra laughed. "You two and your arguments. You know, you do poke fun at him more than me or Astra."

"Well, I like you, and Astra scares me. Everyone else, well it's free real estate!"

"Free real estate?"

"You know, like, it's free reign, I can make fun of them because no one's stopping me, no? You don't get that?"

"I have no idea what you're talking about."

Alyssa rolled her eyes. "Of course. It's slang, a joke, a meme.

Basically means you're free to do something you want to do."

"Huh. Never heard that expression before. Anyway, the rest of the results?"

"Oh yeah. So, it's the same for William's scan as well too. Stable, slight fluid build-up, but nothing to say he's getting better or worse."

"Huh." Nasra folded her arms. "What about the others?"

"Cassian, Nicole, David, they keep getting healthier. I pulled blood samples from them, as well as from Eric since he never got sick. I'll compare them, but for now, I have no idea. The mutated cells seem to be the only difference between the ones getting better and the ones who aren't, but the three who didn't get sick don't have those cells either. And I can't pinpoint what made them healthy yet."

"Do you want to just copy the mutated cells, see if that'll help? Otherwise, I'm also out of ideas."

Alyssa nodded. "I'll look into it. If all else fails I can do that, but I want to find something that will actually last, you know?"

Nasra gave her a pained smile. "I understand. Sometimes you just have to go with whatever will work for now. It's an awful decision to make, but we signed up for this when we decided to go through with the cloning last year."

"I know, I know."

Nasra reached out and pat her comfortingly on the back. "You got this. Now, I'll take these," she took the stack of papers from Alyssa. "You get back to doing whatever it is that you're doing."

"Analyzing blood, a very messy past-time."

Nasra raised an eyebrow. "Messy? You're going to be a terrible doctor if you're spilling it everywhere."

"Messy is the wrong word, you know what I mean."

"No, I don't." She laughed softly. "I have no idea what you're talking about, maybe you're losing it."

Alyssa raised a hand. "Hold on, I am not losing it, I am just tired."

"You're losing it."

"I can't believe you know what *'losing it'* means but you don't know what *'free real estate'* is."

"Well, I have an explanation for that."

"Oh really?" Alyssa crossed her arms. "What is that?"

"Well, my family has this guy, some estranged uncle. Anyway, I can recognize different ways to refer to someone as crazy in many languages. I can't always repeat them, but I know what it means. Like…" Nasra paused, waving her hands. "Whacko! I know that one."

Alyssa laughed. "Wow, that is…" she shook her head. "You're funny Nasra."

Nasra smiled. "Thank you!"

"Of course. Well, I will get back to work, you want to let everyone else know what's going on?" Alyssa asked.

Nasra nodded. "Will do. Good luck!"

"Thanks, I will definitely need it."

23

Control

Nasra stood in front of Astra's door, flipping through the folder in her hands. After making sure that everything was in order, she knocked softly.

"Door's unlocked!" Astra called from inside.

Nasra opened the door carefully, scanning the room for Astra. Nasra smiled when she met the girl's eyes. "Hey, is it a bad time? I can come back if you're busy."

Astra shrugged. "It's a normal day, nothing particularly interesting or terrible. Is something wrong?"

"Well, it depends. Technically, nothing is worse, but we have the results from the brain scans and all our research, what everyone is doing and whatnot. Anyway, Alyssa tasked me with letting everyone know what's going on. Here." Nasra handed Astra the folder.

Astra flipped through it. "Well, that's technically not good, is it?"

Nasra pursed her lips. "Yeah, no, you're right. We don't know how to fix it yet. But we're working on it. Alyssa's running blood tests to see if she can find something to counter it, but for now, we're in the dark. Hopefully, we'll have something soon, we'll keep you and everyone else updated."

Astra nodded. "Hmm. Well, I trust Alyssa. She's a smart girl, I'm sure she'll figure it out."

"Yeah. Well, you know me." She faked a laugh. "Always worrying about something."

Astra reached out to pat her on the back, then hesitated before retracting her hand. "I wish I could tell you something other than don't worry, but I really don't have anything to say."

"It's all good Astra, I know. I'm just stressed."

"You could take a break, you know."

"I know, I know, but I feel like I shouldn't."

"Why? Rest is good for you."

Nasra was surprised to find concern in Astra's eyes. "I don't know I just…" she trailed off, throwing her hands in the air. "I just can't, it wouldn't feel right."

Astra nodded. "I know the feeling. Just, promise me that you won't work too hard, and that you'll go to bed at a normal hour."

"When did you turn into Alyssa?"

"Nasra."

"Fine, I promise."

"That's what I thought."

Nasra gave Astra a curt smile. "Well, I've got work to do, so I'm gonna go. You can keep that, I've already talked to everyone else, and it's just a copy so…" She trailed off.

"Thank you. Good luck!" Astra closed the door behind her and sighed. Every time she thought something was getting better, something went south. She had grappled with her own mind many times before. It was a side effect of living on earth, she was volatile, no matter how hard she tried. Eventually, she was going to snap. She just wanted to be far away from here when that happened. For everyone's sake.

For now, she did what she could. Astra had been monitoring Syn's files on Xavier. Nothing seemed out of place, for now. It looked like he was doing well, though she didn't want him to do well, she wanted him to find her things and get out of there. Astra sighed. Patience was a virtue. Later that week, the authorities would be coming to Torsion and she would finally ensure that nothing would get in her way. Unfortunately, even that didn't make her feel secure.

Astra couldn't recall the last time she truly felt in control. Currently, she was grasping at threads, tying off loose ends before they unraveled. She owed that to everyone. She had never been that sentimental, but something had changed along the way. She considered asking Xavier to ask Cassidy to send her the binder her father had made, but she wasn't even sure if Xavier had told the rest of the siblings about it. Besides, he didn't need that kind of a distraction right now.

Astra dropped the file down on her bed and walked towards the window. She stared, eyes following the curves of the walkways in the gardens below her. She wished it was raining. Rain was a new thing to her. When she was young, rain had been so rare that they had a specific name for it: the time when the planet weeps.

It was a fitting name for the change in the weather of a perfect utopia. Astra however, had grown to love the rain. It was comforting, like washing blood off her hands.

Unfortunately, it wasn't raining. In fact, the sun was shining so brightly, that it pierced through the mostly closed curtains and fell in a thin line on Astra's floor. If she listened hard enough, she could make out chatter from the students enjoying the afternoon. It was beautiful, but Astra didn't want to appreciate the beauty of this planet. It would only remind her of what she was leaving behind.

A loud buzzing noise sounded, causing Astra to flinch away from the window. Her phone was ringing. She slowly picked it up. "Hello?"

"Hi Astra!" came the cheerful voice on the other end.

"Isaac." Astra relaxed, her shoulders lowering and muscles un-tensing. She sat down on her bed. "What's up?"

"I just wanted to check in. There's a lot of nothing going on here. Most of the staff just ignore me."

"That's good."

"I know it's good, I'm just bored. Xavier avoids me too, and it's getting harder to tail him. I'm sure if he didn't already know who I was, I wouldn't be able to find him at all."

"Well, you're not really supposed to interact, that would make people suspicious." Astra looked around the room and her eyes fell on a notebook on her desk. "As it is, Xavier is already under surveillance because he's new."

"I know."

Astra could hear him huff on the other side of the phone.

"Anyway, what's up at Torsion?"

Astra pressed her lips together in a thin line. "Well, there are new developments. Two clones are getting worse, everyone else is getting better. I'm not sure what's wrong, I mean, I have the file, but I did skim it. Alyssa and Nasra are taking care of it."

"How worse?"

Astra rolled her eyes. "You never stop asking questions, do you?"

"I'm not asking a lot!" Isaac said defensively. "And even if I was, which I'm not, I told you, I'm bored."

"Fine." Astra picked up the file next to her. "According to Alyssa, the brain scan shows a small build-up of fluid in the spinal area. They're stable, with no changes in any area. The others are getting better, Alyssa is analyzing the blood of both the sick ones and the immune ones. Oh, and Mary and Elena are trying to modify a MRI machine to monitor brain activity 24/7 without x-rays."

"Fascinating. I mean, that's awful and I'm hoping they get better, but it's interesting to hear and talk about."

"You really are bored, huh."

"I did say that."

Astra sighed. "Anyway, it's very busy. I have Aiken going through files, Zola is swamped with hiring staff, Henry is doing whatever it is Henry does, and I have you guys to worry about." She rubbed her face. "You know, when Xavier told me that we would have full control of the school, the board was just going to instate a new dean soon, that he would make sure was a family friend, he didn't mention how much work it was going to be."

"We're getting a new dean?"

"I didn't tell you?"

"No you didn't tell me. Who is it?"

Astra rolled her eyes. "Like I said, I don't know yet, we won't know until whoever it is is instated."

"That's annoying."

"Yeah."

Isaac was silent for a while. "So, what are you going to do about the sick ones, it's Castor and William right?"

"Yeah. And nothing, I can't do anything, it's not my forte, or my problem. That's what Alyssa and Nasra are for."

"Yeah, but you helped me."

Astra frowned. "What do you mean?"

Isaac sighed loudly. "You know, when I came in contact with your blood?"

"Yeah, I remember that. What about it?"

"I spent time around the other clones, when I had that little bit of your blood in me. I didn't get sick, I wasn't a carrier, and I didn't infect anyone else. So maybe you help Alyssa with her cure, tamper with it, add your blood? You've done stuff like that before."

Astra pursed her lips. "It could work but I wouldn't advise it. It would have to be a last resort. I mean, because of me, you're now susceptible to human disease, though you'll experience a very mild version of whatever you manage to catch. I have an amazing immune system. Keep in mind, the clones don't get human diseases, it would be very weird if they just up and started getting sick from things like the flu."

"It's your call Astra," Isaac said. "Still, you should think about it. What if it works? You've spent your life doing terrible things for worse causes. This might actually help people. Just add your blood to Alyssa's medicine and let her do the rest."

"You say that like it's easy." She paused. "Well, I have done worse." She sighed.

"That's the spirit!" Isaac exclaimed.

"Lower your voice," Astra scolded. "You're going to get caught and I do not have time for that."

"Sorry."

"You should be." Astra took a deep breath. "Anyway, before I forget, did anything important happen on the *'getting my stuff'* front?"

"Not that I know of. Like I said, Xavier is pretty difficult to follow and he doesn't really like me so he only tells me stuff when I pester him."

Astra chuckled. "That sounds like him. I'll get ahold of him later. Thank you for your suggestion."

"You're welcome Astra. I'll let you know if I find anything else out."

Astra hung up and slumped in her chair. She was going to have to make a difficult choice. But what else was new?

24

The Picnic

"Good afternoon!" Elena yelled cheerfully as she burst into the kitchen.

Astra groaned, dropping her head into her hands. "Afternoon Elena."

"Ooh." Elena made a face. "Bad night?"

"You could say that."

"On a scale of one to ten, how tired are you Astra?"

She shrugged, looking up. "Like a six maybe? Seven? I don't know. I was up working late. Trying to make decisions and write notes. I'm pretty sure I fell asleep at my desk around five."

"Ouch."

"Besides." Astra stood up from where she was leaning against the counter. "It's technically the morning because it's still only 11:50."

"Why are you like this?"

"I live to disappoint."

Elena stared at her. "So, is the lunch still on or…" she trailed off.

Astra sighed. "Yes, the lunch is still on. I asked the staff to make a bunch of sandwiches, and yesterday I made potato salad, some pasta, and bought as many bags of chips as possible. All we have to do now is set up tables and put the food out. I think we have lemonade too, and there's a bunch of water bottles. The chef said we can take whatever we want. Most of what I set aside are in those fridges, and then the drinks are in the walk-in." Astra pointed across the room.

Elena walked over to the nearest fridge and opened it, surveying the tins full of food. "Well, the kitchen has no idea what they signed up for, because I will be making sure I get dessert."

"That's what I forgot about!"

Elena whipped around. "You forgot dessert?"

Astra winced. "Technically, I didn't forget it, I just didn't move it. I made like a bunch of cookies a couple days ago and froze them. They're gonna need to be defrosted."

"Oh. That's not too bad." Elena smiled and clapped her hands together. "Let's do this!"

The two moved tables and set up benches on the lawn. At one point, Henry came outside to just watch them. He stood on the sidelines yelling at them to move certain things until Astra chased him off the lawn with a chair. She didn't stop until Henry disappeared inside, yelling threats after him like *'behave or I'll shave your head in your sleep'*, and *'get out or help out.'* Elena collapsed in peals of laughter.

"Oh, I wish I got that on video!" she called out. She lay in the grass staring at the blue sky above her until Astra blocked the sun with an outstretched hand.

"Get up El, we still have work to do."

Elena grabbed her hand, letting Astra pull her to her feet. "Wow," Elena said as she brushed stray grass off of her pants and picked leaves out of her hair. "You're pretty strong."

Astra shook her head. "No, you're just light. I'm pretty sure I could toss you halfway across the lawn."

A wide grin spread across Elena's face.

"No, I'm not going to throw you across the lawn," Astra said.

Elena's face fell. "Why not? It would be funny!"

Astra stared at her. "What's gotten into you? I have not seen you like this, at all, ever."

Elena shrugged. "I don't know. I grew up a pretty happy kid, I mean if you exclude having any accomplishments overshadowed by your older siblings, and your parents attending to your ailing aunt. I love her though, she encouraged me to apply to Torsion. I guess the stress was getting to me when I came here. I don't know."

Elena looked away, following the tree line to avoid meeting Astra's eyes. "I think I'm getting better. I've been journaling, taking daily walks, I'm going to meet with a counselor soon. I mean, I can't talk about everything, but it's a start. I'm–" she paused. "I'm not fully better. I don't know if I ever will be. But I don't focus on it anymore. It's a background thought. No more nightmares."

Astra continued to stare at Elena. The two stood there in silence for a few moments before Astra spoke up. "I'm proud of you El. It's not easy, it never is. I hope you never have to experience something like this again."

Elena finally met her eyes and smiled. "Thanks." She pursed her lips. "Anyway, now that I've made it awkward, do we have anything else left to do?"

"Nope. Just put the food out and wait."

"Sounds easy enough."

Astra chuckled. "Yeah. Okay, do you want to get the food? I'll handle the drinks and defrosting those cookies."

Elena nodded. "Yeah I can do that."

* * * * * * * * *

As people began to arrive, Astra directed the staff to help her distribute food and seat people. She stood at the end of the line, passing out napkins and water bottles. It was easy to go through with her plan, every single person had to go through her. Trash piled up in the provided bins, and with each added empty water bottle, Astra's confidence grew.

She excused herself to the bathroom and just watched the screen as dozens of little dots popped up as the nanobots settled into the systems of everyone who had taken a bottle from her. She smiled, not a happy smile, but a mean one, edges of her mouth turned up just enough to display the unnatural sharpness of her teeth. It matched the malicious glint in her eye.

Now, not only did she now control the students, she controlled the local police.

Astra returned to the event and joined her friends at a middle table. Zola smiled as she sat down.

"Hey, there you are! I was wondering."

Astra returned her smile. "I was volunteering, but I need a break. I didn't know how tiring serving food could be. I mean, you can only go through the motions a certain amount of times before your arms feel like they're going to fall off."

Zola laughed, a throaty noise that sounded almost like a war cry. "You're funny," she said, elbowing Astra in the ribs lightly. "In all seriousness, I'm glad you did this. We get to take a break from all of—" she gestured to the school. "—that." She picked up her half-eaten sandwich and waved it around like a baton. "I don't necessarily like being around cops, they're scary and I'm always worried about Elena. But they're surprisingly nice, and I think everything is going well. I guess people are like that when they appreciate you." She took a bite out of her sandwich.

Astra raised an eyebrow. "Yeah, you're probably right. How is the food, by the way? I know your family has a sandwich shop, so you're probably biased."

Zola shrugged, swallowing before she responded. "Well, it's no homemade bread with sauces we make ourselves, but it's good. The kitchen staff need raises to be fairly honest, we should look into that. We've filled almost all of the spots left by the old staff, so we should see if we have room in the budget for that."

Astra laughed.

"What?"

"Nothing. It's just, you get put in as a temporary staff member and now you practically run the school, and take classes."

Zola made a face. "Eh. I wouldn't say I run the school. I'm kinda like a graduate assistant. Like, I can do most of the stuff, and I get a small stipend from the board, and I don't have to pay tuition, but when we get a new dean, I won't have much power at all. Which will be a good thing, because I am tired. I hate doing the interviews, so don't ever make me do that again."

"Fair enough, you can do other things."

Astra nodded in agreement and returned to her food, looking around the lawn to take in everyone.

As the afternoon faded into early evening, people began to disburse. Astra watched as the last of the cop cars left the property, and as the remaining students and staff started tearing down the set up on the lawn, carrying chairs inside, breaking down tables, and picking up trash that didn't make it into the garbage cans.

Dusk began to settle over the school, bathing the tops of the trees in fading golden light. Astra sat in the grass long after the rest of the students and staff went inside and shadows consumed the outer buildings and roads. As the night life began to stir, Astra just stared at the sky, watching the first stars appear. She didn't move, she just sat there, thinking about Destiny. With the cops under her thumb, she could make sure that no one saw or questioned her if she chose to retrieve the mechanical corpse of her favorite toy.

Destiny was more than just a network of numbers and metal to her, she was proof. Destiny was evidence of the growth, the change Astra had experienced during her training. One of the few things she actually cared about. Maybe that sentiment was bad for her, but she had been brought up with a certain idea of what equality was.

'No one is above anyone, not then, not now, not at any point in time. A title is a job description, and it's reserved for war only. Do not forget that.'

She had learned that lesson the hard way, over and over and over. She had been lectured to the point that she often berated herself for ever believing she was above others because she was smarter. Criticism was the foundation of her ideals, as she improved, her standards skyrocketed. Imperfections were carefully implemented into Destiny's base code, not because she couldn't make Destiny perfectly humanoid, but because she didn't want to. Just like then, when she didn't want Destiny to be too real, Astra didn't want to watch Destiny be taken apart and treated like nothing more than gears and wires. There was a middle ground, there had to be, and that's where the android lived.

Then again, she could also keep them from tampering with Destiny. That was the decision she settled on as she sat in the grass. It started to sprinkle, then rain, then pour, and Astra sat in the grass, soaked to the bone, unmoving, uncaring, just being. She breathed in the wet air and let the sound of rustling leaves and chirping crickets lull her into a peaceful state of mind.

When she finally went inside, it was no longer raining.

25

"That's Classified."

Xavier sat at his desk, dutifully typing away. The sound of his own typing was drowned out among the others in his section, accompanied by scattered chattering. Xavier found that whenever an overseer wasn't on the floor, the scientists would talk as they worked, updating each other on their projects and gossiping about things that they overheard.

He assumed that it was because nothing ever left the compound, as mail was carefully searched, and one day he watched a man get searched and dragged out after they found out he was telling his family what he was doing. He knew his own phone wasn't tapped or monitored, but he no longer sent Astra texts, just in case. He was content to find a blind spot and whisper his findings late at night in between the guard rotations.

Astra kept eyes off of him, still, he felt prickly at all times, as if a thousand people were constantly watching, waiting for him to mess up. He was an intern, the smallest of the employees, but Clay liked him, and Xavier was worried he would get tangled up in everything. If he even faltered, he would be torn apart. So he didn't. He just worked and listened.

He had learned a lot just from eavesdropping on the people around him. Most of the scientists there were his age, or younger, a phenomenon that he was very curious about. The older scientists kept to themselves, a small group of about ten people who always worked in silence and never interacted with the others unless they were passing off reports.

The younger ones reminded him of high school students in the way that they communicated. They would often complain about the manager, or their workloads, discuss their problems in detail, and exchange notes. He once caught two people destroying a computer out of spite. It was entertaining. Sometimes, he'd catch bits and pieces of conversations about the main project, but it wasn't anything that would be useful to him.

One thing he particularly enjoyed was listening to the newer employees talk about their families. They discussed home life, from problems with their parents, to babies being born. No matter how much they talked about work, they always circled back around to their families. One man complained about his wife for a week straight, then he praised her for hours, proclaiming just how much he wanted to see her, solely because he missed her. One day, Xavier passed by that man's workspace and spotted unintelligible scribbles all over the walls and a broken picture frame with the photo torn out. He was nowhere to be seen. Xavier sighed. There was something about being isolated that made these people desperate.

He didn't have the same problem. Sure, he missed his family, same as them. But unlike them, he had been hardened by years of absence. So he kept working, producing better and better results each day. During his chess sessions with various staff members, Xavier's mind would often wander back to his desk and the people who worked around him. Clay would snap at him to focus, and yet, he never lost. With each and every match he played, even if his mind was in other places, Xavier would still counter his opponents' every move.

After his latest game, as Xavier was pulling the sensors off of his forehead, Alejo appeared in the doorway of the room. He smiled at Xavier, and the two fell into a steady rhythm as they walked towards the cafeteria. "I keep reading your results and watching the recordings and it's always the same. How do you do it?"

"Do what?"

"Win all the time? I mean, the monitor shows that you're not always focusing, yet your reactions are instantaneous. That's insane."

Xavier shrugged. "I couldn't tell you how. I just do it."

"Weird."

Xavier nodded, trying to ignore the fact that Alejo was staring at him. Eventually, Alejo turned to face ahead. Xavier wasn't sure if it was because he was satisfied with the information he had gained by trying to read his expression, or if it was because Alejo had almost ran into a trash can.

Rather than sitting alone today, Xavier allowed Alejo to drag him to a table with a few other employees. He had been told to mingle, get close to everyone so that he wouldn't be viewed solely as an outsider. It was something that he was not particularly happy about. Most of his previous infiltration jobs were always done in the background, interacting with maybe one or two people.

Xavier wouldn't consider himself to be awkward, but he didn't have a lot of experience interacting with people that weren't clients and his family. There were social rules in his house, but here? Well, that was uncharted territory.

He slid into a seat next to Alejo and gingerly shook hands as he was introduced to the people around the table. Abby, Ivan, Daniel, Kate, Yejun, Rafe. The names and faces all blurred together. Xavier was certain he wouldn't remember their faces later. He certainly wouldn't be able to match their jobs to their names. He vaguely recalled something about chemical engineering and biomedical science. There was a time where he would've been able to remember everything immediately, but it had been a few years since he had done a job like this. The time off had made him less cautious.

There were certain things that Xavier could do in his sleep, like pattern recognition and reciting 100 digits of pi. He was even good at remembering the summaries of meetings, even if he hadn't been present for them. There was just something about this type of interaction that made his heart race. Halfway through the conversation, he felt like ripping his ears off, just so he didn't have to pretend to care about what they were saying.

It wasn't until one of them—he was pretty sure it was Daniel—said something about androids that he sat up straight and stared. That was something he could get behind.

"—the project itself is going well, but I'm not sure if we're making the necessary improvements."

"Yeah," chimed in one of the girls. "You'd think it'd go faster because of the blueprints we have, but there is a surprisingly large amount of data we haven't even gone through. I mean, the instruction manual was put together by one of my friends, and he barely understands it. Plus—" she paused to gesture with her fork. "—the thing is the size of two encyclopedias, how can he even expect us to master that quickly?"

Alejo chuckled. "I'm sure you'll figure it out, you're smart. Now hush, Xavier here isn't authorized to know about the project yet."

Xavier fought to keep from glaring at him. He forced a smile on his face. "Unfortunately not, I hope to be soon though. That is if I ever get a chance to move past chess."

"You're the chess guy?" one of the men said incredulously.

Xavier nodded.

"Woah. They talk about you sometimes, the computer guys. That must be really interesting to do."

Xavier shrugged. "Not really. I do the same thing every day, run code, play chess, eat lunch, repeat. It's honestly gotten kind of boring."

"Well, I would kill to have that kind of job," one of the girls cut in. "It would be a welcome break from what we're doing. Alejo has it the easiest of us, he gets to work with nanotech."

"What are you doing specifically?" Xavier questioned.

"Well," she started.

"Kate." Alejo said. "We're not supposed to—"

"Oh shut up," she said. "It won't kill you to chill, it's not like he's going to tell anyone, he's the only person who doesn't know what's going on anyway."

Alejo frowned. "Well, when you get fired, I won't vouch for you."

Kate stuck her tongue out at him. "I know what it's like, being left out of things. You know, I used to be in your spot, I was the intern last year, and maybe I'm young, but that doesn't matter. It took me six months to get put on the project, and if you're half as capable as I was back then, you'll get on there soon."

Xavier made an annoyed expression and looked down at his food. "I hope you're right, I want to. From what I've heard already, it's important."

"Everything is important around here. Most of what I do is coding. We have this example piece that we all study and we're trying to reverse engineer it."

Xavier feigned a look of surprise. "You're reverse engineering? I thought that you guys were the ones making this stuff."

"I thought that too when I first got here, but we're not. Some other guy's work, Clay's cousin I think. Anyway, it's hard work, but it's rewarding. We'll get a whole bunch of money when this is all done."

"Speaking of done, are you done breaking the rules?"

"You too, Ivan?"

"I'm not the one who's gonna get in trouble, and you're funny. We don't want to get you fired."

Xavier tuned out the rest of the conversation, just to avoid getting upset. He knew most of what she had told him already, but this made him wonder. What were they going to use Astra's tech for? If the employees were getting paid more for working with the androids, where was that money coming from? Were the androids going to be sold? If so, what for? Would they be weapons? Tools?

The questions monopolized his thoughts from the end of lunch, through the rest of the working day, all the way up until he went to sleep that night. He lay awake just staring at the ceiling, thinking until he couldn't keep his eyes open anymore. There was one thing Xavier was sure of. He had to get access to the project soon, before it was too late.

26

Blueprints and Other Things

"Good morning," Astra said, as soon as she heard the person on the other end of the phone pick up.

"Astra, it is three in the morning. It's not a good morning. I should be sleeping."

"Too bad." Astra could tell that Isaac was annoyed, but she couldn't bring herself to really care. "I need blueprints."

"Wow, so specific Astra," Isaac said. "What kind, which ones, details, I need details."

Astra rolled her eyes. "The blueprints to the facility. I need pictures of them, or enough description that I could map it out myself."

"Why?"

"For a backup plan. In case something goes wrong, it's always good to have exits. Or blow something up. I can't help you very well if I can't see."

"Don't you already know where we are?"

"I can see your general area, how long you've been there, and I've been able to figure out some of the placements of the outer rooms, but I can't see everything. The software doesn't work like that."

"Can't you just, fix that?"

"Is that the sleep deprivation talking or are you seriously that stupid?"

"Rude."

Astra frowned when she heard a thump on the other end of the phone. "What was that?"

"Me hitting my head against the wall."

"Why would you do that?"

"Because I'm tired!"

Astra winced and pulled the phone away from her ear. "Don't yell at me."

"Don't ask me questions at 3 a.m.," Isaac retorted.

Astra rolled her eyes again. "Just get the blueprints to me soon," she snapped, and hung up. She glanced over at her clock. It was still around midnight for her. The time difference was something she'd probably never get used to. Even though the main Duke mansion was several hours behind her, her siblings usually took jobs in various areas close to her. Plus, for some reason, her entire family were night owls.

Astra remembered the late nights where she and her sisters would gather around the fireplace and just be. Reading, knitting, leaving the door to the small library across the hall open so they could hear Yvette composing new songs on the piano. Griffin and Zale crashing the group, diving onto the couch and kicking her off of it. Xavier bringing them cookies. Arya's old camera. Astra still had some of the pictures she got developed.

There were days when their parents would join them. Ares would teach them how to clean a gun and Caliste would simply roll her eyes and tell him to put work away. Back then, Astra still had an accent from trying to get used to forming English words.

"Our language is so much more flowy, it sounds better, and we don't have conjugations," she had told her father angrily.

"Astra, you know a language that is made up of only clicking sounds and hissing and you never said anything negative about learning it. You know one of solely hand signals, and you know one that uses guttural yelling. You have not complained about a single one of those, despite how different they are from our native tongue. If you can learn those languages and be fine, you can get used to this one."

Astra had not brought up a single thing about the English language since then. Even if it made her want to scream every time she tried to pronounce the word *pterodactyl.* 'She vaguely remembered telling Xavier that she thought the word *'yacht'* was stupid, and he responded with ranting about French. Something about how nothing was pronounced the way it was spelled, and she should be grateful that English didn't have gendered verbs. She had asked him why he kept learning French if he hated it, and he said it was because he wanted to.

Astra found that to be a terrible reason, but she hadn't questioned him. He got incredibly grumpy when she did. In fact, Xavier got grumpy about a lot of things, at least when it came to things that he enjoyed. He guarded his comic books like a dragon guarding a treasure trove, and when it came to video games, well if he found out you touched his computer, he'd raise hell. It was one of many things she found to be entertaining.

She glanced back at the clock. It hadn't changed. She groaned. There was something about that night that kept her from sleeping. Maybe it was her thoughts, maybe it was the looming feeling that she was going to be leaving soon. She hadn't gotten confirmation yet, but she would. As soon as they entered the galaxy, she would know.

Astra got up and grabbed her bag. If she was going to be awake, she might as well be productive. The library would be open. It was always open. Astra admired the way that the librarians worked. They refused to close at any point in time, except for major holidays. So, that meant that they worked in shifts to let students in 24/7.

The library spanned twenty-one floors, dedicated to everything from the arts, to languages, to geology, to astronomy, and so much more. This included paperbacks, hardbacks, CDs, VHS tapes, films, and other various forms of written or auditory recordings. Astra was pretty sure that there were stone tablets and papyrus scrolls in the special collection.

When Astra reached the 6th floor, the one where the study rooms started, she headed towards the back. There was a section of tables next to huge windows that opened out over the back gardens. She was pleasantly surprised to find Mary sitting there. "Hello, Mary," she greeted.

Mary jumped and looked up. She smiled. "Hi, Astra!" She was reading a book with wrinkled pages. Astra couldn't make out the title.

"What are you up to?" she questioned.

"Not much." Mary looked back down at her book. "I was bored and couldn't sleep. I've gotten all of my homework done, so really I'm just waiting back on grades. You know, you don't really need to take a masters in civil engineering, and my councilor told me that if I continued I should do architecture, but I really enjoy all my science classes."

"Mm." Astra sat down across from her. "At least you're getting a break, that's good, right?"

Mary nodded. Her curls bounced with the motion. "What about you? I mean, you're not taking classes, what's that like?"

"Well, really I just do what Zola can't. I admire her ability to do so much with so little time, but I don't think I'd like to be in her position." Astra leaned her head on her hand. "It's tiring. Just the applications were a lot to go through, and I only read half of them. Plus with the new staff and helping my brother with the business, I'm stretched a little thin."

"Business?" Mary looked back up curiously. "What kind of business? Also, you have a brother?" Her brows furrowed.

Astra thought that Mary looked innocent, doe-eyed in the face of one of this universes' most terrifying creatures. In that moment, Astra felt that she was the prey, unsure of how to speak, to defend herself from the one thing she feared most: honesty. She hesitated, not sure what kind of answer to give her. "Yes," she said finally. "He does security." It wasn't technically a lie, it was one of many services they offered.

"Like cyber security?"

"Sort of. I'm not really a part of it so I can't tell you the details." Another half-truth. Sometimes she wondered if she would ever get tired of lying.

Mary smiled. It should have been comforting. It wasn't. "Is he any good at it?"

Astra raised an eyebrow.

Mary's smile dropped. "I didn't mean that offensively," she said frantically. "I mean, like, uh—"

Astra laughed. "No, it's fine, I just wasn't expecting that. I would say he's good at it. Our clients keep coming back so I assume so."

Mary's smile came back slowly. She laughed hesitantly. "That's good. Does he make a lot of money?"

Astra shrugged. "No clue, I don't meddle with his finances, he doesn't touch mine. Not my business."

Mary leaned forward. "What's it like? Having a brother."

"Well, I have four of them, so, chaotic."

"Four?!" Mary's eyes widened. "Wow! Sorry if I'm asking too many questions, you just never talked about them before. I know you don't like to talk about yourself, but this is interesting. I've never had any siblings, just Alyssa, but she doesn't count."

Astra laughed again. This time, it was genuine. "I love my siblings, but there are a lot of them. My brothers caused so much trouble when we were younger, I…" she trailed off, laughter dying in her throat. She shook her head again. "I don't see them often anymore. But I think if you met them you would get along with them, especially the twins."

Mary leaned back in her chair. "They sound fun. I've always wanted a sibling, but my parents said no. One was enough or whatever." She made a face. "I wanted a little brother."

Astra pursed her lips. "You could have mine?"

Mary giggled. "You're funny," she said.

"I would sell my youngest brother for a singular French fry, and I don't even really like fries."

Mary kept laughing, smiling hard. "Wow, really?"

Astra shook her head. "No. Even if they annoyed me, even though sometimes they stole my things, I would never. They're crazy, but they're mine, and I love them. They would say the same for me."

Mary sighed. "I'm glad you have that."

"You have that," Astra supplied. "With Alyssa. Family isn't just blood, I think that's common knowledge."

Mary rolled her eyes. "Yeah, I know, but I wish I had an actual sibling. Someone I grew up with, shared secrets with, did everything with… oh."

Astra smiled. "Just realized it, huh?"

Mary nodded. "I think so."

Astra snorted. "I think you need to go hang out with Alyssa."

"You're absolutely right. Thanks for that. You give great advice by the way, you should be a counselor or something."

Astra smiled. "You're welcome." She leaned back in her chair as Mary ran off. She would ponder their conversation until the sun came up and she fell asleep at the table.

27

False Ideology

Footsteps echoed on the stairs and in the hallway as someone entered the lab behind Aiken. He didn't look up, or even move from his seat.

"How's it going Aiken?" Astra asked.

The boy still didn't look up from his work, the current pile of files that Astra had pulled for him. "It's going well, I like reading. I have some more notes." He gestured to a stack of papers across the table from him.

"I'm glad you're enjoying this." Her sarcastic tone was lost on him, not that Astra noticed.

"What are you doing?" Aiken questioned. "I haven't seen you in a while."

"Yeah." Astra sat down and started sifting through Aiken's notes. "I feel like I've spent half of the semester just talking on the phone. You know, I used to hate talking on the phone with people. Sometimes my dad would make me call clients and clarify things and it was really annoying. Some people are just so rude and bossy."

"Hm. What made you stop hating calls?"

Astra shrugged. "I don't know. I think it's because I can't talk to certain people without having to call them. I miss hearing my sisters' voices. And my little brothers, you know them, the twins? They're both adopted, but they're the same age, down to the same day. It's good for them, they will always have each other."

"That's nice." His voice was monotone, but Astra knew he was paying attention. Aiken didn't like eye contact, and when he was focused on something, he could do nothing else. Yet, Astra found that he still paid attention to her, remembering what she said at later dates even if he didn't respond.

"What's up with you?" Aiken asked.

Astra shrugged again. "Not much, I'm just tired, and stressed, you know what it's like. I've got a lot on my plate right now."

Aiken nodded. "Yeah, I know the feeling."

Astra nodded in response and continued shuffling through his notes. Nothing really stood out to her. It was all repetitive, carefully recorded, but repetitive all the same. Reports on Parkes' projects, files on his employees, anger at her family for things that weren't even their fault. She almost rolled her eyes. Leroy sounded so entitled. He had caused so many problems and still played the victim. He still infuriated her. Sometimes, she wished he was still alive so she could punch him in the face.

When she couldn't focus on the notes anymore, she turned to her computer. Aiken wouldn't care anyway, he was too busy with his current file. Even if he did notice that she wasn't working anymore, he wouldn't question it, not out loud at least. Plus, she could remove that memory if she wanted to. Not that she did want to. Astra preferred having Aiken remember things. It made her pay attention to him. She lost herself in the work she was doing, no longer paying attention to what was going on around her.

Aiken glanced up and watched her eyes flit across the screen as she wrote. The clacking of the keys bothered him, but he wouldn't tell her. Not now, probably not ever. It wasn't that big of a deal, not when it came to Astra at least. She was different when she was stressed. It had taken Aiken a while to realize the meanings behind Astra's behaviors. He wasn't used to that, he could read people easily and respond to their actions. Pattern recognition was one of his strong suits, he learned that when he was ten years old.

Astra got tense when she was stressed, and she held herself differently. She was snappier, more formal, and mean. Oh, was she mean. She once yelled at him for walking into the kitchen while she was eating, simply because she didn't want to be disturbed. He was walking on eggshells until he started to pay attention to the way she did things. She had spent so much time in the background, he hadn't thought about watching her.

Astra spent a lot of time in the gardens with her notebooks. The rest of the time she split between the lab and her dorm room. She was perpetually on the phone, talking to people he didn't know, and Aiken knew to avoid her during those moments. She'd get antsy afterward and would take a lap around the building just to think. He didn't want to be responsible for her losing her train of thought. She got irritated when she couldn't finish what she was working on.

Then, there were the times he actually enjoyed being around her. If he found her in the afternoons, sitting in one of the windows, that was a good time to talk. She had been so uptight recently, it was nice to have those moments where he could pretend there was nothing crazy going on. Like he wasn't so angry on behalf of Leroy Parkes, or Astra wasn't getting more and more agitated over something she wouldn't tell him. He'd discuss his findings with her, instead of just leaving notes.

Sometimes, if she was in a good enough mood, he would talk about his family, and she would talk about hers. He was sure that he was one of the only people who even knew that she had eight siblings, and he definitely was the only person who knew all their names.

He was pleasantly surprised to find out that Astra was a family-oriented girl, she didn't seem like the type, not to him at least. She wasn't like Henry who would talk about his siblings whenever possible, and she didn't bring them to school like Zola did with Kyan and Jamal. Aiken would never tell her that she repeated things about her family. He'd heard the same stories dozens of times. He didn't want to make her feel worse than she already did.

For someone who was so intelligent, she could be scatterbrained when it came to things that weren't on the forefront of her mind. If it wasn't paperwork or his notes, Aiken was sure that Astra would repeat it over and over and not even notice. Of course, Astra tended to keep her thoughts to herself, but she could be prompted to talk about the things most important to her. That is, if you brought her a cup of tea and started talking first.

He was grateful to finally use his mother's tea, and he was sure Astra was grateful to have someone to talk to, even if she didn't show it. Astra was sort of like Leroy Parkes in his mind, a misunderstood genius who had no outlet for her emotions. She bottled it up, choosing to tackle her work, rather than her feelings, and while her work was beautiful, she wasn't happy. Aiken looked back down at his file but he didn't read it. He didn't really want to right now, he just wanted to think.

He liked Leroy's work, even if it was insane. That was the best part of science in his opinion, the fact that it was supposed to be outrageous. Something that was made by that kind of person could never be replicated, not in the way that mattered. It would always be missing something, whether it was something in science, or just meaning from the heart of the creator. It wouldn't be the same.

Despite all the trial and error, all the mistakes that he made, there was passion in the way that he talked about his projects. Aiken couldn't narrow down the exact emotion behind the passion, but it was something that felt right. He couldn't help but be attached to the ideals that Parkes had. Sure, the man was kind of self-absorbed, but he deserved to be. He was the kind of person that would burn the world if he had to.

Aiken wanted to get to that point, where he wouldn't have to be afraid anymore. Astra was the same way in his eyes. She was smart, and it would be her downfall if she wasn't careful. Just like Leroy Parkes, she was insane in a way that made her great. She was never scared to take a jump into the unknown, do what no one had done before. He'd seen her codes, he'd seen her notes, he'd caught a glimpse of what it was like inside her mind.

Maybe, just maybe, if he got through Parkes' work and changed for the better, maybe if Aiken became like him–became like them–he would finally be content with himself. Aiken was small in this world. Astra appreciated him, that's why she tasked him with this job, right? After all, she was one of the few people who actually listened to him and his thoughts. He couldn't let her down.

With that thought in mind Aiken forced himself to focus on the files in front of him, tuning out the noise of Astra's typing.

This particular file was full of blueprints from a previous scrapped project, with the same old notes. Something failed, Leroy tried again. If someone got in his way, he got rid of them. Aiken smiled to himself. Something about that made him happy. The more he read, the more he got used to what Leroy was saying, what Leroy wanted. To be on top of the world, now that was a lofty goal. Leroy deserved that, he could have gotten that if he wasn't so prideful.

In that moment, Aiken made a decision. He would do what Leroy Parkes could not, screw the consequences. Except, he would be the one to succeed. Once he did, no one would be able to ignore him, not his friends, not his family, not himself. He vowed something to himself that day: he would make them proud. Not only his friends, but himself. He would not stop until he could look himself in the mirror, scars, metal hand, and all, and not be scared of what he saw. That would be success. That was what it meant to be admired.

Not just looked up to, but feared.

28

Sabotage

"You're going to have to blow it up." Xavier groaned. He didn't really like the idea of having to blow the place up. He wanted to be as discrete as possible in terms of getting out, just in case they'd ever have to infiltrate the place again. Though, in Astra's eyes, Syn was basically done for. As soon as her tech was out, she wanted them torn to pieces.

Xavier didn't mind that part. He liked putting people in their places. He didn't like being watched. Which is exactly what it felt like every single time he ran into Isaac. He had told Astra multiple times that it annoyed him. She hadn't listened, just blew him off and told him to deal with it. Now, Xavier was hyper aware of the boy's presence in every room and hallway. Isaac got around very quickly.

It was interesting, the fact that no one realized Isaac was no longer an android. Maybe they were far too busy with their own androids, or maybe Astra had something to do with it. Though, if Astra had the facility under complete control, he'd be out by now. Unfortunately, that wasn't the case, and Xavier was stuck in a cubical with Isaac in his peripheral vision. He felt stuck, caged.

Even though, for all rights and purposes, Xavier was technically free to do what he wanted now. After a few weeks, he had risen up the ranks until the only thing left was complete access to Astra's tech. Clay Parkes was adamant that Xavier work just a little bit longer before he got the chance to work with the higher-level projects. That made Xavier want to strangle the man. He refrained. It would not be good for anyone if he did that.

In the meantime, Xavier tinkered with lower level stuff, specifically causing small issues with other people's work that set them back just a little bit. No one noticed, they were too busy dealing with the androids and the occasional fire caused by short-circuited wires. Xavier was bored now. Bored of waiting, bored of his repetitive schedule, bored of Alejo rambling until he realized what he was saying delved a little too much into *'outside of Xavier's security clearance.'*

By the time Xavier got his green light from Astra to start really sabotaging the facility, he was ready to burn the facility down with Astra's tech in it. Not that there was anything particularly wrong with the people, but the fact that they stole from his family made him feel sick. He just wanted it all to be over. He knew that Astra was particularly attached to the idea of reclaiming everything that was stolen from her, but he would be fine if she never got it.

Still, he snuck into the main computer room all the same. Astra had told him to plant codes that would slow down the process of reverse engineering her smaller projects, and decoding what made the androids tick. Of course, Clay had Leroy's notes on the androids, but they were just notes. Not everything was accounted for. Xavier reveled in the idea of making the man frustrated. In his opinion, Clay was just too chipper for a man who was partially responsible for so many deaths.

When Xavier got to the computer room, he was shocked to find Isaac there, messing with the cameras.

"What do you think you're doing?" he hissed.

"Making sure that you don't get caught," was the only answer that he got back. Isaac refused to elaborate, it was a trait that reminded Xavier so much of Astra. He groaned, and got to work.

Isaac stood behind him, watching the door as Xavier uploaded the codes, buried them into files, and the framework of the computers themselves. Xavier hated knowing that Isaac was there, that Astra trusted someone who used to belong to a person who had caused them so much pain. If Isaac noticed the way Xavier bit back snarky comments and gritted his teeth when he spoke, he didn't mention it.

When Xavier was done, he made sure to cover his tracks. Isaac followed him out into the hallway, and Xavier's heart dropped. In front of him was Alejo, whose face mirrored the feeling Xavier felt in the pit of his stomach.

"What are you—"

"What are you doing here?!" Alejo spit out, cutting him off. "Are you out of your mind? Do you know how much trouble you'll get me in if they find you?"

Xavier stared, stunned. "What?"

Alejo rolled his eyes. "Did you think I didn't notice that you were causing problems in the main lab? I didn't tell anyone because I did the same things, but seriously. Sneaking into the computer lab late at night? If they didn't know we were causing issues, they probably do now, come on." Alejo grabbed Xavier's hand and pulled him into a side hallway, ignoring his protests. Isaac dutifully followed.

"What are you talking about?" Xavier questioned, not willing to let his cover slip, even when confronted.

Alejo looked past him frantically. Once satisfied with the fact that no one was there, he turned back to Xavier. "Don't lie to me, I've seen what you've done in there, I know what you're up to. You don't have to hide, I—" he sighed. "I used to work for Clay Parkes's cousin, Leroy. That was because I used to be Leroy's brother Isaac's intern. Long story. Anyway, when Isaac died, I was like twelve years old, and back then, Leroy had already started his school and was doing all kinds of crazy things. I learned from the greatest, and now I'm here, because I failed to steal from Leroy a long time ago, and the only way that I can ensure that tech doesn't stay in the hands of people like them is to tear them apart from the inside."

Xavier stared at Alejo for a long time, gauging his intentions from his body language and expression. Alejo fidgeted under his gaze. "Okay," he said finally. "Say that I, we, believe you, what then?"

Isaac hadn't spoken the entire time, but he moved to stand behind Xavier, which made him feel a lot better. Alejo glanced between the two. "Help me. Help me get this stuff out of their reach. I'll make sure they don't watch you, and you make sure they don't catch me."

Xavier looked at Isaac, the only time he had ever asked for his opinion. Isaac nodded. Xavier sighed. If Isaac was being controlled by Astra, then it was Astra who was making that call. If it came to it, he could have her do something about it. Xavier turned back to Alejo. "Fine. But you'll have to prove it. Just to be clear, this doesn't mean I trust you, and this definitely doesn't mean I trust you either," he said, pointing to Isaac.

Isaac nodded again. "That's fair."

Alejo smiled, a relieved one that didn't meet his eyes. "Good. What's with the android anyway?"

Xavier sighed. "That's…" he paused. "…a long story."

* * * * * * * * *

Xavier sat in his room, thinking about his conversation with Alejo, what he had told him, and the shock on his face when he realized that Xavier was a spy. It made everything so much more complicated. Xavier withheld his background from Alejo, but shared his motivations. He hid behind a half truth of Leroy's betrayal, and that was seemingly enough for Alejo.

"That tech was never meant to be a weapon. And it doesn't fully belong to him either."

Alejo didn't question it, and Xavier felt tension leave his body when he realized he didn't have to elaborate. Knowing Alejo used to work for Leroy, even unwillingly, made him sick. From what little Xavier could recall of the stories of Leroy Parkes, he was a strict man who hated most of everything that he couldn't relate to science. He looked down on art, taught that way by his father and his father before him. Though, Xavier could be wrong. Back then he was much younger and he only heard snippets of conversations as his father ranted to his mother about Leroy and how he had betrayed them.

Caliste was subjected to many of those conversations, more of Ares talking at her than with her. She endured them out of love for her husband, and the knowledge that if he didn't get it out, he would get snappy with clients. Xavier distinctly remembered his mother just walking out of the room whenever the arguments became too much for her, telling Ares to come find her when he had calmed down. Every time, Xavier would be sitting with his mother in the living room. Ares would come in, kneel before her, apologize, and ask for forgiveness. Xavier smiled at the memory. He would have done the same for his mother. She was a mad woman in all the right ways.

Caliste never withheld her forgiveness or love, it was more a gesture of respect than anything. The two would retreat to Ares's office to continue the conversation in a proper manner. The phrase *'use your words'* was a common one. She did not tolerate spiteful miscommunication. Caliste had always made sure everyone voiced their concerns and feelings in the household. There was never a moment where someone felt unseen, adopted child, or just a drifter.

While Ares was a soldier, Caliste led the house. Her encouragement of their genius and gentle reminders to actually have a childhood were part of the reason their family survived as long as they did. She was feared among their clients as much as Ares was, for different reasons of course, but she was feared all the same. Caliste didn't stand for pettiness, or excuses. If you did something wrong, you had to deal with the consequences. Most punishments involved writing out your reasonings for what you did. Xavier still followed that rule, even though she wasn't there to read them.

Another thing she was fond of was making them create things. Art was as important to his mother as science was to his father.

Xavier learned several languages, composed and performed his own music on the violin, and was familiar with over 200 forms of poetry. People found this part of him to be endearing. He did not. His mother had explained to him that art helped a person understand the world. The same way a person exercises to be strong, art made him strong. It helped him think. *'Never forget the arts in your works darling. It's far more important to be an artist than a killer.'*

She was right of course, as she always was. Xavier sometimes wondered how much of his mother's intelligence and strength rubbed off on him. Xavier would think of his mother every time he passed an art piece in the hall. Every night when he journaled, he dedicated a section to her. Every morning when he woke up, he hoped that he carried himself the way she did. Caliste Duke was a force to be reckoned with, and everyone knew it. Her love of the arts did not keep her from beating him in fencing or figuring out a problem with his computer before he did. If he had just an ounce of what made Caliste the storm of a woman that she was, that would be enough. If he was anything like her, he was going to live.

29

Warning Signs

Astra paced around her room to the sound of the phone ringing, waiting for an answer. She was jittery, she had called three times previously and every single time she was put through to voicemail.

"Finally!" she practically yelled, as soon as Isaac picked up the phone, his face coming into view on her screen. "I'm going to do it," she said.

"Well hello to you too Astra," Isaac responded. "You should know that I needed to find a spot where no one could hear or see me. Do what?"

"Help Alyssa, use my blood as a cure."

"Oh?"

"Yes. I borrowed her notes and all of her things. I already modified everything. All I have to do is administer the serum myself and that way she won't notice I tampered with it."

There was silence on the other end of the phone. Astra waited patiently to hear Isaac speak up. He said nothing for several minutes. If it wasn't for the video feed, Astra would've thought he hung up. "Well, I'm glad you figured that out," Isaac said finally.

"I thought you'd have a different reaction."

"What kind of reaction?"

"Well, you were quiet for a while."

"I didn't know what to say." Isaac sighed. "I'm glad you're helping though. From what you've told me, they're suffering, and I don't want them to live the rest of their lives in pain."

Astra rolled her eyes. "Yeah, I know," she said quickly. "I just thought you'd be happier, I'm actually doing something you wanted."

"I told you, it was your decision, it was always your decision. What do you want me to do? Praise you for being a decent person?

I mean, it'd be better if you told Alyssa the truth, but you're not going to do that so there's no point in asking. It seems like you're only doing it because I asked you to, not because you want to, and somehow that feels awful."

Astra huffed. "A thank you would be nice."

Isaac fake laughed. "Thanks."

"See, not that difficult."

Isaac tried not to let the bitterness affect his words. "It would be easier if you sounded like you actually cared."

"Well, I don't care. I'm doing this because I can, not because I should. And I shouldn't have to apologize for it, I'm not a doctor."

"I'm not asking you to apologize, I'm just saying you could be happier that you're helping people. Instead you're picking an argument because I don't seem grateful enough," Isaac said.

Astra groaned. "Why are you being weird?"

"Me being weird? You're being weird! Astra, you're taking over the school and controlling the cops as if you're not leaving us as soon as you can? You make us all get attached, knowing full well you're not going to stay. You're not a good person, so don't act like it."

Astra's mouth fell open in shock. "You can't talk to me like that, I own you. "

"There it is!" Isaac yelled. "That's your problem. You're so obsessed with being right and staying safe, you're hurting people. Do you even realize how you've affected everyone?"

"Of course I do!"

"Really? Astra, I've thought about it and I can't just let you sweep this under the rug with everything else. How long? Huh? How long until you're not only covering your tracks but you're controlling them? You're already making Aiken do what you want, what happens when it's everyone?"

Astra was silent for a moment. "You know what, I don't care. What happens to them is not my problem."

"Not your problem?" Isaac's eyes widened, the disbelief showing in his voice. "You are the problem. Everything you've done to help so far is wonderful. But the motives you have? The things you've caused, made people do? They rely on you. And if you leave, when you leave, then what? They're just supposed to move on? What if someone finds out what you've done, uses your work against you?"

Astra shrugged. "Again, not my problem."

"Not your—" Isaac sighed. "You swing wildly between helpful and hurtful. You do something right only to cancel it out. If you don't figure yourself out, I'll hate you forever."

Astra laughed. "And that's supposed to be motivation? Do you really think I care if you hate me? I could make you forget you ever thought of it."

"And you'd have to live with that. Do you want to live with that?"

Astra's gaze softened. She stopped pacing and just stared at the wall, phone in hand, thinking. "No," she finally answered, voice barely above a whisper.

"That's what I thought. Astra, you may not be a good person, but you have the capacity. If you keep this up, you're only going to get worse. And once you realize you've gone too far, it'll be too late."

"And if that happens? What are you going to do, say I told you so?"

"No! Of course not, that's why I'm saying this now. Chill out a bit. Please. I want to help you. But the more you bounce around between controlling and caring, the more problems follow you. Then, you won't be hurting only other people, you'll be hurting yourself. And I may forget this conversation ever happened, because you'll get angry and you'll erase it. But you won't. I know you won't because I know you, and because I know you, I know that you hate being wrong. So let me be the first to say this. When you get caught in a lie, know I warned you. I'm trying to help you."

Astra resumed pacing, thoughts racing. "Really. You want to help me? Even though you just spent the past five minutes berating me?"

"It's not berating, it's constructive criticism! Besides, if not me, who else is going to tell you? Xavier? He doesn't know what you're doing. Your friends? They're either oblivious, or too scared to ask how you're doing. Are you going to let the world burn over this? Think about it."

Astra was silent, stopping once more just to stare out the window at the gardens. A while ago, she had stared to admire the beauty of it all. Now, when she saw it, she felt sick to her stomach. "I'm sorry," she whispered. "I don't—I can't explain it, I'm tired, Isaac. I just want to go home."

"I can't imagine what you're going through, but what I can tell you is that it won't last forever. See, on earth, we have this thing called a support group?"

Astra laughed, and for the first time in a while, it was genuine. "You want me to go to therapy?"

"Maybe!"

"Isaac, I don't think any trained therapist, no matter how good they are, knows how to deal with alien problems."

"No, but they know how to deal with the complexity of human emotion, which by the way, I've started experiencing, and it's weird."

"I know the feeling," Astra murmured.

"Look, whatever you choose to do, again, it is your choice. Just remember that your actions affect other people."

"I know that," Astra said.

"You know it, but do you put it into practice? You of all people should know that knowledge does not equal experience."

Astra paused. "Thanks. You're a good friend."

Isaac chuckled. "I try. Now, go do your thing. And do it because you want to do good, not because I told you to."

Astra nodded. "I will, I promise. I'll try, no, I will be a good person."

"Don't feel bad if you backslide, everyone does."

Astra frowned. "How do you know that, you've been human for what? Less than a year?"

"I've done my research!" Isaac said, defensiveness evident in his voice.

Astra grinned. "I'm just teasing Isaac. I'm going to go, but I'll call if anything changes. Stay safe."

"You too."

Astra hung up, and just stood there, staring at the blank screen. Then, she scrambled to put everything together. She grabbed the two vials from the back of her mini-fridge where she had been storing them and gently placed them in a small Tupperware box. She had filled the empty space with napkins for padding. Astra checked Alyssa's location just to be sure and then left her dorm.

She had decided the best course of action was to use the passageways, which took way longer than expected due to the closed off entrances. The detour took her past the kitchens and into the ventilation system, and by the time she had pulled herself out of the hole in the floor and replaced the tiles, she was sure of what to do and how to do it. She had to be quick. Alyssa was on a lunch break, and she didn't spend much time away from her work. Astra was surprised she wasn't eating in the lab, but she assumed Mary had pulled her away.

Astra grabbed what she needed and moved into the next room, where Castor and William slept peacefully. She hooked the serum up to each I.V., pressed the plunger, and then threw the needles into their designated bucket. She had almost made it to the door before deciding to just take the entire trash with her. She put a new bag into the bucket and then hopped back into the vents. After moving further down the tunnel, she pulled her phone out to check Alyssa's location. Still in the cafeteria.

Astra smiled. Her conversation with Isaac was pushed to the back of her mind as she exited the vents and joined the rest of the students filling the hallways during the transition period in between classes.

Everything was falling into place.

Morals

Xavier sat on his bed with a computer, writing a report about his latest work. He stared at the wall as he did so, fingers flying from memory as he tried to formulate his thoughts. Honestly, he found it pointless, most of what he would tell them was information they already knew. It was like he was in school again, doing busywork to pass the time because no one wanted to deal with his endless questions. Ever since he had started working with Alejo, he expected a knife in his back. Every day he expected to be called to Clay's office, worried that someone would be there to shoot him in the head as soon as he entered the room.

It had been nearly two weeks and nothing of the sort happened, but that didn't stop him from watching. He still saw Isaac in the corner of his eye. He was still suspicious. It didn't help that he was getting closer and closer to his official promotion time. Everything felt like a trap, whether it be a chess match or eating dinner. Xavier kept a close watch on all of his food, never touching something that he hadn't seen someone else eat from or didn't watch getting prepared. Xavier was a proud man, something he was not ashamed of. He would not go out via poisoning.

Every day he waited for a message from Astra, trying to find some way to tell her that he didn't like Isaac and didn't want to work with him. Some days he considered reaching out himself, but Astra was picky about communication, and even busier than he was. He didn't want to have to stress about her feelings alongside his own.

He was in luck though, because as he sent his report away, his phone buzzed. Xavier didn't have to look down to know it was Astra. While she couldn't necessarily control everyone in the facility, she was able to target the cameras and a few security guards from the nanobots Xavier had snagged. It wasn't a lot, but it was a start. Plus, no one messaged Xavier on that phone besides Astra. He hadn't wanted the rest of his siblings to be on a watchlist should he be caught.

After letting it ring a few times, Xavier finally picked up.

"What took so long?" Astra asked.

Xavier rolled his eyes. "I was working."

"Hmm. Do you ever think about the fact that you're sort of helping the people who hurt us?"

Xavier frowned. "It sounds really bad when you say it like that."

Astra chuckled. "Don't worry, it's not that big of a deal. It's just a thought."

"Thoughts can cause problems, especially ones you voice. Now I'm going to be thinking about that all night, thanks a lot Astra!" Xavier groaned. "Why would you say that?"

"It's really not that bad," she said. "I don't know why you're taking it so seriously."

"Well, when you spend most of your time trying to take someone down, hearing that you're kinda helping them puts a damper in your spirit."

"Sorry. Anyway, what new updates do you have?"

"Just the fact that I think Alejo is telling the truth. I don't trust him, not in the slightest, but I think he opposes the Parkes family at least in some way. He seems so adamant that this tech doesn't end up in someone else's hands. Right now I'm avoiding telling him that I'm trying to steal it."

"Good idea, it's best if he doesn't know who he's really working with."

Xavier sighed. "Astra…"

"What?"

Xavier closed his eyes. Part of him wanted to tell Astra how he felt about working with Isaac, the other half of him didn't want her to ever find out. "I don't like Isaac. I mean, he's a former creation of Parkes, plus we have no idea what he's really like. You barely know him!"

"Okay, first of all, calm down. Second of all, Isaac is the only person in the facility you can trust."

"How do you know that?"

"Well, first of all, he was the one who caused the glitch that resulted in us getting into Torsion in the first place."

Xavier sighed. "That's good, but that's not a guarantee."

"I have a guarantee," Astra said matter of factly.

"Oh, really?"

"It's simple really. I'm controlling him with the nanobots. He is physically unable to do anything that could cause you harm."

Xavier's mouth fell open in shock. "What?"

"Convenient isn't it?"

"Astra, do you even hear yourself?"

"What do you mean?"

"Astra, that's awful, you can't go around mind controlling people!"

"I don't see how that's a bad thing, you're safe with him. That should make you feel better."

Xavier face-palmed. "It's not right, okay Astra? It's a very horrible thing to do and you shouldn't."

"I thought we didn't need morals Xavier. You're okay with murder, but you draw the line at mind control?"

"First of all, we're done with murder! Second of all, isn't he your friend? Third, we were working on being better people Astra, what's going on?"

Astra was silent for a second. "Come on Xavier, it's not *that* bad. It's not like he's really human. I mean, technically, he was made. And if he dies, he'll get remade. It's no big deal."

Xavier sat on his bed, stunned. He felt numb all of a sudden, unsure of how to respond. In his mind, this was the absence of humanity that Astra had told him about all those years ago when she first made Destiny.

"Astra, it is a big deal. I'm worried. Remember how defensive you were of your friends when I first came to visit you at Torsion? You were adamant that they were good people and they were smarter than I thought. That they challenged you. What happened to that? What happened to the standards you used to have?"

"That's the thing Xavier, I don't have them, I never had them. It was just easier to pretend that I did."

"Now you and I both know that's a lie."

"Is it?" Astra's tone was accusatory. "Or do you just not want to believe what I'm saying? I think I know myself better than you do."

"You're acting like dad did when mom died, Astra. Using people."

"I'm not sure if you're trying to offend me with that statement, but trust me, I'm far worse. He had thousands of years on this planet, I haven't even had a hundred. Not to mention, Ares was my greatest mentor. I should be grateful you would compare me to him."

Xavier's throat felt dry. He could feel his tongue in his mouth, the urge to cry welling up inside him for the first time in ages. He could feel her slipping away and he didn't know what to do. "What do you really want?" he finally asked. His voice wasn't shaky, he didn't allow it.

"I just want my things back where they belong. That's it. I don't care what I have to do to get there."

After that, Xavier zoned out. Astra kept talking, but he didn't acknowledge it. His ears were ringing, the shock of the change in his sister taking over every corner of his mind. For the first time in his life, he didn't know how to help. He didn't have his mother to coax her into speaking. He didn't have his father who understood Astra more than anyone. He didn't have Arya whom Astra held a soft spot for, and Tessa? Well, Tessa may be good at speaking, but at this moment he doubted Astra would listen. Besides, he had no way of contacting Tessa without suspicion anyway.

When he finally hung up the phone, Xavier sat on his bed in silence. He didn't move to put his computer away or to work on something. He didn't want to think about the phone call, but it was all that he could think about. Isaac had no free will, and Astra didn't see the problem. He was forced to work with people who were actively opposing his family. He was completely and utterly alone.

31

Not Your Fault

Henry knew a lot of things. He knew how to fix a computer, how to knit, sew, and crochet. He knew how to cook most things off the top of his head, and could definitely cook anything if he had a recipe. He knew how to drive, both manual and stick-shift, how to set up a multitude of different electronic devices. He knew how to make most coffees, thanks to a short stint as a barista when he was in high school.

He liked to think that he knew Aiken very well, which is why it stung when he realized. Henry was sure that Aiken had started acting weird ages ago, but he couldn't pinpoint the exact time it started. Henry often got lost in his thoughts. That's not to say that he never paid attention to what people did, but for the most part, he daydreamed. He liked to sit in his dorm and read until he couldn't keep his eyes open. He liked to tinker, watch movies, eat good food, and ignore reality.

His sister used to sneak into his room at night and they would watch TV shows that Henry's mother claimed he was too young to watch. It always ended with him getting scared and them getting caught, but it was still a fun memory. She still sent him show recommendations and he still watched them. He wasn't scared of them anymore.

Henry thought about sharing them with Aiken, but he didn't think that the boy would be the biggest fan of action shows. Or maybe he was. Henry wasn't sure, all Aiken talked about was bees and plants. It had nothing to do with the fact that Aiken didn't understand Korean. Unfortunately, Henry hadn't quite figured out how to put English subtitles on the app he used, so he was sure the gesture wouldn't mean as much.

Henry dragged his way through his morning routine. It was

his turn to watch the brain scan machine that Elena and Mary had somehow managed to create. It was beyond him how they figured it out, he knew he wouldn't have been able to. Yes, he was a computer engineering major, but that's where his expertise ended. He was no good with building things that weren't traditional computers.

He loved helping them, but waking up was difficult some mornings. Henry's stomach grumbled. He checked his watch, hyperaware of the hunger now accompanying his fatigue. If he didn't eat breakfast, he would be grumpy later, but if he did, then he would be late, and Nasra would be upset.

Ever since Nasra had decided he was to be put to work, she had assigned him a bunch of small side projects that ranged from formatting and printer papers to helping her in the lab with the cell samples. Henry was sure he was severely under qualified, but he didn't argue. Whenever Nasra was in the lab, that meant Alyssa was probably resting and he didn't want to cause either of them to get stressed over something unnecessary.

It had nothing to do with avoiding Alyssa and her endless joking taunts. Totally. Nothing to do with the fact that he wanted to come up with better comebacks. Of course not, that would be insane. Eventually, Henry settled with grabbing yogurt from the cafeteria and eating it on the way. He clutched a small cup of coffee in the crook of his elbow as he awkwardly walked down the stairs.

'Why don't we have elevators?' he thought, annoyed. He'd have to bring it up to Elena later. Henry struggled to open the door with everything in his hands. Eventually, he managed to open it, nearly dropping his coffee in the process. He was not surprised to find that Nasra was already in the lab. She had her back turned to the door, fiddling with something that he couldn't see.

"Is that you Henry, or is Alyssa going back on her promise to go to sleep?"

"It's me," Henry responded. He put the coffee down on the

closest table and scarfed the rest of his yogurt down. "What's the agenda for today?"

Nasra turned around, removing the gloves she was wearing and tossing them in the trash. Her eyes were tired, small strands of black hair from her usually neat bun falling out and framing her face. "Not much. The clones have been showing some improvement, so I just want you to keep an eye on them while I'm taking a nap. I'm tired. Make sure that nothing goes wrong. If you see something weird, don't hesitate to let me know. You know all of the alerts and how to read it but I made sure to make a little chart of everything just in case you get confused. I don't care if you work on homework or read, or do anything, so long as you check the monitor every ten-ish minutes. Sound good?"

Henry nodded and took a sip of his coffee. "Sounds good. Go sleep. Bye Nasra."

She smiled and swept past him. Henry pulled a chair up to the monitor and flopped down into it. He did have a book with him, so he read, and the time flew by. Despite having to get up every ten minutes to check the monitor, he was still completely enamored by his book. It had been a while since he had the chance to relax with a classic.

Now, Henry didn't know much about the monitor or the things he was looking for, but he did make sure to listen to what Nasra had said. Eventually, he had noticed a pattern in what she said and pulled books from the library to better understand what was going on. He was by no means an expert, and if someone put him in one of Nasra's classes, he definitely would fail. Still, he knew a little, enough to read the monitor and recognize that the clones were doing better.

That would make Nasra's life easier, he was sure. Henry didn't mind helping her and Alyssa. It gave him something to do other than worry about whether or not his work had been graded. Graduate classes were more stressful than he expected. There were less assignments, but more work to do for those assignments. He still got them done way quicker than normal, churning them out like his life depended on it. In his eyes, it kind of did. Sometimes he felt like his life would be over if he submitted something even one minute late.

By the time Nasra returned to the lab, Alyssa in tow, Henry had finished his book and moved on to reading random medical journals on his computer. He turned around when they entered. Alyssa looked tired too, and she must have been, because she made no effort to joke with him when he greeted them.

"They're doing well," he said, getting up from the chair. "There's nothing weird or wrong with them. I think they're improving."

Nasra smiled. It was a weak one. "Good."

Henry took in her appearance, and that of Alyssa's who was sitting in a chair near the door and leaning her head against the wall. "This is not your fault," he said. "You could not have known that this was going to happen when we set out to do this, and you're doing the best that you can. Everything is going to be fine. They're improving. Please don't put that much pressure on yourself."

Nasra's smile widened. It was more genuine now, still tired, but appreciative. "Thank you," she murmured.

"That goes for you too, Alyssa. Even if you annoy me."

Alyssa chuckled, eyes closed as she slumped in her chair. "Thanks, Henry. I suppose you can get a week off of being the source of my jokes."

"Thank you," he said. "I appreciate it." He sighed. "I really do mean it though. It's not good to blame yourself when things go wrong. Especially if you aren't the reason something happened. This was a circumstance that no one saw coming. Even if we could have avoided this, you can't change the past, so don't act like it."

Nasra raised her eyebrows. "Who died and made you the advice giver?"

Henry shrugged. "No one. I mean, that's what my mother always used to say to me when I messed up during a project or something. You did your best. That's all you can expect of yourself."

"Hmm." Nasra folded her arms. "I should ask you for advice more often."

Henry cocked his head and smiled. "Well, you're always welcome to." Then, he got up and left.

Henry returned to his dorm to find Aiken, sitting on his bed, muttering to himself as he wrote. Aiken didn't look up at him, which was normal. What was not normal was that Aiken didn't even acknowledge him. He was hyper-focused on whatever it was he was doing. Something that was also normal.

What was weirdest to Henry was the fact that it was not homework he was working on, nor was he reading a book. His current read, a green book with a frog on the cover was discarded, having fallen off his desk and onto the floor. Aiken always got his assignments done in advance, and Henry knew he had a major assignment coming up. No, what Aiken was working on was more of Leroy Parkes's files. Henry thought he would have been done by now.

Henry knew a lot of things. It was essential to his personality, being a patchwork of people and interests. He knew how to comfort people, how to fix a toaster, how to get the best discounts at the farmers markets. He knew how to garden, how to dress a wound on the fly, and the scientific names of several kinds of fish. He knew a lot of things, and one of them was that Aiken was acting weird. It had to be just stress.

Right?

32

Spiral

Astra was stressed. She was stressed, angry, and overworked, all of which were her own fault, not that she'd ever admit it. She once again sat in the gardens with her computer, notebook in hand with several tabs open. Her eyes flitted from screen to screen as she watched everything unfold. Most of the students were milling around the grounds or gathered in the library. That happened whenever a major test came up, and one was right around the corner.

It made it easier for her, with no eyes to scrutinize exactly what was going on. Of course, that didn't matter as much now anyway. Astra was grateful for Zola's codes, it made controlling and changing peoples' memories much easier. She was sure she could have done it herself, but that was a theory she didn't have to test. Astra remembered her father carefully changing the memories of her siblings to make it seem like she was the fourth of the children.

In reality, she had been a member of the family long before her mother had even met Ares. She remembered arriving on Earth. Back then, the world was still underdeveloped, even by human standards. She hadn't seen a world so simple since visiting one of the outlying planets in the system for a training outing. She had never gone back.

Then, there was Caliste. Strong, smart, human Caliste. That was something else that Astra remembered very well. She could see it clearly in her mind's eye: the day her mentor introduced her to Caliste. The way he extended Caliste's lifespan so he wouldn't have to live so long without her. How Caliste treated her like a daughter though Astra was far older than her. Astra had grown so fond of Caliste, teaching her Ara'cel customs and explaining away the little things that Ares did that confused her. Caliste was so curious, and Astra loved teaching her.

Of course, Caliste wasn't the biggest fan of the fact that Ares altered their children's memories, but how else were they supposed to explain the fact that Astra still looked 18 by the time that Jaxson was in his twenties? It was a useful trait. She had even lied about her age on her Torsion application. It was easy, and Astra considered herself to be a great actress. After all, human lifespans were like a mere moment in comparison to her own. The only person besides her parents who even knew her real race and age was Arya.

Despite the fact that Astra was older than Arya, she still treated Arya like an older sister. Respect of one's elders or superiors was a human thing, but she didn't mind it. It was just another reminder that she was different. Like many Ara'cel, Arya was wise beyond her years, though she aged like a human and would die like one, simply slower. There were no studies done on Ara'cel and human unions. Ares and Caliste were the first, Arya was the only half-Ara'cel in existence. Sure, Arya's eyes were more on the black side and her skin always had an unnatural blue tint to it, but she was more human than Ara'cel and she acted like it.

Following Arya's example and observing Caliste was how Astra managed to be perceived as human. There had never been a time where anyone thought she wasn't, but she was definitely better at it than the other Ara'cel that passed through the Duke mansion. In fact, she was better at being human than Ares was, and he had been on Earth way longer than she had.

A group of students walked past her, chattering loudly and Astra rolled her eyes. It was unfortunate that her favorite place to work also happened to be one of the most populated areas. She didn't know why, there were flowers everywhere in the gardens, but people gravitated towards this specific spot. At this point, she should start to consider moving spots. She got up, gathered her things, and headed toward the library. Anything to get away from the people. They were too loud, and she didn't want to be distracted.

Most of her time was spent watching people, so when she did have free time, she journaled, or went to the observatory to see if she could catch a glimpse of something that seemed like it was coming for her. So far, she hadn't seen anything. However, that didn't stop her from checking every few days, just in case.

Something bothered her about the way people came and went. They were everywhere, and she hated it. She made a mental note to keep people away from her spot in the gardens while she was there. She wasn't going to just give it up because other people liked it too. When Astra got to the library, she settled into a corner chair on the tenth floor. It was quiet up there, as most students gathered on the first five floors. Everything from six upwards was quiet study zones and never-ending walls of books.

Astra loved it there. There were libraries like this on her home planet, so it gave her a sense of familiarity and security. Speaking of security, Astra decided to pull up the video cameras at the Syn facility, just to watch what was going on. It was funny, the fact that no-one noticed their cameras were hacked. There were days when she spent all her time watching, observing what was going on and seething whenever she caught a glimpse of something that was hers.

She knew her attitude affected the people around her. Students would avoid her, clearing a path so they didn't even have to touch her. Zola often left in the middle of their conversations, not wanting to deal with her when she was like that. Astra didn't blame her. Some of her friends had been avoiding her recently. She had a feeling it had to do with her snapping at them. She really couldn't help it, she was agitated, and nothing could calm her down. At least, not the way they needed. She'd relax for a while, and then something would fire her up again and the cycle would repeat.

Astra switched from the Syn security cams to Torsion's. She watched as the students roamed the halls, moving from one class to another. She spotted Mary working on her thesis in a study room on one of the lower floors. She was absolutely zeroed in on her paper, a half-eaten bagel and a cup of what was probably now cold coffee forgotten beside her.

She watched Mary for a while and then moved on. She scrolled through the hallway cameras, and spent a few minutes on some of the new teachers. They looked just as stressed as she felt. Astra decided she wanted to do something that would entertain her. It was easy: write the code and watch it unfold. Seeing the students fight made her feel just a little better. They wouldn't get in trouble for it. The only person who would care was Zola, and she was all the way on the other end of the school. Astra would make sure she didn't even know about it.

'You can't go around mind-controlling people! Isn't he your friend?' Astra winced. The thoughts had come to her unbidden. She pushed them out of her mind. Xavier didn't get to dictate her choices, he had done that too much when she was younger. Astra rolled her eyes. Not only was she on edge, but any satisfaction she had was short-lived. She was bored. She closed the security cams out and decided to work on some code. She couldn't focus though. Nothing kept her interest.

Eventually, she gave up. Astra closed her computer and placed it in her bag, opting to stare at the wall across from her. Unfortunately, her thoughts could only occupy her for so long. She stayed there, forcing herself to remain unmoving. To outside eyes, it was a testament to her will. In her eyes, it was a normal exercise that many Ara'cel children learned. They were strong in the face of well, anything.

Finally, she got up from her seat and gathered her things. She wandered aimlessly for a while, before turning and heading towards the stairs. She had decided to go to the one place where prying eyes wouldn't find her. Where the one person who never questioned her would probably be.

Per usual, Aiken didn't look up when she came into the lab. He was still reading and scribbling notes. She knew he did it everywhere, though sometimes she wondered why he even bothered to come down to the lab when he could work in his room. He worked in silence, never acknowledging her. She smiled. She felt proud in that moment. The fact that she was able to control him and he was none the wiser was just another thing that made her life easier.

It wasn't until she really looked at him that she noticed. He didn't have his usual expression: furrowed brow, mouthing words as he read. Instead, his eyes were bright, and focused. A small smile twitched as he read. He got up to go grab more files and put things away, and Astra discarded her work just to watch him with a curious expression on her face.

Astra watched Aiken scurry around, eyes tracking his movements, picking up on the rage in his posture, the way he jumped at every noise, paranoia in his eyes. It was only after half an hour of observing him that she realized, blood running cold as she did so. She recognized the pattern, it was so familiar to her, she had seen that kind of shiftiness in someone else's eyes, long before she ever met Aiken. "This is all my fault," she whispered to herself. The poor boy was no longer being controlled just by her, he was being influenced by the things he read in Parkes's work, and she had no idea how to fix it.

33

Promotions

Today was the day, a big one for Xavier. A few days prior, Clay Parkes had given him a date for his promotion. He got ready as usual, knowing that in just a few minutes, Mr. Lavoie would be standing outside his door, waiting to escort him to Clay's office. He thought he would be excited. Instead, his chest hurt. He was not the type of person to be apprehensive, at least, that's what he thought. There was never a time in his life where he was worried of the outcome of a job interview.

Mainly because he had never failed one. There was just something about the knowledge that he was going to be promoted to the main project and working with Astra's tech that made him jumpy. The longer Xavier worked at Syn, the more he became aware of just how long it had been since he actually had a job like this. He decided to dress nicer today, putting on a button up shirt and slacks rather than his usual jeans and t-shirt.

He didn't have to make a good impression. No one really cared what he looked like since there was no formal ceremony, no stage or group of people to cheer him on. He would just show up, get a new keycard and a list of duties, and be given the details of the project by Alejo. He was glad that it was going to be quiet. Xavier wasn't exactly sure how he was going to react when he finally saw Astra's tech.

It would be different than what he was used to. He just didn't want to give any feelings away. Once he was ready, Xavier waited by the door. He had trained himself to listen to people's footsteps and figure out who they were, it made it easier to pick up which one of his siblings were walking past, no matter how quiet they tried to be. Xavier found that Mr. Lavoie walked with a slight limp.

Soon, he heard it, Mr. Lavoie's footsteps coming closer and

closer to his door. Xavier didn't let him knock. He opened the door and gave the older man a curt smile. Mr. Lavoie didn't return it. He simply kept walking. Xavier had learned that the man was one of few words. He had been Clay Parkes's assistant for over two decades, and he was apparently good at fencing. At least, that's what some of the other workers had told him.

Mr. Lavoie was one of the most intriguing people that Xavier had ever encountered. He had mastered the art of mystery, and most importantly, knowing how to keep his mouth shut. Xavier had learned that lesson the hard way. In his younger years, he had talked a lot, spilling family secrets and information to anyone who would listen. That mess had taken quite a while to clean up. Ares hadn't gotten mad at him, but he did make sure that Xavier was punished for it. He was made to stand in a room with the clients and listen, but never speak. He wasn't allowed to interject in conversations or ask questions unless it was with family and he couldn't talk about work in any way. This went on for several weeks.

It was one of the weirdest punishments he had ever received. His parents much preferred putting him to work with the staff or grounding him when he misbehaved. Still, it worked. Xavier was not a silent person, he considered himself to be quite talkative, at least with his family and friends. He just never spoke to strangers that he didn't need to. He still had to bite back sarcastic comments sometimes, but overall, he was good at avoiding the truth.

Mr. Lavoie stopped outside Clay Parkes's office and gestured for Xavier to open the door. Xavier frowned. Mr. Lavoie usually came in with him. Maybe he wasn't allowed to hear about what the project entailed. Xavier had noticed that Mr. Lavoie was rarely ever in the lab, only coming to lead people around.

Xavier took a deep breath and opened the door. Clay was sitting at his desk, leaned back with his feet propped up. Alejo stood beside him with his arms behind his back. No one else was in the room. "Take a seat Mr. Zhang," Clay said, sitting up. "How are you today?"

Xavier sat down in front of Clay and stared straight at him. There was a moment of silence where Xavier gathered his thoughts and composed himself. "I'm doing well," he answered. "I'm prepared for whatever comes next and I look forward to the associated responsibilities."

Clay smiled. "Good answer. As you know, you are getting promoted today. Congratulations."

"Thank you sir."

Clay tapped a folder on his desk. "You'll be shadowing Alejo per usual, who will explain what the project is, what we're doing overall, and what your role in the project will be. You will get a new key card with the highest clearance, and your pay will be increased. Mr. Lavoie will no longer be escorting you places unless it is required, for example, off-site. Your schedule will change, but I will ask that you continue to work in the lab, and do your chess sessions along with these new responsibilities." Clay handed the file over. "Any questions?"

Xavier took the file and skimmed it. It had the same information in more professional writing. It dictated his new schedule, responsibilities, pay, and some other information that probably had something to do with what would happen to him if he shared any of the information about the project with outsiders. He closed the file. "No sir."

Clay grinned and leaned back in his chair. "Good. Alejo, if you will?"

"Yes sir. Come on Xavier."

The two headed out into the hall. By then, Mr. Lavoie was gone, doing who knows what. Xavier was grateful for that perk. He didn't hate Mr. Lavoie, but his constant presence was more unnerving than Isaac's. The two walked for a while before Alejo started talking.

"You excited?" he asked.

Xavier shrugged. "Yes and no. It almost feels like a death sentence with what we're attempting to do."

Alejo chuckled. "It feels like that sometimes doesn't it? Don't worry, we don't have to try anything yet. Right now, you just have to get used to what we're working with."

"Right. So, what is it?" Xavier kept the fact that he already knew the basis of the project hidden behind a facade of curiosity.

"Well, you're already familiar with androids, correct?"

Xavier nodded. "I worked with Isaac before, and I'm familiar with the process and making of humanoid androids but I'm not exactly sure what you're doing with them."

"Well, we're currently hoping to integrate them as helpers. So, teachers, maintenance workers, doctors, etc."

Xavier raised an eyebrow. "And they think an android can accomplish that? I mean, science has come a long way but this argument comes back around pretty much every ten years. Can an AI really do that? I mean, disregard the ability, but what about the emotional connection, the moral side, do we really trust androids to do that?"

Alejo nodded. "I've had the same questions, don't worry. But between you and me, I don't think that's what these ones are being used for. I mean, we're getting the funding because of that sales pitch, but we only have one set aside to act as a help bot. Now, whoever sent you, I'm assuming someone sent you and you didn't just decide to cause problems out of spite, I hope they know that we're making progress quickly. I've been checking the files daily, from those who Clay trusts the most. They have reports about the different things the androids will be used for and their capabilities. Most of these will be used as weapons, perfect soldiers."

Xavier grimaced. "That's what I thought too. That's why I'm here."

Alejo nodded. "You're not the only person who opposed this work. Your chess sessions help us keep the information from leaking, since we were able to modify the security system thanks to you, but some people know. Clay's doing his best to neutralize those threats. No one has been brave enough to attack us outright, but some people have tried from within. Most got caught. I haven't yet, solely because I hadn't helped anyone yet."

"So you're going to sell me out if it comes down to it?"

Alejo stopped. "No! I would never, you're the only person who has even gotten close to getting this stuff out. I believe in you. I'll cover for you, I promise. If you're keeping this tech out of the wrong hands, then we're friends. Besides, I think you're an interesting person, and we should be friends regardless." He smiled warmly.

Xavier stared at him. "Hmm." They resumed walking.

"Anyway, we're almost there. We've got quite the group of workers. You'll be working on the brain components, coding their behaviors and personality, as well as making sure that the "brain" communicates well with the rest of the body. I'd work slowly if I were you. Everyone else is rushing to impress Clay, so we're ahead of schedule. I should be proud of them, but it comes with an odd feeling, you know? If we want to get the androids out and destroyed beforehand, we've got to work fast and cause as many problems as possible."

Xavier nodded. "Got it." He didn't trust Alejo. In that moment, Xavier knew he was working for himself again, careful of what he could say and do. Originally, he had considered telling Alejo that his sister was the one who made the tech and that's why he was sent. Now, he knew that would cause even more problems. Alejo wanted the tech destroyed, and Xavier just wanted to make sure he could get it out.

As Alejo brought him into the bustling workspace and started explaining the finer points of Xavier's new job, he completely tuned Alejo out. The deadline had moved up which meant he had very little time to smuggle the androids out. If he couldn't get the tech out, he had an obligation to destroy it, but he knew Astra wouldn't let him do that unless it was a last resort.

Xavier ran different possibilities in his head, eventually settling on continuing to sabotage the project until he could talk to Astra about what she wanted him to do. He shadowed Alejo for the rest of the day, not really paying attention. All he wanted to do was succeed, and now he had to consider the options. It was no longer an option to just destroy the androids if he couldn't get them out. They were too dangerous to be left alone. He might have to destroy the whole facility.

Recovery

"Deep breath in. And out. In. Out. One more time. In. Out. Good." Alyssa removed the stethoscope from Castor's back and put it around her shoulders. "Alright, that concludes the physical, you're in good shape. How do you feel?"

Castor smiled. "Way better. Honestly, this is the best I've felt in ages."

"Well, that's good," Alyssa said, turning away to add to the notes pulled up on her computer. "It's weird though, you seem to be in better health than when you started. The medicine wasn't supposed to do that."

"Shouldn't you treat that as a good thing?" Castor questioned.

"Yes, I should, and I do. However, I didn't do it, and I want to know why, so I'm going to look into it. You're free to go by the way."

"Thanks Alyssa."

"No problem."

Castor left, slamming the door behind him. Alyssa rolled her eyes. He was always loud. She gathered all of her things and left the lab too, headed towards the library. She wanted to be comfortable while she worked. When she found a table, Alyssa texted Mary to meet her. It had been a bit since the two of them had hung out together, due to the way their schedules were set up. Alyssa juggled her class work and taking care of the clones very well. Mary, on the other hand, tended to hole herself up in her room when she was working.

Alyssa didn't blame her, drawing was difficult, especially when you were distracted. She had already finished her work for the week so she focused on the eight files in front of her. They held the lab results of the clones who had gotten sick, as well as the ones who had immunity. She wanted to find the reason why the clones had gotten so much better, and she wanted to do it quickly. The sooner she figured out why, the easier it would be to track down the person who did it.

She had a lot of questions. Alyssa pulled out a notepad and started going through Nicole's file. Mary showed up at that moment, dropping her bag down and flopping into the chair across from Alyssa.

"How's it going?" she asked.

"I just started, but I do have a lot of work to do."

Mary folded her arms and placed her head on them. "Well, I'm sure you'll figure it out. Besides, it's not like you have to do it immediately, you have time. The clones are perfectly healthy."

"Are they?" Alyssa placed her pen down. "I mean, sure, they look it right now, but we have no idea what will happen in the future. I know I didn't do this, which means someone else did, and that means that we have no idea what they wanted to do when they did it. The addition of whatever it was to the clones' bodies could be lethal in the long run, and it'll be difficult to deal with that."

"So, you're just going to look until you find something that seems weird?"

Alyssa nodded. "Yep. And once I do that, I can trace it back to the person who put it there."

"What if it's not bad?"

"Hm?"

Mary shrugged. "What if it was a good thing? What if whoever tampered with the medicine did it to help you?"

Alyssa groaned and rubbed her face. "First of all, they didn't mess with the medicine. I checked mine already, there was nothing there. Whoever did it injected it into the clones directly, probably while they were asleep. Second of all, if they really wanted to help, why wouldn't they just come to us directly?"

Mary shrugged. "Maybe they wanted to be anonymous. Did

you check the cameras?"

Alyssa nodded. "Yep. I've done everything to search for the person aside from this. The video was corrupt, or deleted. I'm not sure, I'm not a tech person."

"So, it was someone who probably had access to the cameras." Mary grabbed Alyssa's hand. "Hey. We have to start thinking about the possibility of this being an inside job. One of us could have done it. So, maybe we need to look at our friends."

Alyssa paused. She hadn't thought of that. Sure, she didn't know everything about the people she hung around, but she trusted them well enough. They had no reason to harm her or mess with her work, did they?

"Alyssa!"

She blinked. Mary was still staring at her. "Yeah, I," Alyssa shook her head. "I'm sorry, I was just thinking. You might be right. I guess we really don't know people like we think we do. I know it's not Nasra, there's no way, it's not like her."

Mary nodded. "I agree. As for the others, I would count out Zola. She's too busy and doesn't care about the health side of things. Also Elena, haven't seen her in a while, last I heard, she and Henry were experimenting with some computer pieces and haven't left the engineering lab in like three days. Aiken is weird, but he's also obsessed with his file things so I wouldn't count on that. Katya already helps us so it would be really weird if she did it, especially since she talks so much. She definitely would have told us."

Alyssa sighed. "That leaves the clones, which I definitely doubt since most of them were sick or quarantined and…" she trailed off.

"Astra," Mary finished for her. "That's definitely plausible."

"But why?" Alyssa dropped her head into her hands. "I know she's a private person and she likes her secrets, but there's really no explanation for her doing it. She seems like she'd be the kind of person to help by pointing us in the right direction, not messing with my stuff herself and pretending I did it."

Mary shrugged. "Who knows. I'm sure she had her reasons if she did it."

Alyssa nodded. "Do you think I should go talk to her?"

Mary shrugged again. "I don't know. It's not really my thing. I mean, I doubt she did it to harm you, so I don't see an issue."

Alyssa sighed. "Well, no time like the present." She started to pack up. "Wish me luck!"

Mary smiled at her and got to work on her project. "Good luck!"

Alyssa knew the route to Astra's dorm by heart. She had been there several times. Astra always had answers to things that Alyssa couldn't explain, so she had spent nights sitting on Astra's floor, eating food and asking questions. Never once had she seen malice in Astra's eyes. The girl didn't make her feel inferior, or threatened in any way. If Astra was the reason behind the clones' mysterious recovery, maybe she hadn't done it to spite Alyssa. Maybe she just didn't want to hurt her feelings.

Alyssa hesitated before knocking on the door. She was not scared of Astra. Sure, the girl was intimidating, but she was no killer. Alyssa winced internally. That felt wrong to say in light of Elena's current crisis. She finally raised her hand to knock. She had only knocked once when Astra opened the door, causing Alyssa to almost punch her in the face. "Hi Astra," she said, happily. "Can I come in?"

Astra nodded and opened the door wider to let Alyssa move past her and into the room. "What's going on? I thought you were meeting up with Mary today?"

"I did. We were going over some of my results because I didn't want to be alone. Astra, I have to ask you a serious question."

Astra frowned as she closed the door with a soft click. "Why do you sound like that?"

"Like what?" Alyssa's face showed concern, though Astra

could tell she was trying to hide it. Alyssa sat down on the floor and Astra sat opposite of her.

Astra narrowed her eyes at Alyssa, searching for answers in the lines of her face, the way her eyes widened, the stiffness of her posture. "You sound…accusatory."

Alyssa's face crumpled. "Okay, alright, fine. Did you mess with my medicine? The one for the clones?"

Astra's face dropped in shock. She hadn't expected Alyssa to figure it out that quickly, much less come to her about it. "What?"

"Did you mess with the medicine? Be honest, okay. Something was different, and I know I didn't do it. You're the only person who makes sense right now and Mary agrees."

Astra took a deep breath. She was calm. There was no reason to worry when she could erase this conversation and those thoughts from Alyssa and Mary as soon as Alyssa left her room. "I didn't," she said. The words fell off her tongue easily. "Even if I did, I would have run it past you first. It's your department, I wouldn't do that to you."

Alyssa looked relieved, her shoulders un-tensing, a light smile gracing her face. She chuckled. "Okay, well, that's good." She looked down. "I guess we're back to square one."

"Well, I'm busy, so if that's all…"

Alyssa nodded and jumped to her feet. "Yeah, I'm so sorry." She headed towards the door.

"Let me know if you need my help looking for someone who might have done it."

Alyssa nodded. "I will. Thank you!"

Astra closed the door behind her and then immediately went to her computer. She removed Alyssa's memories first, and then Mary's. She coded the thoughts away from both Nasra and Katya as well, just for good measure. When she was done, she couldn't help the feeling of sadness that welled up inside her when she remembered the look on Alyssa's face. She trusted her. Astra looked down at her hands. She didn't deserve that trust, and Alyssa didn't deserve what she was doing to them. None of them did.

35

Kill Order

Xavier rolled his eyes again. He was close to throwing his tools across the room. It was not a good day for him. He had spent the morning in the chess room like usual, and then spent time shadowing Alejo around the androids. Every single time he went into that room he felt sick, every time he touched something of hers, he wanted to rip the skin off his fingertips. He wasn't happy about being around Astra's tech and not being able to take it. It was so wrong in his mind. Everyone saw this as Leroy's work with Clay's improvements. No one knew the truth, and that made him want to hit his head against a wall.

He still hadn't talked to Astra about what she wanted to do with her tech, though he was sure that she didn't want it destroyed. At the very least, she would take their files and any information they had on her things. Astra had told him that they would speak today. It was getting late and he was itching to complain about all that had happened that day.

Finally, they were released. He ate dinner in silence, finishing as quickly as he possibly could. He hurried back to his room, eagerly awaiting the call. Unfortunately for him, that would not come for several more hours. He had almost fallen asleep by the time his phone rang. Once he realized what was going on, he snapped awake.

"It's about time," he said, annoyed.

"I got tied up. Fill me in."

"Well, apparently, the deadlines have been moved up. So, there's a possibility that we may have to destroy the facility if we can't get the androids out before their release date. There's also the fact that Alejo, one of the people I work with, seems to want to help me. He says that he used to work for Isaac Parkes and he wants the androids destroyed. Obviously, I'm not going to let him do that, but he may be helpful in some way."

"I'll look into it," Astra said. "In the meantime, you need to put kill codes into all of your work. The worst case scenario is that we blow everything up. If it comes down to that, nothing can be recovered. As in, even if they get the pieces, it's useless. Do you understand?"

"Yes. It shouldn't be too difficult, right?"

"Just put them in with the stuff you're working on and I'll have Isaac do the rest."

"Okay." Xavier couldn't find it in him to argue with Astra about Isaac, not right now. Something about knowing she was controlling Isaac didn't make him feel any better. If anything, it made him feel bad for Isaac, and concerned for himself. At what point would she stop? Where would she draw the line? Would it be him next? He had no answer for those questions, and that terrified him. He wanted to believe that she would never hurt him, and there was a time when he did. Now, he wasn't sure.

"Any other news?" she questioned. Her voice was dry and monotone. Even on her bad days she had some kind of emotion behind her words. When she was happy, she spoke faster, ditching the formality for a melodic kind of speech that almost sounded like she was going to sing. When she was angry, there was emphasis behind every word, as if she was trying to cut straight through him.

"Nothing important."

"Hmm.

"What?"

"I'm just surprised that Clay hasn't done anything particularly Parkes-like yet."

Xavier frowned. "What do you mean?"

"Well, from what Isaac tells me, there's nothing antagonistic about them. Nothing that he's found that says they're going to use them for weapons."

"Maybe he changed," Xavier said. "Or maybe he's not like Leroy."

Astra scoffed. "Who he is like doesn't matter. All I know is he has what is mine and I want it back."

"You'll have it, I promise."

That night, Xavier couldn't sleep. He tossed and turned, thinking about what Astra told him, what Clay Parkes really wanted with the androids. He worried about the codes he'd have to upload, the things he'd have to do, the people he'd have to silence. Xavier stared at the ceiling for a long time, a single question in his mind. Was he going to be a killer forever? Eventually, he fell into a restless sleep, dreams plagued by blood.

The next morning, Xavier worked beside Alejo. The two were alone in the room, a small lab with pieces of one of the test androids. They worked in silence for the most part, only asking each other to hand over certain tools and to exchange results.

Finally, the silence was too much for Xavier. "Alejo, what makes you want to destroy everything?"

Alejo looked taken aback. "What?"

Xavier shrugged. "I have my reasons, so you must have yours. What made you want to destroy the tech?"

Alejo took a deep breath. "Well, I didn't start out that way. I liked working with this stuff. Then I found out what they were doing. That was years ago. I haven't escaped it yet, and they only get worse. What they want to do with these androids isn't just household help, it's not just workers. These androids are built to be so human, you can't recognize them. They're there to infiltrate and destroy at a single command. The market won't know what hit them. Clay doesn't just want money, he wants control. With these, he'll have it, and we'll be powerless to stop them. Plus, Clay is smarter than Leroy. I think he might actually succeed, unless he's stopped."

Xavier opened his mouth in fake shock. "Wow. That's, that's a lot. How'd you figure this all out?"

"He told me. He trusts me," Alejo said bitterly. "He doesn't leave that sort of information in notes on the computer, but I know. So do a few people in his staff. Obviously I don't agree with him. Originally, I didn't want to have to destroy it all, they're beautiful. I just don't have any other choice."

"That's awful," Xavier said. "I can understand your reasoning now." It was second nature to pretend like he was upset, because he was. Just for different reasons. He saw this coming a mile away, it had been in his head since Astra called him the other night. It was easy to suspect that Clay Parkes was just as ruthless as his cousin, though he hid it better. Xavier hadn't seen Clay outright hurt anyone, not in front of him at least, but Clay had soldiers, mercenaries who would fight for him. He would only get stronger with the androids.

"So, you'll help me? Destroy the tech, all of it?"

Xavier nodded. "Yes, I promise." The lie fell off his tongue easily. He wouldn't destroy it if he could help it. Astra wouldn't want that. He then turned back to his work, getting lost in the motions, thinking about what his next move would be.

Alejo did not. He stared at Xavier. Something about the way he responded was too casual, like he wasn't even surprised. There was once a time where Xavier's demeanor was encouraging and exciting. He was the kind of person that was new, and that made him interesting. Alejo had watched him since the day he arrived, but now he watched him for a different reason. Ever since he had revealed that he was working against Clay to destroy the tech, something about Xavier changed. He was tense, however, not the usual kind of tense.

No, Xavier was angry. Shifty. Scared? Alejo couldn't pinpoint the exact emotions that Xavier was feeling, but he knew it wasn't good. Maybe Xavier wasn't telling him everything. He had promised to help him destroy the tech, but something wasn't right. Alejo stared at him just a little longer before turning back to his station. He was taking a leap of faith by trusting Xavier. He only hoped he wasn't wrong.

* * * * * * * *

Isaac stood in the hallway, pressed against the wall. The guards would switch soon and in that moment, he would need to get in and get out without being seen. He counted the seconds down on his watch, waiting for the perfect time. A man left the room, headed down the hallway to grab his replacement. Six. Five. Four. Three. Two. One. He made a mad dash for the door and slipped inside the room. He barely had a minute to do this.

When Astra had him follow Xavier, she had given him something, telling him to hide it from everyone. It was now, as he inserted the small jump drive into the computer and started the uploading process, that he understood. He couldn't refuse her. *'This is what I use to keep everyone in line,'* she had said. *'It will be my eyes and ears inside once most of the guards are under my control.'*

Isaac finished the upload quickly and ran back into the hall. He walked the opposite direction, ducking into another hall just in time. When he returned to his station, he swallowed the drive, it was the only way to truly rid himself of the evidence. It's done, he told her.

Unbeknownst to him, Astra was already aware, quickly delving into the vaults of information held in Syn's cloud storage. First, she read as much as she could. Then, she copied every single file onto her computer and downloaded it all onto three different hard drives, as well as uploading them to her own personal network. She would be able to access the files anywhere, on and off earth. The best part was that she was the only person who could access them, and the only one who knew.

Finally, after she had double checked everything, she started changing and erasing things. She was going to set them back as much as possible, just in the little details. They wouldn't notice it at first. Soon, she'd have everything she wanted. She just needed to keep Xavier busy for a little while longer, and she'd have her tech back too.

36

Friends to Strangers

Henry turned the page of his book, more out of habit than anything. He really wasn't paying attention. He was currently laying on his bed in the dorms, across from Aiken who was still reading Leroy's files and scribbling notes. Aiken hadn't moved from that spot for hours. Henry had memorized Aiken's schedule, noting the times that Aiken was missing. He only ever left the room for class or to go to the lab.

Henry wouldn't be surprised if Aiken worked on his notes in class. Lately, Aiken would put his projects off until the last minute, choosing the files over his assignments. Henry wasn't sure what had gotten into him. He couldn't be that attached to a promise he made to forfeit his schooling, right? Henry looked at his watch. Aiken's next class was about to start. Just like clockwork, Aiken got up, grabbed his backpack, and left the room without a word. Henry sighed. How could Aiken live like this?

Aiken loved helping other people, it was one of his best traits. Henry could get Aiken to do several things for him, though he always slipped money into his bag or under his pillow when Aiken wasn't looking. It was something his parents had always taught him to do, give money, or something else in return. Asking someone to do something always came with a reward, it would be returned tenfold. Henry tried his best to show that in everything he did. Right now, the thing he wanted to do was to make Aiken happy. To stop seeing the dark circles under his eyes.

So, Henry did the one thing that he thought would help: he looked for Astra. She was not always a predictable person, but there were a few places where she could be. She usually frequented the library, or the gardens, sometimes even the alcoves in the hallways. Eventually, he found her at a corner table in the cafeteria. She closed her computer as soon as she spotted him walking towards her.

As he drew nearer, he noticed the look on her face. He winced. Maybe now wasn't a good time. Then again, she looked perpetually annoyed. "Hello Henry," she said. "What do you want?"

He dropped into the seat across from her. "I just wanted to stop by," he started.

"No you didn't, you want something, what do you want?"

Henry sighed. "Well, don't you just know everything," he said sarcastically.

She looked at him pointedly. "Really?"

"Okay fine, I do want something."

"That's what I thought."

"How'd you know?" he questioned.

"You have a certain look on your face."

"Oh."

She nodded. "So, how can I help you Henry?" She clasped her hands together and rested her chin on them.

Henry sighed. "Well, Aiken has been weird lately. Strange, like he's putting the files over stuff he actually enjoys doing."

"And that's my problem, how?

"He works for you—"

"He doesn't work for me," Astra said, rolling her eyes. "He volunteered. I asked, he said yes, he hasn't complained since."

"Of course he hasn't, it's you, he adores you!" Henry said, exasperated. "He looks up to you because you're smart, and you know everything, and you're friends, he's loyal. He's not going to tell you because he doesn't want to hurt your feelings."

Astra raised an eyebrow. "Really? Or do you just not know him as well as you think you do?"

Henry's face fell. "Are you serious? We're best friends!"

"Are you?"

Henry stared at her. "Fine. Maybe I don't know him as well as

I think I do. But at least I care about him, unlike you. And I can see that he's not doing well. Even if he doesn't realize or doesn't want to voice it, I see it. So please, just tell him to slow down and take a break."

"No."

"No? What? Are you kidding me?"

Astra shook her head and reopened her laptop. "The answer is no, and frankly, I don't see how it's your business. If he's really having a hard time, he can come to me myself, though I highly doubt he will, because you're the only one who has an issue."

Henry stared at her in silence before getting up. "I can't believe you."

"Hmm. Well, that's your prerogative. If it makes you feel better, he really isn't being overworked, he chose this. Any time I see him, he's happy. He likes talking to me."

Henry opened his mouth to say something and then closed it. He had nothing to say, no way to respond. So, he just turned around and walked away. He spent the whole time walking back to his dorm thinking. He tried to come up with some other ways to convince Astra, but he soon settled with the idea that she wasn't going to budge. If he wanted some change to happen, he'd have to ask Aiken. Luckily, Aiken was already in the room when he entered.

Henry almost started immediately, but he decided not to, instead, he greeted Aiken and flopped down on his bed. He waited for a little bit, figuring out how to say what he wanted to. Eventually, he settled on short and to the point. "Aiken?"

"Hm?"

"Why do you spend so much time on the files?"

Aiken looked up. "Because Astra asked me to," he said matter-of-factly.

Henry nodded. "Okay, and does it bother you that she's taking advantage of you?"

Aiken frowned. "What? She's not, what?"

"Well, you overwork yourself. I see you do the files instead of your homework, you're more stressed, anxious, you don't get enough sleep…"

Aiken scoffed. "I don't know what you're talking about. And for the record, I don't put the files before my homework. I get everything completed on time."

"How are your grades?"

Aiken paused. Then his expression changed. "How dare you presume to know how I feel?!"

Henry was taken aback. "Aiken—"

"No! I'm doing fine, and you're accusing me? What, are you jealous or something? If you wanted to hang out with me you could just ask like a normal person."

"I wasn't—" Henry sighed. "I just, you're not yourself and I was worried, so I talked to Astra and—"

"You talked to Astra?" Aiken asked incredulously.

Henry nodded. "Yeah! It's what you do when you think someone is getting hurt. She said it wasn't my business, and to talk to you myself. I know I should have gone to you first, but I thought she would at least be reasonable. If she's taking advantage of you, I want you to know. it's what I would do for any other members of my family."

"You had no right!" Aiken yelled. "We're not brothers, so stop acting like it."

Henry flinched. "I was only trying to—"

"I don't care what you were trying to do, it doesn't matter. All you need to know is that your help isn't wanted, or needed, so just leave me alone!" Aiken turned and left the room, slamming the door behind him. Henry stood there in stunned silence. He didn't move for several minutes, just trying to wrap his head around what had just happened. Finally, he just sank onto his bed and sighed. He had ruined it, the one thing he knew Aiken needed most. He had failed.

37

I Don't Know You Anymore

Xavier sat alone in his room, waiting for confirmation that the security feed was looped. Astra may have had some of the security guards under her control, but Xavier wanted to stay out of sight anyway, just in case. When he got the signal, he left his room and headed towards the lab where the androids were held. It was an easy job. He got in, grabbed the pieces he needed, and got out.

Once he was back in his room, he started examining them. In the lab during work hours, he didn't have the chance to look at the tech closely like he wanted to. Most of what he did was coding: fixing bugs, adding mannerisms, and other small details. Anything that was needed for the *'brain'* was something that he worked on.

Ever since Alejo had brought up the fact that they were supposed to be soldiers, Xavier had wondered whether or not they were more advanced than Leroy's androids. Then, three days ago, he saw the face pieces for the androids and he had almost dropped his computer in shock. Xavier knew what humanoids were supposed to look like. Even with the advancements in technology, if you looked hard enough, you could find something wrong with them, in their eyes, hands, or hair.

These however, were perfect. Too perfect. So perfect in fact, it was like human taxidermy. Even the flaws on their faces looked real. He voiced that concern to Astra, and they set up a time for him to go check. Earlier that day, during lunch, Xavier had searched through all of the files until he found the original blueprints for the androids. As he worked to compare them, it was easy to tell. These pieces were far more advanced than the original androids. They were seamless, the metal pliable and soft, meaning it would move exactly like muscle underneath the synthetic skin.

He didn't know what the older models had looked like when

interacting with humans, since they were never introduced to the public as androids. According to Astra, at least their inner mechanics were flawed in some way, their brains not exactly right. You couldn't tell just by looking at them, but if you stared at them for too long, they'd start to look unnatural. This wasn't a problem with Clay's androids. Earlier, when he had touched the skin, it felt real. Xavier shuddered at the thought.

He loved technology, but it was terrifying to think about being in front of someone that you thought was human, but really wasn't. They were what myths and nightmares were made of. He had seen and worked with all kinds of people. Those whose legacies were blood and violence. Xavier couldn't count himself among the innocent, but at least he had never hurt people who didn't deserve it, not intentionally.

Though, now he saw himself in the androids, like he was looking in a mirror. Trading weapons was just as bad as using them, wasn't it? Even if he wasn't the one to pull the trigger. These androids were built to infiltrate, to spy, to kill. Just like he was, only they didn't have the capacity to feel like he did. He felt awful. Everything he had experienced, his whole life had come to this: hoping desperately that he could take back the things he had done, make up for it somehow.

Xavier noted down all the differences and advancements that he could find and then stealthily made his way back to the lab and returned the pieces. Once he had done that and was back in his room, it was around three a.m. The facility would start to wake up around 6:30 a.m., so he didn't have a lot of time to wrap everything up.

He sent Astra pictures of his notes, and then reset his phone. The notes were one thing. Relaying his plans over text was another. Even if they weren't being watched, he still had to wipe his phone and make sure that no one had seen him coming and going. Once Xavier had checked everything on his computer, he breathed a sigh of relief and called Astra. He leaned against the door, listening to the phone ring. Getting a hold of Astra recently had been a nightmare. She rarely picked up unplanned calls, and took hours to respond to his texts.

"Did you get everything?" he questioned as soon as she picked up.

"Yes. I see what you mean, these are far more advanced than we thought. And you said that Alejo told you they want to use these as soldiers?"

"Yeah, just like Leroy did. Except, they're a lot more suited. Clay seems to have gone about the whole process very differently."

"From what I hear, your chess sessions probably helped a lot," Astra murmured.

"You're not blaming me, are you? Because you told me to do this and I will not tolerate being blamed for something I didn't do."

"Of course I'm not blaming you," Astra said. "I'm just saying. I don't think I thought this through properly. Ugh."

Xavier raised an eyebrow. "Oh, you think? You made me help the people we're trying to steal from, and now they've moved the date of release up!"

"I know! What do you think I'm trying to help you with? Now keep your voice down!"

Xavier groaned and rubbed his face. "Okay," he said. "What do you need me to do?"

"Just, keep an eye on them and cause problems where you can."

"Okay, I can definitely do that."

Astra snorted.

"What?"

"It's just funny. I'm sitting here in the revelation of my worst fear and yet we're making a joke out of it." Her voice turned solemn. "Xavier, these creations were never meant to be anything like humans. They definitely weren't supposed to be weapons. They were a celebration of knowledge and my growth as an inventor, not… this!"

"I know Astra, and I promise, I am doing everything I can. If I can't get this tech out in time, I will destroy it, I swear to you."

"You better."

"You have my word."

"I'll have your head," she retorted.

Xavier frowned. "What?"

"You heard me." Her voice was colder now, angry, like someone had flipped a switch. "If you fail, I will kill you. It's what you deserve, it's what we deserve."

Xavier's mouth fell open. "What?"

"Those androids represent everything I was not supposed to bring to this earth: pain, hatred, war. They were supposed to be art, and they're being used to…" Her voice broke. "If you fail me, you will die, I promise you that," she hissed.

Xavier closed his eyes. He knew that tone, he knew those words. They were as clear in his head as the first time she had ever said them. This was not the Astra he knew. Not the one that he had called his sister, his friend. This was war all over again. He felt sick to his stomach, like the ground underneath his feet was fighting to knock him over. "Don't worry Little Star." The nickname felt like poison in his mouth. "If I fail, I'll kill myself."

Astra clicked the end call button and threw her phone on her bed. She didn't know how to respond to that declaration, so she just hung up. It was easier than admitting she might have gone too far. She walked over to the window and stared out of it. She crossed her arms, leaning against the windowsill. It was raining again, finally. It had not rained for several weeks. Astra had begun to think that they were going to be in a drought.

The sun had just set a few hours ago, so a few students were still outside. She had memorized the layout of the gardens, in fact, she was sure she could recreate them from memory. Astra was sure that if the dry season came quickly, she knew which flowers would die first. Her time at the school had twisted her, changed her ideals, her motivations, her feelings, everything. She was simultaneously kinder and crueler, just from the few years she spent in these halls.

Astra leaned her head against the cool glass of the window and closed her eyes. Her breath was hot on the glass, fogging it up. When she pulled back, it was blurry. She was blurry. As she reached out to rub the fog off the glass, she wondered about her future. Was there anything she could do to make her path forward more clear?

Beep! Astra flinched away from the window. Her phone went off again. *Beep!* Astra picked it up. A message flashed on the screen, perpetually blinking until she opened it. Astra couldn't help the grin from creeping across her face. She closed the message, dropped her phone on her bed and flopped down on it, arms spread out. She laughed, a happy one, the first genuinely happy laugh she'd had in ages.

They were coming. They were close. So close, it would only be a few weeks now. She was going to count down the days, hours, minutes, seconds until they arrived.

She was going home.

38

Questioning

It was the first time he had left the dorm in days. Henry didn't want to stay cooped up there forever, so he forced himself to get up and get dressed. Aiken hadn't acknowledged him the past couple of days, probably expecting Henry to be the one to apologize. He wasn't going to. Henry didn't see why he had to apologize to Aiken, what he said was true and there was no reason for him to be mad.

Even so, Henry blamed himself for it. Still, he could only hole himself up for so long. There were not many places on campus that were truly safe and quiet for everyone. Places where everything felt calm, like nothing would happen that would pull them back into their chaotic world. There was only one that Henry knew well, and so he headed towards his spot in the library. He was annoyed to find that it was already occupied by Mary and Alyssa.

Alyssa looked up as he approached the table, quip dying in her throat when she saw his face. "What's wrong Henry?" she asked.

Henry plopped down in the seat beside her. He folded his arms, laying his head down on them. "Aiken snapped at me a couple of days ago," he mumbled. "I feel awful. He's never done that, I don't know what I did."

"Henry…" Mary reached out to pat him lightly on the head. "I'm sure it wasn't your fault."

"No, it was. I told him he shouldn't be placing so much focus on working with Astra because she's making him stressed and he yelled at me."

"So maybe it's just the stress? I doubt he'll be mad at you for long."

Henry looked up, propping his head up on his arms. "Well, that doesn't make me feel any better."

Mary looked at him, a fond look on her face. "Look, you can't change the past. But I can assure you that everything is going to be fine. Aiken doesn't hold grudges. He'll be back to normal in no time."

Henry sighed. "I hope so."

"Well, if it makes you feel better, you're not the only one who has seen weird things going on around here," Alyssa said.

Henry looked at her. "What?"

Alyssa nodded. "Mary and I talked about this a little bit ago, but I think someone must have tampered with the medicine I used for the clones. I couldn't tell you who or what they did, but whatever it was did way more for the clones than I ever could. They're healthier than ever."

"Shouldn't you be glad then?"

"Well, I am. But it makes me wonder who had access to the medication and why they didn't just come forward. What motive did they have? Is it actually harmful to the clones, that sort of thing."

"Hmmm. Unfortunately, I couldn't help you. Who knows, maybe your cure actually worked better than you thought."

Alyssa shook her head. "No, trust me, I thought of that. But what it did should have been impossible. There's no way."

"What other possibility could there be?" Henry questioned.

"Like I said, someone must have tampered with the medicine or the clones themselves."

"But why?"

Alyssa shrugged. "I don't know, that's why it's weird! Not to mention, apparently, I've been doing and saying things that I don't remember. Like, yesterday, apparently a couple of days ago, I told a teacher that I would help her with some lab reports, and I don't remember having that conversation. In fact, I don't remember that day at all."

Henry frowned, thinking for a moment about his past interactions. "Come to think of it, there's been a lot of unexplained blank memories. I've had a bunch of times where I don't remember conversations, or there's a weird sense of deja vu when I'm working."

"Like you've done something before?" Mary asked.

"Yeah."

"That's what deja vu means," Alyssa said sarcastically. "We just have to figure out why this is happening."

"Do you think it's the stress?" Henry questioned. "Nasra always told me that too much caffeine, not enough sleep, and being overworked can cause a person to burn out and have everything blur together. Though, I'm not sure if memory loss is one of those symptoms."

"I mean, we do work in an environment where we're constantly trying new things," Mary said. "It's highly possible that we did something to ourselves and this is the result."

"But what?" Alyssa groaned. "None of us were used for human experiments. I don't remember taking anything that could cause memory loss, and I don't think anyone in the school would just drug us."

"Has anyone else experienced this sort of phenomenon?" Henry asked. "I'm not really that good at science, but I know that whenever you're testing a theory, you have to have a hypothesis, and you have to collect data that either proves or disproves it."

Alyssa paused. She frowned. "Well, I think I've overheard some students talking about how they missed deadlines because they couldn't remember what day it was, but I think that's normal in this kind of school."

Henry pulled his phone out and started typing in his notes app. "That may be the case, but we should still look into it, just to make sure. Anything else?"

"Well, if this is happening to everyone, then we should see if there's anyone who's not being affected by this," Mary said. "Let's ask our friends first. I know Zola has off today, so she'll probably be in her room, and Alyssa, do you want to ask Nasra?"

"Why don't we just have them meet us here? That way we can finish taking notes," Henry suggested.

"I'll text them right now," Alyssa said.

"Okay, so just to be clear," Henry said. "Alyssa is going to go through the medicine to try to find something that she didn't put in. I'm going to talk to the students, and we're going to have Zola and Nasra do what?"

"Probably just have them tell us their experience. Because if it's happening to all of us, then we need to be suspicious. If it's only happening to a few people, it may not be that bad," Mary mused.

"Memory loss is bad no matter what," Alyssa retorted.

"Amen to that," Zola said as she walked up. "I'm glad I was close, what'd I miss?" She dropped into the seat next to Henry.

"Well, we have reason to believe that someone not only tampered with Alyssa's medicine that she used for the clones, but also our memories." Henry held up his phone. "I've been writing down everything I can to make sure we covered all the bases."

Zola raised an eyebrow. "You think someone is tampering with our memories?"

"Have you not had instances where chunks of time are missing?" Mary questioned.

Zola frowned. "Well…" she paused. "A while back, when the clones first got sick, I had a few blank spaces. Though, to be fair, I haven't interacted with you guys much lately."

Henry's eyes widened. "You're right. The more I think about it, most of what I don't remember has to do with conversations I had with Alyssa, Nasra and Mary. Especially regarding the clones."

"Speaking of, Nasra can't meet up right now," Alyssa said. "She says she has experienced something like I described and that she'll tell us later when she's not busy."

Henry nodded. "Okay, that works. Anything else?"

"Well, I have an appointment with Castor later this week, so I'll check in with him as well," Alyssa said.

"And I can do more research," Henry added.

"Wait," Mary said. "You guys, we have to be careful about what we're saying and doing. We have no idea who's listening or who is truly behind this. It could be anyone, and so you can't talk to just anyone. Be very selective about how you're interacting with people and what you're telling them."

Zola nodded. "I think this all started recently, so I'm going to go through the list of teachers again."

"It has to be someone who has access to the cameras," Alyssa said. "I'm not sure many teachers are allowed to go through them unmonitored, and there's a lot of missing footage that corresponds to the missing memories that I have. I'm sure if you check, you'll find the same for everyone else."

"So, we're looking for someone who had access to the clones, the cameras, and regularly talks to Alyssa, Nasra, and Mary," Henry said.

"Not necessarily," Zola interjected. "If this person is making us forget things, they could be making us forget interacting with them."

"That's ridiculous," Alyssa scoffed.

"No, it's plausible," Mary said.

"Alright, alright," Alyssa raised her hands in defeat. "Fine, we need to look for someone who is smart enough to–"

"Again, not necessarily. Most geniuses who are doing something like this will hide it."

Alyssa glared at Zola. "Wow, you're really contradicting everything I'm saying aren't you?"

"I'm just saying. It could be someone random, or the most obvious person we know. We just have to be careful."

"Great!" Mary clapped her hands together. "Now that we all know what we're doing, I have to go to class." She got up to leave.

“Okay, bye Mary.” Alyssa turned back to the group. “Okay, so I think I’m going to schedule check-ups with the rest of the clones, not just Castor.”

“That’s a good idea. But I think we should also stick to what Mary said, until we can prove that our friends aren’t the ones doing this, we should be careful about who we’re talking to,” Zola said.

“I really don’t think it’s any of us,” Henry said. “At least not anyone here, definitely not Nasra, Katya is too helpful to keep this to herself, and Elena doesn’t interact with the clones, so I think they’re trustworthy.”

Zola nodded. “Okay, fine. But don’t give them too much information until we know more.”

Alyssa nodded. “Sounds good. So…” she said, dragging out the end of the word. “Do you guys want to get lunch?”

39

Caught

Xavier sat at his desk, typing away. He didn't really have any ideas for what he was doing, so he just let his thoughts run away from him. It didn't really matter what he was making anyway. He was getting out today, and therefore, he could get away with slacking. Clay didn't have him play chess today, something that he guessed was Alejo's doing. It kept eyes off of him, so he was grateful.

Eventually, everyone dispersed for lunch and Xavier headed towards the boiler room. That's where he would start. He would set up explosives there, and then move on to the lab to dismantle the androids and move them. There were only four prototypes, so it wouldn't be that difficult, especially with Isaac's help. Luckily for him, the androids were made with a lightweight material. With the proper distraction, they would be able to get all four out and into a truck. By the time anyone noticed, they would be long gone.

Xavier had chosen not to tell Alejo about this, a decision he hadn't told Astra about. He still wasn't sure he could trust him, and he couldn't let Alejo destroy the tech. Isaac was already waiting in the lab for him. Xavier checked his watch. In a few minutes, Astra would make the security go the other way, and Isaac would get to work dismantling the androids.

Xavier stopped at a locker room and pulled a small box out from behind one of the lockers. He didn't know how Astra had managed it, but she had supplied him with a sizable amount of C4 to place around the boiler room. All he had to do was set it up and when they were out with the tech, she would set it off remotely.

Like Astra had said, no one was around. He dutifully set up the explosives around the room and the base of the boiler itself. When the explosives went off, they would take out the center of the facility. A chain reaction would send fire to the heating system, which would eventually cause the whole place to blow. It was an elaborate plan. Plus, if they didn't end up killing everyone inside, Clay Parkes had no way of truly tracking him.

Once he had finished, Xavier headed towards the lab. He found Isaac already almost done with two of the androids. "Go start on the other two," Isaac said, not looking up when Xavier entered. "A driver is waiting for us in the loading bay. Which, by the way, I can't believe they only have one loading bay."

Xavier walked over to one of the androids and started searching for the areas where the limbs disconnected. "Well, I think it makes it easier to monitor who goes in and out. Thankfully, that means it's a lot easier for us, since Astra controls the security team."

"Most of the security team," Isaac corrected. "She's watching us right now I think. But either way, we're not completely safe. You will be, because I promised, but we really have to move quickly. We only have twenty minutes…" he trailed off.

Xavier frowned. "What?" He moved the pieces of the android into a duffel bag and started on the second one, carefully separating its head from its body and stuffing the wires into the hollow space so they wouldn't get too tangled.

"Do you hear that? Someone's coming, this isn't supposed to happen, the change over isn't for another ten minutes."

Xavier turned towards the door, where he could hear footsteps coming for them.

"Oh good, I thought I would find you here– what are you doing?!" Alejo stared at the two, a horrified look in his eye."

"It's not what you think Alejo," Xavier started. "I just didn't know how to tell you—"

"You're taking the androids without me?"

"You'd be safe," Xavier lied, desperately. "We were going to get it off the property so that we could dispose of it without Clay knowing where to look."

Alejo frowned. "You–"

"Please believe me," Xavier cut him off. "You can help us get it out, I just didn't want to risk it."

"You didn't trust me."

Xavier hesitated before speaking. "Can you blame me? I barely know you!"

"Fair." Alejo sighed. "Okay, what are we doing?"

Xavier nodded to the other two duffel bags on the floor. "We need to get these parts in there. There's a driver waiting for us at the loading bay."

Isaac shot Xavier a questioning look behind Alejo's back. Xavier just shook his head. Right now, they had no choice. The three worked together to put all the parts in the bags and secure them in place.

"We need to hurry," Isaac said. "We don't have much time. The guards will switch over soon, and we need to make it to the loading bay before anyone sees us."

Xavier took the lead. "Let's go." He grabbed two duffle bags, swung one over his shoulder and picked up a third one. He ran into the hall and towards the loading bay, careful to slow down and peek around corners to make sure no one was waiting for them. Alejo and Isaac followed behind. Neither were as quiet as he was; Isaac nearly knocked a painting off the wall in his haste.

"Quiet!" Xavier hissed. "We're almost there." He looked around the corner, scanning the hallway to make sure it was clear. Then, he dashed across the hall and slipped through the door to the loading bay. A man looked up as he entered.

"Xavier!" the man whisper yelled.

Xavier recognized him. "Hi Riccardo," he said. "These need to go in the trunk."

Riccardo nodded and took the bags from him and threw them into the back of the van. "You boys are late."

"We had a bit of a delay," Xavier said as Alejo came up behind him and tossed his bags into the back.

"I see."

Isaac threw his bags on top of Alejo's and then closed one of the doors. "I think that's everything. I'll ride in the back." He jumped in, and pulled the second door shut behind him.

"I call shotgun," Xavier said. He got in the passenger seat, and Alejo got into the seat behind Riccardo.

"So, is anyone going to catch me up?" Alejo questioned as Riccardo started the engine.

"Well, that depends on what you want to know," Riccardo said, chuckling. "I'm sure you'll get your answers once we're on the road." He clicked a button and the loading bay door lifted out of the way.

Riccardo was halfway out when the door to the loading bay opened and there was a shout. "Hey! What are you doing?"

Xavier turned to see some men he didn't recognize entering the room. "Step on it Ric, those aren't security."

Riccardo obliged, and the men started running after them. "Stop!" one of them yelled.

Xavier reached under the seat and pulled out a pistol. "Thanks for this," he said.

"We're always armed," Riccardo said, matter of factly.

"What is going on?!" Alejo looked sick to his stomach, his face frozen in a state of fear.

"We're being chased," Isaac yelled from the back. "A truck is catching up!"

Xavier leaned out his window and aimed at the truck's front left wheel. He missed and ducked back inside to avoid being shot.

Riccardo swerved. "Sorry, there was a deer," he said.

"They're right next to us!" Isaac yelled.

"Not helping," Xavier retorted, aiming at the truck's wheels again. He didn't really want to hurt them. Then, they started firing back. The got closer, swerving till they were on the right side of the truck, a few feet away.

A bullet whizzed through the air and Xavier ducked. It hit Riccardo in the chest. Riccardo's eyes went wide and his hands fell off the wheel. Xavier turned to stare at him for a split second, before looking up and shooting the two men in the truck beside him. This time, he didn't miss. The van banged into the side of the truck. Xavier pulled Riccardo out of the chair and clambered into the seat. He rotated the wheel, barely avoiding running off the road. He slammed on the gas, only worried about their safety and the androids in the back. In the rearview mirror, he could see the truck crash into a tree.

In the seat behind him, Alejo was shaking. "We're gonna die, we're gonna die, we're gonna die!"

"We're not going to die!" Xavier yelled. "Just hold on." He drove off the road and into the forest, running over bushes and knocking branches off trees in the process. It would take a little while for the rest of security to get to the other vehicles, so they had some time.

Isaac called Astra, barely able to put her number in with how bad his hands were shaking. "Pick up, pick up," he whispered. "Thank goodness. Astra, you won't believe what happened, we're in trouble, we barely got out—"

"Slow down Isaac! You're incomprehensible. Breathe. What's wrong?"

Isaac sighed, breathing deeply to calm his heart rate. "We were caught. We barely escaped. I don't know what happened, but someone found out. Someone had to have told on us, we were so careful, I don't know how this happened."

"Okay, okay, calm down. You're alive. That's okay. The only thing you can do now is stay safe and come back to Torsion. I'll take care of security and slow them down."

Isaac nodded frantically, even though she couldn't see him. "Okay, okay, okay. I will. I'll tell Xavier and Alejo and we'll get plane tickets and come back."

"Use cash, and catch the first one back. I'll reimburse you when you're here."

"Will do."

"Okay. Are you fine? No one is hurt, right?"

Isaac paused, not knowing if he should tell her about Riccardo or not. "I'm okay, and so is Xavier, I was just panicking for a moment there," he said finally.

"Isaac, you have human emotions now. That's normal."

"I know what anxiety is, thank you Astra. It's just weird. I'm a machine."

Astra rolled her eyes, forgetting for a second that Isaac couldn't see her. "Not anymore."

"Well consider me a computer in a flesh prison! I'm barely hanging on here!"

"Use your brain Isaac, you have one for a reason. Make sure to check in every day so I know what's going on."

"Every day? How long do you think we'll be out here?"

"Well, it should take a while to get to the closest city, and then you have to get a plane. Hopefully, no more than two to three days."

Isaac groaned.

"It's okay Isaac, don't worry. You guys will be fine, I promise."

"Thanks Astra." He hung up and flopped on his back in the trunk, the duffle bags making the experience uncomfortable. However, he was too exhausted to really care. Isaac closed his eyes, trying to level his breathing and slow his heart rate. His whole body felt heavy. Eventually, he fell asleep.

40

Hope in Trying Times

"Katya, have you seen—" Elena stopped in her tracks. "Katya?" The girl was nowhere to be seen in the observatory. Elena frowned. Katya hadn't left the observatory save to sleep for several days now. Elena turned and headed back towards the dorms. Maybe she had overslept. It was a long walk back, but Elena enjoyed the breeze in her hair and the way the sun felt on her skin. It was a good day to be outside. Maybe she'd come work out here later.

The cold air blasted her when she opened the door into the back lobby. A few students were milling around, chattering about test scores and their plans for the summer. Elena was just glad that it was almost over. They had less than a month left of school, and she needed to sleep.

Unfortunately, that had to wait. She had more pressing matters to deal with. As she started walking up the stairs, she groaned. Henry was right. They did need elevators.

When she reached Katya's door, she rapped on the door three times. "Katya? It's Elena, are you okay?"

There was a moment of silence before Elena heard rustling and Katya opened the door. "Hi Elena!" she said. It should have been cheerful, but if anything, it was strained.

Elena frowned. "What's wrong?"

"Nothing!"

"Sure…" she stared at Katya. "Can I come in?"

Katya nodded and opened the door wider to let Elena enter.

"Is Zola here?"

"No, I think she's doing her teacher's aid stuff somewhere. Or she's in class."

"Hmm." Elena set her bag down and plopped into Katya's desk chair. "So, why weren't you at the observatory today?"

Katya shrugged. "I don't know, I just didn't feel like it I guess."

"You didn't feel like it? Katya, you basically live there."

Katya shrugged. "I guess I've just been a little discouraged because of everything that's going on. Henry talked to me about something regarding memory loss, I still think there's something wrong with the telescope, even though I can't prove it, and with the stress surrounding the clones, I'm just…" she sighed and flopped backwards onto her bed. "I'm tired, and I don't want to do anything."

Elena got up and whacked Katya's legs. "Move over."

Katya rolled her eyes and moved so Elena could sit on the bed next to her.

"Kat, you can't just stop doing something because you're worried. You got here, and you can prove yourself. Trust your gut Katya, you got this. No matter what you want to do with that telescope or with your life. I'm tired too, but I keep working, and I know, I know, it's different for everyone, but I know you. You love everything that you do, and you've always pushed through, even with all the obstacles we've faced. I know it's difficult, but this is something that you're super passionate about. I want you to be happy."

Katya gave her a small smile. "Thanks El. I guess you're right. You're a good friend."

"I try. Now, I don't think you have to go back to work immediately, it's always good to take a break, just don't run from it because you think no one will believe you."

Katya nodded.

Elena waited for a moment before moving on. "By the way, I was going to ask you, did you see my blueprints? The ones for the computer that connects to the telescope."

"No, why?"

"I wanted to reference them for one of my upcoming assignments and I could have sworn I left them in the observatory."

"Weird."

Elena shrugged. "It's no big deal, they'll turn up eventually. In the meantime, I have a bunch of floor plans to look over. Henry will not shut up about us getting elevators, and I agree with him, we need them. This school is pretty and all with its vintage aesthetic and all that, but sometimes I just don't want to climb ten flights of stairs to get to my room or to class."

"Hey, at least most of everything is in the same building. I've heard that some college campuses have dozens of buildings and you have to walk miles to get from one end to the other."

Elena grimaced. "I would hate that."

Katya chuckled. The two fell into a comfortable silence for a few moments. The only noise was the occasional chirping of birds outside the window and the AC.

"Can I ask you something?" Katya finally said.

"Sure."

"If I find something meaningful, and I prove that I was right about the telescope, will you believe me? Will you help me with all of that?"

"Of course!" Elena said it like it was the most natural thing in the world. "In fact, if you need or want it, I'll help you look."

Katya grinned. "Thank you, I mean it. I really appreciate it."

"No problem. Hey, you want to see what I'm working on right now?"

"Yeah, that'd be interesting. Is it like a project, or renovations related?"

"Renovations related." Elena reached into her backpack and pulled out a folder. "Here. So, over here, I'm thinking we can move these classrooms down to where the labs in the tunnels were, just by knocking some walls out and clearing space. It'll help with the lighting problem for some of the plants, and not only that, but we'll have a fully underground radiation zone so that we don't have to keep sending those students to a lab that's three hours away."

"Hmm, do you really think using the tunnels is a good idea?"

"Well, so long as we keep the students away from the areas that we work in, we should be fine. We have full permission from the school board, and with Zola as the acting dean, we don't have anyone telling us not to. Plus, we'll be putting elevators in these different sections so they'll go directly to those areas. You'll need a key card, and all other entrances will be blocked off. These doors here will need both a keycard and pin number to get through, and will log who goes in and out."

"That's so interesting," Katya murmured. "I think that will help with the issues some people might have with working in the tunnels, especially since most of the staff don't know about them."

"I was going to capitalize on that in my pitch."

Katya smiled and giggled. "Well, thanks for visiting El, I should probably get to my homework."

"No problem," Elena said. She gathered her papers and swung her backpack over her shoulder.

"Let me know when you get back to work on that telescope. I'll see you around."

"Will do. Bye, have a good afternoon!"

Elena left Katya's dorm and headed towards the cafeteria. She looked through her papers, sorting them in her hand in order of importance. She would also submit some of these plans as part of her assignments. She was working alongside Mary to make sure that it was possible. Elena didn't look up as she turned the corner and collided with someone.

"Oomph."

All of the papers in Elena's hands fell to the ground.

Elena stumbled backwards, almost falling over too with the weight of her backpack. "Oh, hey Aiken," Elena greeted. "I'm so sorry, I didn't see you there."

"Hi El," he said. "It's okay." He grabbed the papers she had dropped on the floor. "How are you?"

She held out a hand to pull him to his feet and took the papers from him. "Thanks. I'm doing good, how are you?"

He shrugged. "Same old things. I'm taking a break right now though."

"Well, I have some free time, and I'm sure you haven't had a lot of time to be around people. Do you want to have lunch with me? I can catch you up on what you missed."

Aiken gave her a half-hearted smile. Though it was small, it was laced with relief. "Sure, that sounds good."

Elena grinned. "Great! Come on, you will not believe what Katya told me about the telescope."

41

Betrayal

Xavier sipped his iced coffee, trying to not let his distaste for the drink show. He didn't really like sweets, and was definitely more of a tea person, but Isaac had paid for it with his own money, and he didn't want to be rude. It was the least he could do. Isaac had proven himself to Xavier, and he didn't deserve his spite or distrust. Not to mention, the other two were probably shaken up by the untimely death of their driver. Xavier put the cup down and stretched. It had been a long night, and the motel beds were extremely uncomfortable. He had forgotten what it felt like, having been so long since he had gone on any kind of mission.

Speaking of Isaac, he was currently trying to get the airline to take cash. Apparently, Astra didn't want them to be tracked. It made sense, but he was used to private planes and people who were always on hand to pick him up if something went wrong. He considered trying to contact one of their clients, but he ultimately decided against it. Clay would be looking for him, and it was best to keep a low profile.

There was a slight breeze, something that Xavier appreciated. It was hot out. For some reason, they had decided not to sit inside the small cafe and instead, sit outside at one of the circle tables. There were no umbrellas, and therefore, no shade. Xavier was not a heat person. He hated summer. Alejo, on the other hand, seemed to love the heat. His coffee was traditional, hot and black, with no cream or sugar.

The last time that Xavier had seen someone drink coffee that way was during a meeting with one of Ares's business partners. That man had consumed fifteen cups of coffee over the course of the half an hour meeting. Xavier was a little concerned about his health. After all, the man had been 70 years old, or older. That much caffeine was probably not good for his heart.

Xavier's eyes flitted around, paying attention to everything, the store fronts, the people who passed him, even children. Especially children. He had been a child assassin before. They were good; no one cared to really watch them so they slipped by undetected. Plus, he struggled to turn the paranoia off in these kinds of settings. This was where he was most vulnerable. The shop fronts themselves were bustling with activity, each one more colorful and crowded than the last. Old women seemed to make up most of the crowd, though Xavier spotted a few families and teenagers among them.

Alejo watched Xavier's expressions as he stared at the people surrounding him. "Hey. What's going on in your head?"

Xavier pursed his lips. "Just thinking." It wasn't a lie. He blinked in the bright light, squinting to look at Alejo against the sun. "There's a lot of people here, it's hot, and it's crowded. Almost makes me miss the facility."

Alejo laughed dryly. "I certainly don't. I haven't been outside in years. This is beautiful. Don't take it for granted."

Xavier nodded. "I suppose it is nice to feel the sun again, even if it's burning."

"That's the spirit!" Alejo scanned the small shopping center for a moment. "Besides, we won't have to be out here much longer, there's Isaac."

Xavier turned around to see Isaac walking towards them with a frustrated look. "They didn't accept cash so they told us to take a taxi to the closest airstrip and see if we can find a pilot. Obviously, that is very far away and costly."

"I could reimburse you if you want," Xavier offered. "I don't have financial struggles, plus I have some saved up. I could pull money from my account, though that might alert Clay to where we are. I'll do it once we get Clay out of the picture."

Alejo raised his eyebrow. "Out of the picture?"

Xavier sighed, turning back to face him. "Clay is trying to kill us. I could probably sue him and put him in jail."

"You'd risk that?"

Xavier didn't have to risk that. He had people who would arrest Clay Parkes simply because he asked them, and forge the evidence later. "Yeah," he said. It was just slightly happier in tone than it should have been.

"Uh huh." Alejo took a deep breath. "Anyway, I'm going to go to the bathroom before we leave, so, I'll be right back."

He disappeared into the cafe, and Isaac took his seat. They sat there in silence for a moment until Alejo came out of the cafe.

"Ready to go?" Xavier asked

He shook his head. "Not yet, I want to check something." Alejo wandered across the street to a small fruit stand and started talking to his owner.

After a few minutes of just watching him, Xavier groaned. "Does he realize that we are on the run? We need to go!"

Isaac laughed. "Yeah, well, sometimes panic makes you do things you regularly wouldn't…" Isaac trailed and his face dropped as he stared over Xavier's shoulder.

"What?"

"Look. Those are Clay's men. I recognize the logo on their shirts, it's a front for the family." He looked at Xavier frantically. "He must have found us, I don't know how. Go. I promised Astra I'd take care of you and keep you safe. You and Alejo, get out of here. I'll slow them down and I'll be right behind you. Go!"

Xavier nodded and sprinted away. "Alejo!" Alejo looked up at the sound of his name. "We gotta go, come on!"

Alejo got up, confused. "What—"

Xavier ran past him. "No time to explain, come on!"

"Wait, where's Isaac?"

"Preoccupied, he'll be right behind us soon. Hurry!"

"What about the androids?"

"They're not as important as our lives Alejo, just go!"

They ran for a few blocks, weaving through the crowd, never looking back. Xavier knew that Isaac probably had a tracker on him so he made his movements sporadic, trying to throw off whoever was on his trail, if anyone was.

"There!" Xavier spotted an alley and turned down it. About halfway through, Alejo stopped. Xavier turned to him. "What are you doing? Why'd you stop, we have to keep going, we have to—" Xavier was cut off by Alejo pushing him into the wall. Xavier, caught off guard, fell, cutting his hand on the bricks. "Wha—"

Alejo kicked him in the stomach. "I'm sorry Xavier. You can't escape, not now. I cannot let you live. I thought I could trust you, but you're just another one of those people who want that technology for their own gain. I can't let you have that, I can't let you survive just to try again and take them by force. So, I called Clay and I let him know where we were. Luckily, they were in the area. And I may hate Clay, but at least I know what he wants with these things. You lied to me once, what's to keep you from doing that again?"

He looked solemn, almost like he regretted it. Alejo picked up a rock from the ground, tossing it in the air to get a feel for its weight. "You know, I really liked you, kid. You had the spark. But, it's better for me to die as a traitor knowing I tried, than to let someone potentially worse get their hands on that tech." With that, he lunged forward. Xavier didn't even have the time to explain. He struggled to process this new information, instincts screaming to fight back, and yet he didn't. He didn't want to hurt Alejo. Xavier heard Isaac yell something behind him that he couldn't make out. Then Xavier was met with a rock to the head and everything went dark.

He had woken up in a chair on a plane with a worried Isaac staring at them. Isaac caught him up to speed, and the information made his head spin.

"I found Alejo off, and then grabbed you and ran into some

people who said they worked for you, who got us on a plane. I really couldn't tell if they were yours or not, but they had guns so I didn't question it. We couldn't find the androids, and I assume they were picked up by the guards. They can't get destroyed easily, so if we choose to storm the place, then we can get them back, so on and so forth…" Isaac trailed off. "Are you okay?

Xavier tried to nod, then winced.

The doctor chastised him for moving. "Your bleeding has stopped, just keep the wraps on until the sticks set. You'll be fine."

As the doctor made his way to the front of the plane to relay that information to Jaxson, Xavier bitterly wondered why Astra hadn't sent a plane for them in the first place.

The plane ride was relatively uneventful. Isaac made him eat, despite the fact that he wasn't hungry. He tried to protest, unsuccessfully. He did have a concussion, but the doctor cleared him to sleep and had a space in the back of the plane cleared for him. Eventually, Xavier fell into a restless sleep. Isaac shook him awake once they landed.

As they exited the plane, Xavier saw Astra first, and then Tessa, Cassidy, Yvette, Jaxson, Griffin, and Zale. He frowned. Astra had called their siblings?

Xavier didn't have the time to dwell on this or greet them before he was struck with a sudden sense of dizziness. His knees buckled. The last thing he saw was Astra's worried face, and his last thought before the world went dark for the second time that day was: *'Really? Again?'*

* * * * * * * *

Xavier opened his eyes. He was back in his room. One of the conference room doors was closed. Xavier walked across the room and pressed his ear to the door. He winced as he heard the conversation that was going on inside.

"We almost lost Xavier out there! If it wasn't for Isaac, he'd be dead, and we're going to sit here and argue about whether or not we should let these people live? They're using my work to make monsters, weapons that shouldn't ever exist, and I'm just supposed to let that slide?" Astra felt her cheeks get hot, but she ignored it. "I will not stand by and let people destroy this world, not when I will take the blame for it. Clay Parkes will die, I will make sure of it." Astra turned and stormed out of the room.

Cassidy grimaced. "That went well," she said sarcastically.

Yvette whacked her on the back of the head.

"Ow!" She whipped around and glared at Yvette. "What was that for?"

"Don't say stupid things," she said, signing aggressively as she did.

Cassidy stuck out her tongue. "It's fine," she said.

Yvette rolled her eyes and took her cochlear implant off. "I don't want to talk to you." She turned around in her seat, crossed her arms, and closed her eyes.

Cassidy stared at her in disbelief. "What? Are you serious, is she serious?"

Jaxson shrugged, laughing. "Personally, I think you deserved that."

Cassidy glared at him. "Rude."

42

Please Don't Go

Isaac flopped down onto his chair and opened his computer. Ever since he'd gotten back to Torsion, he had been swamped with work. Of course, no one had noticed his absence, something he didn't even want to begin to question. However, that did mean he had to do everything on his own, no asking for help. It had taken several sleepless nights, but he had done it, begrudgingly of course.

After the first few days, Astra had banned him from complaining to her, so he spent his time talking to himself. Besides having to catch himself up to speed on what had happened while he was gone, he also still monitored the cameras he had left at the Syn facility. He had done it for Xavier's sake mostly, to keep an eye on him when he couldn't be near him.

Astra hadn't seen the need to keep them up when they escaped, but he ignored her. He stood by the fact that it was good to leave them there, just in case they still needed to sneak in. When Astra told him what her siblings had talked about, he promised to take a look at the cameras. For the first few days, there was nothing, just regular work. Staff didn't even enter the android work room. Today, he expected nothing different.

He shouldn't have. The room was buzzing with activity, drawing his attention as soon as the camera feed loaded on his screen. The audio was awful, but he could still pick up snippets of conversation.

"Keep trying…we can't have any problems right now…due by the end of the week."

Isaac's eyes widened, and he almost fell out of his chair as he scrambled towards the door. He ran to the lab, nearly hitting students on the way. "Astra! Astra, we have a problem!" he yelled as he burst into the room.

"Isaac, I swear if it's another complaint about your work-load—" She frowned, taking in his appearance. She got up slowly. "What's wrong?"

He stopped, chest heaving as he leaned against the doorway. "Parkes, the androids," he gasped out. "The release date has been moved up."

"What?!"

The urge to say *I told you so* died in his throat when he saw the look on her face. Isaac could see the horror in her eyes, which quickly turned to anger. He nodded. Astra's posture grew rigid, hands balling up into fists. Isaac could almost see steam radiating off of her, though it could have just been his imagination.

Her eyes darkened. "We're leaving."

"What?"

"I said I want Clay dead, and I will get what I want!" Astra stuffed her notebook and laptop into her bag. "Come on, there's no time to waste. We have to get on a plane." She strode past him and out the door."

"Wait, what about the others?" Isaac questioned, half jogging to keep up.

"There's no time to wait for them, I'll call Xavier when we land."

"This doesn't seem like the best idea," Isaac said nervously. "I don't even know what we're doing."

Astra didn't answer, she just kept walking, her pace getting faster as she headed towards the exit. "It may not be, but then again, neither is letting a madman release a deadly weapon, so tell me which result you'd prefer."

"Honestly?" Isaac stopped and hesitated while Astra kept walking. He caught up to her, just as she started walking out the door. "I don't like either option. I mean, right now, we are walking into a trap and you don't want to spend 20 minutes waiting for your siblings?"

"No."

"You're not telling me something, are you?"

Astra sighed. "If they come with me, someone will keep me from killing him. Part of reforming our family business. Usually, I would agree with it, it's a great idea, but not here, not now, not for him. This makes sure I get at least an hour head start. By the time they get to me, he'll be dead. That's all that matters." She took a deep breath. Her heart was beating exceptionally fast, like if she talked too fast it would fall out of her chest.

Isaac frowned. "Clay's death is the only thing that matters? Not taking out the weapons you created?"

"That's a secondary mission," she said.

"Astra, what have you become?" Isaac stared at her, trying to read her expression, find some sort of explanation for her actions.

Astra just smiled, never breaking stride, never looking back. Her smile didn't reach her eyes; in fact, it was almost pained. "I have not become anything Isaac. I'm simply doing what I should have done in the first place."

Isaac tried to come up with something to say, but he was at a loss for words.

The rest of the trip to the airport was silent, and by the time they got there, Astra had a private jet lined up. Isaac didn't ask questions. He had learned not to do that early on. You didn't question Astra. You didn't question the Duke family in general.

The flight was quiet, the silence overpowering him. It was suffocating, and Isaac hated it. He hated the fact that exactly one hour into the flight, Astra had called Xavier to let him know what they were doing. He hated overhearing what Xavier said to her, he hated watching Astra walk away towards the back of the plane, still hearing the yelling, even though he couldn't make out the words.

Isaac was used to following orders, but he was also used to breaking rules. Somehow, even though this event was so similar to what he had usually done, he had a funny feeling in the pit of his stomach that threatened to rip him apart. He couldn't recognize it. Though, he had a theory that it was guilt.

After all, he had spent so much time with Xavier, befriending him, protecting him, that this felt like betrayal. Even though he was following Astra, the girl with whom his loyalties should lie. She practically made him, she made the blueprint that created them all. Still, his loyalty to her felt shallow in that moment. Like he was doing the wrong thing. Like he was letting her become something she would hate.

Astra could handle herself, but it wasn't about Astra's protection, it wasn't her life on the line. She was a soldier, she always had been. He was fooling himself whenever he thought otherwise. Astra was an alien, of the worst kind and nature. She was practically brimming with rage that could destroy everything around her at a moment's notice. She was not the kind of person he could fight. She was the kind of person who would snap his neck if he got in her way.

When she returned, he bit back the remarks he wanted to make and took a deep breath. "How much longer do we have?"

"Just a couple more hours."

Her answer was as cold as the look on her face. She was getting angrier by the minute. It was the kind of anger that iced over your heart and left frostbite on your fingertips. The kind of rage that blew in with the winter wind. Astra had always been a storm; she was raised that way. However, she was always angry in the way that flames tore down buildings. She was never like this. Isaac had witnessed her do many things, make decisions that would cause a strong leader to falter, and in all of it, she was fire.

He didn't know what it meant, this cold. It felt like he was drowning in her presence.

When the plane touched down, Astra instructed Isaac to wait. She left alone, and he didn't even try to stop her. She disappeared, and Isaac wanted to do something, but he didn't. He sat in his chair and he waited. He ignored Xavier's frantic calls, the buzzing of electricity in the lights above him, the feeling that he would be at fault for whatever terrible acts Astra felt like committing. He ignored all of it. After all, if Astra returned to her roots for this mission, why shouldn't he?

Astra took the long way, into the forest, weaving her way through the trees, not worrying about the time it would take to get there. It left her alone with her thoughts, a familiar situation, and yet was so foreign. She was ten years old again, running through drills with her fellow trainees, fighting for the first place slot so she could tear a morsel of praise from her superior's lips. Her childhood was a faint touch in her mind. The only things that truly stayed were her orders.

She knew that by the time she reached the facility, Xavier and the rest of her family would be flying in. But she had the upper hand, she always did. She wasn't going to let them take it from her. A faint buzzing noise came from her pocket and Astra frowned. She pulled out her phone. It was Xavier.

"What?" she answered, annoyance showing in her tone.

"Please? Please don't go in without us."

Astra had never heard him ask before. It was weird. Somehow, she didn't feel bad. "It's too late," she replied. She liked holding that over him, dangling the taunt in front of his face. "I'm already here."

"Astra, you really should wait for us. You can't do this, you know we don't want to do this."

"I really don't care about what I should do. I'm going alone. Everyone else can group up when they get here. But Clay Parkes is mine, so don't try to stop me." Astra hung up and shoved her phone into the dirt, burying it deep so no one would hear the notifications go off. She stared at the building through the trees and sighed. She instinctively reached towards the gun holster tucked into the waistband of her jeans. "Well, here goes nothing."

43

In the Dark

Astra made her way carefully down the stairs towards the basement. She must have gone soft during her time at Torsion, where no one gave her a passing glance when she snuck around. Her footsteps sounded and felt as heavy as stones, loud thuds sounding in her ears. She knew it was her own imagination, but one misstep and she'd be dead. Or worse, she'd be compromised.

She could handle torture, she was content with dying, but being the reason her family failed, well… That was salt in the wound. She also didn't want to hear Xavier tell her *'I told you so.'* The idea irked her most of all. Astra just wanted everything gone. When Syn burned, so did her last tie to Earth. The only thing she needed to make peace with. Then, the waiting.

There was a time where she would have left everything in the dust with not so much as a glance back. Where she would spit in the face of those who even dared to call themselves her equals. She was a force of nature and now she answered to insects. If you had told that to her younger self, she would laugh and then rip your tongue out.

She was cruel.

It's what she was born for, what she fought for. Kindness existed only in the darkness, where mercy was letting insubordinates live, and justice was crushing rebellion under her heel. Blindly following in the footsteps of those who came before her, that was normalcy, it was expected. Loyalty was only owed to those who gave her life.

Ares had changed her mind, she knew that. But she couldn't stop focusing on when the switch happened. Was it in the gardens? When Arya had taught her how the dying flowers fertilized the ground and gave way to new life? Was it when she taught Griffin how to build his first gun? Was it when Jaxson comforted her when their first pet died? Astra couldn't pinpoint what it was like to be human. However, she did know that humanity was more like her than she originally thought.

How many people had listened to what they were told, only to find out that it was false? How many soldiers died for a lost cause, how many people were slaughtered in the name of doing good? Would she have been one of them? Every step Astra took deeper into the facility brought a new question to mind, a new worry. If she had experienced this in her early life, she would have requested to have part of her brain cut out and she would face the procedure with a smile.

Fighting for her own freedom felt useless at this point. Until now, she hadn't even considered that if she returned to her home planet, she'd be returning to chains. Oh, she'd be returning to praise, a recon mission fulfilled, getting by as a soldier should, returned to her rightful place, but was it worth it? Would she be happy? Was she even happy now? Did she have to be?

The more she thought about her home, the more she stopped worrying. Instead, she reminded herself of all that she was. The more she stopped worrying, the angrier she got. Rage coursed like fire through her veins. Astra moved almost on autopilot through the halls, no longer caring about the cameras, or the people they would send after her. No, she wanted them to see her now, she wanted them to look her in the face and recognize her. They wouldn't, but at least her image would be burned in their brains. And if anyone so much as thought about targeting her family, she would make sure they never saw the light of day again.

After all, she was here to destroy, and she hoped the fear would be trapped in their faces when she slit their throats. She stopped, blinking, surprised at the thought that passed through her mind. She had not been that bloodthirsty since before she landed on Earth. This was a good sign, wasn't it? She was doing the right thing, returning to her base code. She would be prepared when she returned home.

Astra found the room that her androids were waiting in, and wasted no time in hacking into the computers and corrupting their software. She even planted explosives around the bases of the display cases. She would enjoy watching the facility go down in flames. Now, she wanted to kill. She had a taste of revenge by taking control of Leroy's school. Now, she hungered for more of it.

She only had a few more hours before her siblings arrived to make sure no one escaped the premises. Astra wanted Clay Parkes dead before their plane touched down. She wanted to kill him herself. She exited the room, dead set on the staircase that would lead her to the main floor when she noticed flickering lights down one of the hallways.

She had a feeling she knew what would be at the end of the hall, so she took that route. Clay could wait. Even if he escaped, there was no place in the world he could hide where she wouldn't find him. Not when she knew what he looked like, what he was.

Some may have called it recklessness, she called it a regular work day. Outside the door, Astra noticed a key on the wall behind the desk. She grabbed it and slipped it into her pocket. She stopped at the door and looked up at the camera facing it. She stared boldly into it and mouthed the words *'you lose'* before opening the door.

That's when she found him. Locked in a cell, beaten and bloody. A cold anger in his eyes, an anger she recognized. How could she not? She had felt that pain for years, she resonated with it.

"You're Alejo, aren't you?"

He looked up at her, and behind the anger in his eyes, she saw hopelessness, betrayal, sorrow. He had thought he was safe. "What's it to you?" His voice was monotone.

Astra's mouth flickered upward for a split second. "I know you. You tried to kill my brother. Xavier."

"He was one of them." Alejo spat out bitterly. "He just wanted that tech and it can't go to people like him. He had to be destroyed."

"You're wrong, Alejo. He wasn't one of them, neither am I. He was simply retrieving what is owed. You listen to what other people tell you, and for someone with such a brilliant mind, you're so stupid. You should never follow someone blindly. Not in this world, not in any world. Everyone is corrupt, even your precious teacher."

"How would you know?" he screamed. "I gave up everything, I gave him everything! Isaac told me not to trust them." Alejo started crying, tears streaming down his face, dripping on the ground with small splashes. "The tech must be destroyed, so must Leroy's allies."

Astra stared. If Alejo wasn't one of Leroy's then he must be… Isaac's. Of course, he had apprentices too. And for a moment, her heart softened. She knew what it was like. In fact, she knew better than anyone, but she couldn't risk revealing herself, and definitely not to him of all people. How she wanted to. She wanted to confess that she was wrong, that she knew what it was like to feel slighted by her superiors, to fight for a lost cause and have it burn up around you.

Her composure wavered, something that Alejo didn't notice. His tears almost made her feel sorry for him. Almost. "We're not his allies Alejo." Astra knelt down next to the cell door. "That tech was mine. Leroy stole it. My father claimed it as his own to protect me. Do you know the name Ares? That's my father."

Recognition lit in Alejo's eyes. "That means…"

She nodded. "We are not the enemy, Alejo. In fact, we need your help."

"The past few months, I shared space with your brother and all that I learned was that he was a liar. How do I know you're telling the truth?"

She laughed, a cold sound that echoed off the wall and chilled

Alejo to the bone. He shivered involuntarily. Her eyes glinted as she spoke. "You just have to take my word for it."

"Why should I? I may hate the way I lived, but at least I know I made the choices that lead to my downfall. How can I trust you if I can't trust them?"

"Well Alejo," she whispered. "Better men than you have died because their superiors fed them lies. And with a place like you had… oh." She laughed again. "With great power, there is great responsibility, you know that quote, don't you? But while you may remember that you are responsible for the lives that you take, don't forget about the lives that you've spared." She turned on her heel, headed for the door.

Alejo banged on the door of his cell, rattling the bars. "Don't leave me here! You're supposed to be a good person!" he yelled. "If you're one of them, you have to be!"

Astra stopped, sighing. She turned around and pulled a key out of her pocket, fiddling with it. "Whoever told you that is just as much of a liar as I am. Just because I do good things, doesn't mean I'm good." She dropped the key on the floor and kicked it underneath the bars into Alejo's cell. He grabbed it, but didn't get up, still staring at her unreadable expression.

"Whether you choose to work with us is up to you. I'm only here to help myself, and that's the only reason you are still alive. This road, the life we live, will always end in sorrow. The only difference is the reward you receive, satisfaction for doing the right thing, or a miserable death. So, you can either help us or leave. However, if you try to betray us again—" the look she gave him was cold, cutting straight through him. "I will rip your heart out and feed it to my sister's dog."

44

Something is Wrong

Alyssa was used to being alone in the lab. She had been for most of the time, switching shifts with Nasra to make sure their patients were all properly cared for. This was the first time however, that she was alone since the clones had gotten better. She knew that she was not entirely behind the clones' remarkable healing, and she wanted to know what really caused it.

Every time she had voiced that to her friends, she had gotten distracted by trying to find who could've tampered with it. Now, she just wanted to see what had happened, and she'd go from there. So there she was, in the lab, with only half the lights on, carefully working a microscope to zoom in on the sample of blood she had pulled from Castor yesterday. She didn't know why she hadn't thought of looking at their blood before. Yet, according to Castor, who had asked her during his check-up, she had.

She couldn't remember ever saying that so she just laughed it off and moved on. Still, she was curious. So, she decided to check, just in case. When she finally held the results in her hands, she had an odd sense of deja vu. There was something wrong, something missing. Something her cure definitely could not do. That revelation confused and excited her, but it also made her skin prickle. It meant that someone had gotten into the quarantine where the clones were and tampered with the cure. It meant that someone was working in the shadows, whether against her or with her, she had no clue.

Alyssa messaged Nasra first, meeting the older girl in the hallway just outside the lab. There, Alyssa whispered all her worries into Nasra's ear, including her knowledge that this, whatever it was, was not in the medicine. Nasra confirmed that when she went through the results as well.

"I don't know what to tell you Alyssa, I mean, this should be good."

Alyssa took the folder from her. "I know. It just feels too good to be true, given our track record. I can't help but think I've been here before, doing this same thing. It's weird. Everything seems to be going wrong, and the second we notice, it's like it becomes a background thought."

"It certainly is weird," Nasra mused. It was early for her, she was still in her pajamas, a grey t-shirt and some soft pants with dogs on them. Despite that, her hair had been pulled up into the same perfect, slicked back bun, with only a few strands falling out, due to her running through the halls. "I have no idea, but I'm sure we can look into it. Do you want to ask Mary and Elena?"

Alyssa nodded. "Zola, Katya, and Henry too. Get the whole gang together. Well, as much of it as possible. Aiken is busy and Astra is… somewhere."

"Okay, how about we all meet in the cafeteria in 15 minutes? We can discuss over breakfast? I haven't even brushed my teeth yet so I want to go back to my dorm."

"Sounds good." Alyssa grabbed her sweater and tucked the folder under her arm. "I'll see you there."

* * * * * * * * *

They gathered at one of the corner tables in the cafeteria. It was still quiet, the sun having just risen a few hours ago. With it being a weekend, not many people were awake. The staff had just started to set everything up, so they were lucky they were able to grab food. Most of them were still in pajamas, except Alyssa and Henry, who were both dressed and seemed the most awake.

Alyssa sipped on her coffee, idly stabbing at the waffle she had grabbed from the buffet. "So…"

Mary groaned and rubbed her eyes. "Why'd you have to call a meeting this early?" she whined. "The sun is barely up. I should be resting, I have a paper coming up, and a meeting with my thesis committee later."

"You'll be fine," Alyssa reassured her.

"I can have them move it back," Zola suggested. "I'm sure they wouldn't mind."

"And have the acting dean stand up for me? No thank you, I'll suffer like any regular person does," Mary said.

"Really?"

She sighed. "No. I'm just joking. Please do that, I'm exhausted."

Zola laughed. "Okay. If we had Aiken, I would say ask him about his caffeine pills, but he's off doing who knows what so I think it's best not to bother him."

Mary sighed and dropped her head onto the table. "Would any of you mind if I took a nap right now?"

Alyssa flicked her in the side of the head. "Yes. We need your input. Henry, do you have your notes from back when we talked?"

Henry nodded. "So, I've talked to a couple of other students, and they also report having issues with forgetting things. Not nearly as frequently as us, but it's still weird."

"I agree," Nasra mused. "I haven't had that many issues, but there are instances where I'll forget I've said things to the clones, or I just don't remember things I've done. Especially when it comes to working with the really sick ones, Castor and William. They didn't recover until several days after the cure was administered, meaning there was a window for someone to get in and tamper with them, but I don't remember those days."

"There are days where I forget what I'm working on," Elena said. "And even though I've been told what is happening with the clones, I find myself not knowing the timeline, or really anything important. I basically only remember interacting with Aiken and Astra. Everything else, especially conversations with Nasra and Alyssa, where I remember meeting with them, I don't remember what we were talking about."

"Oh, I looked through the teacher list and the cameras and none of them had access to the security system so they're all out. Most of the students as well. In fact, I think only us and the clones have access," Zola added.

"I know something is wrong with my telescope, I just know. I haven't been able to figure it out, but I'm going to check it out later today," Katya added.

"Do you want help?" Henry asked.

"Sure."

"Cool."

"Can we get back to the medicine problem? I have the results here," Alyssa said. "And…" She set a folder on the table. "I grabbed this from downstairs, it's the last trial folder from Leroy back when we first worked here, along with all the tests we ran when the clones first awoke. I wanted to see how it correlated to what was going on with Castor's blood samples."

"Oh good idea," Nasra said.

She opened the file. "Here's the blood sample results from the initial tests. Everything is normal. Here's where it went downhill, and here's where they stabilized. Every single one who got sick now has a new strand of DNA that doesn't even look human. It could be animal DNA, but I've got to do a test on it."

Katya gasped. "Oh, what if it's not human or animal," she said excitedly. "What if it's extraterrestrial?"

"Not everything is about aliens Katya," Henry said, fake annoyed.

Katya stuck her tongue out at him. "Well, when we find out aliens exist, you owe me twenty dollars."

"Well, whatever it is, based off what Alyssa showed me earlier, the DNA was not added during a time when I gave them a shot, so whoever it was did so after, and either did it without the clones knowing, or erased their memories as well," Nasra said.

"Wow." Zola leaned over to look at the file, then noticed something sticking out near the back. She grabbed it. It was a photo. "Huh. This is the androids back when Leroy started the experiment." She looked over the line of androids. She knew all of them by name, even down to the staff members on either side of the dean. She paused, and frowned, pointing to a dark haired boy near the end of the line. "Wait a second, who's that?" she asked. "Everyone else I recognize, those are our androids and former staff, but I've never seen him. At least, I don't remember seeing him."

Henry leaned over her shoulder. "I—I feel like I know him but I don't know where from or who he is."

Zola sighed. "That is strange."

"Well, I guess it's settled. Something is weird here," Katya said.

"We've established that," Alyssa said. "We just have to figure out who did it, and right now, I think our only options are the two people who aren't here right now."

"Aiken and Astra," Zola said grimly. "That is not going to be a fun conversation."

45

Meet the Family

Alejo stood in the center of a circle made of the Duke siblings, fidgeting nervously with his fingernails. He was used to being higher up in the food chain, so he was not scared of many things. However, having a group of former child assassins who had just burned down his older workplace surrounding him was something he never thought would happen. That feeling of uncertainty consumed him.

There were a lot of faces. Alejo could barely remember all of their names as Xavier introduced him. It made his head spin. After all, he was still reeling from the aftermath of what just happened. It was quick. Astra had left him in his cell and by the time he had plucked up the courage to unlock it, she was nowhere to be seen. He followed the trail of bodies she left behind, but found no sign of her. Eventually, Alejo settled for wandering the halls alone.

He ran into Xavier along the way, planting explosives with a blonde girl who introduced herself as Cassidy.

He helped them knock out security guards, desperate to help the only people he had ever met that were willing to destroy the facility. He had waited too long for that. Alejo only hoped that Astra wasn't lying to him when she said it was her tech they were destroying. They were destroying everything, not even bothering to take notes or files from the facility. When Xavier said that, Alejo got the sense of confusion and stress from him too. Honestly, everything was a blur for him. He was dragged along through the hallways with only a vague explanation of what was happening.

When they were all outside, one of the boys, a teenager with jet black hair and a scar on the side of his right hand, set off the explosives. There, Alejo was met with the sight of Astra with a gun in hand, her neck and face splattered in blood. Xavier, and a man with neon green hair whose name he didn't remember didn't hesitate to start yelling at her.

Alejo tuned it out. It wasn't his place to get involved, and he wasn't exactly all there anyway. It wasn't until he was on the plane that he got an answer. He was surprised to see Isaac standing near the front of the plane as he came in. The siblings pushed past him and Isaac told him Astra had killed Clay Parkes and the guards in his office. Apparently, none of the siblings were particularly happy with her. He learned their names as he went, but none of them really stuck. Then, Astra disappeared to the back to clean the blood off of her and change clothes, and Alejo ended up in the circle.

None of the siblings really trusted him; he could tell from the looks on their faces. At most, they tolerated him. Alejo understood. He didn't expect them to like him. Eventually Astra appeared again and the eyes were off him. He breathed a sigh of relief and flopped into an empty seat. Isaac brought him a wrapped sandwich and a bottle of water and took the seat next to him.

"Stressed?" Isaac asked.

Alejo nodded. "What about you?"

Isaac shrugged. "I don't really get stressed. I'm more worried about what's going to happen with Astra and her siblings. I don't know much about them, Astra didn't tell me, but my guess is she's in a lot of trouble."

Isaac kept him company for the rest of the flight, asking questions about how he was doing, and eventually moving on to talking about himself. Alejo learned that Isaac was a clone, originally an android created by Leroy Parkes, named for his brother, and modeled off of Astra's work. Which explained what Xavier was doing at Syn in the first place and why the family showed up to blow everything up. Alejo wasn't sure why the siblings were mad that Astra had taken the time to murder Clay when they were going to destroy the facility and everyone inside anyway. Isaac said it had something to do with Astra's anger issues and the family not wanting to actually personally assassinate people anymore.

Alejo wasn't sure what that meant. It seemed very counter-productive to kill people at all if they were trying to escape it. He wasn't about to voice that opinion though. He didn't really know these people, and whatever he thought he knew about Xavier had been thrown out the window before they got on the plane. Alejo decided that out of all of them, he trusted Isaac the most. The boy was open and honest with everything; at least, that was what his face and body language said.

When they finally arrived at the Duke family mansion, Astra didn't even let him look at the building for long. She forced him and Isaac into the backseat of the closest car, and got in the passenger side. The instructions she gave him on what would happen when they got there sounded more like incomprehensible noises than words. Xavier drove them, and soon, the house was out of sight. Alejo leaned his head against the window, and promptly fell asleep.

* * * * * * * *

Tessa watched the car disappear from sight then turned to go inside. She pushed the door open and sighed in relief. She took a deep breath. It was good to be home. The rest of her siblings, minus Xavier and Astra, filed in behind her, with Yvette being the one to close the door. It was strange. The lot of them had not been under the same roof in ages. She wished that Xavier and Astra would come inside, but the two had insisted on leaving immediately, Astra wanted Alejo at Torsion so she could keep an eye on him.

Tessa didn't know what she expected. She could have argued that Alejo would be safer with them, in their house, but she didn't have the chance. Besides, Astra had a tendency not to listen when she had her mind set on something. Tessa followed Cassidy into the kitchen. She set her bag down on the counter and sat down on one of the stools. She rested her head against the cool marble of the counter top.

264

"You good?" Cassidy questioned.

"Yes," Tessa replied, voice muffled by the stone. "Just tired. And worried."

Cassidy chuckled. Tessa felt her pat the top of her head. "I know you're worried, but Xavier's with Astra and I'm sure everything will turn out fine."

Tessa groaned. "I know, I just don't like, understand what happened. I mean, we don't even know why she did it, Jaxson and Xavier were too busy criticizing her for it."

Cassidy shuffled around the kitchen. The sounds of cabinets and the fridge opening made Tessa's head hurt. "I know Tess, but I'm sure Xavier has it handled."

Tessa finally looked up. "I can't help thinking about it."

"I know. Do you want a sandwich?" Cassidy turned and yelled out into the hallway. "Do any of you want sandwiches?" A chorus of affirmatives sounded from the lobby where Tessa was sure everyone was removing their shoes and flopping down on the staircase. Cassidy smiled. "You?"

Tessa nodded. "Sure. Turkey please."

Cassidy opened the fridge. "Yeah no, we've got peanut butter and jelly."

"Okay, that works too."

Cassidy laughed and started putting sandwiches together. "Do you think anything will help you not focus on what Astra's doing right now?"

Tessa shrugged. "No clue."

"There's got to be something. Maybe you want to play chess or something?"

Tessa didn't get the chance to respond because Yvette entered the room.

"What are you talking about?" she asked. Yvette had lost most of her hearing during an explosion about seven years ago, and even though she had a hearing aid, she preferred signing. It was a good habit, and the rest of the siblings quickly picked up on it. It was useful in the field, and they could hold conversations whenever their parents weren't looking.

"Astra," Tessa signed as she spoke. "She's not been herself and I'm worried."

Yvette nodded. "Me too."

Yvette had never been quiet until she stopped being able to hear. Then, it was like she was a shadow in the hallways. Sure, she voiced her opinions and thoughts, but rarely aloud, since she couldn't hear well without hearing aids. When she wasn't working, Yvette spent most of her time learning different dialects of sign language. Sometimes, Tessa had to coach her to speak because Yvette was so used to signing. She didn't want to leave Cassidy out of the conversation while she had her back turned making sandwiches.

"What do you think?" she prompted.

Yvette shrugged. "I don't think we should worry too much. Astra may be stubborn, but she always returns to us, no matter how angry she gets. She'll come home, I guarantee."

Tessa smiled. "Thanks, that's comforting."

Yvette moved to hug Tessa. "Have faith, Tess."

Cassidy placed three plates on the counter. "Yvette is right, Astra's done this before. I think Xavier's got it. Now eat up. I don't want my hard work to go to waste. Guys! Food!"

Tessa laughed. "It's just sandwiches, Cass."

Cassidy gave Tessa a scathing glare. "I put my heart into this, Tessa. Be nice."

Yvette giggled and started eating. "She's right, Cassidy's food is made with love," she signed.

Tessa rolled her eyes. She didn't get the chance to quip back because the sound of feet in the hall cut her off. Jaxson, Griffin, and Zale entered the kitchen quickly, and Tessa immediately picked up her sandwich and took a bite out of it. If she didn't eat quickly, there wouldn't be a sandwich left for her to eat.

267

46

Apprentice

Astra tapped her foot against the floor impatiently. She didn't know enough about Alejo to know if he was the chronically late type. However, he was late today, and that annoyed her. She glared at the door in front of her. Zola had decided the best idea would be to put Alejo in an empty dorm room, meant for a teaching position they never filled. Astra had told her he was going to join their research team, and while she didn't seem suspicious of it, she had coded it into her brain for good measure. When he finally opened the door, Astra bit back the urge to snap at him.

"Did you sleep well?" she asked.

He nodded. "I did, thank you."

Astra returned the gesture. "No problem. Come on, we have a lot of ground to cover today." She turned on her heel, not even bothering to make sure that he was following her. "Torsion covers a large chunk of land, around 36 acres, 40 if you include the main building and surrounding small ones, like the greenhouses. The library is connected to the main building, but is 21 stories high. The rest of the school has only 11 floors. It allows us to keep everything in one space. There is a courtyard in the middle of the school, and in the front, but the brunt of the gardens are surrounding the school. There's a surprisingly large amount of forest space that we own."

Alejo moved to walk next to Astra. "Why is it so big?"

Astra shrugged. "Parkes had a lot of money. He also wanted to hide the tunnels below the school."

Alejo's mouth fell open. "There's tunnels under the school?"

Astra nodded. "Yes. Many. Most of them we closed off, but some are still open. Very few students know about it, but I and some of my friends use them."

"Interesting."

Astra nodded again. "Yes. Also, speaking of my friends, you'll meet them today. I think you'll take special interest in the clones, you know, based on what you worked with back with the Parkes family, and if you ever want to know what they were really meant to be like, you can always come find me. I think I have my old notes somewhere, and even if I don't, I've got them memorized."

"How'd it feel?" Alejo asked.

"How'd what feel?"

"Having your tech stolen? Claimed as someone else's, what was that like?"

Astra's face fell, and if she wasn't looking ahead, Alejo probably would have melted in front of her. If looks could kill, the hallway would have been destroyed. "Awful," she said. "Especially since they did the one thing I never wanted those androids to be used for. It's upsetting, watching everything you worked for be wiped out because someone decided they were entitled to it. I guess that's why I wanted to destroy everything they built."

"And why did you kill Clay yourself?" The question was out before Alejo realized, and Astra answered before he could apologize.

"Because I could. Just because he wasn't responsible directly, doesn't mean he's not to blame. He still tried to carry on Leroy's work, and I have a responsibility to deal with everyone who ever worked for or idolized that man." There was a certain sadness in her voice as she ended the sentence. Alejo didn't know what it was.

"So you shot him?"

"Shot and dismembered for good measure. I used to do that to any of my tech that I wasn't satisfied with, so it has a kind of irony to it."

Alejo's mouth fell open again. He closed it quickly, not wanting her to identify his shock. "Was it worth it? Like, are you happy now that you've killed him?"

Astra pressed her lips together in a thin line before she spoke. "No."

She didn't elaborate, and instead moved on to explaining more history about the school and the way that it was set up. Students passed them in the halls, and if they were interested in what Astra was saying, they didn't show it.

Once the two had finished walking around the inside of the school, Astra took him outside, through both courtyards, and into the back gardens. By then, it was already noon, and Alejo was hungry, but he didn't tell her. He was worried that she was already upset for the questions he had asked, and he didn't want to push. After about 20 minutes of Astra talking about the grounds and the smaller buildings, the two finally returned inside.

Alejo was grateful for the fact that the cafeteria food was completely free. His old school did not do that.

After they got their food, Astra led him to a table near the side, next to a pillar, where a group was already waiting for them. Alejo recognized both Xavier and Isaac, but the rest were unfamiliar faces, staring at him with varying levels of curiosity.

"Everyone, this is Alejo Seguar. He will be joining us for the time being. Alejo, this is Zola, Mary, Alyssa, Katya, Elena, Aiken, Nasra, Henry, Castor, Eric, William, Nicole, Cassian, Morgan, David, and Willow. You of course, already know Xavier and Isaac." Astra pointed out everyone as she rattled their names off, but he was sure he was going to have to ask for their names again.

Conversation resumed, and Alejo just sat and listened. He realized this was probably how Xavier felt when he introduced him to his friends at Syn. Except this was worse because he had to remember more names. He sighed and stabbed at his food. This was going to be a long day.

Astra stared at Alejo as he ate, before deciding that he wasn't going to do anything and turning to her own food.

"So what's his deal?" Aiken whispered.

"He used to work for Clay Parkes and was an apprentice for Leroy. Apparently he was really good at it. That's what Xavier said anyway. He said he didn't really like Clay but he tolerated him because of the family business and everything." Astra sighed. "I don't know much so if you're really curious, you should ask him."

Aiken's face lit up. "I think that would be interesting."

"Mhm. Anyway, what's been happening since I was gone?"

Aiken shrugged. "Not much. I've still been working on the notes. There's a lot I haven't covered, but I think I'm nearing the end of the relevant work. Oh, and Katya seems to think there's something weird going on with the telescope so they've been looking into that."

"What?" Astra's head snapped up and she stared at him. Aiken didn't look away from Alejo.

"You're staring," Astra said. "Pay attention. What were they doing?"

Aiken tore his eyes away from Alejo and looked at Astra. "I don't really know. Just that Katya thinks there's something wrong with the telescope and everyone is helping her. Oh, and Alyssa's looking at her medicine because Castor said that she said she was going to, but she didn't remember, and I don't know what's going on with that, but she said something weird was going on with the clones."

Astra continued to stare at him. If Aiken was better at making eye contact, he would have noticed her shocked expression. Luckily, he didn't, and Astra was able to get her emotions under control. She looked down at her plate. "Huh, I'll have to check in with them about that, see if I can help."

Aiken turned to his food. "Yeah, you do that," he mumbled.

Astra ate quickly, and then instructed Xavier to keep an eye on Alejo. She ran to her dorm and started searching through the video feed and her tracking notes to see what she had missed while she was gone. She groaned. It almost wasn't worth it to deal with all of this when she was leaving. Almost. She should have checked when she was adding Isaac back in earlier, but she was so busy she decided not to.

Astra got to work removing memories and coding new thoughts into people's brains. She had only had a little bit of time to do the most pressing parts earlier, now all she had to do was tie up loose ends. Astra paused over a conversation between Elena and Katya. It wasn't technically that bad. Katya needed the encouragement, and if it proved to be problematic, she'd just erase it. Besides, Katya's suspicions were with the telescope, and she had already covered her tracks on the computer. It wasn't pressing, so she moved on.

By the time she was done, several hours had passed. She glanced at the clock on her desk. It was past dinner time. She had just started to get up when there was a knock on her door. Astra frowned. She opened it to reveal Xavier, who was standing there holding a plastic container and a set of utensils.

"Brought you food, I thought you might be hungry." He pushed past her into her dorm. "So, this is your room here? It's nice. Similar to what you've got back home, I guess some things never change, do they?"

Astra closed the door. "No, I like to keep things simple."

Xavier chuckled, turning around in a circle to take in the view. "Only thing you're missing is the scribbles on the walls."

Astra rolled her eyes. "Don't remind me." She took the food from him. "Thank you, you saved me a trip downstairs, I was just about to go get food." She sat down and started eating.

Xavier sat down on the bed next to her. "What was so important that you disappeared? You were gone for a while, and I had to deal with all of your friends. They asked me a lot of questions. Anyway, I just came to say goodbye since I'm about to head home."

"Just work. I have several things to finish up before I leave."

Xavier nodded. "Oh, right."

Astra put the container down in her lap and turned to face Xavier. "Look. It's not like I really like having to leave. But I already have confirmation that the ship is on its way. It's settled."

"And there's absolutely no way that you can tell them no when they get here?"

"I could, but that seems like a waste of resources."

Xavier sighed. "I just want you to be sure that you're making the right decision."

Astra pressed her lips together in a thin line. "I know. I know you're worried and you're going to miss me, but what's done is done, and you can't change it."

"You're going to think about it though, right?"

Astra sighed. "Fine. I'll think about it."

Xavier grinned. "Perfect. I'll see you later Astra. Don't forget to say goodbye to everyone else."

"I won't, I promise."

Then Xavier was gone, and Astra was left with her thoughts, a sinking feeling of unease, and a container full of cold food.

* * * * * * * * *

Xavier stood on the balcony, staring out the long driveway leading up to their front door. Today was the last time that he would see most of his siblings for a while. Part of the reformation included removing contacts from their network, sometimes by force. He wasn't particularly excited about the idea of having to kill more people, but it wasn't his hands getting dirty, and he didn't have a choice. He was surprised that Yvette would agree to it though. She was adamant that she wouldn't kill anyone, just hurt them if they didn't agree with her. Xavier wasn't sure that would work out, but he wasn't interested in arguing with her. She could always call for backup if it got too out of hand.

Griffin and Zale had left already, taking a plane to the middle of nowhere in Asia to meet with some people about taking their weapons off the market. Cassidy would also leave and go to Russia. Jaxson chose South America as the first place he'd visit, and then he was off to the Middle East. Yvette took the entirety of Africa. There were not that many people that they worked with there, so it worked out.

Tessa was the only one who decided to stay. She would help him with the meetings he had to do and send out letters to clients in the area about updated policies. They had also taken on new clients. Xavier had spent weeks writing up the contracts of their diplomatic and guard services. Then there was the problem of actually meeting with their current clients. He had put off meeting with those closest to their mansion for a long time. Everyone he had since met with were from Europe or Australia, and he was not looking forward to having to host those in the nearby city. That was like begging to have someone break in and attempt to kill him.

Some had taken the news of the loss of certain services very well. Some hadn't, and Xavier didn't like being yelled at. Nothing was going to make him change the policies, so he found it all to be a waste of time. The people he was supposed to be meeting with would be arriving later that afternoon, so Xavier forced himself to push those thoughts out of his mind. Instead, he focused on his siblings, and the time he had left with them.

47

Underground

Xavier didn't want to say goodbye. He hated seeing everyone go and not being able to go with them. He had been benched a long time ago. Someone had to take care of the house, and that responsibility had fallen to him after a long argument with Jaxson.

Xavier wasn't mad at him; he couldn't be. Jaxson loved traveling more than Xavier hated being cooped up in the house. He couldn't take that away from him. Astra wasn't interested in the family business, and Cassidy didn't have as much experience. Plus, neither of them really liked to take care of the maintenance. At most, the two sisters would engage with the staff. Every single one of his siblings knew the names and occupations of every member of the staff by heart. It was common courtesy, after all.

Xavier finally turned away and walked back into the house. He wanted to spend some time with Cassidy and Yvette before they left. He found them in the living room. No surprise there. Yvette was sitting at the piano, idly playing a tune he didn't know. Cassidy was curled up on the couch with a book. He recognized it immediately. Dante's Inferno. He didn't know why she liked the book, but it was one of her favorites. Tessa was also there, sitting on the rug with the family's dog: a large Great Dane with a pitch black coat and white paws. Her name was Ursa, after the constellations. Little She-Bear was what it meant, though Ursa was far from little.

Tessa was the only one who looked up when Xavier entered, smiling at him as she rubbed Ursa's ears. The dog's mouth was open, long tongue spilling out as she lounged against Tessa's side. "What's up X?" Tessa asked.

Xavier plopped down on the carpet next to her and ran his fingers through Ursa's fur. "Not much. Just wanted to see those two before they left."

Cassidy acknowledged the statement with a grunt, eyes not leaving her book. Yvette stopped playing and turned around. "Don't worry," she said. "We'll be back before you know it."

Xavier sighed. "I know. I'm just going to be so bored in this house without you. At least Astra kept me on my toes with her pop quizzes."

Tessa frowned. "You won't be bored."

"What?"

"You have like 10 conference meetings split between in person and over the phone. You have clients to review, weapons to reclaim, things to do. You'll probably be so busy that you won't notice when they return."

Xavier groaned and fell back against the carpet, his head narrowly missing the brick surrounding the fireplace. "I do not want to do that."

"Mmm, too bad. It's your job."

Xavier sighed. "I know it's my job. I just hate doing it."

Yvette poked Xavier's cheek to get his attention. "You'll do fine," she signed faster than she spoke. "It's not that bad. It's less work than we have to do."

Xavier nodded. "Thanks," he said. "Not very comforting, but I appreciate it."

"Maybe you just don't like responsibility," Cassidy said from the couch, still not looking up from her book.

"I'm responsible!" Xavier indignantly half-yelled.

"That's not what I said. I said you don't like responsibility, not that you're not responsible."

"What's the difference?"

Cassidy rolled her eyes. "You hate the job because you don't like being in charge of other people, because usually you still have someone above you. Doesn't mean you can't do it, you're just not used to it."

Xavier frowned. "Huh."

Cassidy gave him a quick smile and devoted her attention back to her book.

Xavier glanced at Tessa. "Is she right?" Tessa nodded. Xavier sighed. "Ugh. Well, I don't know what I'm going to do about that."

Yvette shrugged. "You don't really have to do anything about it. It's good to just acknowledge it. You'll get used to it as time goes on."

"I suppose you're right."

"We usually are. That's the fun part of being related to spies. We notice everything about each other, since most of the time, you won't recognize it in yourself." Yvette smiled. "It's not easy, we know. Anything important is difficult, it's worth working for. You'll grow, and figure it out. You'll get insight and encouragement from others. Speaking of which, the binders you found that Father left for us, did you read yours?"

Xavier paused. He had forgotten about them. "Not yet. I haven't had the time."

"Maybe you should," Yvette signed. "There was a letter in mine, there might be a letter in yours. Just read it."

Xavier nodded. "I'll get around to it eventually. There's just a lot I have to do, and as you said, get used to."

Yvette grabbed his hand and squeezed it. "You'll do well, I'm sure of it."

Xavier smiled. "Thank you," he signed.

The moment was cut short by the sound of Cassidy's phone going off. She groaned and closed her book. "It's time, Yvette."

She looked up. "Okay." Yvette dropped Xavier's hand and hugged him. "See you soon," she said. "Bye Ursa." She rubbed the dog's back and kissed her on the snout. Then, she followed Cassidy out of the room.

"Bye," Xavier and Tessa said, in sync. When they were gone, Xavier looked down at his hands. "I don't want to do this Tessa. I want to think we can change, but can they?"

Tessa hummed. "It's not up to them. They will, or they won't and we stop working with them." She looked at her watch. "I think they might already be here. Let me check with the staff."

Xavier let her go without question. When she returned, she had a binder in her hands. Xavier frowned. "What'd you bring that here for?"

Tessa kneeled down. "I thought it might be useful for you to go through it before you meet with the clients. Most of them are here, so I've had them directed to the conference room."

Xavier took the binder from her. "Thank you." He started leafing through it, and as he did so, he wanted to cry. Like Astra's, his binder had clippings of his accomplishments, notes on his performances and hobbies, pictures, messages from his parents, blueprints, and more. Things he had made and done, words of encouragement. Xavier paused at one of the sections. It was banking information. He frowned, skimming the papers there. There was no way. Yet it was true. Xavier was holding information to an account in his name that held millions of dollars. A note was attached to the last page.

Xavier, this is yours. Your inheritance. Your siblings have their own share, so don't worry. It was split equally between you. There are also the family accounts, designated for maintaining the house. I trust you will take good care of our finances. Love, Mom.

"Wow," he whispered. He didn't really have enough time to finish it all, so he tucked the binder under his arm and got to his feet. "Tessa," he called, getting her attention. "Thank you. I'm not sure what I would've done without this."

She smiled. "I figured. Are you ready?"

He nodded. The two walked together down the hall in silence. Xavier took it all in, the familiar hardwood flooring, the new lights he had installed last month, the artwork on the walls, all either made or purchased by his mother, excepting some smaller pieces done by his sisters. This was his, and he had to take care of it.

Finally, Xavier stood before the conference room door. He hesitated, once again unsure of himself. He reached out for the handle, then pulled back. "Are you sure you're not able to come in with me? I mean, if it's a question of authority, I'm in charge, and I can excuse you—"

Tessa shook her head, cutting him off. "No. That's not how this works."

Xavier huffed. "Why not? You're way more diplomatic than I am, it should be you in there, not me."

Tessa rolled her eyes. "You can't run from this Xavier, you chose it, like it or not. When Jaxson offered, you took it, because you knew you had to. No one is better suited for this job, despite your short-comings. No one else can do it like you. And you have to face it by yourself. So get in there. Make our parents proud."

Xavier sighed and reached for the door handle again. "Fine."

"Ah, ah, ah. Wait."

Xavier frowned. "What?"

Tessa looked at him pointedly. "Don't zone out. Pay attention. Take notes, make the clients feel appreciated. They're new to this, same as you. They have to get used to the change, and we have to explain what we're doing and why we're doing it. You cannot lose your temper."

"Okay."

"Promise to behave?"

Xavier nodded. "I promise."

Tessa smiled. Xavier rolled his eyes and shook his head, then opened the door to the conference room.

Teacher

Astra stood in the cafeteria, back to the wall as she watched everyone eat. There were not many people in there at this hour, but those who were there were the subject of her observation. She wasn't exactly sure why she liked observing the students in person when she could do it from the safety of her dorm on her computer, but she liked being there. Along with the students were a handful of teachers, some of whom had papers next to them that they graded as they ate.

One in particular caught her eye. The woman was tall, graceful, with long black hair that fell to her waist. She had thin fingers with sharp nails, and while she seemed confident, she looked a little out of place. Astra grinned. She could recognize those mannerisms anywhere. They were obvious.

"Etaklen," she said, as soon as she was within earshot. The teacher froze and slowly turned around. Her eyes brightened when she saw Astra.

"Etaklen vede," she responded. "Come, sister, sit."

Astra smiled. "Thank you. What is your name? I don't recognize you from the files."

"Seren. And you must be Astra?"

"That is correct."

Seren nodded. "It is a good name."

"Similar to yours."

Seren smiled wider. "I wonder just how many ways the humans have to say stars that came from us."

Astra shrugged. "Many thousands of words I would say. All are common names on our planet. Not that there is much meaning behind them for us. They're just names."

Seren nodded. "So what brings you here, sister?"

"I've been on recon for almost a century. I'm waiting for a return ship, I used mine for parts, then my mentor died so I was trapped."

"Interesting. I have been here for a little less than 20 years. Though, I crashed."

"I'm sorry to hear that."

"Don't be!" Seren waved her hand. "I will rebuild. Though, at this moment, I am not sure I would want to return home."

Astra frowned. "Why?"

"Did you not know? War has broken out among the territories, but it is worse than usual. We fear revolution. I am not a soldier. I do not want to be there should we have to truly fight."

Astra looked down at her hands. "I am, though. I believe it would be best if I went home. I guess this is good timing for me to call for help."

Seren shrugged. "Let that be your prerogative. I hate wars."

"How many have you seen?"

"Many. Hundreds. Not as bad as this one though. It keeps getting worse."

Astra stared at her. "Is home still standing?"

Seren scoffed. "Of course. Ara would not fall even if a thousand wars battered its surface. We are still strong, sister."

Astra smiled. "That's good to hear. So, how'd you even learn about Torsion?"

"Well, I was found by Ares as you were also. I did not ever work for him, but he helped me settle in. I used to work at a small school in America, doing recon on the government there. When I heard that you, Ares's pupil, were in need of assistance, I applied. My name is recorded in Ares's records, so it was easy for me to be pushed to the front."

"Well, I am glad you are here. And thank you for telling me of the war. I saw stars disappearing, but I did not know what it meant."

Seren's eyes grew softer, sadder. "It is unfortunate to hear, to know that so many of our brothers and sisters are dying out there. I hope that this is over quickly."

"As do I." Astra looked down at her hands. "It is good to have one of my own here. It has been a while since I've seen any of my people. It is nice to know that I am no longer alone here."

Seren cocked her head to the side. "You were never alone. You had Ares, did you not?"

Astra smiled softly. "Yes, and no. I worked with him, yes, and he was a good mentor. But he was never at the school, and he died a few years ago."

Seren's face showed shock. "Ares is dead? Oh, I did not know, I am sorry. Have you mourned him?"

Astra nodded. "I mourned for him traditionally for myself, and then again for Caliste."

"Caliste?"

"Ares's wife."

"Ares had a wife?"

Astra nodded. "Yes. She was kind, and she taught me so much about humanity. She died a few years before Ares did, but it seemed fitting to do it for her anyway."

Seren looked shocked to hear what Astra had to say. "Interesting," she mused. "I knew Ares was on probation for something, but I had no idea that it was for marrying a human."

Astra shrugged. "Personally, I think it was a stupid thing for the council to do. I mean, Ares loved Earth, but he also had a daughter, and she never had the chance to see our home."

"He had a daughter too?"

"Yes, Arya. She is also dead. An accident."

"Oh." Seren's face was full of grief. Astra found it strange. This was sorrow for people that the woman was not close to. Two of which she had never met, and yet, she was sad for them.

It was a while before Seren spoke. "Astra, I did not mourn for

Ares. It is customary that I should. Will you come with me?"

Astra raised an eyebrow. She did not expect that. "Are you sure?"

"Yes. It is not something I should do alone. Plus, I think you should do it again. We are meant to do things as a community, right? And you had no one to complete the ritual with?"

Astra shook her head. "No, I did it alone."

"It's settled then. You will come with me."

Astra nodded. "Very well. We can do it in the gardens tonight." She got up. "Thank you, sister. I will meet you in the courtyard at nine p.m."

Seren nodded as well. "Good. I look forward to it."

Astra walked back to her dorm in silence, pondering the encounter. She was surprised at how easy being honest was. Of course, Seren was another Ara'cel, and they were not the kind to keep secrets. However, she had been keeping secrets for so long. Everything spilled out of her like a dam being broken. She couldn't say that she was upset at that happening. She had not truly trusted someone for a long time.

When she got back to her room, Astra gathered the things that she would need to complete the mourning ritual with Seren. It consisted of a few flowers, some water, dirt from their planet, a thin blade, and pure liquid silver. She would also need some of her own blood, though she would deal with that later. The final thing she needed was a traditional outfit. She didn't have it with her, most of her traditional clothes and uniforms were back on her planet. The closest thing she had was something she had thrown together a few years ago for Ares's funeral. Astra had embroidered it herself, just so it felt more formal.

She had to dig to the bottom of her closet to find it: a dress she had sewn herself. It was a gradient, white at the top transitioning to a deep blue-black. She had embroidered stars, flowers, and other planets in their home system along the skirt bottom, as well as small crystals, so it shimmered in the moonlight. When she put it on, it fell a few inches above her feet.

Wearing it felt bittersweet. It was not as beautiful as her home planet's seamstresses could have made it, but she had put her heart into it. It was the first time she had felt close to her planet's culture in nearly 100 years. She waited by her window until night fell and then coded instructions for students to return to their rooms. She didn't want anyone or anything to disturb them that evening.

Seren was waiting for her when Astra entered the courtyard. She was wearing a dress that was so black, it seemed to absorb all the light around her. The only pops of color on it were rays of orange, white, and purple, representative of the explosion of death. She was holding a blanket as well, draped over her hands so Astra couldn't see what she was holding.

Seren tilted her head in greeting. "Etaklen, Astra Ara'cel.

Astra did the same. "Etaklen vede, Seren Ara'cel. Shall we?" She tilted her head towards the garden.

"You lead."

Astra walked through the courtyard, through the back entry, and into the gardens, headed towards her favorite spot. She dropped to her knees in the grass, and Seren did the same beside her.

"Why did you choose this spot?" Seren questioned.

"I like it," Astra answered. "Also, the moon will hit overhead soon. It will make this more familiar."

Seren smiled softly. "You put a lot of thought into this. Ares must have meant a lot to you."

Astra nodded. "He was the only mentor I ever had that was consistent. I switched teachers many times back home. Ares pushed me. They did not."

"It is good to have a teacher who is challenging."

"Mhm." Astra stared ahead in silence for a minute then turned to Seren. "Let us begin."

They set everything up in silence, then transitioned to speaking in their native language. The words felt heavy on Astra's tongue, not just because of lack of use, but because of sadness. She did not want to re-live her father's death. Father. She had no equivalent word for that in her language. Nor one for mother, or family. Just orakki. Union, or unity. There was a word for teacher, but using it felt wrong. It did not mean what she wanted it to mean.

The ritual went on for over an hour, but Astra's heart was not in it. She thought that having Seren there would make her feel better about re-doing the ritual. It did not. She stuttered through speaking. By the time they had reached the closing words, Astra was crying silently. Seren didn't criticize her, which Astra was thankful for. Astra poured the liquid silver out over the dirt and whispered her goodbyes to the moon. When the ritual was over, Seren left, and Astra stayed in the grass. For the first time, she wished that her people had memorials, or even mock graves for those who died. Maybe that would have made it easier.

49

Alien Activity

"So." Zola tapped her pen on the table, staring down at the papers in front of her. "What do you think of the new teachers? Do we need to do anything, is everything going well, what are your thoughts?"

Astra stared at her. The continued eye contact would have made Zola uncomfortable if it was anyone else, but it was Astra, and Astra was always like this. "I think most of them are doing well, considering. Not many were prepared for the sheer amount of young geniuses they had in their classrooms, but they've adjusted to accommodate for that. The clones have reported liking them, which I think is a plus."

"That's good," Zola mused. "Do you think any of them need to go under review?"

Astra shook her head. "There have been no complaints about misconduct, and besides, we should consider firing people as a last resort. We need them to work, and if I have to go into a classroom and teach, I will fake my death and run away."

Zola laughed. "Okay, I'll keep that in mind. Who's doing the best so far?"

Astra sorted through the papers. "This one. Dr. Mark Allen, he's from England, he's teaching freshman psychology and Organic Chemistry I and II."

"Quite a range, huh?"

Astra nodded. "Impressive."

Zola gathered the rest of the papers and tapped them against the table to line them up. "Yep. Well, we still have to review the end of semester surveys, do mid-semester interviews, review new applications, and everything that goes with that."

"Hmm." Astra flashed a smile and got up. "Well, I'll be going home this week to grab some things and visit with my family, so don't expect me to help out."

"Heard." Zola pursed her lips. "But if you're not going to participate in the interviews, will you at least help with the dissertations?"

"What?"

"Dissertations. Students need approval for them to graduate, does that ring a bell?" Zola rolled her eyes at Astra's blank expression. "Never mind. Just go." Zola waved her hand dismissively. "I never get any help in this house."

Astra laughed. "Ask Mary or something, I'm sure someone will be able to help you."

"Yeah, yeah." Zola shooed her out. "Go do your thing, I'll see you when you're back."

Astra shook her head, still giggling. "Bye Zola," she yelled as she disappeared down the hall. Zola didn't respond.

* * * * * * * *

Katya pushed the door to the observatory open, holding it so that Henry could follow her in. "Thanks again for helping, I swear, no one listens to anything I have to say."

"To be fair, no one really knows what you're talking about when it comes to this." Henry gestured to the telescope.

Katya rolled her eyes. "Maybe you're just a little stupid."

Henry made a face. "Don't be mean."

Katya laughed.

"I'm serious." Henry put on a stern look.

"Okay, okay, I'm sorry." She put her hands up defensively. "I take it back, you're not stupid. "

"Thank you," he said, smiling. "So, what's this about anyway?"

Katya shrugged. "I don't know. Elena just told me I should get back to working on the telescope and doing what I love instead of being cooped up in my room. So, I told her I would. I just..." she paused. "Something doesn't feel right about the telescope and everything. I told her that too, and she told me to just trust my gut and look for it. I just…" she trailed off. "It feels like something is missing and I don't know what."

"So you want me to look to see if I catch anything?"

Katya nodded. "Yep. I'll be at the computer, so let me know if you need anything." She walked over to the computer and sat down.

"Will do." Henry strode towards the telescope and started inspecting it. Initially, nothing seemed out of place at first, and then he started to look closer. He frowned. "Katya, come here. Look at this, does this look wrong?" Henry pointed to the base of the telescope. "I don't read blueprints much, but this is wrong. Something is weird here."

Katya felt a weird sense of deja vu at his words. "What?" She got up and looked over his shoulder.

Henry pointed at the base. "This is loose. And if you look up there?" He pointed. "It looks like the lenses are crooked."

Katya frowned. "So, someone was tampering with it?"

"Looks like it." Henry pursed his lips. "I hate to say this, but do you think there's a possibility that one of our friends did this?"

Katya stared at him, considering it for a heartbeat and then whacked his arm. "Don't say that! We've been through so much together already, if someone was going to betray us, they would've already done it and we would've known."

Henry shrugged. "If you say so. Anyway, I think if we use the blueprints and take this apart and put it back together, we'll be able to fix whatever is wrong with it. Why don't you call Elena? I'm gonna take the telescope down so we can get to the base."

Katya nodded. "Okay."

Elena entered the observatory about half an hour later, blueprints and a toolbox in hand. "I heard we had a problem?" she said.

Katya nodded. "Henry said he found something that looked

weird so he thinks we should take it apart and rebuild it and that should fix the issues."

Elena smiled. "Sounds good. I haven't had a big project to work on in a while. And since I've already done this…" she drew herself up to her full height and stretched, cracking her fingers at the same time. "…this is going to be a breeze."

The three made quick work of the base machine, dismantling it and pulling it apart. When they got to the inner parts, Henry pulled the tiny pieces out of the computer. He frowned when he saw an empty vial hooked up to the middle. "Hey, does anyone know what this is?" He held it up.

Katya took it from him. "We would know if it wasn't completely empty. Whatever was inside it evaporated, so I don't think we'll be able to figure out what it was."

"Do you think this is what was causing the glitch in the system?" Henry asked.

Elena grabbed it from Katya. "Well, there's a high probability since there's nothing like this in the blueprints. Anything else weird?"

Henry shook his head. "Nope. Just a couple of fried chips, I think that was probably part of it. They're easily replaced. The only problem is, there have been so many hands on this machine, so there's no way to really tell who tampered with it."

"We could check the video cameras," Katya suggested.

Elena shook her head. "There aren't any in here, at least not inside, only on the doors. Every student has used the observatory before, there won't be any way to narrow it down."

Katya groaned and rubbed her face. "I wish we had good answers."

Elena patted her on the shoulder. "Me too.

Henry grimaced. "Well, now that everything has been pulled apart, it's time to put it back together!" He clapped his hands together. "Let's do this. The sooner it's done, the sooner we have answers."

They quickly got back to work, sorting and replacing pieces so that they had everything they needed. Then, they started putting the base back together. It was a long process. There were hundreds of components, a good chunk of which were tiny screws. Then, they had to mount the telescope back on the top. When they were finally done, Henry connected it back to the computer and rebooted everything.

"There you go!" he said as the computer came back online. "It's fixed."

"Move!" Katya pushed Henry out of the way and pulled up her maps. She knew exactly what she was looking for. Henry didn't, so he just stood behind her, staring over her shoulder. Elena did the same. "That's what I thought," Katya whispered. "I knew something wasn't right!"

Henry stared at her. "Care to share with the rest of the class Katya?"

She pointed at the screen. "Look. There are stars missing. A lot of stars."

Henry whistled. "I never thought the apocalypse would come during my time," he said, shaking his head.

Katya turned to glare at him. "Don't be silly. All stars die eventually. This is probably normal, we just don't know it yet. I know my stars." She looked back at the computer and started messing around with the screen, trying to zoom in on certain areas.

"Do stars typically die without dimming? I'm no astrologer—"

"Astronomer."

Henry made a face. "Astronomer. But you should at least see light from a supernova, right?"

"I know what I'm talking about Henry, it's not the apocalypse."

"Well, Kat, he's got a point," interjected Elena.

"Hush El," Katya retorted.

"Okay, say it's not the apocalypse. What if it's apocalypse adjacent? Are you absolutely sure there's nothing to worry about? Or are you just scared of what you'll find if I'm right?"

Katya turned back around to face him. "I'm not scared."

"Okay, then prove it. Figure this out. If you're right, great, if I'm right, then we have a little bit to worry about."

Katya turned back around. "Tch. Fine. I'll look into it."

"Good." Henry smiled at her. "I miss that wonderstruck look in your eyes. You know, the one where you defended the existence of aliens when I made fun of you for it back when we first met?"

Katya snorted. "Good times," she murmured.

Elena chuckled. "Wow, things were so simple back then."

Katya sighed. "Yeah…" She pursed her lips together. "I'll tell you what. I'll see if there's anything, anything at all, research, notes, maps, that have to do with stars randomly disappearing. And I'll let you know if I see any alien activity." She grinned as she said the last two words.

"You do that. Okay, I've got stuff to do, so good luck, I will see you two at dinner!" Henry clapped his hands and then left.

Elena nudged Katya with her elbow. "Come on. Let's look."

50

Homebound

Astra stood at the bottom of the steps, taking in the sight of the large double doors, looming walls and towering spirals. She closed her eyes and took a deep breath, filling her senses with the sound of birds chirping, the scent of wet dirt and freshly cut grass. Home.

The familiar warmth filled her body when she touched the handle of the worn mahogany door and pushed it open. She was greeted with an empty foyer. It was dimly lit by a set of lights with oil lamp shaped covers. To the left of her was the grand staircase, steps still worn, though the handrail had been replaced. She smiled.

Xavier came out from one of the side hallways, peeking his head around the entrance to see who was there. "Astra! I thought I heard the doorbell."

"Doorbell?" she questioned.

"New addition. Like a silent alarm, whenever the door opens, we all get an alert." He pointed to the ceiling. The arches helped conceal small cameras oscillating around.

"Huh. That is useful."

"Yep. With most of us not home, and only the staff here, we wanted to keep an eye on them. We all have remote access, and you see those holes?"

Astra zeroed in on the circles all around the room. "Yes. They're very well hidden."

"They're gun set ups. If we see someone we don't want there, it's easy to take them out, even if we're not here."

Astra nodded. "All good additions. When are you going to repair the stairs?"

Xavier shrugged. "Whenever someone falls through them I guess."

Astra laughed, smile reaching her eyes. "That would be a sight to see."

"So." Xavier rocked on his heels. "Here to get some things?"

"Yep." Astra headed towards the stairs. "It's been so long, I've missed it."

"We've missed you."

Astra trailed her fingers along the handrail, it felt both foreign and familiar. Xavier followed behind her as they made their way to the third floor. Astra fell into a familiar rhythm, treading the same path she had worn into the carpet years before. When she arrived at her door, she paused. Xavier stood behind her, waiting for her to do something.

"Astra?"

She reached out and touched the doorknob, half-expecting it to burn her hands. Nothing happened. She breathed a sigh of relief and pushed the door open. She flipped the light switch, illuminating her room in cool light.

"Just like you left it," Xavier said.

Astra kicked off her shoes and left them in the hall. She walked carefully across the floor and plopped down on her bed, letting her feet sink into the plush carpet she had put on the floor in front of it; the only protection she had from the cold hardwood in the morning. She rubbed her hands on the soft blanket beneath her, pushing the fibers away from her, leaving streaks in the color.

"It's been so long," she murmured.

Xavier leaned against the doorway, crossing his arms and his feet. "So." He paused, letting the word hang in the air before continuing. "You said you needed to pick up some things?"

Astra nodded. "Yes!" She got up and hurried to her desk. She rummaged through the drawers, occasionally throwing something onto the desk. She disappeared into her closet and returned holding a tote bag. She proceeded to shove everything she had placed on this desk into it. Astra stood in the middle of the room, frowning.

"What?" Xavier questioned.

"I feel like I'm missing something." She started listing things off on her fingers. "I got the journals I wanted, the flash drives, folders, jewelry, a list of books I want to take with me, photos, blueprints, my first pocket knife…" she trailed off. "What am I forgetting?"

Xavier walked over to her dresser and picked up the small blue pebble that was laying on top of it, in front of a small dish full of similar items. "Did you want to take this?"

Astra stared at it. "Oh."

It was sea glass, a trinket that Griffin had found while out on a mission. He had gifted one to every single one of the siblings. Astra held out her hand and Xavier dropped it in her palm. Astra stared at it. It was completely smooth, all traces of its original form lost in the waves that formed it. She wondered if she was just like that piece of glass: made and remade over and over.

Astra closed her hand. "Yeah. I'll take this." She stared at the dish on the dresser. "I'll take all of them." She opened a drawer and pulled out a cloth bag and dumped the contents of the dish into it. The sea glass followed. "It wasn't what I was looking for, but…" she trailed off.

"You'll have something to remember us by," Xavier supplied.

"Yeah." Astra put the smaller bag into the larger one on her desk and then her eyes lit up. "Oh! I know what I'm missing. Come on!" She grabbed the bag off her desk and sprinted past Xavier down the hall.

He rolled his eyes, shut the lights off, and closed the door. "Hey! Wait up!" Xavier followed Astra down to the basement. By the time he got there, she was already rooting through boxes. A pile of papers and hard drives were on the floor behind her. He noticed a few SD cards as well. "Whatcha got there?"

"Just my old project data, some circuits, CPUs, that sort of thing." She didn't look up as she continued going through the boxes.

Xavier sat down on one of the metal tables. "You must be glad that all of your stuff is recovered and safe, huh?"

Astra stopped. "Not all of it."

Xavier furrowed his brows. "What? I thought we got everything. Anything we didn't take, we destroyed."

Astra shook her head and resumed her work. "No. Destiny is still held by the authorities. Technically, nothing bad has happened to her, and they aren't going to experiment with her or anything, but I still don't know how I feel about that."

"Are you sure it's not just sentiment?"

"I no longer care if it's sentiment or not. I should be sentimental."

"Is that why you took those things on your dresser?"

Astra nodded. "Yes."

Xavier stared at her back, knowing that she was probably hiding whatever she was feeling. She was getting better at it, but Astra had never been one to voice emotions to him, at least ones that weren't concern. "I'll tell you what."

"What?"

"If you decide you really want Destiny back, I'll help you steal her back. I'll gather the family and we'll get her and keep her safe for you. Deal?"

The corners of Astra's mouth turned up slightly. "Okay. Deal." She turned around, holding a bunch of circuits and wires. "I think I've got everything."

Xavier raised an eyebrow. "Are you sure you can fit all that in your bag?"

Astra glared at him. "You underestimate me."

"I do not. I have never underestimated you. You can do things I can't even begin to imagine. I have, and always will expect the best and most from you."

"That's comforting," she said.

"I mean it. You are an extremely capable person. Even your

failures are successes in other peoples' eyes."

Astra blinked, not used to the praise. She cocked her head. "Are you still my brother?"

"What?"

"You're different, you think differently. Have you finally grown up? You have never been this positive."

Xavier grinned. "We all grew up. Besides, I think it's time to try new things, and that starts with positive reinforcement."

"Are you going to psychologically fight our siblings to be better people?"

Xavier pursed his lips and shrugged. "I don't know. Did it work?"

Astra laughed. "It did, a little. Remember, it takes a long time for habits to die out. I don't believe in the phrase *'you can't teach an old dog new tricks'*, but I do think it will be difficult."

"Everything we do is difficult. I want to be a better person Astra. I have to be."

"Then be." Astra stood up, the bag visibly bulging from the amount of stuff she shoved in there. "Thank you for letting me get these things."

"It's still your home Astra, always will be. Besides, I can't keep you from something you want anyway."

"That is true."

Xavier smiled at her. "See you around, okay?"

Astra nodded. He walked her to the door, and watched her drive away.

"So, that's it? She's just gone?"

Xavier didn't jump at the sound of Tessa's voice, but his surprise showed on his face when he turned around. "How long have you been standing there?"

Tessa shrugged. "Long enough." She tilted her head towards the door and the tire tracks in the gravel outside. "She needs me, more than you do. She doesn't deserve to be lonely in her last days on earth.”

“I know.” He closed the door and sighed. “Go.”

“Hm?”

Xavier stared at her expectantly. “Go. Go be with her, you’re right, she doesn’t need to be alone. Besides, I’ll be fine. Cassidy is already back, and if I’m really concerned, I’ll call you. I can do this by myself. Plus, Yvette will be here in a few days. If I can survive being knocked out by someone I called a friend and not want to kill him, I can survive telling a room full of killers that we’re not selling to them anymore. I’ll catch you up to speed when you return.”

Tessa smiled. It was warmer, softer than most things he was used to. She reminded him so much of their mother. “You are learning,” she said. “I’m proud of you.”

Xavier rolled his eyes. “You’re still younger than me, don’t forget that.”

“Age does not equal wisdom, neither does education equal intelligence. Your strength is compassion. Be strong, and don’t pick fights with Cass while I’m gone.”

“I know, I know.”

“Good.” Tessa turned and headed for the stairs. “I’ll be gone in a few hours. I’ll let you know when I get back to Torsion.”

“Stay safe,” Xavier called after her. He laughed and headed towards the study. Tessa was right. He was learning.

Sea Glass

Astra sat on her bed, fiddling with the piece of sea glass. The lack of edges was comforting to her, and the coolness of it was relaxing. Was this what it felt like to finally heal? To make decisions for the sake of herself and not duty to others? She was content, in more ways than one. A large fluffy blanket covered her lower half, and a cup of peppermint tea was on the nightstand next to her; not quite lukewarm, but cooled down enough that she could sip it without burning her tongue.

She had finished packing earlier that day, making sure that she could travel light. It was weird, having her entire life in a duffle bag and a backpack, but it was easier to cut ties with humanity if she limited memorabilia. Now, she just wanted to enjoy the time she had left, and finally rest. It would not be a luxury she could have when she finally returned home.

Astra tossed the sea glass in the air and caught it. The more she flipped it, the better she felt. She sat there in silence, the only noises being the dull thwack of the sea glass as it hit her palm, and the sound of her sipping the tea. When she first came to Torsion, she made a point to journal every night, just to keep track of things. Those journals and notes were packed in her bag, alongside the ones she had kept when she first came to earth.

She would probably not have enough time to journal once she was home, but she still wanted to. There were a few notebooks she was gifted with unfilled pages. Her people were not the storytelling type, but they did keep records. It was the only type of art that she was familiar with: history painted and carved into walls downtown, in the lower district. She knew that no one was above another, that was not something that was ever allowed, but artists? Astra knew she probably wasn't the only one who felt a pang of jealousy that of all the engineering and worker types, they had it the easiest.

She was a scientist, a soldier. She wasn't supposed to take part in the jobs of others. That was just one of many rules that her people implemented. Whether it be for strategy or simply because it was an ingrained nature, she didn't know, and she didn't care. Astra was sure that any frowned-on behavior she had excused while on earth would be eradicated the second she stepped onto the ship. Astra flipped the sea glass again and again and again. The best of both worlds was a phrase she heard often from humans. She scoffed. What a joke.

A light knock on the door pulled Astra from her thoughts. She frowned, placing the sea glass on her nightstand and walking towards the door. The person on the other side greeted her with a fond smile. Astra frowned. "Tessa? What are you doing here?"

"Well, I'm still an employee, right? You haven't fired me yet?"

Astra rolled her eyes. "Yes, you're still an employee. I just thought you'd be taking more time at home."

Tessa pushed past her. "And miss seeing you off? Now why would I do that?"

Astra closed the door. "Well, I'm glad you're here. It's nice to see you."

Tessa nodded. "Of course. Plus, I brought you something." She pulled a thick binder out of her bag. "I made Xavier give this to me before I left. I thought you should have it." She held it out.

Astra took it. She smiled softly, recognizing it immediately even though she had never seen it before. She ran her fingers over the gold letters. Astra Aracelli, fourth of the Duke children. Ad Astra Per Aspera. A lump formed in her throat. These words were hand-written, she could tell. She knew her mother's handwriting; Caliste had always loved calligraphy. She had taught Astra some before she died. "This is the binder Xavier found, the one that made him decide to help me."

Tessa nodded. "He didn't want you to hurt anyone because you were angry. He didn't want you to hurt yourself."

"I know." Astra sighed. "I—I don't know what to say. Thank you."

Tessa simply pulled Astra into a hug. "I will always be here for you. I know what it's like, better than anyone. To be alone."

Astra frowned, pulling back. "What do you mean?"

Tessa looked down. "Xavier hasn't told the others yet. That you're leaving. And no one else but him and I know what you are. I mean, I figured it out early on, because I knew our father, but—"

"Wait." Astra held up a hand. "You knew I was Ara'cel and you didn't tell me? Do you know how isolated I was in the beginning? How long it took me to adjust."

Tessa sighed. "I didn't know what exactly you were, but I knew you weren't human. Mainly because I'm not either, and you carry yourself a certain way. Like you're not used to being here. Like you're not supposed to be. Now, I was raised on Earth, brought here as an infant, so I adjusted better but you—" Tessa paused, blowing a strand of hair out of her face. "You didn't have that, I'm surprised no one else noticed."

Astra closed her eyes. "I wish you had told me sooner."

"Do you really?"

Astra opened her eyes again to see Tessa tilting her head with an all too familiar look. "What?"

Tessa rolled her eyes. "You're a smart girl. You know what's going on out there. The war that you're returning to, you may die. I don't want to watch that happen. Astra, you've finally made a life for yourself here, and you're going to give that all up. You're finally happy. You don't have to fight anymore."

"That's the thing Tessa, I'm not happy," Astra said. She moved past Tessa to stare out the window. "I haven't been, not in a while. I just know how to hide it."

Tessa turned to follow her, watching, same fond and yet sorrowful expression on her face. "Yes you have. I've seen you. You know, I may have grown up pretending to be human, but I know quite a lot about my heritage. And I may not be Ara'cel like you, but I've learned about them. Who hasn't, honestly? I think you're switching. Like switching colonies. You're not angry, not like you were. You feel at home."

Astra frowned, turning back to Tessa. "That's impossible. Can't happen. Sorry Tess, you have no idea what you're talking about."

Tessa chuckled. "Sure. Yeah, keep saying that. You've always told me that loyalty to your people and family was because of shared blood, experience, instinct. Which is strange because none of us are actually related. So, if you can associate us with family, why can't you associate us with what you consider to be a colony? I mean, you haven't been home in ages, and from my knowledge, most Ara'cel die after a few years."

Astra huffed. "Okay. Say that you're right, by some wild glitch occurrence, I somehow managed to switch my view of what I consider my colony and people. I have no idea what that'd even entail! I can't stay on Earth, that's for sure. I've already decided, I'm leaving, and there's no changing that, no matter what you or I or anyone else wants." She sighed and plopped down on her bed. "I want to go, Tessa. I miss it. There's security in rules, even if I don't agree with them."

Tessa sat down next to her. "Look, no matter what you decide, I understand. It's difficult, and it's all you know, and, shoot, even I would give up the world to visit my home planet. But no matter what you think, you know, nothing is impossible, not really. I mean, look what you did here."

Astra hummed. "I don't know, I really don't know. It's not something I can just accept as fact, Tess. You think it's easy, because you're smart and you're loyal and you're trusting, but I was raised with a certain set of ideals. I can't just throw that out the window because something makes sense."

"I'm not asking you to. I'm just saying you should think about it. We question our ideals every day, we live in regret of what we've done, we weep for the things that never happened, so if we can do that, why can't you question the people who raised you?"

"It's—"

"Don't say it's all you've ever known, I know that. But everyone else in the family is turning around and disposing of what we've been taught because we found out it's wrong. People are corrupt, parents lie, don't you see that? If I'm wrong about this, fine. But I think you need to question people's motives more often. Not just the people you're up against, but the people who send you out."

Astra was silent for a bit. She sat there, repeating Tessa's words in her head, ignoring the feeling of Tessa's eyes burning a hole in the side of her head. "Stop staring at me," she said, finally. "I can't think when you're staring."

Tessa huffed and turned away, settling on staring at the wall. "That's an excuse Astra, and you know it."

"You're not going to let up until I accept what you're saying, are you?"

"Nope."

"Ugh." Astra rolled her eyes. "Fine. I'll question them, I promise. I'll look into it when I get there."

"Good."

"But—" Astra looked at her pointedly. "—you have to promise me something."

"Anything."

"You're going to watch over the school when I'm gone, you're going to keep these people safe." Astra held out her hand. "Deal?"

Tessa took it, shaking firmly. Her hands were cold. "Deal."

52

Revelations

Aiken sat staring at the man sitting across the table from him. Ever since Astra had brought Alejo to the school, he had been intriguing. Aiken trailed him as soon as he got there, inserting himself into conversations and just listening to the stuff that he said. He had learned quite a few things about Alejo since he'd been there.

One, Alejo had worked for many members of the Parkes family. Two, Alejo was 30 years old, and still looked like he was 18. Three, Alejo was probably one of the smartest people that Aiken had ever met. He was fascinated with the way Alejo thought and worked. Aiken hung on every word the man said. With this sort of information, and the things that Aiken wanted to do, he thought that Alejo would be a good ally. Plus, it was difficult not to idolize him.

It had gotten to the point where Aiken spent time with Alejo every day, just because he wanted to listen to the things he said. Alejo might not have had the level of intelligence that Astra possessed, but he was still a genius in his own right. Alejo spoke like he'd seen things Aiken couldn't even dream of, but it was in a way that he wasn't used to. Astra did the same, but Aiken listened to her like she was speaking of a nightmare. Alejo was speaking of a dream. Aiken knew he wasn't good at relating to people, so he pushed forward with the only thing he knew the two truly had in common: Leroy Parkes. One day, Aiken asked him to go through the files and help him take notes. Alejo jumped at the chance.

"I've always wanted to take a look at his notes, see what kind of crazy ideas he was coming up with. He never let me see them when I was an apprentice," Alejo had said.

Aiken was happy. He felt like he finally made a friend who actually would actually understand him. Getting Alejo to work with him was easy. Getting him to talk was a completely different thing. The two worked in silence for the most part. Aiken itched to start questioning him, but he didn't know how to start. He didn't want to scare him off before they had the chance to get close. Eventually, Aiken decided on asking him about his favorite parts of working with the technology.

"What was it like? You worked with some of the greatest minds in the world, utilizing technology that should still be fantasy. I mean, for you it was probably just another day at work, but for me?" Aiken paused, eyes wide, imagining it. "I would kill just to see it."

Alejo shrugged. "It was really intense. I never really thought of it like that, because I had been working with the Parkes for so long. I mean, yeah, people fought to get in, but I got used to it. I suppose I did also enjoy just being around it. You're right, that stuff was super advanced. It takes a genius to do it, and we definitely couldn't have done it without having examples. I mean, we barely did it with the examples. I'm surprised that Astra was able to do that, it's incredible. She did something that no one else in the history of well, ever, did. She made humanoid androids, nanobots, advanced computers, codes, basically everything we ever worked with." He chuckled. "Now, hers is a brain I'd love to get into."

Aiken frowned. "Astra? No, no, the Parkes family made that stuff, it was Leroy's work."

Alejo looked surprised. "Oh, she didn't tell you?"

"Tell me what?"

"That she made that stuff. Leroy stole it. Like he stole a lot of things. Sure, he replicated it, continued to work with it to make the androids you are used to, and so did Clay. But he didn't come up with it." The bitterness and guilt in his voice was lost on Aiken as he tried to process this new information.

"How could Astra have come up with tech that a 70 plus year old man used for over 20 years? She's 20 now." Aiken stared at him. "That's impossible. I mean, Astra's smart, but technology like that was breakthrough decades ago. Leroy is the only person who could have, there are articles about it, people look up to him! That's false, it has to be!"

Alejo raised an eyebrow at him. "…Okay." He shrugged. "Look, Leroy's lied to a lot of people. My guess is that Astra's been lying to you too. And I wouldn't blame her. That tech is the type that people kill and die for. I almost did."

Aiken sat there in silence, shocked.

Alejo sighed. "I probably shouldn't have told you that. She must have had a reason for not saying anything. Then again, her family is scary. I've never been that worried about whether or not someone was going to kill me, and I interviewed with Clay Parkes during his executioner phase." Alejo laughed. "Now that was an experience. You should be grateful you didn't have to work for him. He was harsher than Leroy back then."

That would have been something Aiken would have spent a while questioning, had he not been in shock. He was too busy absorbing the fact that Astra was behind the technology that they fought so hard to understand.

"What was it like working for Leroy? I mean, you must have admired him, even with his flaws."

Alejo's gaze hardened, eyes narrow, a vein pulsing in his forehead. "Actually, I started out as an apprentice for Isaac, Leroy's brother. Isaac opposed everything that Leroy did, and I know why. In the end, he died for it, and I ended up working for Leroy shortly afterwards. I never truly wanted to work for him, I hated him. I was supposed to kill him! But Isaac told me not to, he said he couldn't live knowing that I did."

Aiken gritted his teeth at that, not wanting to let his distaste for the sentence show through. "Oh," was all he said, quietly. "Well, at least you're out, right?"

Alejo nodded. "Yep. I finally have some freedom. For the first time in ages." He smiled as he said it, but Aiken didn't return it. They continued to work in silence. This time, Aiken didn't look at Alejo with admiration. He looked at him with vengeance. He clenched his pencil tighter as he wrote, slightly moving his arm to shield his work from Alejo's eyes. He no longer thought that Alejo spoke of the Parkes family like working for them was easy. The more he replayed Alejo's words in his mind, the more he recognized the disappointment in his voice, the tiredness. Alejo hated working for them. He hated the Parkes in general. Everyone except for Isaac, and Aiken didn't know anything about Isaac Parkes.

He didn't know what to think anymore. On one hand, he still trusted Astra with everything in him. Sure, she lied to him, but she always had good reasons for it. On the other hand, Alejo could be lying to him and Astra might not be. He was torn. Aiken was used to getting lost in translation. He wasn't the best at communicating, and he spent most of his life with his mother and grandmother, learning how to become a beekeeper. His time at Torsion had hardened him. In fact, Aiken was sure that he was a better person now. Only now, he was hyper aware of how much he still didn't know.

Aiken did his best to hide his feelings. Thankfully, if Alejo noticed, he didn't say anything. Then again, Alejo didn't know him well enough to pinpoint what was wrong. Aiken was grateful that he didn't. His tells would be caught by Astra; she would've called him out hours ago. He'd have to avoid her for a few days so that when he went to her, he wouldn't be overwhelmed. Eventually, he excused himself and ran up to his dorm room. Aiken didn't know what else to do; he wasn't good at concealing his emotions.

He was lucky that Henry wasn't there. Aiken wasn't sure what he'd say if Henry asked why he was upset. Though, at the moment, Aiken wasn't sure he would even have to worry about that. Henry hadn't spoken to him since he had told him to stop working with Astra. There was a part of him that wanted to listen to Henry, but the urge to make Astra happy was stronger. He still didn't know if he could trust Astra, but something was pushing him to. He didn't want to question it. Not to mention, Aiken didn't know why Henry still wasn't speaking to him. It wasn't like Aiken hated him for suggesting he take a break from working with Astra. Though, maybe he could have been nicer about telling Henry no. Henry could be sensitive at times.

He didn't have much time to dwell on what was going on with Henry. He needed to focus on Alejo. Aiken's awe and respect for Alejo, his obsession with him, was replaced by something much darker. He would confront Astra later, or maybe he wouldn't. He couldn't believe she had lied to him. Everyone had lied to him. Aiken needed closure. If he didn't figure something out, he was going to explode. He wanted, no, he needed, Alejo dead. He was willing to do anything to get there.

53

Deathbed Confessions

Aiken lay in his bed staring at the ceiling. *'I never truly wanted to work for him, I hated him. I was supposed to kill him! But Isaac told me not to, he said he couldn't live knowing that I did.'* Aiken muffled his scream with a spare pillow before throwing it across the room and hitting Henry on the head. Henry didn't react, still deep in sleep. His snoring never used to irritate Aiken, but he had the sudden urge to strangle Henry.

Aiken shook his head. What was he thinking? He wasn't angry at Henry; Henry hadn't done anything wrong. It was Alejo. Alejo was the problem. Alejo was the one who wanted Leroy dead. If he had wanted Leroy dead, what was keeping him from killing Aiken? After all, he was taking after Leroy, studying his work, he wanted to be him. Aiken clenched his fists. It would be in self-defense if he killed Alejo. Kill or be killed, right?

He thought back to all his interactions with Alejo. He was nice. Strange, a genius for sure, an odd and free thinker, but he was nice. Still, Aiken hated him. He hated looking at Alejo so much that he avoided him for the past week. Every nerve ending burned to wring the man's neck. Alejo didn't represent himself, no, Alejo represented a threat to everything that Aiken was working toward. If he had any chance at all to finish what Leroy started, any chance of bringing him back, he had to get rid of Alejo.

Aiken slipped out of bed and headed down to the lab. He almost expected other people to be in there, but it was quiet. He almost missed working side by side in silence with Astra. That thought left his head immediately when he spotted the files he had left out on the table. Every single one of the notes that he had given to Astra were laying neatly in a stack next to one of her projects. Aiken picked them up. As he began reading through his notes, he found it harder and harder to keep control of his own anger.

He slammed his fist down on the table. Alejo would face his rage, no matter how long it took. Aiken sat down at one of the lab computers and started looking through his notes on poisonous plants. He wanted Alejo to die painfully, and most importantly, he wanted to make sure that people wouldn't trace it back to him. There were a couple of different types of untraceable poisons. However, Aiken didn't want to use an easy one. He wanted Alejo to suffer.

Aiken had been researching plants and poisons since he was a child. It was one of few things that kept him company when he used to be bullied in school. He would never willingly hurt someone, but he liked to know that at least he could defend himself. It also made his science teacher happy.

Luckily for him, he knew of the perfect plant that would do exactly what he wanted. *Cerbera odollam*, the suicide tree. Toxic, relatively unknown by scientists world-wide, and practically untraceable… Aiken smiled. With a few tweaks, he could double the poison's effectiveness. If he slipped it into the man's breakfast, Alejo would be dead by midnight. Plus, Aiken knew just where to find it.

* * * * * * * * *

A week later, Aiken, along with his imported kernels, locked himself in one of the unused labs. Aiken put gloves on and then carefully removed one from its tube with a pair of tweezers. He had paid a lot of money to get these so quickly. One was already fatal, five would make it even quicker, and a lot more painful. Aiken stared at the kernel for a moment before dropping it and the others into a bowl. The easiest way to get this to Alejo would be in food, something very sweet or spicy, and using a mortar and pestle to grind it up would limit the possibilities that he could be traced. After all, everything he bought was planned out carefully.

Aiken had traveled over thirteen cities away, wore very plain clothing and made little eye contact with the cashier. He had made sure to keep his back to cameras, bought the kernels in a store under the guise of making pesticides, and paid in cash for the entirety of his trip. He had sanitized the lab thoroughly, hadn't touched any school-owned equipment, and planned on disposing of the tools immediately afterwards in one of the many dumpsters in town. He had planned this out perfectly, and tomorrow morning, he would execute his plan.

Early the following morning, Aiken left his dorm with a pep in his step, poison in his pocket. Astra was gone, so he left the latest notes on the desk in her dorm room. She was a very neat person, he noted, something they had in common. He thought she would be proud of him for finally taking action. He was protecting himself, protecting them. Astra would admire that, in fact, Aiken was sure that if he told her his plans, she would help him.

Aiken couldn't sleep last night, he tossed and turned, fantasizing about watching the light in Alejo's eyes fade. The cafeteria was pretty quiet when he entered. It was easy to slip into the kitchen unnoticed. One thing about Alejo was that he was very picky. His food had been specially made by the staff since he got there. According to Astra's brother, who Aiken thought was just as, if not more closed off than her, he had the same done for him at his old workplace.

The staff paid Aiken no mind as he headed towards the walk-in fridge. He had studied the blueprints of the school enough to know where the cameras were, so he was able to stay out of their view. Once he was in the fridge, it was easy. There were no cameras in there, and Alejo's food was labeled. He always ate something savory or spicy, so Aiken knew that he wouldn't notice the taste. Even if he did, Alejo would just add more spices or eat it without complaint. He didn't like to bother the chefs.

Aiken put on some gloves and mixed the poison into his food. Then he grabbed a yogurt and some fruit so that he wouldn't arouse suspicion by leaving empty handed, and left the kitchen. He snagged some pancakes on his way out of the cafeteria, and once he was in the main hall, he ducked into a hidden passage. It was one of the few that they opted not to close off, and Aiken was grateful for that. He had hidden some cleaning supplies in a nook a few feet down the passage, and he spent a few minutes carefully ridding the vial and the spoon that he had used of his prints along with any traces of food or poison. Then, Aiken tucked them into a plastic bag and followed the passage all the way down.

It spit him out in the gardens, and Aiken enjoyed every second of the 20-minute walk down. He dumped the contents of the bag in one dumpster, and then disposed of the gloves in another across town. Finally, he dropped the plastic bag in a puddle and rubbed it around in dirt and mud before throwing it in a trash can at a grocery store. He then spent what seemed like an infinite amount of time scrubbing dirt out from underneath his fingernails.

When Aiken returned to the school, he sat in his dorm reading for hours. He didn't want to risk being seen with Alejo in his final hours. Especially since he would have to hide the evidence later that night. Alejo's room had a passageway into it, like most of the dorms in the school. Why Parkes felt the need to put everything in one giant building with secret hallways was something that Aiken hadn't yet discovered. All he knew was that it was extremely useful, and because of it, he wouldn't get caught. Yet another reason to admire the man.

When night finally fell, Aiken faked sleeping until Henry returned to the room and his snores signaled the fact that he was out cold. Aiken slipped out of bed and carefully opened the window. It would be the best way to avoid the cameras. He hopped on the ledge, closed the window behind him and crawled along the side of the building until he reached the next window: an empty dorm room. This one used to belong to a PhD student who had ended up getting in a car accident and quitting halfway through the semester. It would stay empty for a while, which was perfect for Aiken.

He had discovered that the room had a passage connected to it when he had went to clean it out the previous month. The staff had a lot on their plates, and Aiken loved helping people, especially when it involved cleaning. He was through the passage and into another one in no time. Aiken sprinted through the walls of the school, heart rate elevated, and not because he was running. He was so elated that he wasn't even out of breath by the time he got to Alejo's room. He entered quietly, though Alejo wouldn't even have heard him over the sound of his own labored breathing. Aiken stood over him triumphantly. Alejo had collapsed in the middle of the floor, reaching for the doorknob.

Aiken smirked. He was so weak that he couldn't even call for help. Aiken grabbed Alejo and lifted him, draping the boy's arm over his shoulder and pulling him into the passageway. As the mirror that served as the door swung shut behind him, Aiken heard Alejo groan, attempting to speak. He just smiled wider.

"Don't worry," he said, the satisfaction apparent in his tone. "This will all be over soon."

Aiken dragged Alejo all the way up to the roof. "I couldn't just leave you to die in your room," he said. "Then they'd know it was murder." He climbed up onto the ledge and pulled Alejo up with him. "But now, you get to take the blame for your own death." He removed Alejo's arm from around his neck, holding the boy steady so he could look him in the eyes. He reveled in the fear, the pleading that Alejo couldn't voice. "It's what you deserve."

Then, Aiken let go, and Alejo, unable to stand, topped forward. Aiken watched him fall, almost in slow motion. The sound of his body hitting the ground with a sickening crack was like music to Aiken's ears. He didn't linger. He stopped for a moment to admire his work and then he left, disappearing through the passages, back through the windows, and into his own bed. Aiken fell into a deep slumber with a smile on his face. This time, his sleep was easy, the image of Alejo's bloody corpse burned in his brain.

54

Go-Getter

She was never going to catch a break. Astra stared down at the message on her phone, an email from someone she barely knew. Attached to it were about a dozen pictures of people and messages depicting plans to steal Destiny from the authorities. Astra sighed. She had been hoping to avoid this. It was payback after all, and in their eyes, she deserved it. Her family had destroyed their facility, burned it to the ground, murdered multiple innocent employees. If they could be considered innocent in any way.

Astra put her phone down on her desk. She looked out the window. The sun had just come up, welcoming what should have been a normal day. Astra turned, grabbing her phone and bag as she left her dorm room. She only had a few days to intercept Destiny before she would be gone forever. Astra was never going to let that happen. She would rather die than lose Destiny. This attachment was something she couldn't bring herself to get rid of, not anymore. It was almost like the android was a part of her. She had already lost so many pieces of herself. Sometimes, Astra wondered how many she could lose before she stopped being herself.

It didn't take long to find Tessa, face buried in a book as she curled up in one of the library's big chairs. When Astra told her what was going on, it was like a switch flipped behind Tessa's eyes. That was it. Tessa called Xavier while Astra pinpointed Destiny's exact location. While they waited, Astra laughed to herself. It was like she was constantly saying, *'No, I'm not coming back.'* Then, she'd turn around and call for one last mission. Letting go was a lot harder than she had anticipated.

She and Tessa didn't leave their place in the library until they got confirmation that their siblings had arrived. The eight of them crammed into a corner booth in one of the local diners. Astra was sure that if the place had been full, the lot of them would have gotten stares. She knew that her siblings were an odd bunch. From Jaxson's neon green hair, to the scars on Zale's hand, to the assortment of styles, ages, and faces at the table. They were so different, but they knew each other so well. Astra used to be able to say that she wouldn't trade this for the world. Things change, and she found herself mourning, rather than listening to Xavier speak.

He noticed of course, because he always did. Xavier didn't bother to stop talking to catch Astra up on their plan. He would tell her on the road. He rolled his eyes and pointed to the map that Astra had handed him earlier.

"Okay, so, we'll have Griffin, Zale, and myself distract the officers while Astra hacks the cameras. Jaxson and Cass will retrieve Destiny, and then leave immediately. She should be in evidence lock-up with the rest of the Parkes related stuff, but prepare to be surprised. We don't know, she's a highly advanced piece of technology so they could have put her in a more secure part of the building. Our sources do say that she's still there. If worse comes to worse, there's an officer inside who will help you. You'll be able to recognize him easily. Tessa, you stay in the car, you'll be our getaway driver. Yvette, you're going to be back-up for Griffin and Zale. We managed to get a second car, so if they get in trouble, pull them out. If anything goes wrong, scatter. Regular procedure. Any questions?"

The siblings shook their heads, and Xavier smiled. "Let's go then!" He grabbed Astra by the elbow and pulled her back as the siblings paid and filed out of the diner. "Something's wrong, Astra. You're not paying attention."

Astra hummed. "I was just thinking."

"You need to put that on the back burner, Little Star. You can't be out of focus for this. It was your mission, therefore you have to be at your best."

She sighed. "I know, I just…" she trailed off. "I'm not ready."

"Not ready for what?"

Astra hesitated. When she finally spoke, her voice was soft, just above a whisper. "I'm not ready to say goodbye to her, Xavi."

"Why would you have to?"

"I can't take her with me, can I?"

It finally clicked in Xavier's head, and his eyes widened. "You're going to destroy her, aren't you?"

Astra nodded. "I won't be here to make sure that she's safe. I can't trust anyone to guard her." She looked up at Xavier. "No offense of course, but you're only human. Humans make mistakes."

Xavier chuckled. "None taken. I know how much she means to you."

Astra elbowed him in the ribs and started walking. Xavier shook his head and caught up to her. The two still walked slowly, trailing behind the group. Astra smiled slightly.

"So you understand, right?"

Xavier nodded. "It's official?"

Astra nodded. "I think… I wanted to stay, I fought with it, went back and forth until I couldn't deny it anymore. I don't belong here, and yes, you will always be my family. I love you all and you mean the world to me. However, it is impossible for me to imagine a world where I'm okay with staying. I tried talking myself into it. And people will probably try to talk me out of leaving all the way up until I do. It's how the world works, Xavi. Not all of us get the luxury of being able to do anything besides surviving. I've wanted to leave since I got here. I don't think I'll ever lose the urge, I just spent my time putting it off."

Xavier nodded. "I respect it, and you. But that doesn't mean any of us will be happy about it."

"You don't have to be."

"I know."

They stopped just short of the car and Astra shoved her hands into her pockets, fidgeting with the fraying strings lining the sides.

"Do you think they're ready? To move on?"

Xavier shrugged. "I couldn't tell you."

"We were built for war, Xavier. I'm not sure any of them, even Tessa, will be able to handle this new chapter."

"I'll be there for them, you know I will."

Astra nodded. She left Xavier and hopped into the passenger seat of the black car that Tessa was currently driving. Jaxson, who was sitting behind her, reached over and flicked her in the back of the head. "Jack!" she yelled.

"What?" he questioned, innocently. "Just like old times." He smiled, something that Astra couldn't see as she adjusted in her chair, huffing.

"You're the worst," she grumbled.

Jaxson just laughed, and then Cassidy and Tessa joined in. Astra cracked a smile, then eventually caved. They exchanged jokes and stories as they drove, and Astra wanted nothing more than to pretend nothing bad had happened. That illusion was shattered as soon as the car stopped and Jaxson and Cassidy jumped out. She immediately pulled up her computer and started hacking the cameras. Then they were gone, disappearing into the building like the shadows they were born to be. Astra was left with Tessa in the seat beside her, and a lump in her throat.

"Something wrong?"

Astra didn't look at Tessa. She didn't have to. "I'm worried. I feel like I'll never forgive myself."

Tessa hummed. "It'll take a long time. But we'll always love you, you know that. It's not something easily taken."

Astra fiddled with her thumbs. "What's wrong with me? I need so much reassurance, as if I'm a child who's making friends for the first time."

"I think we've spent so long suppressing everything. It's good to be sad, it's good to be in pain, it means you're healing."

"It doesn't feel like healing," Astra mumbled. The two spent the rest of the waiting time in silence. Astra could feel Tessa staring at her, but she ignored it. She didn't want to get into the details, something that Tessa always pushed for. She just wanted it to be over. She wanted Destiny destroyed, and she wanted to go home. She always wanted to go home. Now Astra knew for sure this time, that she would be running forever.

It didn't take long for Jaxson and Cassidy to return, Destiny's body in tow. Astra moved to the back, just to stare at it, tracing the cold metal of her face. Jaxson flopped next to her, and Astra turned.

"What?"

"Why didn't you say something?"

"About what?"

Jaxson glared. "About leaving! I can't believe that this is the first time I'm hearing about it, and it's from an off-handed comment from Tessa. You didn't think that maybe we'd like to know?"

"I was going to tell you—"

"When? When it was too late? Did you just think that you could put it off until the last minute? Well, you can't and it's too late now, don't expect me to say goodbye." Jaxson huffed and returned to his seat. To him, that small outburst was equal to a rage-induced rampage. A singular tear slid down Astra's face and she looked back down at Destiny. Destiny was going to burn, just like all the things Astra created. At least it meant that her family would be safe.

When they got home, Astra stayed in the car for a few minutes, waiting for the rest of her siblings to arrive. They didn't, but she did get a confirmation that they were on their way, and that was enough. Astra eventually made her way to the basement and just stared ahead at the furnace as Jaxson and Cassidy tossed Destiny's body in. Cassidy glanced at her with a pained expression. Jaxson couldn't even look her in the eyes.

Astra turned and ran towards her room immediately, not wanting to stand around watching Destiny's body melt in the furnace, or face the anger and the pity in the room. She locked the door and paced around for several minutes before finally stopping and reaching for the item that weighed heavy in her pocket. Astra stared at the piece in her hand, face illuminated by the moonlight streaming through her open window. Light glinted off the silver, emphasizing the scratches, evidence of age and use. She didn't feel a single bit of remorse for her choice, and not only that, but she was glad. The processing chip she held was her only memory, a treasure she had to protect: Destiny's brain.

55

Memorial

It was already late when Xavier and Astra left the mansion to visit their parents' graves. The cold air nipped at Astra's cheeks. It reminded her of both her homes: training and school, Ares making her run in the snow, the sparkling streets of her home planet. Her conversation with Tessa had left her with a sense of urgency to say goodbye for good. Xavier hadn't questioned it when she had called. Astra was just glad she didn't have to explain herself. When they arrived at the graves, they just stood there, sharing the silence. It was comforting, knowing that she was safe. But sooner or later, she had to break the news.

Astra turned to Xavier. "You know Xavi, if I die, I want you to bury me here. Well." She paused. "You know what I mean."

Xavier looked at her, brows furrowed. His gaze slowly turned to understanding and he looked away. "You're really not going to stay, are you? Last chance, no turning back?"

Astra shook her head. She stared down at the headstone bearing Ares' name. It was an empty grave and no one bothered even to bury something there to pretend.

"I expected it, don't worry. I wanted you to change your mind, but I can't make you. I can't say I'm not disappointed, but I'm not surprised either."

"Tessa tried, and though I wanted to, I just can't. I'm not sure why, but it feels wrong. I fought it for so long, going back and forth, but I just can't."

Xavier nodded. "I understand. You have a strong ideal. Getting to your goal takes the forefront, no matter how you have to get there."

Astra hesitated. "It's not like I want to leave—"

"—but you have to, I know."

She looked down. "Is it fair? To want something you can't have?"

He shrugged. "I couldn't tell you. We're selfish people, Astra, it's how we were made. Ultimately, the decision is up to you. I will miss you immensely. I'll miss your advice, your anger, your presence in our home. I have said things to you that I never meant. Since Arya's death, you have been constant, always taking charge, always there, even if you weren't home. I think I was jealous of your leadership."

"Xavier. You were always better at taking charge."

He rolled his eyes. "No I wasn't. They don't listen to me."

"Yes they do, and they respect you. It's just not easy to show it sometimes. We've never been the best at being genuine."

Xavier laughed. "Well, if you ever want to take over…" He trailed off. "You will always have a home to return to if you want."

Astra gave him a soft smile. "Thanks, Xavi. I will keep that in mind should I ever have the chance to visit." She stood up and then knelt beside Caliste's grave. "Hello, Mother," she whispered.

Xavier put his hand on her shoulder. "They loved you, in a way that I can't express. They were good people."

"Good?" Astra looked up at him. "They weren't good. They were efficient workers and proper parents but they weren't good. Good people don't do what we do for a living." She turned back to the gravestone. "They were survivors. And so are we."

Xavier pulled Astra to her feet. "You can't hate this forever."

"I don't. I know who I am, and what I've done. I'm not ashamed of how I lived because it made me understand the world in a way I never would have. I am a harsh person, Xavi. I was raised to enforce the rules. It's hard to unlearn something that is a part of me."

"It doesn't mean you'll never change, does it?"

"No. But for now, I can't put anyone else in danger. I'm already close to breaking as it is. You've seen it. I cannot be the reason that you burn."

"We wouldn't blame you."

"No?" Astra stared at Xavier, holding his gaze for what seemed like an eternity. She finally turned away and looked up at the darkening sky and sighed. "We should probably head back to the house."

Xavier bit back the words he wanted to say to her and fell in line with her. The two walked together, keeping pace, and for a moment, they both pretended they were their younger selves, scheming together again.

"What do you think you'll do now?" Astra questioned.

"What Yvette told me to do. Right what we've wronged, start a new journey."

"The path to peace is difficult."

Xavier nodded. "I know. I'm willing to work on it though."

"With everyone surrounding you, you'll succeed. There's no other option is there?"

Xavier grinned. "Yeah, I don't think Yvette would let me fail. She's optimistically forceful like that."

Astra bumped Xavier with her elbow. "Even without me you'll be in good hands."

When they returned, Astra found her siblings waiting for her. Some of the staff gave her smiles and shook her hand or waved goodbye. Astra then turned to her brothers and sisters and melted into their embraces. Jaxson met her first.

"Hi," Astra said, staring up into Jaxson's face. "You came."

"Hey." He smiled at her. "Look, I know I said I wouldn't say goodbye, but it was wrong of me."

Astra buried her face into Jaxson's shoulder. "So you all know?"

"Yes."

Astra pulled away. "I'm sorry we couldn't have told you sooner."

Jaxson laughed. "It makes sense. Dad was always the secretive type."

"He did what was best for us."

Jaxson shrugged. "Maybe. At the very least, he loved us and taught us how to survive." Jaxson held onto Astra's shoulders. "Stay safe, sis." Then he disappeared into the depths of the house.

Cassidy found Astra next and enveloped her in a hug. "I'm sorry," she whispered, over and over in Astra's ear.

Astra returned the hug and closed her eyes tightly. "I don't blame you, okay? I love you Cass."

When Cassidy pulled away, there were tears in her eyes. Astra turned to find Griffin standing behind her. She smiled softly and took his hands.

"Is this goodbye forever?" he asked.

Astra shook her head as she hugged him. "No, no I promise. I will see you again."

Zale came up behind her and hugged her silently, and then Astra came face to face with Yvette.

Neither spoke for a while, they just stared at each other, waiting for someone to take the initiative. It ended up being Astra who swept her sister into her arms.

Yvette held on tightly. "Don't go, please. We'll work together again, just stay. It won't be the same if all of us are here and you aren't," she said. Her voice was soft and hoarse. Astra squeezed her eyes shut tightly, trying not to cry.

After a minute, Astra finally pulled shook her head. "You know I can't stay, Yvette, plus, Tessa already tried to convince me. I have a job to do."

"And what about us?"

"You'll be safe. You will keep Xavier in check, and you will do what we've been meaning to do for a long time. You are the change I longed to be, Yvette, don't forget it."

"Promise me you'll be okay. That once you've finished the job you'll stay safe."

Astra nodded. "I promise. I said I'd visit when I'm able. That may take years, but it'll be worth it."

Yvette looked down. "I—"

"Don't say it. I know you think you can convince me, but you won't."

"You always were the stubborn one."

"And you took after me." Astra grabbed Yvette's hand and squeezed it. "I'm so proud of you."

* * * * * * * *

When Astra returned to the school, it was in reserved silence. It was a weekend so right now, no one was awake, and she was alone. That was something she was grateful for. Astra decided to walk around the school gardens, thinking. She was content in her choices, content with the idea that she was not going to stay. Her family loved her, and she loved them, it was not something that could be lost easily. But she did not have it in her to abandon her chosen path now. She chose her home planet. Earth was beautiful, but it didn't belong to her.

About 15 minutes into her walk, she saw it in the distance: a dark shape near one of the walls. It was difficult to identify exactly what, or rather who, it was until she got closer. She smelled it first, the dirt, the rot, the blood. Astra ran to it and dropped to her knees in front of the body. It was Alejo, face down on the ground, blood pooling out of his head around his body.

Astra flipped him over and shook him but he didn't respond. She could feel that his bones were broken in several places, the joints of his arms twisted at an awkward angle. She could see the visible crack in his skull, but she wanted to believe there was a chance. She started to panic, something that she hadn't done in a very long time. Astra knew he was dead before she even checked for a pulse, but that didn't stop her from searching for it. A burning heat welled up inside her, and she didn't even try to stop it.

That's where Tessa found her; crying in the grass in front of

Alejo's body, scorch marks in the shape of hand prints on the walls and the grass in front of her.

Tessa placed a hand on Astra's shoulder, then withdrew it, wincing in pain at the heat radiating from her body. "Astra," she said. "What have you done to yourself?"

Astra shook her head, the tears falling faster. "Tess," she wailed. "I don't know who I am anymore. This is my fault. I could've saved him. I knew, I knew he was going crazy, and I didn't stop him and now Alejo's dead and it's all my fault."

Tessa knelt in the grass beside her. "You're Astra of the Ara'cel, you're the smartest person I know. You are brave, but if you continue on like this, you will kill yourself."

Astra stared at Alejo's body in front of her, and the sight of his blood spilling across the ground, soaking the dirt. "Tess, I can't stand this." She turned to look at her sister, and Tessa gasped.

Astra's eyes were black and her tears left bright blue streaks on her cheeks.

"Astra…" she whispered.

Astra nodded. "I know, I know, I'm dying, I've been dying, and I. Do. Not. Care." She turned back to Alejo. "I want to go home," she screamed. "Please! Just let me go."

Tessa threw her arms around her sister, ignoring the searing pain from the burns that her sister was inflicting on her in her grief, and held Astra until she could no longer stand the heat. Astra stared into the distance, tired, and scared, and wishing for relief. All she wanted was to be herself again. She knew that wouldn't come until someone found her. So she cried in the grass with Tessa beside her, until she couldn't cry anymore.

Epilogue

Katya once again sat in the observatory next to the telescope. At this point, it was her comfort spot; even if there was nothing to find, the least she could do was feel safe. It had been a rough couple of years, and yet she was proud. Proud of herself for surviving, for taking that jump into the unknown. Most importantly, she was proud that she hadn't listened to her father. She was thriving, and she knew that soon, she would prove him wrong. She just had to wait.

Katya pulled out a pen and her notepad and started sketching. It was a hobby that she had picked up recently, so she wasn't that good at it, but it was relaxing. She didn't want to tackle learning how to draw people yet, so Katya drew scenery. Above all, she loved to draw space. It was a little cliché, learning how to accurately portray the night sky, but she didn't care.

After all, if she could learn how star maps worked, she could learn how to draw the view outside her window. With her phone open to the reference photo in front of her, and the comforting silence settling into her bones, Katya carefully began to trace an outline onto the paper.

She started with the trees, the tips of which brushed the horizon. The winding path between them was easy enough; no one really cared about the shading of the bricks. She left the sky blank for now; she'd fill it in with color later. Katya focused on the moon: not quite full, and yet still large enough for her to see the darkness of the craters that speckled its surface. Katya switched to marking places where she'd like to leave stars. She went slowly, matching each white dot perfectly to the photo in front of her.

It didn't have to be accurate—it was just a drawing after all— but something made her want it to be right. It was strange; she wasn't usually a perfectionist. Katya switched to colored pencils and shaded the sky in a mix of blues and purples. She smudged the colors together, grateful that her clothes were dark enough that the excess pigment wouldn't show up. By the time she had finished, hours had passed. It was already noon, and Katya's stomach began to growl. She ignored the pangs in her stomach and grabbed a granola bar out of her bag. She moved on to sketching a new photo when the beeping started.

Initially, she ignored it, figuring that it would stop eventually, but it didn't. Katya started to tune it out, telling herself that she would look at it later. The insistent beeping grew louder. Katya frowned and groaned. She threw her paper down and pulled up the video feed. If the computer didn't have her attention before, it did now. Something seemed to be falling through the atmosphere, headed straight toward them. Katya smiled. Finally, she would have something to look forward to.

If a meteor landed close enough to the school, she could be the one to claim it and the students at the school would have their chance to get a foot in the scientific community. She ran toward the telescope and looked through the lens, carefully adjusting it to track the falling rock. It was a strange-looking thing, and every so often she'd lose it. Still, there was no doubt in her mind that whatever that thing was, rock or something different, she was going to be there when it landed.

Katya scrambled to find her phone and called the one person she could think of. "Pick up, pick up," she whispered.

"Hello?"

"Astra! Get down here, I found something on the telescope you might be interested in, and I need your help programming something to keep track of it until it lands."

Astra hung up immediately and raced towards the observatory. She needed something to keep her mind off of the numbness she felt. She still hadn't found a way to tell the others that Alejo was dead. Astra found Katya with her eyes glued to the monitor when she got there.

She approached the chair and leaned over Katya's shoulder. "What are you looking at?"

Katya pointed. "Look! I think it's a meteor, but I can't really tell, it's falling too fast for me to really focus on it."

"So you want me to track it?"

"Yeah, I want to be the first person there when it lands."

Astra nodded. "Okay. Move." She sat down in the chair and started entering parameters into the computer. After completing it, Astra curiously opened the video feed. She probably could have made the computer focus on it if it wasn't for the sinking feeling that she knew what it was. Shielding technology was not a strange concept to her; in fact, she used to work on it herself when she was younger.

Meteors were a popular cloaking choice that all pilots were a fan of. It was a universe-wide thing—all planets had meteors sometimes—and it was the easiest to do in terms of the element of surprise. Astra shook her head. She was probably overthinking this. Just because she wanted to go home, didn't mean that the people coming for her were in danger or were planning to attack. She would get a message from them soon, and all would be fine.

That's when her phone rang. "Hey, Kat, I'm going to take this. I have the tracking program up, it'll give you an alert with coordinates as soon as it hits, okay?"

"Okay!" Katya waved her hand, still glued to the telescope.

Astra rolled her eyes and left the room. She pulled her phone out of her back pocket and answered. "Hello?"

No one answered. The ringing just got louder. Astra pulled the phone away from her face and what she saw confirmed her worst fear. It was not a phone call. It was a distress call. Astra turned back towards the open door to the observatory where Katya was still watching the telescope, and the video feed was still up on the computer.

Astra sighed. *'Well, so much for being discreet.'*

To Be Continued In...
ZENOSYNE

This excerpt is taken from *Zenosyne.*

Scheduled Release: December 2025

O

Prologue

BEEP. BEEP. BEEP.

The jarring noise of the siren drowned out everything save for frantic screaming of orders and feet pounding against the main deck. Atria stood at the bridge overseeing the chaos beneath her. She rolled her eyes. *'Or'en are so excitable'*, she thought. It was unfair to her to have to work with them, but her star cluster was deemed too small to control a ship this size.

Typically, the council wouldn't send them into war, they were not good at following commands when too many things were happening at once, and fought amongst themselves constantly. Unfortunately, they were short on soldiers, and the Or'en, no matter how many problems they caused, were grunts. They were expendable.

In a way, so was she. Of course, they wouldn't be particularly happy if she died, the Ara'cel hated to lose any of their people. Really, being expendable only meant that she and the other Retriever-led hubs and associated clusters didn't have to fight unless there was something drastically wrong. They usually stationed themselves on the outskirts of planets and galaxies with known Ambassador and Spy clusters. From there, they would monitor and collect Ara'cel, debrief them, and send them out again. Right now, her job was to make sure that all available Ara'cel returned to their planet.

So far, roughly ninety-eight percent of the teams and deployed Ara'cel had been retrieved, but they were still picking up stragglers. Atria's star cluster was small compared to others with her job. The overseeing officer of their star cluster didn't exist, thanks to the amount of Ara'cel on the ship. Technically, she was the highest ranking, due to the fact that she also led the overall hub ship on the outskirts of the galaxy, but that didn't matter. There were 75 members of her star cluster, mostly engineers, soldiers, and retrievers like her. They used to have an ambassador, but he was recalled several months prior for some emergency that she wasn't allowed to know about.

Sometimes it was best to keep certain missions hidden, just in case. Atria knew for a fact that no one other than the field agents themselves, and of course the Ara'cel knew the meaning behind the colors of their arm bands. It made reconnaissance easier if no one else knew what your purpose was. Groups of mixed colors always had an Ara'cel overseer who knew who everyone was, if they couldn't have a fully Ara'cel team. In training, field agents were taught that it was forbidden to discuss their jobs. The last person who even requested to talk about it was shot.

Atria turned away from the chaos beneath her and walked over to the control panel. The siren didn't belong to their ship itself, but rather the dropship that was currently entering the atmosphere. They were losing control of the engines. Even if they landed at that speed, it wouldn't kill the people on board, it would just be frustrating to deal with. Earth was an at risk planet, meaning they were not supposed to find out about aliens for several hundred more years.

If anyone picked up on the ship, they would have a problem.

"Atria, the dropship is entering too fast."

Atria paused, then glanced over her shoulder, black eyes boring into the ones of the man standing behind her. "I know, Corvus." She took in his appearance, the grey uniform and the yellow band around his arm that told her he was an engineer. She turned back to look over the rail. "Are we able to slow it down in any way?"

"We are working on it Atria. In the meantime, I suggest telling the Or'en to calm down, the noise is distracting the engineers."

Atria nodded. "Send a few soldiers down to calm them and get that dropship to slow down. If it doesn't, tell them to implement safety measures and hold on tight."

"Will do." Corvus turned and disappeared, leaving Atria alone on the bridge.

She walked towards the guardrail and watched the soldiers enter the crowd below. She rolled her eyes. If only she had been given a calmer backup team, like Xals. They wouldn't have this problem. Atria turned on the closest computer and pulled up the signal that was radiating from Earth. It was a classic call signal, a general message that screamed *come get me* to whoever was in the area. Atria was lucky she was the first one to catch it. Ara'cel often coded their names into the signal and Atria was looking forward to greeting Astra as soon as she set foot on board.

She had been in the same starting class as Astra, back when they first entered school. Even though they didn't end up in the same group, they constantly worked together. The two had gotten along and Atria considered the girl a friend. Astra's uniform was folded up, waiting on a nearby console to be returned to its owner. Atria reached up and touched the band around her arm, a deep green to Astra's black. They had several successful missions together in the past, being stationed on the same planets and ships. Before Astra was assigned to Ares on Earth, Atria had once hoped Asta would join the ambassador team on her own ship.

Atria's watch beeped and she tapped it to open the com line. "Yes Corvus?"

"The drop ship is slowing down, but it will still crash and cause some damage. Permission to send down another ship to assist?"

"Granted. Be quick about it."

"Will do. Are you able to take over for one of the engineers? Pyxis will be joining the second team to assess the damage."

"I can do that. Keep me updated. Go with them."

"Okay. Anything I should do while I'm down there?"

"Make sure everything is finished quickly. We are already behind on schedule, we cannot afford to wait here for more than a day. Also, do not leave the damaged dropship behind. Attach it to the second one if you have to. Make sure to take a security kit with you, there's no doubt now that the ship has been seen, so you have to leave something for the humans to find. Do your best to not get seen, I do not want to go home to a lecture."

"Understood. I will have an update message for you in two hours." Corvus ended the call.

Atria spun on her heel and headed towards the engineers' station. She couldn't wait to hear about Astra's recon to earth.

Acknowledgements

Alright, this is my second book, and part of me wants to just copy and paste the acknowledgements from the first book because I've been working on this for over two years and I am TIRED. That's not fair though, so here I am.

First off, I want to thank everyone who helped make this possible. So many people put their hearts into it, and I'm so grateful for you guys. I had an awesome team who read, critiqued, formatted, made art, sent encouragement, helped me promote, and I am so in debt to you guys. I had immense support in this, and I'm incredibly honored to have such a remarkable group of people around me.

As always, thanks to my friends, family, fandom, and my teachers for the motivation. Thanks to my cover artist Jessica, and to Effie who reformatted it for me. Thanks to Riley, who did the interior formatting, I know it was a pain and you were so patient. An extra special thanks goes to my developmental editor, Ariana. I had the privilege of being her first developmental editing client, and it was a great experience. I love you guys.

Ad Astra Per Aspera!

Pronunciation Guide

Astra Aracelli (As-truh Are-uh-kell-ee): Computer Science, Engineering, and Programming/Data Analysis Major

Aiken Frost (Aye-ken): Earth Science Major

Nasra Dabiri (Nas-ruh Dah-bee-ree): Neuroscience Major

Elena Valdivieso (E-leh-nah Val-dee-vee-eh-so): Mechanical Engineering Major

Hanbin 'Henry' Lee (Hen-ree): Computer Science Major

Zola Reed (Z-oh-lah): Computer Networking and Communications Major/Acting Head of Torsion University

Alyssa Clark (Ah-lis-ah): Health Sciences Major

Marilyn Anne 'Mary' Newman (Mare-ee): Civil Engineering Major

Katya Leonova (K-ah-t-yah Lee-oh-noh-vah): Astronomy and Astrophysics Major

Clay Parkes (Cl-aye): Owner and CEO of Syn Research Facility

Willow (Will-oh): Engineering Major

William (Will-ee-um): Accounting Major

Morgan (Mor-gun): Chemical Engineering Major

Cassian (Kas-ee-un): Chemistry Major

Castor Allen (Kas-tor): Environmental Engineering Major

Isaac Kim (Eyes-ick): Computer Engineering Major

Enlai 'Eric' Huang (Air-ick): Engineering Major

Nara 'Nicole' Arai (Nih-kole Ah-r-eye-ee): Physics Major

David (Day-vid): Molecular Physics Major

Xavier (Zay-vee-er): Astra's brother. Not a student.

Cassidy (Kas-a-dee): Astra's sister. Not a student.

Tessa (Tes-uh): Astra's sister. Not a student

Jaxson (Jak-son): Astra's brother. Not a student.

Yvette (Ee-vet): Astra's sister. Not a student.

Zale (Z-ail): Astra's brother, Griffin's twin. Not a student.

Griffin (Gr-ih-fin): Astra's brother, Zale's twin. Not a student.
Alejo (Al-eh-ho): Lead researcher at Syn Research Facility.

Glossary

ARA'CAL

Ara'cal is the native language of Astra and the Ara'cel people, natively known the Ara'ttnav (lit. home people). It's the sole language used on Ara, as other dialects have never been created.

Ara — home
Cal — language
Cel — from/of
Etaklen — Greetings
Nav — person
Tt — plural prefix
Vede — also, as well

Sera Amoroso is the self-published author of The Makria Cycle. She's a freelance editor, college student, cosplayer, linguist, tea enthusiast, and avid reader. She spends most of her time at home with her dog, Minnie.

She has been writing stories since she was ten years old. Ever since she got her hands on books such as The Lord of the Rings, and Enders Game, she wanted to publish one of her own. Finally, multiple scrapped ideas and discarded drafts later, she did it.

Torsion, her debut novel, kicks off The Makria Cycle trilogy. She's also been featured in the anthology Aphotic Love, and the 2024 edition of The Dragon Bone Journal. When she's not writing, she can be found reading, creating languages, and playing games with friends.